Trapped
in
Time

The only hope for the future lies in the past

Lee Hardesty

Artwork by Tom Edwards
Editing by Jason Letts, Shannon Kidd, Jonathan Wright

Paperback ISBN: 978-1-968963-00-2

Hardback ISBN: 978-1-968963-01-9

E-book ISBN: 978-1-968963-02-6

Table of Contents

Trapped in Time

The only hope for the future lies in the past

By Lee Hardesty

Acknowledgments

I never set out to write a novel. It was my intent to encourage my friend Tom to write it since he was at least vaguely literate. I was supposed to help him with the math. Somehow this evolved, or mutated, into my becoming the author and his becoming a reader and cheerleader. Tom helped and made suggestions throughout the book, and it would never have come to be without him.

Shannon Kidd was one of the first readers of the book and bravely volunteered to do a line edit of the manuscript, mainly to ease her pain at the numerous errors in grammar throughout the first draft. I don't think she realized what she was getting into, but she gamely held on until almost the end.

I found Jason Letts through Reedsy. He was willing to work with a first-time author and did an extensive developmental edit on the book. I highly recommend him. He was very thorough and gave extensive advice, which made the book far better than the very rough draft I handed to him. Jason was available on short notice. He worked fast and finished the edit a week ahead of schedule and did a fantastic job even when it was well outside his normal comfort zone; he's not really a gun guy. If you ever have a book project, I don't think you could do better than to hire Jason Letts.

If you notice that the latest version sounds better it's because a fellow named Jonathan Wright polished it fixing all the errors. You can also find him on Readsy.

The cover, which I think is fantastic, was done by Tom Edwards from England. I also found him on Reedsy. I had a great deal of trouble finding someone who could draw a dinosaur. In a world full of Photoshop magicians who know only how to cut and paste, he is one of the few remaining genuine artists. He did an outstanding job of bringing the scene to life in a cover reminiscent of the books I grew up with in the 1980s. If you ever need artwork, don't mess around. Start by calling Tom.

Shortly after I finished the first draft, I stumbled across a local writers' group at the library. It is run by Russ Hall and W. C. Jameson, both widely published writers in fiction and nonfiction. Give them a search on Amazon. The best way to describe my experiences there would be to say that I didn't know what I didn't know. This book probably never would have come to print without their help and guidance and the support of the other members of the Lago Vista Writers' Group.

Ray Seibert of Advanced Concept Design is a publisher I met in the group. It started with his announcing that he was going to publish a collection of ghost stories and was looking for submissions. That led to three anthologies being published on Amazon and was an interesting experience in learning to write on command and deliver on time and on target. Although I did not accept his offer to publish this book for me, he was kind enough to guide me through the hurdles of doing it myself. Again, it probably never would have happened without him. Check out his library of work on Amazon or on Audible.

Prologue

The Dig

Roger Hoffman, 65
2024 Dinosaur Park, UT

Dr. Roger Hoffman stared out to the west across the arid land with the unsettling feeling that time was slipping away.

The view from the hill gave him a long vista all the way to the horizon. The older man stood on a gentle shoulder that was slowly eroding into the plain below. The weather was still hot, but the rains would come. Soon this season, as so many before, would be over. He just hoped they would be able to recover this find before the year ended.

He took off his hat and wiped the sweat from his balding head. He had been bringing his students here for ten, no, twelve years now. Dr. Hoffman looked down as his pupils knelt on pads, chipping away at the soft stone surrounding the fossil. His knees no longer allowed him to work like that.

After so many years in the sun, he now did most of his work at a table in the museum, sorting through trays of fossils others had dug up long ago. So much was still unclassified. The two real discoveries that he had made in his career had both been found there, overlooked decades earlier, but it wasn't the same as being in the field. It wasn't the same as digging. Nothing matched the satisfaction of using your own hands to coax these ancient bones from the stone where they had hidden for millions of years.

Several other groups were working at different sites nearby, but most of them wanted to be here. This was the most complete find they had made this year. Some of the other work being done was admittedly more important. Susan had found a pair of early mammals that had died curled up together in a burrow. The little creatures were probably the most important find they had made and could make her entire career. It would almost guarantee her PhD. But everyone wanted to work the big bones.

Turning away from the sun, Hoffman looked back at the students sweating as they meticulously exposed what was once the most feared creature to walk the earth.

It didn't look like much now—patches of plaster covering sections of the spine. Some of them had already been removed, pried up and carried away down to the main camp below to be crated for shipping. There was one femur and part of the pelvis. Most of the tail was missing. He thought there might be the upper section of one of the arms and both scapulars. Quite a few ribs remained, but the skull was gone.

Such a pity! There was nothing like finding a skull or even a mandible. If only they could have found one of its jaws full of those long sickle-like teeth, but as they dug into the hill, it simply ended. They had extended the excavation into the hillside to no avail.

Two of his students were working, soaking epoxy into the broken fragments of ribs to try stabilizing them. Another group was working along the spine, carefully isolating the vertebra from the surrounding strata.

"Professor," said Jeffery as he peered up from where he was kneeling, squinting through what seemed to be impossibly thick Coke-bottle glasses. Could the poor boy not find a pair of sunglasses to fit his myopia? "Professor, there's something here." He was pointing at a section of the beast's spine that he had been laboring over.

The professor came over and examined the area. The vertebra in question was broken, shattered in fact. The anatomical alignment was still fairly good. *Well, nothing's perfect, but I wonder how that came to pass*, he thought.

"Well, yes, it is rather badly broken, but it looks like most of the pieces are still there. Don't try to separate it all now. Wrap it all in plaster, and we'll clean it up when we get it back to the university. That's a good boy..."

"No, Professor—look." He pointed to... something. It was a different color from the surrounding fossilized bone or the soft gray stone that encased it. Jeffrey scooted to the side to make way for the professor to kneel. Bending down like that was painful.

Once Hoffman had composed himself, he pulled the wide-brimmed hat off his head and wiped his brow. Yes, there *was* something there. It was an erratic. The body had been covered by a fine silt, but an oddball can always wash down any stream bed in a flood. It was certainly wedged in there. Odd shape. He reached into his pocket and took out his glasses. He hated growing old, but it seemed better than the alternatives. With a sigh, he bent down a bit closer to peer at this little intruder.

One often found anomalous stones, gastroliths, in the digestive track of some herbivores. The question of whether these were intentionally swallowed to aid in digestion or consumed by accident was still under debate in the community, but they had been used as evidence for migratory patterns stretching thousands of miles. This was different. Gastroliths were unknown in carnivores, and this one was embedded in the spine.

The surface was flakey, a dark red with green leaking into the surrounding stone. Part of it crumbled as he scratched at it with the dental pick that he had picked up from where his student had left it.

The inside seemed more solid. It was truly odd. He couldn't decide what it was. He scratched at it harder. It was soft, and as he scratched at the back of it, the outer layer came away, leaving bright scratches.

He sat back on his heels, peering at something that could not be, his mind trying to resolve the contradiction between what his eyes saw and what could not be true. Slowly suspicion began simmering inside him.

Hoffman looked closely at the matrix that encased the vertebrae and the intruder. The stone was homogeneous. He scraped at it, blowing the dust away. He could not see any seam or line where someone might have tried to cement the... no, he couldn't say it—cement "it" into the rock of their dig.

He reached into the pouch on his belt and pulled out a small bottle of water. He carefully wet the matrix, looking for the edge where some prankster had tried to perpetrate this hoax. There was none.

Roger Hoffman's mind became very quiet as he looked down at what could not be, and it occurred to him that the tiny bones Susan was sifting from the site a quarter of a mile from here might *not* be the greatest find they made this year.

Someone had shot a dinosaur.

CHAPTER 1

A Bit of Meat

John Hamman, 43
Cretaceous

God it was hot, but the heat would bring the animals. They would need water. Hell, he needed water. John Hamman reached down for the canteen resting beside the pack on which he sat. It was half full— best to put it out of its misery. This could be a long day, but they had another. He offered it to Manny. The Black man smiled and shook his head, as John knew he would. He would not drink until John did, and when he did, he would not drink as much.

This was an old ritual between them. How many years had they done this? He had tried getting Manny his own canteen, but Manny had assumed it too was John's and that he was just carrying it for him. One day he would get Manny to drink first before his bwana. For now, he lifted the canteen, turning his head so Manny could see him take several large swallows before handing it over. Manny smiled before raising it to his lips, careful to take less than his master.

Manny's face seemed to split in two, bisected by his wide grin as if he could read John's mind. John had harbored the suspicion that Manny really did possess such a power. He had accumulated more than a bit of evidence over the years. He even asked Manny once outright, but the man had just grinned even more widely, laughing silently just as he did now, laughing at John, just as he laughed at all things great and small.

He had never known anyone so happy or content in life. Clearly, Manny's people still possessed a secret that John's had lost. He had never seen a people who took such delight in simply being, regardless of where they were or what they were doing.

And to think that John's grandfather had owned slaves. He might well have owned Manny's uncle and called him property. The thought, that you could possess a person as you might possess a horse or a cow. Easier to lay claim to the wind, and yet more than a few people back home would consider Manny to be lower than such animals.

John pondered what his own father would think if he could see them sitting here sharing water from a canteen like brothers beneath the shade of these ferns, as they had done so many times in so many lonely places. He could still remember his father beating him for drinking from the "colored" fountain. John's father would have an apoplexy if he could have seen his son grow up to spend so much of his life among these people.

Manny handed back the canteen. He had drunk just under half of what was in it. John shook his head as he raised it to his mouth to finish the water. Sometimes the best place to keep it was inside you. He could have predicted that, no matter how thirsty Manny had been, some things were as certain as the rising of the sun. He put the canteen back in its pocket on the side of the pack.

He turned to peer out through the gaps in the large ferns. Even with a good rifle, hunting required a little bit of attention. Best to remember that even though you were the hunter, you could easily become the prey. Nothing had appeared during this short, silent exchange. Manny had already turned back and stared out over the dry plains behind them, a slight smile on his face.

John's big double rested across Manny's lap. He had carried it and other guns for John for so long that John could barely remember him without one. There had been a time when John would have taken it from Manny to hold himself so that it might be quickly at hand, if in fact something decided to stalk the stalkers. But that time was long past.

As with so many things they had never discussed, it was a mark of trust that Manny took more pride in than any authority he might ever be given. That trust had never been betrayed, and more than once John had heard the concussion from behind him as a big ten gauge or rifle was emptied at a charging lion or elephant that had stalked up their trail, intent on mayhem.

In his own arms John cradled the three seventy-five. The gun was really too big to shoot meat with, but it had the power to drop anything that might look on them as dinner, and it was a flat shooter. The three seventy-five was like an old friend. He had owned it for a long time and held it in his arms more often than he had held any woman he had known. The rifle had been made for him in England by Holland & Holland after the war. The action was superb. It had a long relief scope mounted forward of the action on the barrel. The magnification was only four-power, but it didn't slow down his shooting up close. John would never admit it to anyone else, but he thought his sight might be getting weaker. He was actually thinking about going in and letting a doctor fit him with glasses.

John couldn't see the river from here. There wasn't much to look at anyway. The width was less than a quarter of its size right now. It had been a long dry season. He didn't want to be that close to the river. Too many things were prone to show up there, it being the only source of water in the immediate area. No, right now John wanted a bit of meat and a little privacy, and he would not get that at the river's edge.

To the west of him the low escarpment that overlooked the river bottoms was broken by a slope leading to the water. Above was a drier plain. The drop-off wasn't huge but enough to make the slope to his west somewhat attractive. He was actually a good ways from it, better than a quarter mile, but there would still be more traffic here as wildlife made the trek toward the water.

Perhaps he was being overly smart. John liked to think of it as being subtle. He hoped it would not look like a trap, mainly because it wasn't much of one. He was essentially sitting in the middle of an open plain, a spot he hoped would see a bit more traffic. Then again. perhaps he had overestimated the use the path received. But it's like they say—you only need one. And in the afternoon their vigilance was rewarded.

The herd was small, seven in all, headed for the river in a slow, meandering path. They would want to drink their fill and be away before it became too cool. The hunters preferred early evening.

There were four females, a bull, and only two calves, not many young. It had been a hard year, hard for bigger herds to find food, and small herds were more vulnerable to predators. This group had probably lost at least one or two calves already, and they might lose one more member today. It all depended on how close they wandered to his patch of ferns.

John thought about moving toward their path, but he couldn't do it without being seen. How would they react? He wouldn't normally be a threat. He thought about simply standing and casually wandering in a path that would cross in front of the herd to get a bit closer. They might ignore him, or they might veer away. Some things spend their lives hunting; some things spend their lives *being* hunted. Both get very good at what they do. Better to sit tight.

He didn't like watching animals that he was stalking too closely. Some of them seemed to have more sense than they should. Watching would not make them take a path nearer his hide, and it might hurt his chances if they felt his gaze on them. He had seen Manny freeze sensing prey or danger when there was absolutely no way he could have known. Hell, John had felt it himself at times and learned to trust it. So he turned and sat, not looking at the herd and trying not to think murderous thoughts.

He waited perhaps ten minutes before turning to check on what he hoped would be their dinner. Hmm—not so bad. As far as he was concerned, they could walk right up and graze on his bush. They weren't overly bright.

It looked as though they would pass nearby. He settled himself down to wait, opened the bolt, and emptied the magazine of the three hundred grain solids. The reach would be a bit long, and he wanted a good boat tail bullet. He reached into the left pocket of his vest and pulled out three cartridges over three and a half inches long. The more pointed two seventy grain spitzer bullets would not slow down and would reach farther with less drop. He had long ago sewn tubes into the backs of his pockets. He didn't like the idea of brass glinting in the sun.

He put the three rounds into the magazine and closed the bolt, watching the Mauser action strip the first round and lock it into the chamber. The bolt felt smooth as silk, with no sign of sand or dirt in the action. He flipped on the safety.

John looked out to the north, thinking about where they would likely pass and where he would take his shot. The wind was light out of the northwest. Not much of a crosswind, not for the heavy bullet. It would leave on its way at over 2,700 feet per second.

While he had the time, he tried to estimate the distance to different points. The shot was going to be a bit of a reach. Careful to stay behind cover, he peered through the scope at a cycad that was kind enough to present itself. He was zeroed at three hundred yards. The bullet would break around 200, where it would be only about five and a half inches high, but after it passed through his zero it would start to drop hard.

He motioned silently to Manny, who came forward and knelt where he indicated. Kneeling behind him, he laid the rifle upon Manny's right shoulder as if it were a shooting rest high enough that he would be able to shoot above the brush. He could not make such a long shot unsupported.

He again scoped the target area and made his final decisions as to how high he would hold, depending on their path. It could be from as little as thirteen inches to as much as three feet at the far side of the clearing. He guessed it would take up to three quarters of a second for the bullet to reach the target.

He took one last long look through the gaps in the ferns. Yes, the herd of was coming. Yes, they were staying in the open away from the cover along the path he had guessed. They would pass through the clearing he had chosen.

He settled down on his knees behind Manny to wait. He didn't want to have to move once the herd was closer. Manny could probably do this forever, but John became uncomfortable, aware of a pebble under his left knee. He gently wiggled his knee to the side to relieve the pain.

Finally he caught sight of the leader of the herd, a bull, followed by what was probably the alpha female and her calf. John watched their gait as they passed, counting, trying to estimate the lead he would need on the shot. They were passing through the far side of his range. It would be a long shot.

He wanted one of the females without a calf. One of them passed, followed by the second mother. He would take the last one. She was slightly smaller than the others. He concentrated on taking long deep breaths.

As she entered the clearing, he started tracking with her. He had almost twenty seconds as she crossed the clearing to take his shot. He would try for behind the shoulder, the heart and lungs. He didn't trust the drop enough to go for the spine. He focused on the holdover and began to pick up the lead as he followed with her. The gait was a little uneven, but he tried to average it out.

All the world disappeared outside the ring of his scope and the sound of his breathing. Manny had done this for him so many times over the years that they needed no words. Without being told, he started to pick up John's breathing, in and out with him. When John paused, smoothly exhaling half of his breath, Manny did the same.

He didn't pull the trigger. It chose to break all on its own, clean and crisp, as he pressed back on it. All John knew was that the world had changed.

Firing a big gun was a rude experience. There is no way to stay on your target. It's like a discontinuity in the universe.

He was throwing the bolt, pulling the long action all the way to the rear, ejecting the case onto the ground next to him, and stripping another round from the magazine into the chamber. He got back on the scope as he heard a meaty thud echo back to him.

Running animals. Rising dust. It was hard to see. The cover near the ground hid her from view, but she was down kicking in the dust, raising a cloud that did not follow with the rest of the herd.

Better than he had hoped for. If she stayed down, they would not have to chase her. He did not know where he had hit. Maybe he had gotten the spine after all, but she wasn't running.

Manny turned back to him with another enormous grin. Once, John might have tried to pretend that he had planned that shot placement, but they were long past that. He shrugged, lifting the rifle off its resting place on Manny's shoulder.

Now the question: Sit and wait or go and see? From here he would at least have good line of sight on her if she got back up. If they started moving in, they would lose sight of her. Better to wait and see. If she wanted to lie there and bleed, he was not inclined to dissuade her.

He laid the rifle on his pack and got out the other canteen for another drink. There might be whiskey tonight at the camp, but the water passed back and forth between them was the real celebration. It looked as if she was going to stay down, maybe take her last nap. He decided to send Manny back to the camp for porters to help carry the meat.

It was best to have a bit of help when you butchered a dinosaur.

CHAPTER 2

Hired

Robert Brown, 24
1962 New York, NY

It was very unusual. The Hammans were very unusual, but they were also by far the largest and wealthiest of all of the firm's clients. The amount of business they did through the firm surpassed all other clients combined. They were very successful in all their ventures. They were also very private, almost reclusive, and liked to keep their names out of the spotlight.

So when the Hammans said they wanted to quietly arrange for the education of a young man, no one had made any objections. A few discreet phone calls to the university had insured his acceptance. A small endowment could go a long way to opening doors for anyone. No one had been able to determine any connection between the Hammans and this young man. It was as if they had pulled his name out of a hat.

His progress was discreetly followed as he attended school, but then the Hammans insisted that the firm offer him an internship. No one had ever made such a request before. Clients did not dictate the policies or hiring of the firm, but the Hammans had made it clear that if the law firm wished to continue representing their business dealings, then they would accept this young man and assign him to work on their account. It was also made clear that their names were not to be attached in any way to this decision.

He had proved to be a bright young man but in no visible way extraordinary. He did not stand out from the rest of his class and would not have garnered any special consideration if it were not for the Hammans' special patronage.

There had almost been a revolt when upon his graduation the Hammans insisted that he be made a permanent part of the firm and be assigned to their account.

They attended the celebration welcoming him to the firm, expressing to him how pleased they would be to have him working on their account. Mrs. Hamman seemed particularly pleased by all of this. She was very old now, and rumors were circulating about her health, yet she was well dressed. He could see that she had once been very attractive.

One thing seemed out of place. Instead of a pearl necklace, she wore a large tooth on a leather cord around her neck as if it were the finest pendant.

She was very warm toward him, taking his young hands between her own, not wanting to release them. She insisted on rising from her wheelchair to greet him and took him into an embrace in her old arms as if he were a long-lost friend. He accepted all of this gracefully, and Mrs. Hamman beamed at him as if he were her own son.

No one really understood the Hammans, but they had practically built the firm. Their business was the cornerstone on which it was based. Every effort would always be made to accommodate them.

It was not long afterward that Mrs. Hamman passed away. The entire firm turned out for the funeral, which was a surprisingly small, private affair. Robert Brown stood respectfully with his coworkers, having no idea of the role this woman had played in his life or why.

CHAPTER 3

Childhood

Jenny Hamman, 8
1976 San Francisco, CA

The book was wonderful. It was full of pictures of gigantic beasts in swamps and monsters fighting each other. She sat cross-legged on the floor with it before the fire. It was Christmas, but the new doll was forgotten in favor of the book.

Her parents were sitting on the couch talking to her grandfather. He didn't come to visit very often, but when he did, he always brought her presents—sometimes books, sometimes other things.

After her parents went into the kitchen, she climbed up onto the couch with her grandfather and asked him to read to her. The names in the book were long and hard. He said they were Latin and that it was good to know them, but they were really too long, and most people called the dinosaurs by other names.

As she sat beside him, he turned the pages while reading to her. But he also told her things about the animals in the book. He said a lot of the pictures were wrong. Most of them did not live in the water of the swamp and were more like giraffes living on land and grazing on the trees. The people who wrote the book didn't really know what they looked like because they had never seen them and mostly had to guess.

He pointed to them and told her about them—what color they were and how they liked to hunt or care for their young. He said a lot of them didn't look like reptiles but were more like birds with as many feathers as scales.

When her parents came back into the room, they said Grandpa shouldn't be filling her head with silliness and that she should ignore his stories. Everyone knew dinosaurs were big, stupid lizards. That was why they had died out. They were cold-blooded and couldn't compete with modern animals. Her grandfather simply smiled and winked at her when they turned away.

He asked her which one was her favorite, and she had pointed to the big one with the long neck. "That's Mokele-Mbembe. He lives in the forest or on the plains. They're like elephants. They eat so much that they have to move around all the time or they will eat the whole forest. They can feed off the tops of the tallest trees, like a giraffe."

He turned the pages and told her about Emela-nt ouka. Its name meant "Killer of Elephants." They were brave defending their herd and their young. They were like the rhino and would charge anything with their horns.

When he turned to the page with the scary one killing the other dinosaur, she asked him "Is it real?"

He smiled down at her kindly. "Yes, they were real and very scary, but they generally don't hunt anything as small as little girls!" She giggled as he tickled her, and she missed the slightly sad look on his face.

Growing more serious, he said, "The real danger was its smaller cousins. They hunted smaller dinosaurs more the size of people—or little girls. They hunted in packs like wolves." Her grandfather told her how they would stalk their target. One would show itself, distracting the prey or trying to make it flee into a trap set by the rest of the pack. He told how they always attacked from the side and the rear.

She stared wide-eyed, spellbound, as he described how they could trail their prey and stalk them by their scent, even in the dark of night when all the other dinosaurs were asleep, curled up trying to stay warm. They had feathers like birds and large eyes that let them see in the dark. Shivers ran up and down her spine as he spoke.

"Do you want to see something?" She nodded quickly. He leaned over to the side in an exaggerated way to see if her parents were coming. When he saw that the coast was clear, he leaned back in and put his finger to his mouth for silence, reached into his jacket pocket, and pulled something out. It was a necklace made from a leather thong with a big ivory tooth on it. Her eyes grew wide.

"Do you want to hold it?" he asked, then placed it in her small hands. It wasn't as heavy as it looked, worn on the point.

She looked up at him and he solemnly pointed to the picture of the monster biting into the other dinosaur's neck with its big teeth. He took it back from her and stared at it fondly before putting it back in his pocket. He had a sad expression on his face when he looked at her.

"What's wrong?"

Her grandfather hugged her, "Nothing." He kissed her on the top of her head before turning back to the book.

Soon her parents made them come to the table for dinner, but she first went and put the book on her bed for later. She would learn all the names of all the dinosaurs.

Her grandfather sent more books over the years and sometimes other things. The first fossil he brought her was an ammonite. She turned it over and over in her hand as he told her about how it had been locked in stone for millions of years. From then on it lived on the shelf next to her bed with the books.

1977

Her parents didn't want to let her have it. It wasn't fair. Her grandfather maintained that it was only an air rifle and that every kid should have one. It was a Crossman Pumpmaster 760.

They said it was inappropriate for a young girl and that she could not have it in the city. In the end they compromised. She would be allowed to keep it, but it must remain at the ranch with her grandfather. She could use it only under his supervision.

Later, looking over the sights at the small paper target as she knelt behind the stump, she slowly pulled the trigger as her grandfather coached her on her breathing. Nothing had ever felt so right.

The hand guard was the pumping lever. She had to pump it ten times, and the last few were really hard, but it was worth it. Slowly she got better, and she would never forget the first time she hit the bull's-eye on the small target.

She had pinned that target to the wall with thumbtacks as if it were an award from school.

The next morning when they snuck out together and came back with a small brace of squirrels, her mother had almost lost her mind. There had been yelling. In the end she said Jenny had to butcher them herself. Her mother seemed to think that would be punishment for her.

Her grandfather led her out on the back porch and took out his knife. It seemed so big to her. He told her stories of it and how it had belonged to his grandfather, a Texas ranger. He teased her, grabbing her by the hair and pretending to scalp her like an Indian. She squealed and they both laughed.

He used the knife to show her how to skin and clean the squirrels by peeling the skin off them, almost like stripping off a sock. They cleaned the carcasses in the sink to the horror of her mother, and he showed her how to stuff them with celery, the only valid use for the plant. They cooked them stacked head-down in the slow cooker. Her mother didn't eat with them that night. That was when she seemed to give up the fight.

1981

She was eleven when he died. He was very old, and his heart had finally given out. They bought her a black dress. She didn't like it, but she wore it for him. There were so many people there. It seemed so alien, so unlike him. The large church, the service, all these people talking about what a great man he had been and all the things he had done in business. Did any of them know him at all?

No one talked about how he could shoot a squirrel from ear to ear high in a tree so that it would drop dead at your feet. She did not even recognize this man they spoke of. She almost asked her mother if they were at the right funeral.

Afterward, her parents went to a lot of meetings. She could hear them yelling on the phone as she was in her bed. They seemed very angry. His ranch and all his business dealings had been placed in a trust managed by a law firm. Her parents had been expecting them to be left to them. She got the impression it was a lot of money.

She felt lost, alone. She mostly sat in her room. She would reread books her grandfather had given her, books about the dinosaurs they had both loved and ones about faraway places. He brought her books about the great hunters he had known from the wilds of Africa. He used to tell her stories of them and all the places they had hunted together.

Sometimes he showed her old pictures of them from his time in Africa. He grew sad occasionally while looking at the pictures. He would try to cover it up, telling her something funny, but she could tell he missed them. He would tell her stories of the wars he fought in and the friends who had died. Now he himself had died.

Was he with them again, riding over the dusty savanna under that hot sun? Was he with his wife again? He had shown Jenny a picture of her. She was very pretty. He told Jenny that she had been named after his wife, who died long before Jenny had even been born. Jenny had never met her grandmother, but she could tell that her grandfather still loved her very much.

1982

Jenny's grandfather had always come on her birthday. He would not come again. She almost jumped up when she heard the doorbell ring, thinking that somehow it was all wrong and he had come back to her. She heard a lot of talking in the living room, but she could not make any of it out until her parents began raising their voices. They sounded angry. Eventually things quieted down.

She did not know the man her parents brought into the room. They said he worked for her grandfather and would be doing things on his behalf. He asked he and Jenny be left alone. Her parents reluctantly left and closed the door.

The man looked down at Jenny as tears rolled down her face. This was not her grandfather. How could anyone hope to replace him? She didn't want anything to do with this man.

"My name is Robert Brown. I worked for your grandfather. He asked that I do things for him from time to time since he can't be here himself. He wants you to know that he has always and will always love you. Even though he is gone, he left some things for you."

Kneeling down in front of her as she sat on the bed, Robert said, "He wanted you to have this." He pulled out the necklace and showed it to her. "He hopes you will always remember him, and he wants you to have this to remind you that he will be looking out for you."

She took it from him, turning it over and over in her small hands. She remembered when he had shown it to her. He had teased her, telling her it was a dinosaur tooth. She took it and placed the worn leather cord around her neck and looked up at the man.

He said some other platitudes but seemed uncomfortable. Finally he excused himself, leaving Jenny alone holding the necklace left to her by her grandfather.

* * *

The man was as good as his word. From time to time she would receive things from Mr. Brown, books that had been left for her or bought for her. Later she was given hunting licenses for different types of game. At first she tried to get her father to take her, but he had no interest in hunting at all. They found a guide company that specialized in youth hunting. The game became larger over the years.

Her parents never understood why her grandfather would have left her a trust to pay for such a hobby or why she was so enthusiastic about it. But these were things left to her from her grandfather, things he wanted her to have and have the chance to do.

Mr. Brown came every year on her birthday before the end of school. Sometimes he would arrange trips for her or take her places. She never knew what her grandfather had left for her, but it was something from him, almost like the things they used to do together. And even if he was not there with her, it was something he had left for her.

1988

When Jenny graduated from high school she received a letter from a safari company in Kenya inviting her on a safari to hunt cape buffalo. Her grandfather had left it to her as a graduation present. It was the first of the "Big Five" and her first trip to Africa. Her grandfather had spent much of his life there. She would never forget her first night lying in a tent, listening to the night's sounds and hearing a lion in the distance.

*   *   *

Upon returning home from Africa, Jenny found a scholarship waiting for her at Wyoming University for her to major in paleontology. She never questioned her decision and started that year. She excelled in a field where women were as common as hens' teeth. Even more than her fellow students, she liked being in the field. When the field seasons came around, she was the one selected for the internships at the dig sites.

The years that followed found her at dig sites all around the country and eventually all around the world. She wasn't the best at playing the political games of academia. She might not be given grants or selected to lead teams, but they always wanted her on their team. She was becoming well known as the one who always came back with the bones.

CHAPTER 4

Broken

John Hamman, 43
Cretaceous

Manny returned with a dozen men and news from the river. A large herd of trikes had moved down to the river near the camp. They were mean animals with about the same personality of a black rhino but about three times the weight of one.

Unlike the rhino, they traveled in herds. It might be worth moving the camp farther away from the river. They would move on in a day or so, but he didn't want to be that close to the trikes.

They fed on the ferns that covered the plain. They ground them up with their jaws like a cow chewed its cud. When they spread out looking for food, he didn't want members of the herd wandering into camp.

He had stood watch over the kill. No predators made an appearance. The animal never stood up or tried to move off, and by now he was quite certain she never would. But just to be on the safe side, he unloaded the 375 and reloaded it with heavy round-nosed solids. He traded it to Manny for the big double and moved in toward the kill.

She was lying where she had been hit. He could see the wound. Frothy blood ran down from it into the dust, turning the ground black. It was a lung shot. She was quite dead. On examination, he found that the bullet had passed through both lungs but had missed the heart. It smashed the shoulder bone on the far side and had not exited. It was the broken shoulder that had grounded her. Not his greatest shot, but it had been rather long.

The butchering went quickly. They removed the hind quarters, the two forelegs, and one side of ribs. It was all they could carry and would feed the camp for a week. The meat was slung under poles carried by four men each, and they headed back to camp.

In a little over an hour the porters began singing as they walked. This was actually a good way to avoid contact with most animals and even most predators. Most would avoid a larger group and tended to avoid louder noises that they were unfamiliar with. So sometimes it was best to go forth boldly singing a song—even when you were carrying several hundred pounds of meat.

They were still out of sight of the camp about half a mile away when they heard the first gunshot. John took off at a run toward the camp but knew he was too far away. Manny ran beside him. Although he could have outstripped John, he would never leave his side. The one shot turned into a volley, then another, and then became more ragged and sporadic. The shots stopped before John crested a small rise and looked down on the camp.

Two of the trikes were down inside the camp, and another was a few hundred yards away. People were moving around, but he saw several bodies unmoving on the ground. All the tents were down, and supplies were scattered everywhere. This was precisely what he had been afraid of and why he planned to move farther from that herd.

They had missed the party. Slinging the big gun, they walked down toward the camp, trying to catch their breaths. It occurred to John that he was not as young as he used to be.

Going from man to man, he found three of them dead, but one was still breathing with a badly broken leg. They brought a stretcher, and tying a rope through the injured man's crotch to the stretcher, John fixed a loop around the man's ankle and drew the leg down toward the end with a hitch.

He tightened it several times as the muscles relaxed, drawing the leg out and putting tension on it. Without the tension splint, the pain would make the muscles contract, driving the jagged ends of the bone past each other into the flesh.

They needed to get him back to a doctor if they were to save his life, if not his leg. Waiting, he watched the man's toes. Pinching them, he could see them refill with blood under the nails. That was good. The circulation still worked.

Standing up, he looked around and saw that the camp was in shambles. With the beasts' poor eyesight, the large tents had drawn most of their wrath. It was a small group, maybe a family, that had decided to charge through the camp.

The men in the camp got off two volleys, and then it had degenerated into mayhem. It was fortunate that no one had been shot. There were four casualties, but everyone else seemed to be unhurt. He called out to the headman, not to rebuild the camp but to pack everything up. They were moving. Better late than never.

He wanted to be farther from that herd before more started to spread out grazing. They were worse than hippos. He went to what was left of his own tent. He untied it and started pulling it off what remained of his possessions.

Everything in the tent had been thoroughly trampled. This was not good. His cot, chair, and small table were smashed. One of his fowling pieces had been stepped on and bent, the barrels destroyed. He found his pack. It was torn open, the seam split from where it had been trampled.

Only one thing in the pack really mattered. He opened the special waterproof pocket in the top of the pack and smelled the acid immediately. That wasn't good.

He looked inside. With a shirt wrapped around his hand, he began pulling out what was there. The batteries were smashed, the acid leaking everywhere. The material of the pack was already falling apart. The device appeared undamaged but was becoming discolored from the acid of the battery.

He pulled it out onto the ground and poured some water over it from a canteen. He had to use some of the water to wash his hands off as well as they had started to burn. The batteries were another story. He always carried two of them, just in case. Both cells were completely smashed. In truth, it was the one part of the device he understood.

The original power source—he couldn't really call it a battery, as it was far too small—was long exhausted. It made electricity, and a normal cell of the same voltage served the same. Now, looking down at his battery and its backup both lying smashed on the ground in front of him, he felt a cold shiver run up his spine. They were in trouble.

CHAPTER 5

Funeral

Robert Brown, 43
1981

John Hamman's funeral was even smaller than his wife's. It was held in New York. The church was old, predating the skyscrapers around it, but the body would be sent to be interred in Africa on his estate, there with his wife, who had preceded him by almost twenty years. This was the conclusion for one of the richest yet least-known men in the world.

Robert Brown sat quietly in the pew along with other junior members of the firm. Looking over across the aisle, he could see the handful of family members: Hamman's daughter, her husband, and a young grandchild sitting there quietly crying. He had worked on the Hamman account for almost two decades and yet he never really knew the man.

Robert had to drag his attention back to the service. The priest in the pulpit was still speaking: "As we celebrate

the life of one of the greatest industrialists of our age..."
Robert found himself wondering about the truth of the man.

Hamman was an enigma. Few men gathered that much
wealth and power without coming into the spotlight of the
world stage. It was almost as if he had set out from the
beginning to make sure he stayed anonymous and had
structured all his business dealings to conceal his success.

Robert had worked alongside the other members of the
firm creating the shell corporations that his business
operated under. At times he wondered what he was
concealing, but he had never been able to find evidence of
any crime.

He had been a client for more than forty years.
Hamman contacted the firm in 1938, shortly before World
War II, to assist in the immigration of Jews from the
European continent. He assisted in the smuggling of an
unknown number of families out of Europe before—and
some said after—Hitler controlled all of western Europe. He
gambled wildly with his money in those years, and all his
bets paid off, almost as if he knew what would happen.

"A leader and a pioneer in the nuclear industry, leading
the way to energy independence..." As the man in the pulpit
droned on about Hamman's accomplishments, Robert
couldn't help but think about some of the wilder rumors
surrounding John Hamman. *If these people only knew the
truth about the man.* The stories read like some kind of spy
thriller.

It was said that he was involved in the US acquiring
the Uranium ore from the Congo before the Nazis could
capture it. He was an investor in Union Miniere du Haut
Katanga, which controlled the Shinkolobwe mine. He
persuaded Edgar Sengier to stockpile the highest-quality ore

in a warehouse on Staten Island and to hold another 3,000 tons on site in the Congo rather than to send it to Belgium.

The Germans captured all the ore that had previously been sent to Olen for processing and used it in their own nuclear program. But thanks to Hamman's efforts, the US was able to transport the ore remaining in the Congo to America for the Manhattan Project.

Would the US have been able to build the bomb without it? It probably would have happened eventually, but it never could have been done in time to be used in the war without Hamman's ore.

He had worked with the Office of Strategic Services, the OSS, and William "Wild Bill" Donovan to protect the shipments and prevent smuggling of ore to Germany. Some said he worked with Donovan to form the organization that was the precursor to the CIA. Rumors circulated that the association had never ended.

Robert thought back to the old man he had met only a handful of times, always been nervous in his presence.

Older members of the firm told stories of Hamman working with the OSS hunting down Nazi diamond smugglers in the wilds of the Congo. The Germans were transporting industrial diamonds out of Africa for their war effort. It was a key strategic resource for the cutting and grinding of the new harder alloys. Some said it played as large a part in defeating the Reich as bombing the ball-bearing factories.

Even as old as Hamman was, Robert could still see the old man in running gun fights through the jungle. He had that larger-than-life aura about him that made you believe even the wildest rumors. Once or twice Robert had seen the old man eyeing him speculatively. It had made him want to scurry away.

Who *was* John Hamman? Robert thought back over what he actually knew to be true. The firm had handled his business dealings for years.

He acquired the mineral rights to large tracks of land that were critical for uranium mining and oil production after the war. He was part of the founding of ARAMCO and the Arabian oil fields. He located and was an early investor in kimberlite pipes in Africa and Canada and owned mineral rights on land where they were beginning to mine the rare earth metals in Africa now being used in the growing semiconductor market. And he was an investor in numerous companies, all of which had paid off spectacularly, including those with names like IBM and Apple.

Throughout all of this success, he went to great lengths to avoid drawing notice to himself. The firm worked for him setting up and managing the shell companies that held his interest.

Now the old man was dead, and the firm was to administer his estate.

CHAPTER 6

The Lodge

Jenny Hamman, 31
2002 Nairobi, Kenya

The old man looked into the fire. It crackled merrily in the large fireplace warming the room. The warmth was good. His old bones ached in the chill of the night. Tonight she would come. It had been so long waiting. He leaned heavily on his cane as he stepped forward to look at the items on the mantel piece: pictures of times gone by, mementos, all the things of a long life well lived.

His eyes settled on a box with a glass front. He opened it and took out one of the two knives displayed within. He turned and spoke briefly to the servant behind him, who nodded as he handed him the large knife. The young man hurried away on his errand. Leaning on his cane, the old man settled himself into a large chair and composed himself to wait, as he might wait for the animal to come to the waterhole. Tonight he would see her again—one last time.

* * *

The letter was a surprise. Jenny had not heard from her grandfather's law firm for years. She thought that had all been settled long ago. When she flew to New York to meet with them and settle the remainder of her grandfather's estate, she had no idea what they wanted to discuss with her.

This man had played a central part of her childhood, but she never understood why he had left so much to her or the way he did it. Now in her mid-thirties, she thought all of that was behind her.

It was more than a shock to find that her grandfather had a large property in Kenya with an estate that had been cared for all these years and was now being passed to her. The one requirement was that Jenny must travel in person to take possession of the property on the 15th of February 2002.

She flew into Nairobi. A young man picked her up at the airport. Upon meeting her, he very solemnly addressed her as "Bibi," which confused her, as it was a respected honorific, meaning "lady of the house," "mistress," or "mother." It was the female form of *bwana*, meaning "boss," "leader," or "master."

He introduced himself as Kamanny. He had been born on the farm. Kamanny's grandfather was chief of the village that was on the farmland. His grandfather had worked for the bwana for many years.

They ate and then left directly. Jenny tried to engage Kamanny in conversation, but he had that deferential standoffishness of some of the employees who still thought of themselves more as servants than equals.

The farm was large, over ten thousand acres, and had its own native population living in a village on the land. Or maybe it would be better to say that the farm grew crops on the village's land, as it had been here long before the farm.

They drove all day, mostly in silence with Kamanny pointing out things along the way, like the boundary of the property, the herds, and water sources, all of which he was very proud of, as if they were his own. After all, he had been born there and would probably grow old and die on the land. Perhaps he belonged to it. They had to stop to refill the tank on the land cruiser from jerry cans.

It was dark by the time they arrived at the lodge. Lanterns around the house lit up the wide, shaded porch. As Kamanny pulled up in front, people were lined up on either side of the path leading to the house. As he walked Jenny down the line, Kamanny introduced them to her. The retinue included cooks, groundskeepers, house servants, and the foreman. All bid her welcome and called her "Bibi."

Jenny had come here simply to dispense with an old forgotten property left to her by her grandfather. Instead, she found a thriving, well-managed farm and a rather large house that had been maintained perfectly in her grandfather's absence, as if they expected him to return at any time.

As Kamanny walked Jenny up to the door, he unlocked it for her with a large brass key and pressed it into her hands, stating, "Welcome home, Bibi." Holding the door for her, Kamanny motioned her within. As she entered, he closed the door behind her.

Jenny was in an entry hall with a gun rack on one wall and a coat rack on the other. The floors were hardwood, polished with long use. It was rustic and felt more homey than formal. As she continued inward, she admired the trophies and skins adorning the walls: all the normal species of African game. She then turned through an archway into the main hall. It formed the main living area with large, overstuffed chairs, bookcases, and a large rug made from the tawny hide of a... what was that?

She walked closer, her gaze fixed on the skin forming the rug on the floor. It was not right. Nothing was that big. The head was affixed. It had to be a joke. It was a tiger but more like a lion in color. The head didn't look right, and it had... it was fake. Someone had made a fake saber-toothed tiger throw rug.

She bent down to look at it. It did look very real. Lifting the head, she tried to see how they did it, what they had made it from. The teeth and the skull had obviously been preserved, but it looked real. The giant canine teeth were part of the skull, and they were real teeth. She had seen many bones and many skulls, and this was obviously a real skull. The skin was preserved and reattached to the skull, but the skin was also a real hide.

It wasn't possible. This was a saber-toothed tiger pelt... which someone had made into a throw rug. All the hair stood up on her neck with the feeling that she was being watched. Jenny slowly turned her head and looked back over her shoulder to the opposite end of the room, where a large fireplace cast a cheery glow, warming the room from the chill of the night air. It was a tall room with a high-vaulted ceiling.

The house needed that room to hold the head that was above the mantel of the fireplace—she was looking up into the maw of a Tyrannosaurus rex head mounted above the fire place.

"Welcome home, Bibi," called a new voice. She jumped, turning to one of the large chairs. Jenny locked eyes with a small old man sitting silently, almost lost in the shadows. No, not small but very old. "We have waited for you for a long time." The old man's eyes seemed to peer through her, as if looking into the very center of her being.

Jenny felt as if she were staring into the eyes of a lion. Frozen in place, she replied, "What *is* this place?" She could barely force the words out.

"Your home, Bibi." She glanced up once again, but her eyes were drawn back to the old man's as he assured her, "Yes, this is real ,as real as any dream." Slowly he leaned forward, pushing down on the arms of the chair, and rose to his feet. Taking a walking stick, a knobkerrie, from beside his chair, he motioned to her. "Come, Bibi."

As she came to his side, he put one hand on her shoulder, leaned on her, and at the same time led her from the room, down the hallway, and out into an enclosed courtyard.

"Do not worry, Bibi. All is as it should be, and all is as it will be, and all is as it has been. Be brave. Be strong. Be good. God smiles on all." With that, he led her into the center of the courtyard, where a small pile of equipment was in the center on the bare ground. He stepped back, leaving her there alone.

"I don't understand. What is all of this?" Jenny asked. She stared at the old man as he walked back to the side of the courtyard.

"The caterpillar does not understand the butterfly. It is good to have seen you again, Bibi. All is as God wishes."

Jenny heard a beeping sound at her feet. She looked down at a glowing red light and watched it turn from red to green— and then all the world changed.

When the bright flash faded, the darkness of the African night returned, leaving an old man leaning on his cane staring into an empty courtyard. It was done. The story was over. The story had begun. A melancholy sadness filled him. He stood there for a long time as the night sounds returned.

Finally he turned, making his way back into the house. Soon his work would be done. He thanked God for letting him fulfill his tasks, and he prayed for the young woman, that she might have the strength for her own.

CHAPTER 7

Harry

John Hamman, 19
1914 London, England

John was in England when the war broke out. He never intended to join the army, much less someone else's army. He never wanted to go to war, and certainly not someone else's war.

It was all Harry's fault really, the big, tall bastard—Harry and a lot of English beer. John vaguely remembered some girls being involved somehow as well, promising them he would help and "do his duty, if not for their country then for the world."

The chubby girl kissed him for that. The prettier blonde had already attached herself to Harry as he waxed on elegantly in the very refined accent he had picked up at Beaumont College.

John didn't think the brunette had "done her duty" by him, but his memory of the latter part of the night was a little vague. He did remember standing in front of a large desk in the recruiting office in front of an elderly English officer. He and Harry were both still very drunk. John remembered wondering if the man had fought against Napoleon but couldn't recall what year that was.

Harry did most of the talking and helped hold John up. He did swear to having been born a British citizen—a lie—under the glare of the old man, who seemed offended by this claim. But the old man let John sign the papers and swear an oath to "faithfully defend His Majesty, His Heirs and Successors... against all enemies." He also swore to obey the authority of "all generals and officers set over me." And with that, he was in it for as long as the war lasted.

Harry walked him over to a bench, but John didn't remember anything else until waking up in a barracks with a British drill sergeant standing over him, yelling at the top of his voice. Harry was nowhere to be seen.

John did later learn that Harry had somehow managed to wrangle some sort of commission through one of his school friends and was now an officer in the artillery.

That courtesy was not extended to John. He was now in the infantry, the lowliest grunt in the British army, and was by his instructors' evaluation "the most useless, incompetent, worthless waste to ever aspire to take the queen's shilling."

For the next two months John lived in an unknown circle of hell, one of a thousand other men from the same town that he had volunteered in. They were all formed into a pals' battalion.

He was seriously rethinking his life choices but didn't have long to ponder his plight. Their abbreviated training was cut short. Soon he was being handed a pair of boots, which did not vaguely fit and were almost unwearable, and associated other bits of "kit."

He was then loaded onto a boat with several hundred others, like so many cattle, for transport across the channel. He seemed to spend all his time on trains. The food was a crime. Mostly he remembered never knowing where he was or what he was doing and simply followed along with all the other men he was being shipped with.

John did finally seem to arrive somewhere. Men from their group had been dropped off at various points. As their numbers grew smaller, finally it was his turn as some nameless officer pointed at John and a group of other men and ordered them off the train.

He eventually learned he was in Belgium. They were replacements for casualties at the northern end of the line. They were hustled along out of what looked to be a perfectly nice town and marched most of the day toward the front.

It was raining, and he began learning about mud. He had not understood the term before, but he was about to become intimately familiar with it. And they finally handed him a rifle, one taken from a pile beside a tent that was the hospital. It would be generous to call them well-used. He was not at all certain it would fire. So began his first experience on the Western Front.

John didn't see Harry again for several months. They had managed to exchange a few short letters, but Harry's experiences seemed to be a little different than his own.

Harry would ramble on about "the cause of the world's progress" and "the honorable advancement of his soul." John just saw mud—mud and rats the size of his mother's dog. If the world's progress was being advanced here, he didn't know how. And John found himself far more interested in trying to keep his feet dry than in the "advancement of his soul."

He learned the nearby village was called "Ploegstreert," but he never did learn how to pronounce it properly. He learned which bars sold the most watered-down wine, which bakeries used the most sawdust in their bread, and which of the young—and not so young—women carried the pox. He assiduously avoided all three as he watched his trench mates fall victim to the same.

He supposed it was a fairly typical war. The lines were stagnant in that sector, and they saw little fighting, at least since he had been there, but they were already hearing rumors of a big push planned for the summer, talk of breaking the Hun and smashing their lines. He was quite certain that whoever was saying that was not peeking over the trench line at the machine gun emplacements.

One day he was bending over a smoky fire made from some wood that they had scrounged trying to cook their lunch when he heard a familiar voice call, "So there you are!"

He looked up to see Harry in a remarkably clean uniform standing on the planking in the bottom of the trench. His smile was like a ray of sunshine shining through the cloudy springtime sky. Suddenly the mud did not seem as cold, the smells as bad, nor the day so dreary. They embraced, and soon it was as if they had never parted and were still in the local bar where they had first met in England. Their conversation continued as they traded stories.

"So what's this then?" someone bellowed from behind them. Turning, John found nothing less than the brigade commander and his aide standing behind them. John had seen him only at a distance, but his round face with bulldog cheeks and the large Mauser pistol at his side made him unmistakable.

Apparently he had decided to do a tour of the trench line and was more than a bit curious as to the unknown officer he found consorting among his men. John stood at attention as they talked.

The last he ever saw of Harry was a glance over his shoulder as Harry was led away in the wake of the commander toward his bunker. He never got the chance to speak to Harry again.

It was only a few months later after the big offensive started in France when he received notice that Harry Butters had been killed. Artillery had landed directly on his gun position, and Harry and all of his men were killed instantly. John also got word that he was being redeployed to the same battle happening along the River Somme.

CHAPTER 8

The Trust

Robert Brown, 43
1981 New York, NY

The men sitting in the conference room were baffled. As the will and the instructions within it were read, they became more and more confused. None of them had seen anything like this. It was as if the man were trying to run his own company from beyond the grave.

An entire stack of envelopes filled with instructions was in the middle of the table, each with a date on it. They were to be opened on that day, not before, not after. The instructions in those envelopes were to be followed to the letter. One of the greatest fortunes of their time, and Mr. Hamman expected it to be managed by instructions written sometimes years in advance.

A board would handle day-to-day operations, but the letters superseded all its powers. The contents of the letters would be known only by the firm, and the firm would instruct the board of these overriding instructions.

The senior partners looked at the first letter dated that very day. The eldest member pressed a button on the intercom and said, "Please send him in." The doors at the end of the room opened, and Robert Brown walked in looking confused and a little nervous. He was forty-three years old and was being called before a meeting of the senior partners.

"Please sit down. You've been with us for some time now, ever since your bar exam. Your performance has been outstanding, and you have done excellent work on the Hamman account.

"Now with the death of John Hamman, the account is moving into a new phase. This firm will be the executor of his estate and will be in charge of managing his interests, including all his business assets. If you accept this offer, you will become a full partner and be in charge of carrying out... certain special instructions in his will."

A stack of papers was placed in front of Robert, including a lengthy NDA. Reading through it, he wasn't sure he had ever seen anything so binding. The consequences of breaking it would be beyond severe. Nothing else was said. They simply placed a pen beside him and waited.

Robert was confused by all this. None of it made sense. He looked at the head of the table, where the senior partner sat, a man he had never even spoken to before.

"I don't understand. Why me? Please understandI am very honored and very pleased to be elevated like this, but why me? You have numerous other associates with more seniority then me who are even more familiar with the account."

The head of the firm simply looked at him, having just offered to make the man's fortune. Dozens of lawyers in the firm would, quite literally, kill for this opportunity.

"The instructions in Mr. Hamman's will were very specific. They require that this offer be extended to you. You will accept this promotion to this position and all the tasks that go with it, or you will be terminated immediately. If you cannot perform your duties, then this firm has no need for you. Have I made myself clear?"

Better to emphasize the stick than to let the man suspect the continued association of the firm with the Hamman account, and its long-term solvency depended on his accepting the offer. It would not do for him to realize the upper hand he had in such a negotiation.

Robert Brown's throat was suddenly very dry. Every eye in the room rested on him. A cold shiver ran up and down his spine as he picked up the papers before him. He took his time looking through all the documents carefully. The terms for compensation were generous to say the least, an extra zero in the number for his salary. He actually wondered if it was a mistake. He almost asked, but it occurred to him that if it was an error, it would be to his own benefit to sign it.

Everything else was routine, except for his duties. It was notably vague in that regard. It felt like a trap. If anything ever actually crossed the line into illegality, he could of course refuse. He could not be compelled to break the law, at least not by this paper. He picked up the pen and began signing his name. The whole thing felt like some kind of Faustian bargain.

When that was completed, the papers were placed in a folder, and he was handed a copy of the will. After reading it, he stared in confusion at the stack of envelopes in the center of the table.

The senior partners—now *his* partners—handed him the first, which they had opened that day. It included financial instructions, as well as instructions to make Robert a partner in the firm. It placed him in charge of a special trust set aside for Hamman's granddaughter and said that Robert would be responsible for carrying out "special instructions" on behalf of the estate. What had he gotten himself into?

Inside the first envelope was a second sealed envelope addressed to him with something in it. He felt a bit of apprehension opening it, and a necklace slid out. It was a simple leather thong with a single large round tooth on it. He remembered seeing it around Mrs. Hamman's neck.

There was a piece of paper with a single sentence on it: "Please give this to my granddaughter."

CHAPTER 9

Note

Jenny Hamman, 31
Cretaceous

The light of the setting sun in her eyes was blindingly bright. What the hell? It was nighttime. How could Jenny be looking into the setting sun? Where were the buildings? Where was the courtyard? Where was the old man? Where was she?

She stood there in a daze, looking around her at everything that could not be. She was standing on a wide plain as the sun sank into distant hills. This wasn't even Africa. The trees were wrong. The landscape had a scattering of ferns.

She turned around in a circle, coming face to face with what was behind her. She stared at the impossible, what she had seen only as a fossil, a plant no human being had ever seen. It was a Bennettitalean. It almost glowed in the warm light of a setting sun, lit up against the dark eastern sky. Jenny reached out and ran her hands over the leaves, which had died out millions of years ago. As the sun sank below the horizon, she knew she was not in Kansas anymore.

The night came quickly near the equator. As she dug through the pack at her feet, Jenny found a headlamp and tent. She didn't really want to use a light and managed to put up the simple A-frame tent in the growing darkness.

Dragging the rest of the pack inside, she closed the flaps and tried to assess what had happened. She could not make sense of any of it and tried to deal with what she could control.

Jenny turned on the headlamp and took stock. She had a rifle, a Winchester Model 70 in 458 Lott with express sights, not unlike rifles she had carried on big-game hunting trips, although she had always favored Remingtons. In the pack was a selection of ammo, soft points and solids.

The second weapon was something strange. It was a shotgun, but perhaps the strangest one ever made. Jenny had actually seen one at Shot Show but had never seen one anywhere else. She had not realized any were produced or sold. It had an odd name. She thought it was called a Neostead, named after its South African designer. She had played with a prototype at the booth.

The only word she could think of to describe it was *backward*. Everything on it was the reverse of every other gun on the market. It was, however, the smallest, most compact, and highest-capacity shotgun in the world. It was built upside down with the magazine tube on top—only instead of one magazine tube, there were two. The thing was short. It was a bull pup, meaning that the barrel went almost all the way back to the shoulder. The trigger was well in front of the bolt and used a transfer bar. It ejected downward like an Ithaca, making it ambidextrous. And the best part of all was that the pump action ran backward.

She released the slide and pumped it. The barrel slid forward, opening the chamber. That was so weird, the exact opposite of how God and John Browning intended. She pulled backward, closing the chamber, and dry-fired the gun. That would take some getting used to.

Jenny pushed a button, and the back end of the magazines popped up. She fed several of the shells into the tubes and practiced cycling the slide. They fed and ejected smoothly as long as she remembered how to pump the damn thing.

The contrast with the Winchester was severe. The Neostead was all plastic. Jenny thought it was an ugly little thing. Fully loaded, the gun was a bit heavy, but with the double magazine tubes, one could stuff 13 3-inch shells into it. It gave her a little chill to think that she would need such a gun. This wasn't for hunting—it was a defensive weapon.

The sidearm in a drop holster was a Browning High Power. That was something she knew well. It was one of the highest-capacity nine-millimeter handguns on the planet, a solid design that had been around since before World War II. This Jenny knew she could trust. The magazine was fully loaded with hollow points. The left-hand side of the belt held two more magazines.

On the other side of the belt in a long scabbard was a knife. Jenny knew that knife. It was her grandfather's, and if the stories were true, it was his grandfather's before him. Her grandfather had carried it through two wars.

She had seen it on his belt, often tucked in diagonally behind his back, all her life. He had taught her to skin her first kill with that knife. She ran her hands over the staghorn grip. It had a brass cross guard, and she did not have to pull it from the sheath to know a brass guard wrapped around the back strap on the blade. The brass was nicked—he had told her once it was used to deflect blows in a knife fight in Abilene, Texas. With that one thing Jenny knew all of this was real.

The pack was military issue of an older style, built on an external frame in military woodland camouflage. It sat high on her back, above an equipment belt with various pouches on it. Jenny preferred an internal frame with a good waist belt, but it was not overly heavy. In addition to the holster and knife, the belt held a large canteen, a well-supplied med kit, and some other survival equipment, like a fire starter.

The tent was a simple A-frame with no floor. It was not as good at keeping the bugs out, but if a large predator started pulling it away into the brush, you wouldn't be trapped in it.

The pack also held some dehydrated food, iodine tablets, two canteens full of water, a compass, a small cooking kit, matches, and a fire starter. The oddest things she found were two large batteries and some wire leads. They were sealed inside vacuum-wrapped plastic along with what looked like a pair of film canisters.

Then there was the device—cylindrical, about eight inches long, and a little discolored on one end, as if it had been stained or corroded. Dials surrounded it, what looked like a display and a button. Jenny turned it over in her hands. It had to have been this that had brought her here. If only she could reverse it to take her back.

The final item was a note:

Dear Jenny,

Don't mess with it! Put it down!

Looking at the thing in her hand, Jenny carefully put it down on the ground in front of her.

> *Even if you could reset it to return you to your own time, you would be sealing your own fate. I'm sorry for all this, but I have no choice, and in truth neither do you. I need your help. I do this not just to save myself but to save you as well. You see, at this time your mother is not yet born, and if I remain trapped in the past, she never will be. This is something you must do.*
>
> *You have probably realized most of this, but I will spell it out for you. The device you have in front of you is a time machine. It allows you to travel into the past and return forward the same number of years. So if you stay here a week, you will return a week after your departure.*
>
> *I have used it for years to explore the distant past. But on one of my trips something happened. The technology of this device is far beyond my understanding, but as advanced as it is, it still runs on electricity. Batteries. It runs on batteries, and it needs a fairly large amount of current to operate.*
>
> *On one of my trips originating in 1938 I had an accident, and both of the batteries I*

carried with me were destroyed. The device, the same one you hold in your hands right now, was undamaged, but I had no means to power it. I, and all the people with me, were trapped in the past.

We were saved—not by our own ingenuity, but by another. By a woman. By you. I have always known this. From the very first time I came to see you, I knew this day would come, a day when I would have to ask you to save me and yourself from my own errors.

I have tried to prepare you in every way I could for what you must do. The woman who saved all of us that day was the most extraordinary person I have ever met. And although I have not lived to see you grow into her, as I knew I would not, I have faith in you, in the person you have become, in the person you will be.

I will tell you all I can to help you, but I have little to offer you. The device is fairly accurate in both space and time, but that is relative to the great distance of years you have traveled. The setting is not that precise. The location is also somewhat inaccurate.

When you travel, you tend to drift in location. The distance is relative to the millennia covered but random in direction. It seems to be mostly east or west. You could be anywhere within thirty miles of us. We could be over the next hill or tens of miles from you.

It is also uncertain when you will arrive. You might be there weeks ahead of our arrival. You could search an area only to have us appear behind you in an area you have already searched. Or we could have already been there for months awaiting your rescue. We could be twenty or thirty miles to the east of you or to the west. The drift seems to be less north to south, but it could still be ten miles either way.

It's not hopeless. I can tell you what I remember and what your past/future self told me. I pray it turns out the same for you this time as it did for me in the past, but any small quirk of luck may change the course of fate.

I will not pretend to understand this or how it works. I can give you landmarks for you to seek out. There is a river. It runs north to south. Listen carefully. I use the terms north and south based on what the compass you have with you will read.

In the time we are in, the poles have reversed. I have seen this on other trips, and honestly it's almost a fifty-fifty chance which way a compass will point at any time in the past when viewed on a large-enough scale. Do not be surprised when you see the sun rise in the west and set in the east. But the river runs from the north to the south.

We were camped about two miles south of a large horseshoe bend in that river on the east side, about half a mile east of the river. It's not a wide river. It's at a seasonal low, only about one hundred yards wide. I pray you are also on the east side. Some of the things that live in the water are aggressive in this time. Even getting water from the river can have its perils. It was the beginning of the dry season when we arrived. Water sources were drying up, and the river was becoming the only source of water in the area.

In my past we had been here for two weeks, about halfway through our planned stay, when the accident happened. We were trapped here for another month before we were found.

You had been here for three weeks when you found us. You had searched over a large area. As far as you could determine, you were about twenty miles west from your point of arrival when you struck the river. You struck the river about five miles above the horseshoe bend I described. The route you had taken in your search was far from straight, but that was your best determination of our relative locations when you arrived. Again, I do not know if this will hold true.

Find the river. Seek a large bend with its loop to the east. Look for us half a mile back from the water. The river has more than a few such bends, but it's the only landmark I can give you on this plain.

Do not try to travel on the water. Stay well back from it. All the large animals are drawn to it for water, and that situation will *worsen as the season progresses. I am sorry. That is all I can tell you.*

Go to the west in the direction of the rising sun. If you do not strike the river in three days, try the same distance to the east. Once you strike it, try to the south first, but we could also be to the north.

I have no other advice to give to you other than to keep your rifle on you and loaded. Some of the beasts here are big, but you can generally see them from a distance. The most dangerous are the smaller predators. They tend to be more active hunters and can travel in packs. Do not disregard the risk of some of the herbivores. Some are as aggressive as any cape buffalo.

Good luck. Godspeed. And please hurry. We had an injured man with us, and I pray we might save his life.

John Hamman, Granddad

CHAPTER 10

Tube Alloy

Ms. Hamman, 34
March 1941
University of Birmingham, England

He had saved Rudolf a seat. Otto was good about that. They often had lunch together in the cafeteria. When they did, they always spoke in English. It would have been nice to relax into his native German, but their accents alone drew enough attention to them.

"Ah, you made it. I was losing hope. But I see you were a bit late for the meatloaf."

Otto cut his slice in half and slid a portion over onto his colleague's plate. Meat was rare enough to make that a very meaningful gesture. It did add a lot to his otherwise rather dreary tray of vegetables.

The English had been very welcoming, taking them in during their time of need, but the food was rather lacking. Wartime rationing had done nothing for a country already famous for a rather bland diet. Otto hoped his friend would have good tidings for him.

Otto added, "You had a meeting with Oliphant? Did he say anything about our security clearances? Will we be able to join... the other project?"

Rudolf shook his head. "Yes, I met with him. We did not discuss that. He wants more calculations." Rudolf took a bite of his meatloaf, chewing it slowly, savoring the fatty taste of what was at least partly beef.

"It's his way of letting us help, since he can't admit to it openly. What was it this time?" As he picked up his tea, wishing it was a dark coffee, Otto did acknowledge that they were lucky to have real, if weak, tea.

Rudolph shrugged with exaggerated casualness. "He wanted to know about solutions to Maxwell's equations in a hemispheric cavity. How is your work going?"

Otto spooned up some of the peas, holding off on another bite of the meatloaf. "A question that, of course, has nothing to do with microwaves. As for me, I can't make it work. Maybe if I had better equipment... It was only demonstrated in Germany, and Klaus Clusius was not trying to produce any significant quantity. I honestly don't think this is a practical method for separating isotopes in any significant amount, and I don't see how it could be scaled up even if I had the equipment." Otto was becoming frustrated.

A woman's voice addressed the pair from behind. "You've got to be the ones."

Otto looked up behind his friend with slightly widening eyes. Rudolf turned in his chair to find himself looking up at a very attractive woman. Not a young girl but someone with the strength and bearing you get from seeing more of life. She was dressed very stylishly in what was clearly expensive but understated clothing.

They both scrambled to get up out of their chairs. Her face split into a smile, and the room seemed to become a bit brighter. Rudolf lowered his estimate of her age to... thirty.

"Please—don't get up. May I join you?" she asked.

"But of course, madam." Otto rushed to pull out a chair for her, but she was already doing that for herself.

With a broad smile she said, "You must be Otto Frisch and Rudolf Peierls. I'm sorry, but I couldn't avoid overhearing the accents. Close your mouths, boys. You'll catch flies. Mark Oliphant was telling me about the two of you. I'm here working with the Academic Assistance Council. They have been helping to settle some of the people we have been helping to get off the mainland. We've also been helping them with some of their funding."

She winked and smiled again. She clearly had an American accent. Was this woman a party to smuggling people out of Nazi-occupied Europe? This was not what they imagined an OSS officer to look like.

"So how are things going for you two? Mark said he assigned you to the Tube Alloy Project," she noted.

"We are very grateful to be here and are happy to help in any way we can." It wasn't only the proper answer; Rudolf meant it.

"But you'd rather be part of Rad Lab," she responded. "It's okay. I talked to Mark. He told me he was still waiting on your security paperwork. Don't be so eager to switch departments. What you're working on right now could be very important. In fact, it could be the most important project of the war. The amount of energy could be almost unlimited. Have you calculated how big a mass would have to be to sustain itself?" She was no longer smiling and seemed to be trying to peer within the men as her eyes scanned back and forth between them.

Who was this woman? His paper on the subject wasn't classified, but it wasn't common reading outside a rather small field. Rudolph shook his head. "That's a dead end. That calculation has already been done. Francis Perrin decided you would need a mass of forty tons of the oxide. There are ways it could be made to work with a lower mass, but we are still speaking on the order of ten tons. I myself did the calculations for an ideal scenario of a sphere of pure metal, not oxide, and it is still on the order of tons. There is no way you could deliver something that large. It can't be used as a weapon." He wondered who this woman was that she would even be familiar with such a subject.

"Are you so sure?" the woman asked. "You might be thinking about this all wrong. I recently spoke with Bohr. You know there exist more than one isotope? Did it ever strike you as odd that it reacts to both fast and slow particles? Bohr thinks the rarer 235 is the more reactive of the two. You need to rework your calculations for a ball of pure 235. I know it's difficult to separate." That drew a grown from both of the men. "It's a hurdle, granted, but sit down and do the math."

She was deadly serious now. Her eyes bore commandingly into them with a purpose. Rudolph got the sense that more was going on here than they understood.

Otto was slower to pick up on what was happening, or he was more dismissive of her as a woman. He should not have been so quick. After all, it was his own aunt who had discovered the mechanism behind fission. "Young lady, the lesser isotope is very rare. Even if you could somehow separate it, I assure you, not enough 235 exists in the crust of the earth to make such a device."

She glared at him. "First, I don't think the mass will be nearly as large as you believe. Second, we already have the ore in America. With a fission cross section of one point two four Barn, 235 is much more reactive than natural uranium. It's that 0.7 percent that does all the work. Do the calculation." She seemed to be losing patience.

"What is a *Barn*?" Rudolf felt as though he wasn't keeping up with the conversation. It was a new and uncomfortable feeling.

For a moment she seemed to be confused. "It's a measure, 10^{24} centimeters squared. Look—calculate how big the sphere would be and its mass, plus its explosive potential. How long does it take to blow? That will give you an idea of the power we are talking about." She started to stand up, and Rudolph scrambled to get up with her.

"Sorry—I didn't get your name," he said. She seemed ready to disappear as quickly as she had arrived.

"Mrs. Hamman of the Hamman corporation. Look—run the numbers. I have to go. Time is a'burning." Smiling at some private joke, she was gone, her heels tapping on the floor as she disappeared from their lives.

Rudolph found the number in a copy of *Nature*. It wasn't the one she had quoted, but it was close enough that he didn't think she could have guessed at it. He also found no mention of it being measured in "Barns." What a strange name for a unit of measure! Maybe it was an American thing.

When they were done, they both sat staring at the sheet of paper. She had been right. The mass was small. The power was almost beyond comprehension. It could be expressed only in abstract numbers. He could not connect in his head what the explosion of thousands of tons of TNT would mean.

When they sat down to write their findings up, Rudolph typed the document himself. He did not trust anyone else with this information. He made only one carbon copy.

They took it directly to Oliphant. Looking down at it as it lay on the desk, Rudolph thought it might well be the most important document ever to have existed. He and Otto never spoke of the young woman or saw her again.

It was several years later when Rudolph once again heard the term Barn and had its recent adoption explained to him along with the source of the name. When the fission cross section was finally determined to a high accuracy, the number was the one she had used years before, not the preliminary one he had found in that paper. He thought about that sometimes but never mentioned it to anyone. He never learned anything more about the strange woman, and no one ever knew about the part she had played.

CHAPTER 11

Somme

John Hamman, 21
1916 Front Lines, France

There wasn't enough air. There never seemed to be enough air—too many men packed into too small of a space. They said the big shells sucked all the oxygen out of the air.

John didn't know about that, but far too many men were packed like sardines into the bunker. Even men with no hint of claustrophobia could lose it in here. You didn't hear the big shells landing outside—you felt them as dirt sifted down through the boards of the ceiling. It was something beyond sound as the air and your whole body were compressed with the concussion.

Men went insane at the mere idea of one of those landing directly on the bunker. They had had to strangle a man last week. They had killed one of their own. No one spoke of it. It drove them all a little mad. Perhaps it was meant to. By the time the barrage lifted, they would be ready to pour from the bunker simply to taste the air again. They would flood out and up and over the trench line toward the enemy to escape the bunker.

Their officer stood by the oil lamp at the front of the bunker looking at his watch. John didn't know if the time had come or if his time had run out. All he knew was that he had to get out of this bunker even if it meant he would die, as long as it was in the open air. He couldn't really look down in the dark and press of the bunker, but he could feel the gas mask container on his belt, the pockets of ammunition, the bayonet, his canteen.

The lieutenant was staring at his watch. He lifted the whistle from around his neck and brought it to his lips. The sound was loud in the confines of the bunker. It was time.

The bar slid back, and they poured out along the trench. He could see men flooding from other dugouts along the line, out into the night air. So many star shells were bursting above them that it might as well have been day. Why bother attacking at night? The light of the flares cast eerie shadows from the barbed wire and filled the scene with an otherworldly light.

"Fix bayonets!" The command echoed all along the line. They all gathered under the berm. Beyond it was no man's land and the death that awaited them with an 8mm bullet.

The whistle was loud, but John didn't hear it over the roar of the men, the roar that was emanating from his own throat. The men scrambled up and over the trench line into a wall of machine gun fire cutting down the men to his left as it walked across their line, and then he was tumbling forward into the mud below the berm and line of tracers.

He remembered charging forward over the broken ground pitted with more craters than the surface of the moon. Bullets cracked around him as another man fell on his right.

Artillery shells were landing, raising great fountains of dirt into the air, leaving behind fresh craters on top of the ones already there. Artillery rounds burst above their heads as hot shrapnel cut into the ground all around them.

A human wave rolled forth, stumbling, clawing, crawling across the broken ground through the obstacles of barbed wire and tank traps.

Off to his right he could see one of them. The roar of the engine and grinding of the great tracks could be heard even over the artillery. Its machine gun hammered continuously at the enemy line, and as he watched, one of its side guns fired with a great flash, leaving a ringing in his ears. Sparks flew and ricochets whined crazily off the beast's armored hide as the Huns' machine guns ineffectively tried to penetrate.

He angled to his left, not wanting to be so close to something attracting that much fire. With all the many ways to die this day, the random death from a ricochet seemed most ignominious.

He heard a whistling sound, as if the very air was being ripped apart, and the artillery began falling on them. The concussion knocked the wind from his lungs. Dirt rained down on him, and he crawled forward, his rifle lost as he blindly tried to get away when he crawled over a ridge and fell headfirst down a steep slope into a large crater.

He landed with a sodden splash at the bottom in stinking, rancid water. He came up gagging and swam toward the side, clawing his way through the mud out of the water up onto the forward slope.

John tried wiping his eyes, but his arm was covered with mud. Dead, bloated bodies floated in the water. The smell was overpowering. The natural urge to vomit was abated only after several involuntary dry heaves were beaten back by his desire to survive this night.

Another shell landed off to his left with a huge roar, and more dirt rained down on him. Part of the side of the crater seemed to collapse, threatening to bury him. Tracers streaked overhead. The water was cold, and he was not sure how he could get out of the crater. The slippery, near-vertical walls were like a trap.

Another star shell burst overhead, and as he looked around, he realized he was not alone. Someone else was in the crater with him.

The man was on his belly, as if he had slid back down from his own efforts to climb from the crater. John's bayonet was gone with his rifle.

He pulled his knife from the sheath in the back of his belt. It had been his grandfather's, and the stories said he had fought off Indians with it. Some stories said he had scalped them with it. He had bought it from a blacksmith named James Black in Arkansas on his way to Texas, and he had always sworn it was the finest knife he had ever owned.

The man was not in uniform, at least not one he recognized. He had a helmet on, but it was not English. It was closer to a Hun helmet. And it had something on the front of it.

Crawling closer, he rolled the man over and found him to be quite dead. A bullet had struck him in the face. The helmet had a small camera on the front of it. He could see the lens, but it was smaller than any other camera he had ever seen. The man had another camera attached to a stick with a loop around his wrist.

The clothes he wore were not any uniform John had ever seen—not the khaki of the British, the gray of the Germans, or even the blue of the French. The best way he could describe them was as of a mottled brown with splotches. He couldn't be sure with all the mud and the wavering light from the star shells, but he could almost swear the cloth had patterns dyed into it to resemble leaves. Or it could be the mud that inexorably covered everything.

His helmet was not of any make he knew. It was not made from metal but something thicker, almost like a pith helmet. He also had something on his chest like some kind of armor plate. It was thick but not heavy enough to be metal or anything that might stop a bullet with pockets all over it.

Who was this man, and what was he doing here in the middle of a war? He wore no insignia, no badges of rank. The only thing on his uniform was a patch, a strangely stylized "X" with a clock face in the background, on his left shoulder.

Scraping some of the mud away, John opened some of the strange pockets on the man's chest. They did not close with buttons, but the flaps pulled up with a ripping sound to reveal a small device, cylindrical about eight inches long with a series of dials around it. It had been grazed by a bullet, cutting a deep grove through the first few dials.

It didn't look like a grenade. It didn't have a pin. He twisted some of the dials. They turned, and a red light came on, almost like a tiny electric torch but shedding little light.

The artillery barrage seemed to have passed over him, but then it started over again. This time he could see them burst in the air in great white clouds. Gas! Nothing was more feared.

Dropping the strange device, he reached down to his side and found nothing but tatters. A piece of shrapnel had torn through the container, spilling out the only thing that could save his life during a gas attack somewhere on the battlefield.

He frantically searched the stranger, but he could find nothing resembling a mask. Beyond the edge of the crater he heard a loud *whump*. Death in a white cloud rolled over the edge of the crater and down toward him. Then there was a chiming sound, and everything changed.

* * *

It was over five hours later in the quiet before dawn when John crawled his way out of no man's land and back to the line. Calling out to the men not to shoot him, he finally dragged himself up over the berm and into his own trenches.

The men there could not understand how it was that he was shivering with hypothermia on a warm summer night. The ice in his hair and in his wet clothes was melting quickly in the warm air. The doctor had more difficulty in explaining what appeared to be frostbite on his fingers and toes.

He was not the only man to find his way back that morning. All of them would be scarred for the rest of their lives by what they had witnessed, but none of them had seen anything to compare with what John Hamman had experienced over the last few hours.

CHAPTER 12

Tooth

Robert Brown, 43
1981 San Francisco, CA

It was a nice house in a neighborhood of nice houses. The lawn was immaculate. It looked so much like the residences on either side that he had to check the number to make sure he had the right address.

Robert Brown sat in his car for a long time flipping through the papers, telling himself that he was getting them in order. He was procrastinating. He didn't know why he was here. Why had he been chosen to do this? He had met these people only briefly at the funeral as he filed by in line to give his condolences. None of this made any since. If John Hamman wanted to provide for his granddaughter, Robert could arrange for schooling or anything else that the child might need. There was no need to come all the way here for this errand.

Ringing the doorbell, Robert Brown waited with his briefcase in front of him. As he saw the man approach through the glass, he braced himself for the confrontation to come. He had gone into contract law because he didn't want to deal with things like hostile witnesses, only to find that corporate officers could be as full of vitriol as any indicted criminal. He much preferred to deal with paperwork from his desk.

The conversation that followed contained more than a bit of animosity. It was understandable. The girl's parents could not possibly be aware of the vast fortunes at stake, but they had always known that Mr. Hamman was wealthy, if eccentric. They had probably expected to inherit from him upon his death, as there were no other relatives.

The fact that everything was being held in a trust for their daughter was certainly unexpected. The fact that it was structured in a way outside of their control was maddening. The check Robert delivered to them was somewhat appeasing. It should be, with the amount of zeros in the number. The agreement they had signed allowing for special considerations on behalf of their daughter was quickly forgotten.

He dreaded the next part of his task far more. He felt uncomfortable as they led him down the hallway to the room with drawings of dinosaurs taped to the door.

He did not like children. They were loud, messy, and this one was crying. He did not know how to console a mourning child. He felt trapped as they closed the door, leaving him alone with her. He reached into his jacket pocket and grasped the strange necklace as he looked down into her tear-stained face.

CHAPTER 13

First Night

Jenny Hamman, 31
Cretaceous

Jenny turned off the headlamp and settled into the tent, thinking. The night was still with fewer night sounds than in the Africa of her day. As the night wore on and the temperature dropped, it became almost silent, except for the wind.

She did from time to time hear the rustling of small animals near the tent, undoubtedly the small mammals that survived unnoticed among the giants. *Good for the little guys. Hang in there. Your time will come.* One of them might be her great, great, great... great ancestor. In her time the night was when the world came alive, as all the wildlife came out to feed and hunt, free from the oppressive heat of the day.

Many of the animals here were cold-blooded and did not move around well in the colder parts of the night. Jenny knew that would not be true of all. Paleontologists knew from the sectioning of bones that they were much more vascular than the bones of cold-blooded reptiles. Some of the predators had high-enough metabolism that they were probably warm-blooded and could maintain their body heat into the night. The larger herbivores had enough mass that it would take much longer for them to cool down. What did all of this mean? What did she really know?

Using reptiles as an example, she knew they liked a certain temperature range. They didn't function well if their body temperature rose above or fell below that range. Was this true here?

Some dinosaurs were small, but some of them were beyond massive. With greater mass, they would cool and heat more slowly. They could be active later in the night than you might think if they were big enough. But would it take longer for them to warm up in the morning? Would the heat of the day be too much for them? Did they have other ways to control their temperature? She thought of alligators yawning.

Then there were the predators, which had higher metabolisms. Would they stop hunting in the night at all? How would they deal with the heat of the day? Would they have feathers? That was the current theory, that some of them were feathered to one degree or another. Which ones?

She tried thinking back to her grandfather. He had spoken once about that, but it was many years ago, and she wasn't sure which ones he had said were feathered.

Over the last two decades fossil records had shown evidence of feathers on theropods, which included all the nasty bipedal predators. Many of them were probably covered or at least partly covered in downy feathers for insulation.

They had evidence of larger feathers on the limbs. They might have been for display, but one other idea was that they were used to cover and keep the nest of eggs warm through the night.

The impression of skin from larger animals showed signs of scutes, horny plates like the surface of birds' feet or the skin of rhinos or elephants. They may have been bony enough to act as armor. As they grew larger, they may have outgrown the need for insulation. Would the older animals still retain any feathers, perhaps a crest? No one was sure how far it dated back, so other branches might also have some form of feathers.

She tried to wrap her head around where she was, what had brought her here. She thought about her kindly old grandfather and his visits. She tried to remember every time she had seen him and what he had said as she looked back on the things he had taught her.

He had known, all that time—the slightly sad look she would sometimes catch on his face as he watched her. The money he had left her made sense now, always pushing her toward this point.

What would have happened if she had not come here? What would happen if she failed? If she died here, would her grandfather have disappeared on one of his trips? Her mother would have never been. Her father would have married someone else. He might have had a child, but it wouldn't have been her, would it? It boggled the mind to imagine all this cascading history stemming from this one moment, disappearing and being rewritten. It gave her a headache.

She didn't have the right kind of mind for this. Maybe one of those theoretical physicists could wrap their head around all the contradictions. She had talked with one of them at a luncheon, and he had tried explaining quantum theory to her, but she tuned out after he tried turning it into an analogy about a cat in a box.

She was here. She could feel the ground beneath her. She could hear the wind outside her tent. The rodent digging under the bush to her right was real. The Bennettitalean she had touched today was real. And everything said that what she had to do was real.

It was late when she dozed off with the certainty that the day to come, and many that were to follow, would be memorable.

CHAPTER 14

H & H

John Hamman, 24
1919 London, England

London looked the same, but the feeling was different. People were quieter now. Fewer shops were open. He had a nice lunch and the beer was still good, but being here made him think of Harry. John missed him. It wasn't the same walking these streets alone or sitting down in a cafe and turning, expecting to see his friend.

John made his way west toward the Mayfair district. This was a higher-class area. The residences were much larger and more elegant here. He made his way along Bond Street. The shops were upscale. This was the home of Sotheby's auction house and Tiffany's. He found Bruton Street and turned south down it.

He had a plan that had started with a set of billiard balls. One was missing. John had gotten to talking to another man in his regiment who was a piano-tuner. They had talked about ivory and its growing scarcity. The man had told him that the big tuskers were being hunted out. It was becoming harder and far more expensive to buy new ivory. There might come a day when keys could not be made for new pianos.

The men had laughed, but John thought back to that night on the Somme. Many men, the lucky ones who lived through it, had nightmares from that night. John's dreams were different. He also dreamed of the great furry beast he had seen with its long, curving tusk.

He had almost frozen to death, soaked to the bone in that cold wind that blew on what should have been a warm summer night but was instead a cold, cloudy day in a strange land he did not know.

John shivered on the barren hillside. The wind blew cold out of the north, bringing flurries of snow, as he watched the beast that could not exist feed below him on the empty plain.

John shivered on the street, dragging his mind back to the present, to the now.

The war was now over, and like untold thousands of men, he was now free once more to pursue his fortunes wherever life might lead him. In other words, the British government had discharged and unleashed hundreds of thousands of men on to the country with no jobs, no employment, and no plan.

For those with families to welcome them, this was a warm homecoming. Many who had held positions before the war were able to return to their work. But many of those jobs had been filled over the last few years while they were gone, or those businesses had collapsed under the stress of the wartime economy.

What followed was predictable. Unemployment was high. Jobs were low. For someone without ties or family to support him, the outlook was bleak. John needed to get out of this country as fast as he could before his savings ran out.

All of this led to the plan. The European colonies had heavily culled the elephant herds to protect their new farms, killing hundreds of animals at a time. This led to the ivory trade.

As the older bulls were killed off, there were no more jumbos with massive hundred-pound tusks on each side. To be sure, the country still had elephants, but it took eighty years for an animal to grow hundred-pound tusks.

Supply was collapsing, and the price of white gold was going through the roof. The herds that once roamed Africa might be gone today, but if someone could somehow go back into a distant time when they roamed all over Africa... someone with a gun who knew how to shoot might be able to do well for himself.

There, Holland & Holland. Even then, it was legendary for its firearms. Harris Holland had passed away more than twenty years earlier, but the company endured and continued producing the finest firearms in the world in some of the most powerful cartridges. If you hunted game birds, you could find no better shotguns in the world. But today he was looking for something a bit bigger.

It had been more than a year since he had contacted them, sending them what amounted to every penny he had in the world to secure one of their double rifles. He would have felt quite silly if he had died in the meantime. Now it was ready, just in time for the end of the war.

The shop was smaller than he expected. He was used to gun stores with racks of rifles lining the wall, counters and displays, shelves of ammunition. This was different. It was more like a sitting room. A large fireplace with a painting of Old Man Harris above it dominated one wall. To either side were gun cabinets with glass doors but only a half dozen rifles on display. A desk and a few comfortable chairs were the only other furnishings. When John entered, a distinguished man with a graying beard and waxed mustache in a three-piece suit came in from another room to greet him.

"Can I help you?"

John was wearing his best uniform. It was clean but a little worn. He was feeling a bit underdressed. "Is this Holland & Holland, the gun-maker?"

"It is. Do you have something for me?"

John realized the gentleman thought he was some sort of delivery man.

"Actually, I hope *you* have something for *me*. My name is John Hamman, and I've been corresponding with you about acquiring a rifle. Is this your storefront?" John tried not to fidget and hoped this would not end with his being thrown out on his ear.

"Ah, the American." The man seemed to relax a bit, as he could now place John in his social hierarchy. John had seen this before. England was still very much a class-based society. They seemed to believe that everything would run smoothly as long as everyone stayed in their place.

Being a foreigner put John in a slightly different category, outside their normal strata, less than an Englishman but more than a commoner. Being an American, John found he could associate with almost any level of English society but would be treated more with amusement, as an oddity, than as an equal. However, wasn't really constrained by their class system.

"Yes, I believe your rifle is ready. Please have a seat." He pulled on a rope and then joined John in one of the large overstuffed chairs.

A maid came in with a decanter of whiskey and glasses on a tray. It was very rich and peaty. John did not want to think about how many years it must have rested in a barrel to become that smooth.

What followed was half an hour of polite conversation in which the man inquired about how John had come to be in his country's uniform, then about the war and his future plans.

John explained he was preparing to leave for British East Africa, where he planned to try his luck at the ivory trade as a hunter. The man seemed quite amused.

"Well, that certainly explains the rifle. I dare say it will do you good service there." He seemed tickled at the idea of hunting commercially for profit. John was sure most of the man's clients paid extravagant amounts of money to do the same for sport.

The ivory trade was in fact quite large, but it was beneath him to acknowledge that. They spoke of the other rifles John was taking with him.

Eventually the man stood and pulled the rope again, and a butler came in carrying a beautifully lacquered wooden box. It was placed on the table and opened before John. There in a velvet-lined pocket made to fit was an engraved double rifle.

"Five hundred Nitro Express, as you requested." The man picked it up and mounted the barrels. Handing it to John, he added, "Your rifle."

It was gorgeous. The engraving was of elephants on one side and rhinos on the other. John had thought about asking for something else, but they would have thought him mad if they had known what he expected to shoot with it.

John had never held anything this beautiful in his hands. He had never held anything this valuable in his hands either. He looked down at what amounted to two years of his salary.

The man politely inquired, "Tell me—do you have a sidearm?"

"I have a Webley Mark Five that I plan to carry."

The man granted that was a fine weapon but that it was prone to jamming in dirty environments. "Could I show you something we have just gotten in?"

John was more than a little intrigued. "Certainly. I would love to see anything you might have that would be of interest." The man excused himself and left the room briefly, returning with a rather large leather holster and belt, from which he drew a strange weapon.

At first John thought it was a cut-down double-barrel shotgun, but then he realized it had four barrels. A pepper-box? As a latch was pushed, the barrels opened downward on a hinge like a shotgun.

"It's a Lancaster in 455 Webley. It's only four shots, but the mechanism is completely contained. Only the trigger and the firing pin holes are open. It's far more reliable than a revolver in dusty environments. They were popular and did good service in the Sudan. This one recently came into our possession along with some other pieces in a collection."

It had an extended trigger that acted as a set trigger. It was heavy toward the front, but the man assured John that the barrels registered well. John had never seen such a design but bought it along with the rifle. Considering where he was going, he didn't think he could have too many guns.

CHAPTER 15

Survival School

Robert Brown, 44
1982 New York, NY

The senior partners of the law firm sat around the conference room table. The president sat at the head of the table with a large simple manila envelope in front of him. As he looked down at it, with the instructions and the day's date written on it, he shook his head, trying to imagine what the old man had been thinking.

He picked up the letter-opener and sliced through the sealed envelope. Taking out the documents and reading through them, he saw that they contained financial instructions, written more than a year before, for his company.

He read them aloud to the other senior partners, who took notes on all the instructions that must be passed on to the board of directors who were in charge of the running of Hamman's various companies. Half of the instructions did not make any sense. "Buy Sony... what the hell is a 'CD'?"

Finally, at the bottom was another sealed envelope. It was addressed to Robert Brown. He stared at it and then passed it to the man on his right. On it went to the most junior member of the firm. Robert sat there, uncomfortable, as all eyes turned to him as he opened the envelope. The papers within detailed his tasks in the administration of the trust set up for Jenny Hamman.

The first page instructed him that he was not permitted to discuss the following documents or contents therein with any other person, including members of the firm. As he explained this, the disapproving looks that bore down on him made him want to wilt in his seat. Returning this cover letter to the president, he read onward silently as the board looked on.

His brow furrowed in confusion. None of this made any sense. This couldn't be right. He had to do *what?* Robert wasn't sure this was possible or for that matter if it was even legal. Why on earth would John Hamman want this for his granddaughter? He stared down at the instructions and then self-consciously slid them back into the envelope.

He desperately wanted to ask them what this was all about. The instructions were very clear that he was bound not to discuss it with any other person. It also made clear the consequences if any member of the firm deviated from the instructions. "Please continue." The rest of the board stared at him in displeasure and then turned back to the other matters at hand.

He heard nothing the rest of the meeting as the other board members discussed stock options and how to structure the purchases through subsidiary corporations.

He had been expecting to arrange for private schooling. He had even been compiling a list of possible institutions. He had not expected this. As the meeting went on around him, his thoughts were turned inward, trying to imagine where he would find a primitive survival school that would accept a twelve-year-old girl.

CHAPTER 16

Morning

Jenny Hamman, 31
Cretaceous

Jenny woke before dawn, the air still cold. Reaching up, she touched the tent above her head. It was real. She was here in the past. She thought back to the note and all that it implied, what she had to do.

It was still chilly. That was good. This would probably be the safest time of the day. She pushed the sleeping bag off her. She had not zipped it up or taken her boots off. She did retighten them from where she had loosened the laces last night.

Jenny untied the front of the tent and slowly pulled the flap back to look outside. You never knew what you might see if you were quiet. It was still dark but she didn't hear anything.

She climbed out and began breaking the camp down. The sky was finally lightening when she had everything packed away. The batteries were sealed in plastic in a pouch on her belt. The rifle was strapped to the side of the pack. Releasing two Fastex buckles would free it. The Neostead was on a single-point sling around her shoulder. She could shoulder it on either side or let it hang, where it would point to her lower left. She had bird shot in the chamber and number #4 in one side and 00 buckshot in the other.

Jenny took her first real look around as the sky grew light and the sun began cracking over the horizon. She looked at the compass. Sure enough, it said that the sun rose in the west. That meant the needle was actually pointing to the south. She knew this was entirely possible from geologic data, but it was different to see it in person. It was reassuring. If it had not been reversed she would know that she was in the wrong time, perhaps by millennia.

The sun was rising above a line of hills in the distance. From the distance she judged them to be fairly large. She thought she could see the land rising to meet them.

Could there be a river running at their base? She couldn't see any sign of one. If the river was bordered by hills, she thought he would have mentioned that. Instead, he spoke of meandering horseshoe bends. That sounded like an open plain. Looking to the east, the plains rolled away as far as she could see. That looked more promising, but it also meant she was on the wrong side of the river. That could be a problem.

It was possible the river was on the far side of those hills, but again that would still put it close enough that she was sure he would have used them as a landmark. Or she could be much farther from him then he had estimated. Best to follow the watershed downhill away from the range of hills to her west.

She put her back to the sun and started out away from the hills. As she did, she detoured by the Bennettitalean that she had appeared beside. She reached out and stripped a handful of the seeds from the plant. If she lived through this, no one would ever believe what was growing in her garden.

Walking with her back to the sun gave her good light to see anything she was approaching. She carried the shotgun at low ready, though she had not seen any of the fauna yet.

The land was open enough that she made good time. As she walked, she chewed on a protein bar, not wanting to waste the morning hours cooking something more substantial. It was chewy, requiring an effort to masticate. The flavor left a lot to be desired and was hardly worth it, but she knew she could march all day on a couple of them.

As much as she yearned to explore this world, she was more than aware of the hazards that might lurk here. The sooner she found her grandfather the better. They should leave this place as soon as possible.

As she walked along she cataloged the flora around her. The idea of the seeds stuck with her, and as she walked she would do the same with other extinct plants as she passed by them. Of course, not all produced seeds or were bearing at this time, and she could not stop to dig anything up. Not here, but perhaps if she found her grandfather, she might be able to pick up a larger souvenir.

It was still early when she saw it—curled up in a ball under a fern. She wasn't sure what it was. It was covered with feathers like those of a bird, but she could see a long neck turned and tucked under its arm, which was covered with long feathers, almost like a wing. It was her first dinosaur, and it was lunch.

She thought about the sacrilege of what she was about to do as she raised the shotgun. She was about to kill an animal that had been extinct for millions of years. She wished she had ears.

The roar was loud. The barrel was not overly short, but the bull pup configuration put the muzzle too close to her ear. She wished for her Remington. The blast blew the thing over, and with one spasm it went still. She walked over to examine her kill.

It was small, a bit larger than a chicken. It had long feathers on the back of its arms and larger feathers on the end of its tail. The rest was covered with more of a down, clearly for insulation. With its smaller size, it probably had issues with body heat during the night. The head was not overly large. The mouth was more beak-like, reinforcing its birdlike appearance.

She knew what this was. Collections were full of examples. It was a Caudipteryx, or something closely related to it. She wondered what would be in its stomach. The thinking was that it ate mostly plants and seeds but was opportunistically omnivorous, preying on insects and small animals, maybe on some of the small mammals living in this time.

For that matter, what time *was* she in? Jenny was fairly sure that she was in the Cretaceous, probably the early to middle. She turned back to the dinosaur. It caused her pain, but she cut the head off and held it upside down to drain. One thing she could say was that the heart was persistent, and she thought she got most of the blood out.

She sat about plucking it. Again, this felt like a crime against science, but she would think more about specimens and less about lunch later when she wasn't trapped here. She thought about plucking it while she walked but didn't want to leave a trail of fresh feathers behind her. So she sat on her pack as she worked and thought about the ridiculous situation she was in.

Once the animal was plucked and gutted, she could see it much more clearly. It was a Caudipteryx, or a close cousin. She really wanted to dissect it too see the full skeleton. What an opportunity! But she buried the evidence with a small trowel from her pack, wrapped the thing in a bag, and put it inside the pack for later. She would bury all the evidence she could of her passage. She didn't want a larger predator to pick up her trail.

The sun was up now as Jenny continued on her way. The plain was flat and dry. Wind blew dust around her feet. The ground cover was sparse, consisting mostly of various types of ferns. Grasses had not really developed in this time period, and the soil was not as stabilized. Erosion must happen much faster here.

As the afternoon progressed, she started spotting some fliers. At first there were only a handful, circling high on thermals as the day grew hotter. They were far enough away that she could not identify them. Their behavior implied that they filled a place in the ecosystem like the vulture. They were probably searching for carrion.

She was debating what to do about food. She didn't want to cook anything at a fixed camp, so in the early afternoon she stopped and decided to cook her kill. Best to eat it now when there was no sign of larger predators and the land was open enough that she could see anything coming.

The prospect of something being attracted to her tent in the night was unappealing. She decided she would make only cold camps. She wasn't sure if a fire was a good idea or not. Most animals were naturally afraid of fire, but it would also announce her presence.

Another thought occurred to her. A nocturnal predator might do well to hunt with infrared vision. In the cold night, larger prey would hold enough thermal mass to make them stand out against the cold ground. Snakes hunted warm-blooded rodents that way.

The point was that a fire would be even more of a beacon in the night. It was a moot point right now with little to burn, but a fire at night might be a mixed blessing. She had a small stove with three bottles of propane. It should be more than enough as long as she used it sparingly. Water might prove more of an issue.

She stripped the meat off the bones of the small dinosaur and put it into the pot to cook for stew. A packet of chicken noodles filled it out nicely. In the end, it did taste very much like chicken, and she didn't think that was because of the noodles. This family was the direct ancestors of birds.

As she ate she couldn't help but play with the bones. So strange to handle what she had previously only chipped from stone. It was a big meal. She forced herself to finish it and buried the remains. Washing her hands in the dirt, she shouldered her pack and marched onward.

CHAPTER 17

Philby

Kim Philby, 30
September 1942 London, England

Kim Philby sat back contentedly in his chair and listened. He was good at that. It was his job, listening and hearing what was actually said. That was the real trick. It was one thing to listen to people's words but something completely different to hear their actual meaning.

People said so much, but to look underneath it to the truth took a different set of skills. That was part of what had made him such a good reporter. It was what made him so good at his present job and his other job, the one no one could know of.

That was the other secret—to be the person you were supposed to be, to believe the things you were supposed to believe. No one could see through that face because it was real, as real as the things you truly believed, as real as the person you truly were. As long as you could keep those things separate, no one could ever see through you.

He sat and listened. The beer was good, which always helped, and the man across from him was his friend. Philby had helped him and advised him. He had shown the man how to form the very organization, the newly minted OSS, that he was betraying with every word without even knowing it. Why would he ever question or suspect? And later, when Philby was alone, he would write up every word to be sent to his real masters to support his real loyalties.

"He had been bugging me about it for years. How he and this fellow Sengier had this ore—that it was important. All the way back when I met him in '39. He was a partner in this mine, and I thought he was trying to sell it, like anyone would, but he kept insisting it was important. I mean, I'd never even heard of this stuff. What did it matter about purity? He was always bugging me to tell people about it. Well, it finally came up in a meeting. Top priority, critical to the war effort, all that. You should have seen their faces when I told them I knew someone selling it, that he had been storing it in New York for two years trying to find someone in the government to buy it. I thought this guy Nichols, Kenneth Nichols, was going to fall out of his chair. This big secret announcement of this mission to find this rare element... When I told them right there that a guy was selling it by the ton over on Staten Island—I should have asked for a raise."

Why was this so important? Why did the Americans want it? This mine in the Congo. Perhaps someone should look into that. And how did they know it was so important? Everyone used radium for watch dials, for everything. That was important, but the waste ore left over? What were they doing with that? Anything being made that high of a priority at that level had to have some meaning.

Those thoughts fell by the wayside later as they continued talking. It was disturbing, the amount of intelligence the Americans had. Someone in the network must be compromised.

One operation in particular stood out. He had a hard time keeping his face composed as the man across from him told him of one of his own plans. That alone would be disturbing, but this plan was not yet in operation. He had not initiated it yet. He had not yet reported his plans to anyone above him. He had not written anything down. He had not in fact discussed it with another living soul. He had conceived of it only the other night.

And here it was being laid out in front of him in detail. He tried to ask about the source, but the man was cagey about where the information had come from. That was not uncommon—knowledge of the source of information was often guarded more closely than the information itself. Still, he must know.

How could this be? Could it be a guess? Was he trying to entrap him by telling him of all this? Maybe they had struck on the same idea as his own. But the other operations they had compromised were real.

And what about this fellow at the mine? How had he known about the desperate need for what had been tailings, basically wastage, two years before America had even started to seek it for some secret project. Could they be connected?

It crossed his mind that they had somehow learned to read someone else's thoughts, but if that were the case, why were they having a beer in a warm pub instead of having this conversation in a cell? And why would they be disclosing their knowledge of these plans to him? To flush him? They had all they needed to take him in right now if they had tied any of this to him. But then where had it come from? And how the hell did they know the details of the plans that he had dreamed up himself, lying in bed, the other night?

He knew beyond a doubt that no one else in the world shared this knowledge. It was almost as if they could see into the future. But that was as absurd as the idea that they could read minds. He must write up a report for his superiors but wasn't sure how to do it without sounding too crazy.

He waved to the barmaid and ordered another round. He had to keep "Wild Bill" Donovan talking. He had to find out the source of his information.

CHAPTER 18

Nairobi

John Hamman, 24
1919 Nairobi, British East Africa

Passage through the Suez was swift, as the area was now secure, and the freighter made its way through with little delay. They were not the most comfortable accommodations. John did have his own bunk in a dark unventilated compartment that he shared with five crewmen. Not exactly POSH, but it was all he could afford with what remained of his funds.

His companions were not the friendliest, being of rough demeanor and bearing more than a few scars. He would have been surprised if there was one among them who did not have a price on his head somewhere.

John thought the only reason his throat was not cut and his body slipped quietly over the side was that he had no more to be stolen than any of them. He made sure to keep nothing on himself, never to leave anything in his bunk, and he always slept with a knife in his hand under the pillow.

It was an interesting trip. John spent as much time as possible on deck or in one of the break rooms that the crew was fed in, retiring only later in the evening after the temperature had dropped enough to make the compartment tolerable. He woke up early and slipped out before dawn. It did allow him to spend most of his time admiring the African coast that they followed after passing through the canal.

They encountered only one storm, early on as they passed through the Mediterranean. The storms there could be surprisingly violent for the size of that body of water. The ship rolled drunkenly. At times John wondered if it would right itself again.

They were all confined below deck, and everyone was sick, even the old sea hands. John ate little and kept down less. Even water refused to stay down. The storm lasted four days, which he supposed was blessedly short, but by the end they were all like trapped animals in a cage.

The only thing that kept John from killing one of the worst offenders was his own weakness. He wasn't sure he could stand long enough to cross the room to finish the man. As it happened, John did not need to bother.

A violent fight broke out between several of the crew over one of the interminable card games they all seemed to engage in. John was propped in a chair in the corner, trying to keep some water and crackers down, when it started.

He had no idea what provoked it, but when he looked back, all four men seemed to be engaged in a free-for-all. If there were sides, he could not distinguish them.

One man was knocked or fell down, and the other three were on the fallen man, stabbing with their knives. John didn't know how many times the man was stabbed, but all three men were bloody when they finally tired and stepped back to examine their work.

No one said a thing. Someone fetched a piece of canvas, and the body was wrapped where it was against the wall. It was never moved and stayed there for another day and a half until the weather calmed and the seas permitted the body to be carried out of the room and without ceremony dumped over the side. As far as John could tell, that was the end of the matter. It was a lesson. In this land, do not fall. No one tolerated weakness here.

John was more than ready to disembark when they sighted the port of Mombasa. The British had built docks that the ship could pull up to, and over the next two days it was unloaded.

John was very happy to be off it. He splurged on a hot bath at what passed for a hotel near the docks. The men in the port were not that different from his travel companions. They fit the description of pirates all too well.

He found that they were holding the train for the ship to be unloaded, but the clerk pointed out that there would be nothing for it to carry and no point in its departure until that was done. John realized he was in a slightly different world with different rules.

Fresh and clean, dressed in his newest safari jacket, safari boots, and mandatory pith helmet, John thought he made quite a sight—a proper "white hunter." He saw to his baggage being loaded and then boarded the train.

The two passenger cars had rows of benches on one side and an aisle on the other. The rest of the car was filled with Black and Indian workers. It was stuffy, and John tried to open a window only to find that the smoke from the engine blew in. The other passengers made their displeasure known, and he quickly secured it. It was about then when John heard a voice behind him.

"My word—who are you?"

John turned to see another white man dressed in a lose shirt and wide-brimmed hat looking him up and down. He was a bit taken aback as he introduced himself and learned that his traveling companion was one Berkeley Cole.

With a "Come on then," Cole led him forward through the door in the front of the coach. They had to step across the gap to the next car, which was a coal car, and Cole led him to a narrow plank running down the side of the car. "Watch your step." The men continued to the engine.

The engineer was an old, grizzled man who greeted them warmly. And the stoker was a large, smiling negro. Introducing John, Cole asked if they could pop forward.

"Suit yourself." Berkeley led John forward once again along a narrow service walkway along the side of the engine. "Watch out. It can be a bit hot."

He led them past the boiler to a sort of basket with a bench seat on the very front of the engine. John felt like the figurehead on the prow of a ship as it cut through the waves, only here it was oceans of grass.

"My good man, I'm rather sorry about this, but it must be done."

He snatched the pith helmet off John's head and tossed it, sending it sailing out into the grass, lost forever. John let out a squawk of protest, but Cole ignored him and took the wide-brimmed hat off his own head and planted it on his new acquaintance.

"There—much better. Keep that. You look a little pale and will need a bit of protection from the sun until you get a more healthy brown."

The view of the plains was spectacular as they lounged in the sun, the smoke from the engine being left far behind as the wind from the passage blew in their face.

John couldn't believe the richness and variety of game. They crossed the famous Tsavo River, where lions had killed so many workers on this very rail line. They did not see any lions. As they rolled along, Cole pointed out all the different species and told John of them, and John told Cole of his plans to become a great white hunter and to make a living hunting elephants for ivory.

Cole was a very well-bred member of the English aristocracy, son of the fourth Earl of Enniskillen, and was able to control his laughter with a straight face. He merely stared at John slightly wide-eyed.

On realizing John was serious, he simply said, "I see."

They rolled into Nairobi shortly before dark. Cole was met by several Blacks and spoke to them rapidly in their own language, motioning toward the baggage car. "Best come along with me to the club so everyone can get a look at you."

"But my bags—"

"Yes, yes, I told them to take them to the hotel. I'm afraid we don't have any rooms open at the club right now. This way. Let's go get a drink."

The club turned out to be a pink stucco building, the Muthaiga Country Club. Cole led John into the bar and preceded to introduce him to everyone there. This was the heart of white society in Kenya. The dining room was rustic, and the meal was the best John had had in weeks.

Cole become engaged in conversation with a tall, lanky man named Denys. John wandered over to a broad lounge area to the great fireplace that warmed the chill from the night air. Engraved in the stone above the fire were the words "Na Kupa Hati M'zuri."

"'I bring you good fortune,'" John heard from behind him. Turning, he found a distinguished older man. He lifted his cane and pointed at the inscription. "It reads, 'I bring you good fortune.' Hugh, Hugh Cholmondeley. People here insist on calling me Lord Delamere, but please call me Hugh."

"John Hamman. I arrived on the train." They shook hands.

"Yes, the American who wants to hunt ivory." John stared at him. "Please—it's a very small community."

"And he founded it. This is the man who founded the entire country. Isn't that right, my lord?" It was Denys. Cole stood behind him, smiling and enjoying the interplay.

"It's one of the dangers of growing old. Eventually you predate everyone around you. The other annoying part is that the young people around you eventually grow big enough that they can no longer be spanked," Lord Delamere said as he looked down, grinding his cane into the floor.

"Have you thought about where you are going to live?" Lord Delamere persisted in ignoring his friends as he continued the conversation. "You are eventually going to need some land."

"And now he's going to turn you into a farmer like the rest of us." Cole was more than a bit amused as Lord Delamere tried to convince John to settle on a farm. He said he could arrange the purchase of a quantity of land near the Ngong hills. "Soon he'll have you as a part of his 'set.' He tends to collect people he finds interesting. I don't think he has an American yet."

The conversation evolved into a card game around a small table in the corner, which ran late into the night. John eventually made his excuses and bid them good night. When he left, he saw no sign of the game ending any time soon.

On leaving, John realized he had no idea of where to go. He knew in theory he had a room somewhere in the town but had no clue as to where it was. He had to go back in and ask the doorman where the hotel he was staying at could be found. As it turned out, not knowing the name of the hotel was not an impediment, as there was only one.

It was remarkably nice. The Norfolk was the only stone building with a tiled roof in the town, built in a classic Tudor fashion in 1904 and boasting forty rooms, a billiards hall, and a French chef. At the desk John found that he had already been checked in, and all his bags had been sent to his room.

The walls were covered with pictures. Many of them were of people posing with trophy-size animals they had shot on safari. John was sure some of them must have been famous. One stood out to him. As an American, he was unmistakable with his mustache and glasses. A whole section of the wall was dedicated to his trip, showing pictures of huge elephants, rhinos, and lions.

Above them on the wall hung two rifles, both lever actions. One was an 1894 with its tubular magazine under the barrel. It had a Maxim suppressor screwed to its barrel. The other was an 1895 with its box magazine. John had never fired one. The idea of being able to load it with a stripper clip, as he knew some of the Russian soldiers had done during the war, was intriguing. He didn't see the feed lips on this gun. Under it was a small plaque that simply read, "Big Medicine."

John stopped in at the bar to see if he could still get a nightcap before retiring and found it was still open and patronized by a tall man in dusty clothing. Wearing an ammo belt around his waist, he turned out to be a Swede, one Baron Bror Fredrik von Blixen-Finecke, otherwise known as "Blix." He was also some sort of baron. It seemed that everyone here was some kind of second-string aristocracy. John was getting the impression that Africa was the agreed-upon dumping ground for all the unwanted nobility of Europe. He was beginning to wonder if he would find a Russian princess working as a barmaid.

Blix was the only person not to make fun of John or his plans. He talked about safaris, the men John would need, where to find game, and how to hunt them. He said John should try his luck in the Maasai Mara, or the Great Rift Valley.

The Mara was more open. You could see farther. But if you really wanted elephants and big ivory, you had to go into the dense jungle where they fed. Shots were at point-blank range. You needed a big gun, and you would get only one shot before it trampled you. Trying to find and track them in that environment was a nightmare. He had an idea of trying to spot them from the air by plane and directing the hunting parties with message canisters, as they did in the war.

He argued that the money from now on would be in guiding, not in the ivory itself. He was already very drunk, and the evening ran very late. At some point John must have gone to bed, but he didn't remember doing so.

John's next memory was of a banging on the door of his hotel room. Light was streaming in through the window. He realized he was still fully dressed and stumbled to the door, which continued to shake under the assault. He opened it to find the man from the bar last night. He couldn't place his name.

"There you are! I've been looking for you everywhere. Good—you're already dressed. Are you ready to go? I've found you a man."

"What? Who?" John tried to rub the sleep from his eyes.

"He's Kikuyu. His name is... well, even I can't pronounce it. Just call him 'Manny.' You should bring your hat. You'll need that," he said, picking it up off the bed and handing it to John. "Manny will find some men for you. They'll fetch your bags down. We should get breakfast before we go."

He seemed to take John's never-unpacked baggage from the steamer to be his preparations—for what exactly was unclear. John felt as if he were being drawn along in this man's wake. When John stumbled down the stairs after him, he found that breakfast was champagne and pink gin at the bar.

By the time they had finished their repast and walked outside, they found a large lorry waiting for them with a number of Negros milling around it. They walked up to find a tall Black native with eight others lined up behind him.

"This is Manny. He'll be your man. He'll take care of everything. Just let him handle it." One other stood out from the rest, tall and lanky. Alone among all of them, he held a spear and shield. He looked different from the rest. He felt different from the rest. The others did not go near him. "That's your tracker. He's Maasai."

John looked at the man, who was silent, unsmiling, unmoving, like a statue. He made John uncomfortable. None of the other men went near him ether.

Manny came and addressed John: "Hello, Bwana. These men belong to you." John had no idea how to take that comment. Manny motioned deferentially for him to enter the back of the lorry. John found that all his baggage, still not unpacked, was already in the bed of the truck.

Manny had John set himself down on a stack on rolled-up blankets as a pillow, and all the men began piling into and onto the truck. Some sat, but most had to stand. Two even sat on top of the cab with their feet dangling over the front of the windscreen. The overloaded lorry fired up with a sputtering roar and began lumbering ponderously down the street out of town. John had been in Nairobi for less than a day. It would seem that he was off on his first safari.

They followed a road, such as it was, until it became thinner and thinner, until they were driving across the open landscape of Africa. Late in the day they reached an open, slightly rolling plain dotted with scattered patches of trees, the Maasai Mara. The lorry pulled to a stop, and people began piling off, unloading bundles and packs and John's baggage. Blix unloaded two crates himself.

"I took the liberty of picking you up some provisions." He sat down one full case of whiskey and one of gin. "I should be back to pick you up before they run out. You can pay me back from the ivory. At some point you'll have to get a lorry of your own. Best of luck. Try not to get yourself or too many of your men killed."

With a cheerful wave, he and his men loaded back into the truck and were off, leaving John's men, Manny, and John in the middle of the Mara with a stack of supplies. John watched the truck and its small dust cloud disappear into the setting sun.

CHAPTER 19

Colorado Survival Institute

Jenny Hamman, 12
38°46'17.2"N 105°10'02.6"W
1982 near Cripple Creek, CO

*S*hit, *shit, shit, shit, shit.* Jenny repeated this mantra as she ran up the rocky trail and assiduously avoided tripping on the scree. Tripping now would be bad. She chanced a look back, and her pursuer was still there.

She was alternating between careful stalks and ferocious runs toward Jenny that always stopped short as Jenny readied the log she had picked up to defend herself. The stalker was at least 150 pounds of pissed-off mountain lion.

What Jenny had done to piss her off, she didn't know. Somehow in the midst of her panicked thoughts Jenny imagined that the mountain lion had babies somewhere nearby. Who knew, and why that mattered at that moment, she had no idea, but that was for another time one when a pissed-off, overgrown cat was not trying to eat her.

Jenny heard a voice echoing through the canyon. It wasn't her imagination or some long-lost prospector's ghost. It was the voice of her wilderness survival coach, the oddly named, or perhaps aptly named for this particular incident, Reuben Angry Lion.

"I'd find a tree if I were you," the voice said with not a small bit of humor in the delivery. "You might want to hurry. She looks angry and outweighs you by quite a bit."

Thanks, Reuben. What an asshole, she thought. *Find a tree, find a tree, find a tree.* There on the right was a tree with some lower branches she could reach with a jump.

She veered off the trail and jumped into the tree, grabbing the lowest branch, and climbed as if her life depended on it, as it may well have. The mountain lion was right behind Jenny and started following her up the tree.

Once Jenny had gotten about ten feet up, she turned and brained the beast right between the eyes with the trusty log she had managed to hold on to throughout the climb. That took the fight out of the cat. She didn't fall out of the tree but hung there for a minute with her ears tucked back with an angry and somehow disapproving look on her face.

Jenny's beloved Mr. Cuddle Bunny had many a time, given her the same look at home when he was perturbed with some imagined slight.

With a low growl to let Jenny know she had decided to leave her prey alone as long as Jenny stayed far away from her area, she descended the tree and ambled down the trail back to wherever the hell bitchy mountain lions went after a busy morning of terrifying young girls.

Jenny could still hear the echoing laughter of her tormentor, Reuben. How was it that she was in the middle of bum-fuck Egypt, Colorado, and still surrounded entirely by assholes?

Jenny yelled into the air, "I'm glad you're having a good time, Reuben, you fucking wet wipe."

The laughter abated long enough for him to reply, "Such language from such a young woman—it's not fitting." The laughter resumed, and if such a thing were possible, at an even higher volume.

Other kids from Jenny's high school were in Acapulco or Hawaii. Some sat at home and played video games. Some even went to summer camp. She had to assume their summer camps involved things like swimming and whitewater rafting and assiduously avoided the angry mountain lion chase event she had had the opportunity to experience.

Jenny thought of Mr. Brown sitting in the Midnight Rose Hotel and Casino in Cripple Creek at that very moment, sitting in the air conditioning, sipping a cold drink, and undoubtedly complaining about the accommodations, as he was apt to do. Jenny swore that he would object if you hung him with a golden rope. He'd turned self-pity into a high art form.

There she was, up a tree, scratched, bruised, filthy, and sore, wearing moccasins she had had to sew herself and a positively horrible Native American-pattern tunic that she had fashioned from buckskin that fell to her knees.

Jenny realized her ass was hanging out, as Native Americans didn't wear underwear, and she'd not been able to figure out how to make a pair of pants. So a knee-length dress type thing it was. She could now see the downfall of this type of clothing as she tried pulling her skirt out of the branches before Reuben could see her bare-assed in a tree and most likely fall over dead in a fit of uncontrollable laughter.

That voice, filtering through the gorge, filled Jenny with a level of hate that a girl her age should never know. "Daylight's burning. Come on, Squeaky. Let's get going."

"Squeaky?" Jenny called.

The voice answered, "That's the noise you were making running up that trail. That's your Indian name now."

She responded angrily, "That's some bullshit. That's not even a thing—you just made that up."

The echoing voice responded between fits of laughter, "Ancient Indian rules—I didn't make them up, Squeaky, but it's my sacred duty to observe them."

"I hate him. I hate him so very, very much," Jenny grumbled as she carefully lowered herself down from the tree.

CHAPTER 20

Afternoon

Jenny Hamman, 31
Cretaceous

S he started seeing the dust in the early afternoon. It was a herd moving east toward what she hoped was the direction of the river. They were not moving fast but were overtaking her and looked to be passing near her.

Jenny decided to hunker down and found a spot on a small rise where she could sit down in the shade of some small bushes with a good view. As she sat in the shade, she knew she would blend in and, if she was not moving, almost disappear.

She was not afraid of the herd, but herds often had other less friendly things shadowing them. She pulled out a small monocular. The clarity in it was excellent. It was hard to see through the dust, but as they grew closer, Jenny began making them out. It was some form of Ornithischian. They were quadrupedal. It was hard to narrow it down beyond that. They were not her main interest.

They had company, as most herds did. She could see the predators paralleling the path of the herd, looking for the young or the weak straying too far from the safety of their brethren. As they grew closer, the size became more apparent. These were big animals, only slightly smaller than an elephant. The hunters were larger, some form of theropod. They weren't the famous Tyrannosaurus but a close relative.

Jenny watched them cross the plain below her. As they came closer and the wind picked up a bit, carrying away the dust, she could see them better through the glass. She thought she could see a bit of a bulge on their noses. They might be Muttaburrasaurus.

The herd had already passed when the hunters made their move. She heard them call to each other as they moved in. They charged, trying to scatter some of the creatures from the back of the herd. As the herd broke into a full gallop, everything dissolved into clouds of dust.

The herd charged away and the dust began settling, revealing a scattering of creatures. Most of them were able to escape, running to catch up with the herd, but two were cut off. They tried standing together but had no chance against the predators that moved to surround them.

One tried to make a break for it, but two of the theropods sprinted after it. One hunter tried cutting it off, and as it turned to escape, the other hunter pursuing caught it by the rear leg, bringing it down. The powerful jaws must have broken the bone outright.

Soon they were both on it and the animal's fate was sealed as the second hunter locked its jaws around the animal's long neck above the shoulder. The loud bellowing honks of the dinosaur ended.

The other ornithopod was surrounded. The hunters moved in, snapping at it. It tried fighting back, swinging its tail at one that tried to take it from behind. The predator pulled back, but as it was distracted, another attacker charged it from the front. It tried dancing away, but the jaws clamped down on its shoulder, and at the same time the one behind it lunged back in, seizing one of its legs. It tried to keep its feet but was dragged down on its side, and the killing jaws with their long teeth seized onto its neck. It died silently, kicking futilely in the dust.

Jenny watched as two others returned to join in, feeding on the kills. She had not expected dinosaurs that large to hunt in packs. She wondered if they hunted larger herbivores like the bigger sauropods.

She waited until she was sure that all the members of the pack had joined in on the kills. Predators rarely passed up an easy meal, even if it was comparatively as small as her, but if they had a kill, they rarely abandoned it for anything else. It wasn't that they weren't greedy. It was more important to protect their share from the other members of their own pack. It was about the competition between pack members. This was Jenny's chance to move on and be ignored.

She gathered her pack and moved from her spot in the shade, taking one last long look through the glasses. Would she find these bones someday after she returned across that vast space of time? Would someone dig these scattered, cracked bones from the stone and wonder about the fight she had witnessed?

As she moved off, she made sure to angle off, giving the herd's path a wide berth. She did not want to have anything following that herd pick up her scent trail.

She thought about the battle she had witnessed between animals larger than anything walking the world she came from. How had her ancestors survived among these giants? By being small. By hiding below their notice. She didn't think there existed a mammal bigger than a large rat in the entire world at that time.

How close had it come to her species never existing at all? If it had not been for a small twist of cosmic fate, none of those little rodents would have ever grown any larger.

Her whole world and all the animals that lived in it would never have existed if this world had not been destroyed. She owed everything to a random piece of space rock that even now orbited somewhere out there in the cold night.

Could those mighty predators ever conceive that one day their undisputed reign of this world would end? Would her own people, the rulers of their own world, pass into history, and how would it happen?

As Jenny moved away at a brisk pace, wanting to put distance between herself and the conflict she had witnessed, she began noticing fliers circling above the recent battle. They would have to wait their turn. They looked large, but she could not judge their sizes so high in the sky, riding the thermals above the plain.

The silhouettes were wrong, but they seemed to fill the same niche that vultures did in her time. Strange how some things change but everything stays the same.

She did not stop moving as she took another drink from the canteen. She would not hunt again this day. The noise was too much of a risk with that pack of predators in the area. She would eat from her pack tonight without cooking at her campsite.

The sun was moving toward the horizon. She had lost a couple of hours watching the hunt. It would start getting dark in another hour, with no sign of a moon rising. She would like to continue her march into the night, but the headlamp would be too much of a risk. The smaller predators would be more active in the early parts of the night. It might be best not to be moving around in the early evening.

She kept moving until she started losing the light. Once it got harder to see, she began looking for a place to conceal her tent. She wanted to find some larger bushes or ferns that would hide her from a casual passerby.

It was becoming quite dark by the time she had it up and had moved her pack inside. She unrolled the foam pad and settled down, pulling the sleeping bag over her. She did not climb inside it. The night was not that cold, and she did not want to be confined.

Jenny listened to the night sounds. She had seen things this day that no one had witnessed for millions of years. And even then, they had been seen only by her grandfather and his men. They were out there somewhere right now, looking up at the same sky. Did they have any hope, stranded in this foreign time? They could not know that she was here. They must be scared. Had anyone ever faced such a hopeless situation?

She thought of all the things that had led her here, her grandfather and everything he had said and done. Looking back, she was sure he loved her. It was also clear that everything he had done for her had been leading her to this, preparing her for this-the books he brought her, teaching her to shoot, to hunt.

She tried thinking if there had ever been anything between them that had not been part of his plans for her. Somehow it made her sad to think that every moment between them had been a part of some kind of grand plan.

She did not notice as tears ran down her face in the dark. She could not believe there had been nothing else between them. She remembered times when she had caught him looking at her, that sadness in his face.

She would see him again, the man who had been lost to her since she was a child. But it would not be him. It would be some younger him, someone who had never known her, a stranger who one day would become the grandfather she had loved. Would it be as strange for her as it had been for him? What should she tell him? Would she change the future with every word, or was that already part of her future, her past, and would it change everything if she did not?

All of this was too complicated. Trying to think about it tied her in knots. Somehow she fell asleep, lost in her memories.

CHAPTER 21

First Safari

John Hamman, 24
Cretaceous

John watched the cloud of dust disappear into the setting sun. He felt a little lost. This was what he had been aiming for. He had an expedition party ready to go on a safari but wasn't sure what to do.

Should he do it? He could stay here and look for elephants. He could shoot ivory, as if that weren't adventure enough for any man. John looked at the waiting faces turned to him. The men were unsure. Manny's gaze was warm and trusting, and the Maasai's like a statue. This was it. He might as well make a start. He looked around, so be it.

"Manny, do any of them speak English?"

"No English, Bwana. I speak very good English. Do not worry, Bwana. They know what to do." Manny's grin was wide, filled with supreme confidence in himself, in John, and in all the world.

How could John say any of this in a way that they would understand? "Can you explain to them that we are not going on an ordinary safari? We are not going to hunt here. We are going to go to a place very far away. We will hunt animals they have never seen before."

Manny grinned broadly. "We hunt all kinds of animals, Bwana. It does not matter. All is as God wills it." John didn't have any response for that. He couldn't imagine how they would respond to what was coming.

He told them to gather around. If he was going to do this, it was time. John set the dials and took one last look around at this landscape. As the last light of the setting sun dropped below the horizon, a light came on, and there was a beep. Then everything changed.

* * *

It was hotter. The sun was high above their heads. The sea of grass was gone and in its place was a dryer landscape, dusty with a scattering of ferns and some larger plants. In the distance were taller trees.

John wondered how they would react. Would they scream in fear? Would they attack him as some kind of devil? John's hand was on his gun. The men did none of these things. They hardly reacted at all. They looked around with curiosity, but that was all. Manny asked, "We hunt now, Bwana?"

"Yes, this is where we will hunt."

Manny turned to the Maasai, saying something John could not understand. The man turned and started running with a long, steady stride toward the groves of taller trees.

"He will find water, Bwana. There will be good hunting here." The porters began picking up the bundles of supplies. John grabbed his guns, the big double and a Mauser karabiner 98a. He took out the ammo and loaded them both.

"I will carry for you, Bwana," Manny said solemnly, as if it had some greater meaning. John looked at the two guns and handed Manny the heavy double. He bowed his head briefly and took up station on John's right, a step behind, a position that he never left for all the years to come.

They marched across a land they did not know in a time that was not their own. Manny and John led the way with no particular direction in mind. They followed in the same direction that the tracker had gone, following in his wake.

The porters of their small train followed after. Soon they began to sing. John was somewhat shocked by this. It was not exactly how he imagined stalking quietly through the bush.

John turned to Manny to get him to quiet them, but he said, "Do not worry, Bwana. It is a good song." That seemed to settle it. John was the amateur there.

John was a little disappointed. They didn't see any large dinosaurs but did scare up a few things. They flushed out a few small dinosaurs as they walked. The dinosaurs would streak out from groups of ferns as the column got close. It was like flushing jack rabbits out on the plains back home.

At first John thought they were birds, like little ostriches. But they had long tails with more feathers on the end of them. Their heads were like lizards' on long necks that they held lower than an ostrich. They could raise their heads up high to look around but generally carried them low and kept low when they took off running. They ran on two legs and were fast. John thought they could out-distance a jack rabbit. What he first took to be wings were shorter arms with long feathers on the back of them. John drew a fowling piece and slung the Mauser over his shoulder. He got four of them as they walked along.

They did in fact have teeth, not a beak, and were about the weight of a large hen but taller with longer legs. They tied them to the packs as they went, like game birds. At least there would be something in the pot tonight.

Late in the afternoon the Maasai returned. He stood up in front of them off to the right from behind a bush where he had been crouching. It was unnerving. Manny walked toward him and they spoke. It was more than John had ever heard the man say. Manny came back, but the Maasai continued standing there.

"He has found water, Bwana. He say there is a creek bed, but it is dry. It runs into a water hole. It is not dry. He say there are many footprints at the water hole. The footprints are very big. He does not know these footprints. There is a place to camp."

John nodded and said that was good. The Maasai tracker turned and ran in front of them. They followed, and he came to a small hill with some larger ferns with short trunks like a tree.

Manny said, "He say the water hole is a half mile that way. We camp here, Bwana?"

John took that as a suggestion. "Yes, we'll camp here."

"We gather wood? We get water? You bring gun, Bwana?"

"Yes, I think that's a good idea. I'll bring gun." He left the fouling piece in the camp, and the Maasai led them toward the tree line. Four of the porters came as well, carrying water barrels, hatchets, and short machetes.

The trees were tall, far taller than anything else they had seen. They looked modern. The trunks were perhaps a bit thicker than those of normal trees. They were conifers, and if John had seen them back home, he wouldn't have thought them out of place.

John slowed as they moved into the trees. He traded Manny for the big double. The damn thing was heavy, but its weight felt good in his hands.

The feeling was different under the branches, out of the sun. It was cooler. John saw his first fliers. He was not sure if he would call them birds. They did fly, but then they would land on the side of a tree and cling to it with all four limbs, like squirrels. Their cry was more of a hiss, and they also had teeth and lizard-like heads.

The porters chopped deadwood and made bundles of it to carry back. John turned to Manny and said one word: "Water."

Manny looked at the tracker, and wordlessly the Maasai led the two of them deeper into the woods. The land sloped down slightly, and at the far edge they came to a rock shelf. The stream had run along below the ledge. The grove was in the bottomlands below the shelf. A deeper pool had formed here where a bend followed the wall. It was brushier here, but nothing moved.

The Maasai knelt in a more open trail leading to the water. Manny and John joined him, and he motioned to a large footprint, outlining it with the motion of his hand. It had three toes and was eighteen inches long. He started outlining other tracks, some of different shapes. John looked out at what he could see of the horseshoe-shaped pool.

He turned to Manny. "Is there anything in the water?" On second thought he added, "Crocodile."

Manny turned and said one word to the tracker, who turned and looked over the water and then turned and stared back at them. John took that to mean there was no way to know the answer.

John turned back to Manny. "Bring the men. Fetch water." Manny left as they watched over the water hole. Nothing moved. The Maasai was like a statue. His eyes never left the water.

Manny returned with the porters and the water cast. John motioned for him to wait as he got set up by a tree. The drop-off where the stream had cut into the side was about two feet. The low level left a small, sandy bank beside the water. It was as good a view as he would get. The tracker stood on the other side with his spear raised as the workers, one by one, filled the small barrels.

Nothing exciting occurred. As they pulled back, John made them lay the barrels down so he could drop iodine tablets into them. It would spoil the taste, but he did not trust that stagnant pool. Water in Africa was bad enough. He hated to think what bugs might lurk here in the past. He sent the porters back to the camp with instructions to build a fire. Hopefully that would keep the animals away here, as it did in their own time.

John wasn't sure how to do this. He tried explaining to Manny what he wanted. The tracker led them along the stream bed to the right, where the stream had undercut a medium-size tree that had fallen across and was leaning against the rock ledge on the other side.

They had a ladder up the twelve-foot wall on the other side. It was more awkward than it sounded, but soon they were all safely on the escarpment. Looking out, John could see it was more of a dry plain here, uneven as it sloped down to the edge.

They returned to the pool. The top of the ledge had no cover, but to the right side it was a bit flatter, and they could lie down on their bellies with little showing over the edge. It gave them a decent view of most of the pool. They could not see the far end around the bend. The early evening air was still.

John didn't know how sensitive the animals would be to smell. Would they even react if they caught the men's scent?

The ground was rocky. Small pebbles bit into John. He couldn't seem to get comfortable. His neck quickly grew tired, and he wound up resting it on his arm. None of these things seemed to bother the other men. The sun grew lower, and they continued to wait.

John had imagined something more exciting. The sun was setting behind them and was still lighting up the tops of the trees, but everything below them was in shadow and getting dimmer. It was that time when the sky was too bright to allow your eyes to adjust to the darkness on the ground. Soon they might have to give this up. John did not fancy walking back to the camp in darkness.

They heard movement in the trees. Something was there, but John could not see anything. Then to their left, movement. He could see a head, strangely shaped. It had what looked like a bill, almost like that of a duck. The skull protruded backward behind the neck, almost as if it were trying to counterbalance itself. All John could see was a silhouette. The head was about eight feet off the ground. It stayed there, swinging back and forth.

Would it come forward? Would he get a better shot? John slowly shifted the big rifle and pulled the gun into his shoulder. It didn't seem to notice the movement. It came forward a bit but then stepped back. It also was cautious about the water. John thought, *There's a lesson there*. Then it hopped. It landed on the mud of the lower bank with its forelegs in the water.

John could see it now. It looked awkward. Its hind legs were larger than its forelegs, but it seemed to be a quadruped. Its large, heavy tail balanced the front half of the body. It waited, looking both ways, then lowered its head to drink.

John had completely forgotten what he was doing. He sighted down the barrels of the gun but could barely make out the front sight. The range was short. He aimed as best he could. He didn't know where the animal's heart was. Most of its weight seemed to be balanced on its large hind quarters. In a moment of inspiration, John shifted his aim back to the hip and pelvis. The big rifle roared, kicking into his collarbone like a mule.

He looked up, reorienting himself in time to watch the animal drop. It let out a long, deep honking sound, almost like a foghorn on a ship. John tried getting the gun back into position. He drew himself up onto his knees, kneeling and lifting the gun to his aching shoulder and tried to sight again. The beast was down and had rolled onto its side away from the men. He sighted in the chest below the armpit. The gun fired again, or perhaps *detonated* would be a better word.

He found himself on his back, having rolled backward when the gun fired. John sat up and looked again. The beast was still down on its side. Its legs were still kicking. He opened the action, the cases ejecting, and fumbled for more cartridges. He closed the action and sighted again, bracing his arm on his knee to try to help support the weight of the big gun. He tried for a spot a bit lower, and the gun roared again.

He was once more looking at the sky. Sitting up with the gun in his lap, John saw that the beast was no longer moving. That was good. He was not sure he could have fired again. He slumped there, looking down at his kill in the water. John had just killed a dinosaur.

CHAPTER 22

Shooting Instructor

Robert Brown, 45
1983 New York, NY

They fidgeted. Everyone's eyes were fixed on the door. Robert Brown squirmed in his seat. He could feel the eyes of the other partners on him as well and was not able to meet theirs. He focused on the legal pad in front of him, the pens ready to take notes.

When the group heard the door opening, every head turned to watch the man enter the room. The senior partner carefully locked the boardroom door before walking to the head of the table. All eyes were on the manila envelope in his hand. As he opened and read the contents to the partners, everyone kept meticulous notes on the instructions.

Whether they were actively involved in passing these financial instructions to the board that ran the Hamman company or not, the people there hung on every word. If the information in this letter, written three years before, turned out to be as prophetic as the last set of instructions, fortunes were in the offering.

Many of them did not understand what the letter spoke of, but they were going to find out. No one in the room had ever heard of ARPANET, the Advanced Research Projects Agency Network. The talk of Internet service providers, IP addresses, servers, and routers meant nothing to them, but they would be on the phone as soon as they left the room researching these terms and what they might mean.

When he came to the end, a second inner envelope was passed down the table to Robert Brown, sitting at the end of the table. Robert felt like a plant withering in the sun under their gaze. Again, he passed back the cover letter to the partners and then sat back to read the documents entrusted to him.

Eyes flitted toward him as they wondered what was contained in these documents. If it was anything like what was being read aloud, they desperately wanted to know its contents.

Every year he seemed to disappear for months on end, and no one knew where he went or why. Some of them thought about having him followed, but none wanted to risk the consequences. The only thing that prevented a rebellion was the lack of any sign of him prospering more than the rest of them from this information he was privy to. In fact, he seemed less than enthused, sometimes even depressed by what he read.

Robert stared at the papers in front of him. Was the old man serious? The instruction in the letters were becoming more and more outrageous. Why would he want such a thing? Was it even legal? How was he expected to arrange something like that?

In the meantime came more pressing questions, asking for clarifications on the instructions, and the spelling-out of terms occupied the rest of the partners. They could not leave the room until he had finished reading his instructions. He began making notes of what he would need to do before returning the instructions to the envelope to be disposed of by the senior partner. Research firearms laws in various states...

A debate had broken out over the commercial viability of this new Internet between two of the partners. Meanwhile, Robert Brown was worried about how he would find a combat shooting instructor who would work with a thirteen-year-old girl.

CHAPTER 23

Hunted

Jenny Hamman, 31
Cretaceous

J enny was awake early, lost in thought waiting for the dawn to come. She could not get back to sleep so she got up, turned on the headlamp, and started fixing herself a meal. Now in the early-morning hours when it was cold would probably be the safest time to risk cooking.

Nevertheless, she made sure her gun was at hand. It was good to have a hot meal, even if it was made from dehydrated eggs. Some things were a crime against nature. No one had ever managed a decent dehydrated breakfast meal. By the time she was done, the horizon was beginning to lighten. She had the camp packed up before the sun crested. As its warmth lit the world, she was already on the move.

The terrain was changing. It was becoming a bit hillier, and she thought the slope was trending downward. She was seeing erosion features moving in the same direction she was going. All good signs. Then she came to the edge of a step. It was a small shelf, and then the hillside dropped away gently to a lowland with heavier vegetation.

She recognized what this was. It was like in Utah. A large lake had been there thousands of years ago, and this had once been the shoreline. In Utah a geologic feature had given way, and the lake had drained in a flood, cutting through the ridge that had contained it.

Looking down, she could see where the richer silt fed the thicker growth of ferns. The wind had scoured the richer soil from hilltops and ridges and concentrated it in the lowlands between. The plant life grew much heavier there.

Somewhere out there would be the river. There would be more wildlife, more dinosaurs, from now on. She took out a monocular and scanned the land below but couldn't spot any movement. She knew they would be there but didn't know what they would be.

She cycled the action on the shotgun, ejecting the birdshot she had in the chamber and loading a round of 00 buck shot. Any meeting in there would get very personal very fast. She pocketed the bird shot and reached up to pull another round of buck from the sling on her shoulder to top off the magazine. She was as ready as she could be.

Jenny hopped off the shelf and started down the largest of the ridges, following on its crest to stay out of the heavier foliage for as long as she could. She kept the shotgun at low ready, now with the safety off.

When she got down into the bottomlands, it was not as dense as she feared. It did not really hinder her movement too badly. Sometimes she dodged around denser thickets. The issue was that it shortened her sight lines.

Most of the surrounding area was still covered in various forms of fern, but they grew much taller. Rather than being to her knee or waist, here the average height was her head or taller. Some things reached over twenty feet.

She made a greater effort to move quietly and focused on her hearing. Sometimes your ears or your nose would alert you before you could see your quarry. She recalled stalking a lion in tall grass. She had been young. She had not done that again. This time *she* felt more like the prey.

For all her misgivings, nothing happened, at least not at once. She went on like that most of the day. Her movement was slow but steady. She felt it was better to get there alive than to rush to an early demise. Her feeling of unease never left her.

It was late in the afternoon when she heard it for the first time. It was... a bark? But higher pitched than she would expect. It came from some distance behind her.

She froze and listened intently. Something else, an answer from behind her but off to her right. Something was following her. Something was hunting her, and it was not alone.

What to do? Running was pointless. Any predator here could easily run her down. She had to make a stand, and whatever it was, she had to kill it.

She needed longer sight lines to shoot. Looking around, she headed to her left, slightly uphill. The ground was a bit higher there, and she hoped the cover would be less. She didn't have any hope of eluding them by changing direction. If they were following her trail from that far back, they were probably following her scent.

It wasn't much of a hill to die on, but the higher ground was drier, and the ferns grew a bit lower. She would have more room. She heard them again, at least three, maybe more. That was fine. If they wanted to be assholes, she was ready for them.

As she moved onto the higher, more open ground, they seemed to hold back. They preferred to surround and corner their prey in the brush. She guessed that most of their prey tried to stay in cover. Jenny was not playing that game.

The ground was rockier here, as the wind had blown away more of the silt, leaving behind the larger stones. Nothing grew higher than her waist, leaving no cover for them.

She finally got a look at her pursuers. One of them came forward to the edge of the heavier brush. It was behind a large cycad. All she could really see was its head. If she didn't know better, she might have thought it to be a bird at first glance. It was feathered with a heavier plume on its head that ran down the back of its neck, but the mouth was a dinosaur's, not the beak of a bird. She was willing to bet it was full of teeth.

Based on the height of the head, it was a little taller than her. Looking down, she could see one of its hind feet past the trunk of the cycad. She could see the claws, including the one particularly long sickle-shaped one on the inner toe. It tapped that toe impatiently, eager for the hunt, the kill. It was a theropod, one of the raptors.

It stared at her, letting itself be seen. It was trying to flush her, to make her run. It wanted to run her down. That was probably how it hunted most of its prey and why she knew above all else that she could not run.

She had to flip the script. She had to make them move. She could hear other movements. It had friends. She could not see them but knew they would be moving to surround her.

Time to make them play her game. *Let's see how they like this.* Jenny made sure the selector switch for the magazine was to the right for the magazine full of buckshot. She wished that both magazines held 00. She raised the Neostead and placed the sights right on the creature's face. *Smile and wait for the flash...*

The gun bucked back into her shoulder. These were not light loads. The head disappeared behind the cycad with a screech, higher pitched than she would have expected. She saw a tail whipping the ferns as it thrashed on the ground.

Automatically she cycled the action, feeding another round of buck. The dinosaur continued to scream and writhe in the underbrush.

She pivoted, looking for a charge. Nothing happened. Perhaps that had given them pause. She pulled another round off the sling and topped off the magazine. Shotgun matches were all about the reload.

Modern animals were afraid of gunfire, at least the ones that had been hunted. Even animals that had never encountered guns were startled by the noise, but they did not know to fear it.

The charge came from the right, low and fast like a lion, kicking up dust as it accelerated faster than a racehorse.

She fired at the attacker and hit it, but it didn't even slow. It was bipedal. All the locomotion in this thing was in the hind legs. Hitting the shoulder didn't cause it to crash and roll like a lion or even turn it.

She cycled the action and dropped to her knee for a lower shot. The gun kicked again as she fired into its chest, but it was too late. The thing struck her full speed, bowling her over and sending them both tumbling across the ground. She was down.

Another one came from her left, low and fast. She fired from the ground, hitting it in its chest and shoulder, watching the feathers explode and leaving a red hole.

Her second shot went right down its wide-open mouth, and the raptor piled into the ground. She emptied another round into the raptor that had knocked her down. It was trying to get up to come for her when her shot opened up its chest. The dinosaur flopped backward.

She scrambled under the weight of her pack to get up on her feet. Two more were behind her. They had stopped and were watching. Her first shot caught the one on the left in the neck, and it collapsed on the ground.

The other jumped sideways, and her shot missed. Or at least she could not see any sign of a hit. Cursing, she pumped the action again, but it clicked empty. She had to flip the lever on the top of the gun to the other side to feed the #4.

Her target was staring at its pack mate. She fired two rounds into its face, and it fell back flailing and screaming, its whole head a ruin.

Jenny ran the action again, wishing she had loaded both magazines with 00 buckshot. She turned in time to see one of the raptors launch itself. Its leap seemed impossibly high. It was coming down on her, its hind legs pulled up in front, and she could see those big claws cocked back ready for the kill.

She turned and lunged, trying to get out from under it. Too late. It landed on her back, knocking her to the ground. She sprawled on her face with the weight of the dinosaur on top of her.

She could hear her pack rip open as everything spilled out around her. The sling kept the shotgun close, and she grabbed it, twisting under the animal to try to bring it to bear.

All she saw was wide-open jaws coming for her head, and she shoved the gun between them to block the bite. The jaws clamped down sideways with tremendous force, crushing the magazine tubes and the barrel. At the same time, she felt a ripping pain in the back of her leg as one of its claws found its mark, opening up the back of her thigh.

Screaming, she turned her head away, burying her face in her shoulder as she pulled the trigger. The barrel exploded, rupturing in the raptor's mouth, when a three-inch magnum load fired with nowhere to go.

Searing pain erupted in her shoulder, neck, and the back of her head. All she could hear was ringing in her left ear. She was disoriented. She tried to orient herself and to think through the pain and ringing in her head. She found the Fastex buckle on the chest strap of the pack and slid out of it, or what remained of it.

She crawled away from the dinosaur that was thrashing on the ground, hitting the release to drop the ruined weapon. Its mouth and jaws were mostly gone. She crawled, incapable of much else.

Jenny stumbled to her feet, trying to draw the browning pistol from the holster on her leg. It was hard to hold the pistol steady with the ringing in her head.

Another pursuer was circling around her. It was more cautious, but smelling the blood, it knew it had the kill.

Her left leg didn't want to work. She could feel blood running down her leg. She brought the gun up, trying to aim, but she couldn't seem to hold it steady.

The dinosaur circled her. Were there others nearby? Would they be attracted to the noise or repulsed by it? The smell of blood and death filled the air. She knew anything in the area would be drawn here looking for a meal. If she could get away...

She held the handgun with both hands. The gun was loaded with hollow points. She had to deal with her leg. All this creature had to do was wait.

She heard barking from the west. More were on their way. This was not good, but it was what saved her. The dinosaur, hearing more of its kind approaching, tried to move in to secure its own kill.

It charged. Holding her ground, she fired with both hands. It was all she could do to empty the gun center of mass. She got only seven rounds off before being bowled over by its charge.

They rolled backward together, ending on their sides. She was able to bring the gun up between them under the beast's chin and pulled the trigger three more times, firing up into its skull. Blood sprayed in her face, and her left eye burned as something from the muzzle blast struck her skin. All she could hear was ringing. The animal spasmed, clawing frantically as she rolled away from it.

She crawled blindly away from the dying animal. Looking up, she forced her eyes open and crawled on all fours into a mass of ferns. She made it about thirty yards until she was at least out of sight.

She fumbled with the med kit on the back of her belt and managed to pull the zipper, and a Ziploc bag with a pressure bandage and packets of QuikClot dropped into her hand. She reached around her leg and tore the pants leg open. Peering around to her left, she could make out the wound with her right eye. The gash was about four inches long, bleeding freely, but at least it wasn't pumping.

She tore open the larger package and pulled out the syringe, yanking the cap off the end, and gritted her teeth as she pushed the end into her wound. It raked down the back of her leg, turning into a deeper puncture at the bottom. She pushed in the plunger, irrigating the wound, and tore open the bandage. She paced the sponge impregnated with QuikClot over the wound and, holding it closed as well as she could, wrapped it tightly with the pressure bandage. She downed two of the capsules of wide-spectrum antibiotics from a sealed packet. It hurt, but the bleeding stopped.

The pain gave her the clarity to start hobbling off the hill and down into the thicker brush. She needed distance. She had to break contact. She had made it one hundred yards when she heard their calls. They had found her kills. Maybe that would keep them busy. Would they eat their own dead?

She collapsed against the trunk of a cycad. She had lost her pack and most of her gear. The only gun she had left was the High Power, and it was down to a little over two magazines of ammunition. She had her father's belt with his knife and canteen on it. The batteries were in the cargo pocket on her right thigh and the device in her left.

The bandage was controlling the bleeding, but she looked down at the blood on her leg and boot. She could not afford to be leaving such a large blood trail. She scrubbed her boot and lower pants leg with dirt, trying to clean the blood off. She washed her hands with the sandy soil, trying to get them clean and to remove the smell of her own blood.

She had to move. They seemed to still be in the clearing. She could hear more calls now. But sooner or later one of them would find her trail.

She pushed herself up to her feet. She had to get away from here. Her leg would support her but did not work well. The muscles of her quadriceps were fine. She could push her leg straight, but the muscles on the back side of her thigh were not taking any orders. Good enough. She hobbled away to the east. Somewhere out there was the river.

She heard the barking of the dinosaurs behind her. At first they seemed to still be at the site of the battle, but soon it was clear that some of them were following her. She heard them calling behind her to both the left and right. She thought she was starting to recognize their hunting calls. It was time to pick up the pace.

That was when she came to the edge of the feeding area. Suddenly the foliage opened up before her. It was as if something had mowed down and plowed the ground before her.

Something had eaten all the ground cover in a stretch several hundred yards wide. The ferns had been bitten off at ground level. The larger plants and trees had been torn up by their roots and were half eaten. Something, or a whole herd of them, had grazed everything down to almost bare ground. She heard the barking grow closer behind her. She had nowhere to go.

Jenny started running as best she could across the ground. She would not die here. Then she saw it—a nearby mound. Maybe. If she could only make it there before they broke cover. It was big, but was there enough of it? No one had ever seen it before. Only the ones from carnivores had been preserved.

It wasn't like a cow patty. It was balls more like from a deer or rabbit. They were about the size of basketballs and dark green with the fiber of the plants they had eaten. It was a big pile of sauropod scat. It had to be—nothing else could have produced something this massive. It must have been standing still and grazing as it relieved itself.

She made her way around to the far side, looking for some kind of hole or gap. She started burrowing, pushing the balls to the side and sliding in between them. Pulling them back over her, she curled inside the mound.

The smell... it wasn't really the smell as much as the air. The smell was so thick it seemed to displace the air. It was hard to breathe. Could she asphyxiate in this mound? What an ignoble death! It might be better to go down fighting.

Those thoughts were driven from her mind when she heard them. She could hear the barking coming closer on all sides now. They seemed to be passing her, and then she heard one right outside her hole.

A shadow passed over her. She could see it through the gaps between the balls as it blocked out the sun. It barked and then continued on around the pile, circling it. Then silence.

The sounds of the hunt seemed to move farther away. She had no idea of where they were. She couldn't risk climbing out of her hole. It seemed hard to get enough air. Her head began spinning, and darkness closed in around her.

CHAPTER 24

Camp

John Hamman, 24
Cretaceous

John ran his hands over the great body. It was the largest living thing he had ever seen in his life. Well, it *had* been living. Even in death it was a wonder.

Its heart still tried to beat, and the last of its blood flowed like a waterfall down its side, over his hand. It was warm in the rapidly cooling night air. John looked at his hand, almost black in the last fading light. Wasn't that wrong? He thought they were cold-blooded reptiles. Shouldn't their blood be cold, like some giant snake or lizard? He laid his head against its great chest, feeling the warmth of the body and listening to the final beats of the animal's heart.

Manny returned to the camp to fetch the porters. They had heard the gun, and six of them met him at the edge of the wood. They took a picture with the camera on a tripod, of all of them with the dinosaur. John stood by the head, which they propped up so its strange shape could be seen.

Manny stood on his right and the Maasai on his left, with the porters lined up behind the body to their left. John posed with the big gun. The flash was tremendous, blinding them all. John thought this scared his men more than anything else that day.

Butchering took them well into the night and was done by lantern light. They saved the head, though John had no idea what to do with it. They took the meat for the camp. The porters had to cut poles to carry it, as if one leg were a full-size animal.

It was late as they marched back into camp, singing. John was even beginning to learn some of the words. This was apparently very amusing to the crew.

Tents were set up in a circle around a fire burning and smoking in the middle. They could see it as soon as they left the woods as a guide home.

A camp chair and a plate of roast dinosaur from the little hens they shot earlier that day were waiting for John in front of the fire. It was lean like a game bird and tasted mostly like chicken. A reptile should taste stranger than that, but he had never seen a reptile with feathers. Were these damn things birds?

John broke out a bottle of the whiskey. That was what he really needed. A large glass of that put everything right. He must thank Blix. It even helped the pain in his shoulder. He stumbled to his tent, settled down onto the small cot, and blew out the lamp. He was out before his head hit the pillow.

The next morning, light was streaming in through the tent flaps, but John swore he had only barely dozed off to sleep. He was awakened by Manny gently shaking his shoulder. "Come, Bwana."

John was still looking around in confusion as Manny turned and left the tent. The whiskey may have helped his shoulder, but it had not been kind to his head. John managed to sit on the edge of the cot. That bastard. He was going to kill Blix.

John looked down at himself. He really must stop sleeping in his clothes. He realized he had been wearing the same clothes on the ship before he'd even set foot on this continent. He had worn the same suit on the train ride to Nairobi. He'd still been wearing it when Blix dragged him out on this adventure, and he'd been wearing these clothes yesterday when they hunted—of all things, a dinosaur. He had yet to even remove them.

Had all that happened in forty-eight hours? John started to leave the tent but retreated back inside upon facing the glaring sun. He found his hat and tried again. Was the sun brighter in this time? Surely it had never been so bright before. The little camp was busy. The crew had built racks and were smoking meat over a fire.

Manny, the finest person in all creation, appeared with a steaming cup of coffee. John sat on the camp chair in front of the tent and tried to get his bearings. He poured a bit of the whiskey from the bottle he found beside the chair into the cup, and the world got a little better.

John stared at the bottle. How had the level gotten so low? He shook his head and set it back down beside the chair in what seemed to be its home.

Manny appeared once more before John with the Maasai. "Bwana, he say you come. Bring gun. Big animal."

John tried to focus on Manny, asking, "What kind of animal?" He quickly realized this was a truly useless question. The man could have no knowledge of the animals in this time. But to John's surprise, he got an answer.

"He say big elephant. Giraffe eat trees. He call it 'Mokele-Mbembe.'" It would seem they were already naming the wildlife here.

John pushed himself to his feet. "Bring guns. Let's go see 'Mokele-Mbembe.'"

He carried the double this time, not sure what they might be walking up on. They headed to the right along the tree line and walked for some time.

John heard it before he saw it, sounds of cracking, crashing, and ripping. He saw the top of a tree shake. They came over a small rise and saw them.

There were three of the beasts. Two were what John hoped were fully grown, and one was slightly smaller. One of the big ones had ripped a sizable limb off a large tree and was chewing on it. Another took a large bite out of the top of what John could only describe as a palm tree and was chewing on the foliage.

He could not begin to describe the size. They were quadrupeds. They had long necks and long tails. They must have been one hundred feet long. Their legs were like tree trunks. The barrel of their chests must have been twenty-five feet in diameter.

The Maasai led them forward. They walked almost up to them. Any closer and John would not have been able to see them. As it was, he had to crane his neck and turn from side to side to take the beast in.

They completely ignored the humans, who were ants in comparison. The Maasai seemed to know this instinctively.

John wanted to touch one. How could anything be so enormous? They never stopped eating. He walked up to it slowly. Well, he walked up to one of its legs. It was round like a barrel but bigger than a tree. He reached out, and the skin felt slightly rough, almost pebbly, like the skin of an elephant.

John thought it might squash him for having the temerity to touch it uninvited like that. One of them lifted onto its hind legs, balancing on its tail to reach the new growth at the top of the tree. It ripped and tore at the limb, and then the body came down. When the forelegs struck, the ground shook. John retreated for fear of being turned to jelly beneath their feet by accident.

Manny was staring at John wide-eyed, and they all backed away. It was easier to observe them from a bit more of a distance. They were going to need bigger guns—much bigger guns. John did not think they could scratch, much less kill, one of those things. He could not imagine even the 500 penetrating deep enough to reach the heart of that thing, even if he did know where to aim. He thought of how thick the bones must be. How could they ever do enough damage to bring one down?

They returned to camp about midday. John's stomach was ready for a real meal. He sat down once again in his camp chair, and magically a plate appeared with a steak and potatoes.

John thanked the man as best he could, but the man simply smiled and backed away. He couldn't understand a thing John said but must have understood the sentiment. The steak was good, richer and less like chicken, but it was still a pale meat, not red like a cow.

John was feeling much better. He thought they were doing quite well and asked Manny if they could find some smaller game since Mokele Mbembe was too big. Manny went off to consult with the Maasai.

John dug into his pack and pulled out another of his little treasures that he had salvaged from the war. It was an oversized holster, longer then a proper handgun. The leather holster was attached to a wooden board of the same shape. He opened the flap and drew out his prize, a Luger pistol with a long barrel. It had an adjustable sight, like that of a rifle. It was chambered in nine-millimeter parabellum, which the Germans had favored. He loaded the two magazines.

The interesting thing about this weapon was that one could slide the end of the piece of wood that was the backing of the holster into a dovetail on the back of the grip of the pistol, and then you had a tiny automatic rifle. John threw a thin belt over his neck and now had a handy little weapon. He came back out of the tent to find Manny and the Maasai waiting for him.

John took the karabiner from him and put it over his shoulder. They would see what they could find. The Maasai turned and took off at a jog. They followed along behind at a more leisurely pace. John had no illusions about being able to run all day across the plains. They skirted the edge of the forest and walked a good distance.

They then saw the tracker squatting behind a large fern with a short barrel-shaped trunk. John stopped and studied the land in front of them. Finally he spotted movement.

A small group of dinosaurs was ahead of them, feeding among the ground cover. They appeared to be herbivores, four-legged and more balanced than the one they had shot before. They were shorter than John at the shoulder and not as heavily built as the previous kill. Their necks were not as long, and the heads lacked the long extension back over the neck. They had long tails that they held out almost straight and could rise higher off the ground.

For some reason John got the impression that they were not fully grown. Were these adolescents? They didn't have any feathers that he could see.

The hunters shifted to come up behind the cover that the Maasai was squatting behind. As they knelt, John thought about what to do. He counted eleven in the group. Maybe this was a chance to change things up a bit. He figured the group could spare a couple of its members.

Crouching low, he moved toward the group, trying to keep a patch of cover between them. He moved as quietly as he could, the ground soft and sandy beneath his feet. He started around the patch of ferns to the left. Manny, as always, followed him. The Maasai moved to the right.

They were close. John could hear them call out to one another, the sound not nearly as deep and resonant as the dinosaur the night before. They were just ahead.

John looked back at Manny, who smiled broadly back. Holding the stock of the Luger into his shoulder, John stepped out from around the corner. They were now about thirty yards from the animals.

John put two rounds into the side of the nearest one and then switched targets, putting three more into the next. Both dropped. John saw movement to the side, and a spear flew through the air and struck another in the neck.

The injured dinosaur backed up, trying to get away from its enemy. It tried biting at the spear but could not turn its shorter head enough to grasp the shaft. It stumbled, its forelegs collapsing under it, as blood poured from the junction of its neck and shoulder. Its rear legs dropped as well, and then with a bellow it rolled on its side, the spear pointing into the air. The rest of the little herd pounded off across the plain.

They had meat from last night but might be able to turn this into something else. They still didn't know much about this place or the creatures that inhabited it. They now had a little bait, and John was curious as to what it might bring. Examining the kills closer, they had what looked like a beak filled with flat teeth. The fore feet had large claws. Could they be used for digging?

They retreated to the edge of the forest where it was shady and cool to see what the day would bring. That put them about two hundred yards from the bait. If John stood behind a tree, he could see one clearly and the tops of the other two.

He stowed the Luger back in its holster, extended the strap, and hung it around his shoulder so it hung behind his hip out of the way. He took up the Mauser and checked the chamber and then moved the sight up a notch to the 200-meter mark.

It was a fine gun. John had carried an Enfield in the war, of course, but the 8mm was a bigger cartridge. He liked this shorter gun that he had liberated from a guard at a rail station. Unlike the normal service rifle, it had fit nicely in his duffel.

The hunters all made themselves comfortable and prepared to wait. John was fine with a more relaxed pace after the last two days and sat there chewing on a bit of jerky. He wasn't sure what was in it, but it was spicy, and the salt satisfied a need within him.

Late in the afternoon they began getting some attention. "Buzzards" started circling, but they did not look like any birds John knew. Soon two of them were circling above the bait.

They were much bigger than any birds he had ever seen. John could not get an accurate sense of scale, looking up into the sky. As they got closer, his estimate only got bigger.

When they landed he was utterly shocked. They were bigger than the planes in the war. Still, even after they landed and folded their wings in, they must have stood twenty feet tall to the top of their heads. Each had a long neck, and the head was enormous with a crest on top of the skull. The head alone was longer than John was tall. The wings were more like a bat.

The animals did not stand on their rear legs as would a bird with its wings folded, instead leaning forward on the elbow in the wing as a bat would. John could see no feathers, reinforcing that bat-like impression. For all of their size, the body was not all that heavy. John supposed there must be limits if it were to become airborne. Still, the scale of the things...

They bent down and started tearing at the kills. John took aim at the larger one. When it lifted its head with half a dinosaur in its beak, exposing its chest, he fired. The winged beast staggered, dropping the carcass from its mouth, and let out a loud cawing noise.

John cycled the bolt and fired again. The other feasting dinosaur looked toward the sound of the shot and turned to take off.

John stared, speechless at what followed. He had seen an albatross take off once, and this made that display look graceful. It faced into the wind and began a lumbering hop that ended with its back legs desperately trying to keep up, running across the ground as the wings made three desperate flaps before it lumbered into the air.

Even then, John was convinced it would crash before it gained enough altitude for its ridiculously long wings to get a full sweep. He stared at the thing slowly gaining altitude as it disappeared into the distance. Only then did he turn back to see the first one still flailing on the ground. He put a third bullet in its chest, and it finally went still.

All three of the men approached and circled all the way around the creature, studying it. They still couldn't grasp what they were looking at. It was on its back at this point. They grabbed the wings and stretched them out. The length was huge. The wings had a membrane like that of a bat and had only bone on the leading edges. At the elbow of the wing was a clawed hand. That was what it stood on, and then a single bone extended to the wingtip.

John sent the men back to the camp. Manny brought the camera. They had to back up to get the whole thing in frame as the men held the wings out. They took another picture with John posing with the head. It was indeed bigger than him by more than two feet.

John tried to get one of the men to lay down in the mouth as if he was being eaten by it—but he could not persuade any of them to pose for such a picture.

The group harvested meat from what remained of the kills they had made earlier and took the head, which took two men to carry. And they butchered what they could from the corpse. The bones were incredibly light. John noticed that some of the men had brought those back as well.

He wasn't sure what they were going to do with all the trophies.

CHAPTER 25

Combat Shooting

Jenny Hamman, 13
1983 Arizona

Mr. Brown picked her up on the day following the last day of her seventh-grade year with very little explanation, as had become her expectation of these forays planned by her grandfather before his death.

Jenny always had a mixture of anticipation and dread as she counted down the days. She received a letter three weeks before with a suggested packing list and very little information.

She surmised from the packing list that she was going somewhere warm. She was bringing sneakers and hiking boots, so at least this summer she might get away without running bare-assed through the woods with an Indian tracker laughing at her the entire time.

Robert showed up like clockwork at her front door at 12:00, as prearranged. She swore that next year she would stand there and open the door at 11:59:59 and catch him reaching for the doorbell.

"Where are we going?"

As usual, Mr. Brown replied, "You'll know when we get there, won't you?"

They traveled to the private executive airport and boarded—unusually, a twin-engine prop plane instead of the normal corporate jet.

"Why aren't we flying the corporate jet?"

"This plane is designed for short takeoffs and landings. Where we're going doesn't have a paved airstrip."

The plane was louder than the jet and a lot colder, as for some reason the pilot kept his window open the entire flight. Conversation was almost impossible. Jenny surmised that Mr. Brown had designed it to avoid being bombarded with her never-ending questions.

About three hours into the flight, the plane dipped its nose. Looking out the window, Jenny saw no sign of an airport, only desert as far as the eye could see. They circled what looked like a dirt road that someone had scraped out of brush with a bulldozer.

Large flaps extended from the back of the wing as it turned in to land. As they touched down on the rough strip, the whole plane shook, and the engines roared when the pilot reversed the props. They left a cloud of red dust behind them all the way down the landing strip until they stopped at the very end. Jenny's ears rang with the incessant noise of the past several hours.

She squinted through the small window and saw an older man, almost her grandfather's age, with iron-gray, short-cropped hair and a face more weathered than her grandfather's if that were possible.

The man walked over and leaned into the door as the crewman lowered the air stair. He yelled into the cabin, "Come on, di di mau! I'm not getting any younger! Offload and throw your shit in the back of the truck!"

He didn't offer to help or linger in the door. By the time Jenny tripped over the pile of duffel bags, he was already back in his truck, looking out of the window impatiently.

Between Robert, the pilot, and her, they managed to load all the bags into the truck and crawled into the front cab with the dour old man. Dour he might be, old he might be, but Jenny got the distinct impression that this was the kind of man who "chewed railroad spikes and spit out nails," as her grandfather used to say.

They had no more than closed the door when the man stomped the accelerator. They were off down a gravel road at a speed far higher than was safe.

"Welcome to the world's premier combat shooting facility," he said. "I'll be your private instructor for the next six weeks. I've never done a one-on-one course before, but then again I never saw that many zeros on a check all at the same time either." He laughed.

He took them to a large two-story bunkhouse. The bottom floor was mostly one large open room with a lounge area, but the rest of it was lined along both sides with what looked like workbenches.

Several men were sitting on the couches reading, and a few were at the benches with various weapons in differing states of disassemble. All eyes turned to them as they entered the room.

The looks turned from curious to puzzled as they examined Mr. Brown, who did not look like the normal patrons of this facility. Their eyebrows rose even higher as they turned to Jenny. What kind of man brought his daughter with him to a training course like this?

"This is the common area. You can sit around and jaw if you like. You'll be assigned a bench to clean your weapons. PT 0500, breakfast 0600, lunch twelve hundred, and dinner is at 1900." Turning to Jenny, he added, "Your room is upstairs. You're in 9."

Almost as an afterthought, he turned to Mr. Brown. "You can stay in 10, across the hall. Don't get in anyone's way." He led them upstairs to a very small room with a cot, a small desk, and a chair. He dropped a pile of books, a calculator, wind meter, and weather station onto the desk. "You'd best start studying. I'll be back at 0500. There will be a test."

Jenny scowled at his back as he walked out of the room.

"Thank you for welcoming me. I'm very pleased to be here!" she yelled at his back as he disappeared down the hall and down the stairs.

"Welcome to Rear Sight, the finest combat tactical shooting academy in..." The voice echoed back up the stairs to Jenny as the man walked away. *Asshole*.

She stared at the pile of books. School was supposed to be over. She thought they were learning to shoot. Where were all the guns?

She learned that 0500 meant in the middle of the night. She was woken up by a fist banging on her door. She had hardly gotten any sleep as she was up late cramming for his "test." Her scowl was every bit the match of his when she answered the door in her footy pajamas.

Breakfast was preceded by an hour of "PT," as he called it. She had other terms for it. This was not her idea of a fun summer adventure. What the hell does doing jumping jacks in the middle of the freezing night in a dusty-ass desert have to do with shooting? And about that, weren't deserts supposed to be all hot and have camels and things all over? It looked like this year might actually be worse than the last.

To his amazement, Jenny passed his test. She had kept Mr. Brown up all night forcing him to explain the math to her. Why did there have to be math in shooting? It wasn't fair! Shooting was supposed to be fun. Her instructor looked at her suspiciously, but he said she had passed and earned the right to pick out a gun.

As they walked to another building, he explained that they had paid for her to take the full course load of all four disciplines, which was why she would be staying there for six weeks. She would be trained in combat pistol, rifle, shotgun, and long-range shooting. As such, she would need a full complement of weapons.

He side-eyed her and muttered something about midgets. He was walking too fast for her to catch up to kick him.

When he unlocked and opened the door, Jenny thought she had died and gone to heaven. The long building was lined down both sides with racks of guns—every kind she could imagine and ones she had never seen before.

Every wall held racks of weapons, and they even hung on the wall above the racks if they were too big to fit. At the far end a huge gun sat on its own tripod. It took up the whole end of the room.

"We'll need to find you something that will fit and work for you... No!" She was pointing emphatically to the M-2 Browning 50-caliber machine gun at the end of the room. So began the negotiation. "First let's settle on a rifle."

"I want to shoot that one," she said, pointing again to the big 50.

"No," he repeated.

"Why not?"

"Because that one is a crew-served machine gun and not on your curriculum."

Jenny screwed up her face. Instead of continuing to whine, a thoughtful look came across her face. "Can I shoot it if I do really good in the course?"

He thought about that. No way was she going to do well enough to impress him. Hell—he would be surprised if she didn't give up and head home halfway through training. God knows that enough full-grown men had done so.

"Okay, here's the deal. You pass the course and impress me enough, and we'll see about letting you rock and roll like the big boys."

She beamed back to him and said, "It's a deal."

She was already walking down the rows. "It will need to be something that will match your stature and length of pull... "

She pointed to another, and he sighed as he took the FAL from the rack. "You have to be able to move with it."

He hung the sling around her shoulder. The barrel went "thud" as it hit and dragged on the floor. She scowled again as he put it back into the rack and took down a mini-14. He looked at her and had her hold it and sight down it. He looked at the fit and shook his head as he took it back.

Walking down the line, he paused and looked back at her and took down a Car 15. He pushed in a button, compressing the stock, then slid it out one notch. He had her aim down it as he walked around her, studying the fit and correcting her stance. "That will do."

Next they moved to the other side of the room, where the wall was covered with handguns. "We'll need to find you something that won't be too big for your hands, with manageable recoil."

"*Dirty Harry*!" She had found a Model 29 and was reciting lines from the movie as she aimed at an imaginary crook. She needed both hands to fit around the large grips of the gun to hold it.

The instructor shook his head as he eyed the options on the wall. There were revolvers smaller than the Model 29 with frames small enough for her hands, but the recoil would be harsher than an automatic. He took down and examined a 1911 in 38 super. He started walking over to her as she defeated the hoodlums, to test the fit in her hands.

"It's heavy," she noted as she held the gun out. The frame was still too big for her hands front to back, even with the thinner grips.

"The weight will help to make it manageable for you. But the grip is still too big."

"I'll use Grandpa's gun. It's the one he taught me with. It's a... Sig P 210? We brought it with us," Jenny responded.

He paused. "That's interesting. They're good guns, even if they're in 9mm. That might be a good fit for you."

As she continued playing with the twenty nine, he went over to a rack of shotguns. Working his way down them, he looked for something he had not had to use for a while.

The banker had insisted that his wife take the course with him. It was the last time he had a woman take one of his courses, for good reason. It was still there. He pulled out an Ithaca 34 defense model in 20 gauge with a shortened stock. He called her over and checked its fit.

"I have a new type of sight you might like to try. It's an occluded eyesight. You'll need a pad to raise the comb, but I can have the sight mounted by the end of the week."

He led her over to a rack of bolt-action rifles and took down one that was hanging on the wall above the rack. It had a camouflage stock and a large scope on top of it.

"This is an M40 A one in 308. It's the standard sniper rifle used by the Marines, but it's rather heavy." Putting it back on the wall, he looked down the rack until he found another rifle with a wooden stock. "This is something new. It's in a new cartridge, 7 millimeter 08. It's the same Remington 700 action but quite a bit lighter. It has a higher muzzle velocity, and the 145-grain bullet has a high ballistic coefficient. Do you understand what that means?"

"It means the bullet won't slow down, and you can shoot bad guys from a really long way away!"

He couldn't help smiling. "I'll get a scope mounted to it."

* * *

"What's your target?"

"It's a silhouette. It's... thirty inches tall."

"What's your range?"

"It's... one mil—" Jenny consulted her card with the table on it. "It's... 833 yards."

"What's your wind?"

She had measured it here with the wind meter, but she knew that was not what he meant. She turned the focus back to about halfway to the target, 400 yards. It was blurry now, but she focused not on the target but on the waves in the image. "Left to right. They're blowing almost straight across the image."

"Are they still wavy or straight?"

"Wavy."

"That's about ten miles an hour. What's your hold?"

Jenny hated math. It took her longer than it should. She knew he was getting impatient when she finally answered, "4.4 mills, and 1.6 left. It will drop... 143 inches?"

"Is that a question?"

"Yes! Is that right?"

"I don't know. Why are you asking me? It's *your* rifle, your dope, your pencil, and your shot. Send it and find out."

Asshole. She didn't say that out loud. Jenny dialed in the hold on the turrets and settled in behind the rifle. The image through the scope became her whole world. She breathed and then slowly let half of her breath out. She watched the image jump with each heartbeat. The trigger broke, and the image jumped and disappeared.

She got the scope back on the target in time to see a puff and a dark smudge appear on the left side of the target.

"Hit! Nine o'clock," he called as he watched the wake of the bullet track through the air all the way to the target in the spotting scope.

It was a full two seconds later when she heard the gong of the bullet striking the steel target. Her laughter might have been a little maniacal as she looked through the scope at the target. She could not see that his grin matched her own.

*   *   *

The scream resounded through the building. She looked up from the book she was holding and jumped down from the chair to run across the hall. Mr. Brown was in the corner of the room. "What's wrong?" He pointed frantically to the center of the floor, where a scorpion was crawling across the floorboards. She knelt down. It was a nice, big, fat one.

She looked at him concerned. "Did it sting you?"

"They can sting? Kill it!"

She looked at him condescendingly and went over to get an envelope. She then coaxed it onto the paper and captured it under his water glass. She carefully picked it up and carried it down the stairs.

"What happened this time?" asked one of the men sitting on the couch, comparing load data.

"He found a scorpion in his room. Look—it's really fat."

"Nice one. Are you going to keep it?"

"Somehow I don't think he'll let me." She sighed as she carried it outside the bunk house.

* * *

"Shooter ready?"

A nod of the head, tense ready. The horn sounded. The butt of her rifle left where it touched her hip, coming up to her shoulder, front sight on the target. The light rifle jumped twice in her hands, but the front sight did not leave the target. Two fresh holes appeared in the A zone. She transitioned smoothly through the next three targets.

She left her position at a dead sprint and ran to the next hula hoop on the ground. She kneeled and tried to control her breathing as she aimed at the 300-yard target.

It took three tries to get a hit on the first piece of steel. After that, she had the hold and had no problem making hits on the next three. She missed only once.

Jenny ran again, another hundred meters to the next hula hoop on the ground. Now she was only two hundred yards from the targets, but her breathing was harder. She missed the first shot. *Slow down, control, hit*. She got the next three with no misses.

Running, she had to go down through a wash and up the other side to the next shooting position. Now she was really panting. It was hard to keep the sight steady on the target even at 100 yards.

She hit the first two targets on the first try before her bolt locked open on an empty magazine. This was where her misses cost her as she dropped the rifle to hang from the sling, drawing her handgun. The 210 was more than accurate enough to hit the targets at this distance if she could do her part.

Struggling to control her breathing, she aimed with both hands in an isosceles stance and smoothly squeezed the trigger. It took four shots to hit the third target. The fourth she got in two.

Angling to the left, she had to climb over the 200-yard berm and down again to a plate rack at 25 yards. She changed magazines along the way and was ready when she got to the ring.

"Die, commies!" She hit all the targets with the first shot, knocking them over one at a time going down the row of plates.

The RO hit the button on the timer. "Unload! Show clear!" He called out her time. It was not the fastest time in the class, but it put her in the top quarter.

The others looked on with begrudging respect at the little girl who had beaten them with her mouse gun. As her instructor marked it down on his clipboard, he had to admit that the girl was coming along.

* * *

It was the last day. A deal was a deal. She had done better than anyone had any right to expect of a girl her age. He felt a pang of regret that she was leaving. He mused that with some more training and a bit more focus, she could be the first top-tier female shooter, not only in the women's class. He bet she would be able in time to hold her own with the men.

He made her help carry it as he would pick up one end, and she would struggle with the other. They carried it in pieces from the truck. First the tripod, then the receiver, and last the barrel, which he made her carry by herself.

They hauled over an entire ammo can of ammunition. The targets were set up all over the hillside, silhouettes of men charging toward them. He showed her how to check the head space and load the gun.

He screamed at the top of his lungs, "Gooks in the wire! Gooks in the wire! Kill those motherfuckers!"

She swung the gun around to the left, and holding the grips tightly, she depressed the double paddle triggers with her thumbs. *Kaboom, kaboom, kaboom!* "Die, you evil dink bastards!" she roared, trying to match the volume of the gun.

The big rounds blew through the plywood targets as she traversed the gun cutting them in half. He smiled like a proud father. All too soon the belt ran dry. She looked over, realizing what had happened. "Is there any more?"

"I brought another case," he said, shaking his head.

She barked, "Don't just stand there! Reload before we're overrun!"

There might have been a tear in his eye as he ran to the truck and heard her laughing and yelling, "You want some? How about you? Plenty more where that came from. Come and get it!"

It was probably the smoke from the machine gun.

CHAPTER 26

After-Attack

Jenny Hamman, 31
Cretaceous

Jenny woke up gasping. Air. She needed air. She was being smothered by something. She started pushing all around her. Something fell away from her face, and she sucked in clean, fresh air, one lung full after another, as she remained there resting, breathing.

Jenny realized the air was actually *not* so fresh. It was only relative. She started realizing where she was and froze in fear. Were they still here? She was warm, but the air outside was nice and cool. It was dark. As her eyes adjusted, she could see stars in the sky. She didn't recognize them. They didn't look right. She strained her hearing, but there was nothing. The night was quiet.

Were they warm-blooded enough to hunt at night? Everything said yes. The way they moved implied a high metabolism, and they certainly had enough insulation with the feathers.

Could they see in infrared? Her body would almost glow in the dark in this cold night. In a world filled with cold-blooded animals, Jenny would glow like a beacon in the darkness.

She couldn't stay here. Not only the smell but the idea of being in a literal dung heap was repulsive. It was a warm, safe place to spend the night, but she simply could not do it.

She started pushing the balls off her, making her way out of the pile. It was mostly dry, but she was sure she looked a sight. Most importantly, this would without a doubt cover her smell. She didn't know what other senses her hunters had, but she knew they tracked by scent. This was her chance. If she could get out of their territory before dawn, she might still make it.

Jenny tried standing and fell back down. Her leg would not support her. It would not straighten. She had to work and stretch it to get it to let go and straighten all the way.

She awkwardly climbed to her feet and managed to stand. Somewhere out there was the river. She took a couple of hobbling steps and then forced herself to stand erect.

Her leg made her slow. The moon was a waxing gibbous, almost overhead. It was still early in the night. She made her way across the wide swath that the grazing heard of sauropods had made passing through to who-knows-where. She wished she could have seen them. Brontosaurus. It was one of the first names she had learned as a child.

Of course, Brontosaurs were from an earlier time. The family had grown to include many others, some much bigger, but to her all sauropods were brontosaurus, her favorite dinosaur. Her grandfather had called them something different. "Mokele-Mbembe"? He had given them an African name. Now that made more sense. Perhaps if she found him, he would tell her the story behind that.

She reentered the cover on the other side. The moon lit the scene around her, casting crazy shadows. She knew the moon was actually closer to the earth in this era, but by how much? How much shorter would the month be? She couldn't tell from looking at it.

It was open enough that she could see to make her way. Her mind conjured horrors in every shadow. A monster under every tree. She couldn't let her mind run away from her. She was in the territory of a large pack of aggressive predators. She also knew the density of animals on the ground in any environment was low.

She would have to be profoundly unlucky to stumble across their pack in the dark. As long as she didn't follow game trails or something stupid like that, the odds were that she would be fine.

Slowly, Jenny trudged on through the night, trusting in the cold to help keep her safe. She drank from her one remaining canteen. She had lost blood but knew she would need the water tomorrow as well.

She did not know how long she walked. It occurred to her that she also didn't know how many hours were in a day here. The earth's rotation had slowed as energy transferred from the earth to the moon. She knew the days would be shorter here, but not by how much.

Her mind wandered as she continued marching along with her slow limp. She checked the compass around her neck. It had a glow in the dark needle. She was able to keep a roughly easterly direction. It might be her imagination or the poor light, but it seemed that the vegetation was getting denser and taller.

Could the land be getting wetter? Was she getting closer? She welcomed it, even if it meant she had to take more detours around the darker patches. It would be much easier in the light, but the cold night was hers. Even with the chill, she welcomed it. Her kind were meant for this. They owned the night and the cold in a way no reptile ever could.

She wished she had a crutch, a cane, a walking stick, anything that would help. All she could do was press on.

The dawn found her stumbling along under taller trees, and some of them were now actual trees, not various forms of overgrown ferns. Conifers grew here. They were new on the scene, relatively at least. But like her kind, they along with the grasses would one day dominate this world.

The ferns would be pushed aside. And with them whole new forms of life would emerge. Once the grasses evolved as alternatives to the tough, fibrous ferns, animals would no longer have to be so huge. The size of the dinosaurs was based on the size of their guts. The carnivores grew in proportion to the herbivores, big enough to hunt whatever was their prey.

As the morning became warmer, Jenny started looking for a place where she could stop. Finding a particularly thick patch of growth, she wormed her way into the middle of it and was able to hunker down between the larger ferns, where she was concealed. She took another drink from her canteen. She would have to find water soon.

She went through her pockets. She still had the batteries. The device was still there. She found another power bar and started eating it. Reconsidering, she broke it in two and put the other half back into her pocket.

She still had the browning pistol but had only two full magazines and one partial. While she was thinking about it, she swapped a full mag for the partial and put that one back into the pouch on her belt. She had her grandfather's belt and his knife in a sheath on the left side. The compass was still around her neck. One leg of her pants was in tatters.

She decided to wait to look at her leg until she was ready to move on. She didn't want to rest here with any more blood smell than she had to. She took another antibiotic. At least she had a good supply of those. But she was not looking forward to cleaning the wound. Jenny curled up and gave in to her exhaustion, falling asleep in the middle of a thicket of large ferns.

It was late afternoon when she awoke. She slowly opened her eyes and kept still, listening intently for any sign of dinosaurs in the area. She heard nothing.

Looking up through her ferns, she saw a bird. No, not a bird but a dinosaur. It landed on a large branch, grasping not only with its feet but also with the claws on its wings. They were the thumbs of the animal. It was small, and she recognized it immediately. It had two long feathers forming a twin tail. A Confucius ornis.

The museums had many fine specimens showing the twin feathers that made it so distinctive. They always reminded her of the scissor-tails she saw in Texas in her childhood. She wondered if it was male or female. One theory held that only one gender had the distinctive long-tail feathers.

Unlike the earlier proto birds, it had a bill without any teeth. But most importantly, it fed on aquatic animals. It liked water. She watched it closely. When it took off, she noted its direction until it was out of sight.

She could not put it off any longer. She took off her belt and opened the rest of the contents of the other pockets. The large main pocket held emergency supplies, and the two side pockets housed additional materials: antibiotics, analgesics, a suture kit, tweezers, hemostats, and some spare bandages.

The first thing she did was to take one of the pain-killers. This was going to hurt. She didn't want to damage her pants more than necessary. The bandage was actually on over the pants fabric, so she had to remove it first. Her leg ached. She didn't doubt there would be more to come.

She removed her pants and got her first good look at her leg. It was a mess of clotted blood. She poured a little of her water on the corner of the old bandage and began cleaning the wound. It took a lot of work to get rid of the congealed blood. The QuikClot had made a mess of it.

She had to stop several times to breathe and wait for the dizziness to pass. By the time she was done she felt exhausted, but this was only the beginning.

She opened the suture kit. It contained sterile sutures pre-threaded on small, curved needles, a pair of sterile gloves, and two syrettes of lidocaine. She cleaned the outside of the wound as well as she could with an alcohol wipe and began to inject the lidocaine along both sides of the wound. Poking at it, she was relieved to find it blessedly numb.

Now she had to get this done before it wore off. Taking up the hemostats, she fished out the first of the sutures and started to work closing the tear in her leg. It was awkward working on her own leg, but she did get the wound closed.

How aggressive would the bacteria be here? In theory, her modern immune system would have an advantage over older strains of bacteria. On the other hand, everything here was so old it might act as a novel infection. She could be killed by the smallest scratch. She would have to trust the antibiotics. She buried the bloody bandage but reused the elastic wrapper with a fresh gauze bandage.

She settled back and rested after taking another of the pain-relievers. When she was feeling better, she used one of the remaining sutures to sew up her pants. It didn't look much better than her leg when she was done.

Dressing, she accepted the fact that she needed to move. Her canteen was now empty since she had used the last of it cleaning her wound. But she knew water was somewhere nearby and had an idea of the direction.

It was a small, stagnant pond, already halfway to being dry. She stopped and waited, trying to spot anything that might be lurking. Not seeing any danger, she cautiously approached the water's edge and filled her canteen. She used a piece of her shirt as a prefilter to try catching the worst of it before it went into her canteen. She dropped two iodine pills in the canteen and shook it. Her water filter was lost, so the iodine would have to do.

As she turned to leave, she spotted something she recognized. It was a young sabal palmetto, or sabal palm, perhaps the longest surviving species of that family, now only newborn in this world. Her favorite name for it was *swamp cabbage.* She pulled out her grandfather's knife and began to cut it off as close to the ground as she could. She needed the heart.

Jenny then withdrew from the pond. Once she was far enough away that she felt safe, she found a place to make a fire.

She peeled the section that she had cut from the young plant, exposing the core. She roasted it over the fire, her back propped against a tree. Her leg hurt. Once the heart of the palm was nicely golden brown, she cut it into sections and was able to munch on the pieces. It took her mind back to a summer she had spent in Florida. Not bad, if a little bland. It would be much better if it had some sauce to absorb flavor from.

Jenny didn't want to move. Her leg ached, but she needed to get away from her fire. She levered herself up and moved off deeper into the forest, looking for a safer place to spend the night.

CHAPTER 27

Dangers in the Night

John Hamman, 24
Cretaceous

The men arrived back in camp at sundown to find a roast turning on a spit above a fire. John noted that they would probably have to go for more wood tomorrow. He sat down in his camp chair with a fresh bottle of whiskey and a much smaller glass than last night. Soon, a plate of sliced meat was brought to him.

John sat back thinking of how strange life had become and how well they had adapted to it. They had been here for only two days, but he felt that they should return soon. This was only meant to be a test. It would be best to come back with a larger party.

They had seen some amazing things, but he worried that they had been lucky so far. They had not encountered any of the truly fearsome beasts these times were known for. What would they do then? Could they really cope with just one double rifle? Would even the 500 prove enough against what they might find here?

The encounter with the behemoth this morning had shaken him. It had been peaceful, but elephants were also herbivores, and they were not peaceful. Buffalo were herbivores, and they were definitely not peaceful. In fact, they were notorious as some of the most aggressive animals of his time. If Mokele-Mbembe was out there, there would be a lion large enough to feed on it.

His mind made up, John set his empty plate aside. Tomorrow they would return. They still had to hunt for some ivory to pay for this charade and cover what they were doing. Who knew how long that would take?

They had a lot of meat in the camp. That may have been what drew it. The fire had been allowed to burn down low to cook the roast. They should have kept it higher. If they had been back home and had more men, they could have built a wall of thorn bushes around the camp. But their group was small, and nothing like that seemed to grow here.

There was no sound, only a flash of movement, and a shape leaped over one of the tents, landing in among the group. It seized one of the men by his arm and began dragging him out of the camp between two tents, ignoring the rest, to a place about thirty feet beyond. The man screamed piteously all the way.

John had put all the rifles in his tent, intending to clean them. He rushed after the beast into the night. It was dark beyond the tents.

He drew the Lancaster from the sheath on his right leg. He couldn't see clearly, but from the man's screams, John thought the beast had dropped the man to the ground and appeared to step forward, pinning him with its foot as its head bent down to devour its prey.

John couldn't see his gun, much less the sight, so he pointed the long barrels at the monster and squeezed the trigger with both of his fingers cocking the gun.

The flash was bright in the darkness, like a flashbulb from a camera lighting up the scene before him. The predator was about half again John's height, like a much larger version of the small things they had hunted. It walked on its hind legs, covered with feathers, a long crest running down its back. But unlike a bird, its maw was filled with razor-sharp teeth it aimed down at the man's head. He was pinned beneath its foot, screaming. John saw all this in the flash.

He fired three more times, not knowing if he even hit it. The battle was lit by bright flashes, but in between it was darkness, their vision totally ruined.

John saw the beast turn toward him. The last flash revealed that it was charging at him, its maw agape, then darkness. It hit him, bowling him over with its mass, but John thought it was as blind as himself at that point.

He heard a battle cry from behind, and something leaped over him. He heard an angry squawk from the dinosaur. About then Manny arrived on the scene with one of the camp lanterns, and John saw the Maasai standing over him with his shield and spear. He had buried its point deep in the monster's chest, but it gave no indication of caring.

John reached and drew the Webley from the holster across the left side of his belt. He scrambled to the side to try getting a clear shot. He emptied all six rounds into the beast's chest without really aiming.

It staggered to the side, and the tracker stabbed it again at the base of its neck. The beast fell over on its side, and the man stabbed it over and over again until it went still.

John staggered to his feet, looking around. Both of his guns were empty. He went to the fallen man, calling for Manny to bring the lantern.

He was alive. His arm was bleeding badly, and blood welled from a wound on his chest. They carried him back into the camp, and John called for the fire to be built up.

They laid him down moaning next to the fire. The man had deep puncture marks in his upper arm where it had been in the beast's jaws. The bone was not broken, and although blood was running freely, it was not pumping. They did what they could for him.

He cried out when they washed the wounds with gin. At least John had found some use for the stuff. They wrapped the wound tightly with bandages from a small medical kit. On his chest were scratches and a deep puncture into his left pectoral muscle.

John went back out to examine the enemy. It was similar to the small game they had hunted, from the same family of animals but much larger. Its head was quite big with powerful jaws. If it had wanted to bite the man's arm in two, it could have done so easily, but it had not wanted him to get away.

Its body was covered with down, and it had large, long feathers all along its back. But the beast lacked the large feathers on the arms. It did not have the same bird-like appearance. The tail was heavier, without large feathers at its tip. It became bare like a rat's tail. On its toes one claw was larger than the rest. That was what had dug deeply into the poor man's chest.

John went back to the fire and made his decision. They would not wait. He told Manny to have the men break the camp. They would return now to their own time.

They would camp there where at least they knew what dangers they would face. A lion seemed paltry in comparison to what lurked here.

It took over an hour to break all the camp and gather everything together. John made them all stand around him as he set up the device and triggered it, taking them back to their own time.

CHAPTER 28

Jo Bob's

Robert Brown, 46
1984 New York, NY

Robert Brown sat at his desk in his private office. He looked over at the bottle of Melox setting on his desk, and his stomach turned over.

His door was closed. He was on the phone long distance. Around him every other office door was closed and mostly locked, as every member of the firm demanded that their stockbroker buy Apple at any price. No one knew what a Macintosh was. No one in the world had heard of such a thing, except for the people who just left the conference room.

He had gone to law school. He was a lawyer. He liked being a lawyer. He liked the order of it, the predictability. However, he didn't know if he was a lawyer anymore.

After years of working happily on this account, filing corporate paperwork, arranging mergers and acquisitions—lawyer things—he was now in charge of this. After being elevated to a full partner in the firm that he had worked at for years, he now felt like an intern running errands.

What bothered him was that they were errands he didn't understand. None of them made sense. Why would John Hamman, one of the richest men in the world, insist that his grandchild attend a survival school? Why would he be so insistent that she learn how to shoot? Did he think that a thirteen-year-old was going into combat?

In theory, one day this trust would mature and she would be the richest woman in history. When would she ever need to know how to make moccasins?—which brought him to his current struggles.

Robert was desperately searching for accommodations near Jo Bob's Wild Game Processing and BBQ in a rural Texas town of fewer than a thousand people. He spoke into the phone, "There has to be something. A hotel, a bed and breakfast, even a motel?"

The sole member of the chamber of commerce, one Bo Bohannan, also the owner, operator, and chief mechanic of the only filling station in town, was less than helpful with Robert's queries.

Perhaps he should speak louder. That always helped people understand you. Trying to speak very slowly, hoping that there was some kind of misunderstanding or bad connection preventing the man from comprehending him, Robert asked, "Where... do... people... stay... when... they... come... to... your... town... for... business?"

In an even more pronounced and slow response, complicated with a strong Texas drawl, Bohannan responded, "We... don't... have... that... round... here." This might be the worst year ever.

CHAPTER 29

Gibraltar

William "Wild Bill" Donovan, 60
Gibraltar November 1943

The rain beat against the plane in a dull roar as the C47 pushed its way through the storm. Donovan tightened the belt across his waist and leaned back against the wall of the aircraft. He could feel the whole airframe vibrate with waves of rain. The plane lurched up and down. All the cargo was secured, and the belt was the only thing that prevented him from being bounced off the top of the cabin.

The two young officers across from him were ghostly white. One leaned forward with his head in his hands, and the other had his eyes squeezed tightly closed, his lips moving as he recited some kind of rosary. All three of them had emptied everything from their stomachs long ago.

It was a hell of a night to be in the air. After all they had been through, it would be a sad ending to die in a plane crash. Looking forward, Donovan could see the two pilots through the cabin door, lit by the instrument panel as they fought the controls. He hoped they could get it on the ground. He didn't think they had enough fuel to reach an alternate landing area, at least not one with better weather. The storm had been unrelenting.

He heard the engines throttle down as they approached their destination, the pilots chasing the needle of the directional beacon, even as it was drawn off by every flash of lightning. They were going in. Donovan could neither see nor hear the drama that his life depended on. All he could do was sit and wait while their lives rested in other hands. He listened to the engines throttle up and down as they tried to stay on the glide slope. He let out a breath he had not realized he was holding when the wheels finally touched down.

When the rear doors opened, he let the two young men stumble out of the plane first. Pushing his fedora hat down on his head, he stepped out into the rain. He could see nothing in the darkness and the rain beyond the handful of airport lights and the headlights of an army jeep half hooded with blackout filters. "This way, sir." A young officer took his arm and led him to the jeep.

As they drove off from the airport into the darkness, following the narrow road more by feel than by the wholly inadequate headlights, he looked up at the sky. The lightning flashed, revealing the dark looming shape of The Rock towering over the skyline. By the time they had been through three checkpoints and reached the entrance, he was soaked to the bone.

The tunnels were dark and cold, cut from the living limestone and lit only occasionally by dim electric bulbs. The chill seeped into his sodden clothing. He clutched the leather attaché case under his arm, praying that at least his papers were still dry. A multitude of soldiers moved through the tunnels as so many ants. He had no idea where he was in this warren. They passed through an internal checkpoint, where his civilian attire drew more than a few curious looks.

The tunnels were slightly more illuminated here. Everyone they passed at this point was some form of officer. Finally he was led into a larger underground gallery where a number of men stood around a long table. Maps hung on all the walls.

He waited by the entrance as his guide went forward to report. All the faces around the table would be recognizable to anyone in the Western world. This was the heart of the military effort of all the allied nations. The man with thinning hair looked up from his conversation to stare at him.

Eisenhower called from across the room, "You look like a half-drowned dog. Change into something dry and clean yourself up before you get anything wet." He nodded to the side toward an alcove. It held bunk beds occupied by sleeping officers, one snoring loudly.

Donovan was able to change into some khakis that were brought to him along with an only slightly dirty towel. Once he was no longer dripping and had combed his wet hair, he returned to the table to find only General Eisenhower and one other man rummaging through the papers and photographs he had brought from such a great distance.

"You picked a hell of a night to join us, Bill. I would normally ask how your flight was, but I'm just glad you got down in one piece." Eisenhower leafed through the aerial photos, stopping to study one in greater detail. His aide was reading through the report.

"I've been a little out of touch, General. How have things been going?"

Ike looked up at him from above his reading glasses. "Your information proved spot-on. A resistance group out of Austria, the CASSIA, was able to get close to the target and confirm your suspicions. It's the primary development site for their new superweapons. They are all autonomous—no pilots. One is a jet-engine-powered aircraft with a large warhead. The other... is something different."

So Hamman's information once again proved to be correct. Donovan wished he knew where and how Hamman learned everything he seemed to know. And he wished Hamman would be a little more discrete about talking of these things in front of his wife.

Sometimes Hamman even let his wife lead the conversation and answer questions as if she were the one delivering the information. First the oil fields, then this Peenemunde place no one had ever heard of before. And now Heavy Water? What the hell was that, and why did it elicit such excitement, almost panic, when he reported it?

"How is it going at Ploesti?" Donovan redirected.

The general growled under his breath. "Not well. Operation Tidal Wave is continuing, but it's a tough nut to crack. It's a long way for our bombers. We've had some losses." He turned back to the first photograph and reached for a magnifying glass on a stand. He placed it over the image and leaned to look down through it. "The bad news is from Europe. We've spotted a launch site. It's a rail, looks like a goddamn ski ramp, just like how you described." He looked up suspiciously at that. "The Brits are panicking. They're worried about it being used as a gas attack or maybe something biological, maybe something worse." He trailed off with a sour expression. "If they're building one, I'll bet they're building a hundred of the damn launchers. The Brits want us to bomb them all."

Ike continued studying the aerial photos. "Operation Hydra went well. I don't think they'll be building anything on that island. We're preparing for the next phase. We're calling them 'Crossbow Operations.' We are designating the launchers as 'Noball' sites. The Brits want us to devote 40 percent of our air assets to stopping these attacks, but that's not striking against anything that would help us win the war."

Donovan wanted to change the subject. "I bring better news from up north. I think we can label Operation Gunnerside a success. I have intelligence that key equipment was damaged at the electrolysis plant. Production has ceased, but they still have a rather large supply on hand, and they could conceivably repair it. I recommend we bomb the hydroelectric plant. They might also try to transport the supply they already have to Germany. We should be on the lookout for that." He wasn't sure how to broach the question, but he needed to understand if he was going to do his job. "Sir, what is this stuff? This 'Heavy Water'? Is it a poison?"

Eisenhower paused as if unsure about whether to answer. "It's key to something they want to try to develop. If we can block their acquisition of it, we may stall their development project."

Development of what? Donovan knew better than to press when the general was that cagey.

Eisenhower's eyes drilled into him now. "I don't suppose you'd care to divulge the source of your information." It wasn't quite an order.

"Sir, you know sources are even more closely guarded than the information they provide." Time to deflect again. "What about the rail yards? Did you do an overfly of any of the sites? If we knocked out the rail system leading to the... prisoner camps, we might at least slow their... operations."

More than a bit exasperated, Eisenhower replied, "I know what you think they are. We did task a plane to overfly one of the sites you specified." He didn't meet Donovan's eyes. "The official evaluation of the aerial photos was that they were inconclusive." Eisenhower turned to him, waving one of the photos. "Thank you for bringing these. Go get some sleep. It looks like it was a long trip." He turned away in dismissal.

One of these days Donovan was going to have to have a long talk with Hamman. This story about "far-reaching business interests" was getting a little old. How did he acquire all of this information? It had crossed his mind that Hamman could be a German spy, but the information he had given them over the years had been so good that it almost felt as if he were handing them the war on a silver platter.

If Hamman wasn't a German, then who was he, and how did he seem to know the inner plans of the Third Reich? If they all lived through this war, Donovan swore that one day he would learn the answers.

CHAPTER 30

Ivory

John Hamman, 24
1919/8,000 BC

They reappeared in their own time. It was night here as well, a dark, cloudy one with mist closing in around them. John looked around in the pool of light thrown by their two lanterns. They along with all their belongings were all there. He could not tell if they were in the same place from which they had left. It was some hours before the horizon began to lighten and even longer before the rising sun burned away the morning mist.

John was worried for the injured man. They needed to get him back to Nairobi, to a doctor, but he had no idea when Blix would return. He also had nothing he could actually show for their time there. He had no ivory.

John looked over at the crates and all the liquor remaining. He tried to estimate how much longer they would last, even at the prodigious rates of consumption that someone like Blix was capable of. He did not like the answer. He did not think they could expect him for at least another two weeks. John turned to Manny.

"How long till Blix comes back?"

"No time soon, Bwana." Manny was not smiling when he said this.

"How many elephants would Blix shoot on a trip like this?" John needed to keep up their cover.

"Sometimes none, Bwana. Sometimes many. Sometimes three or four bulls," he said with a shrug that seemed to indicate the randomness of life.

They would have to go hunting. But first they must do their best for their man. John told Manny to have half the tents pitched, including the big one. Three of the men would stay here with their injured companion. The rest of them would hunt for ivory.

John told him to make sure the Maasai stayed in camp as they would need him. With that, he pitched in on the setup. Trying to make sure the injured man was as comfortable as possible, John left him lying on his own cot in the big tent in the care of his companions.

John gathered everyone else a short distance away. He asked Manny to explain that they were going to hunt for ivory now, but they would do it a little ways away from there.

He thought they had a better idea of what was coming this time. They did not seem scared and waited passively. He set only the first working dial. This had been his plan all along. The land may be almost hunted out today, but it might be easier going back, say, ten thousand years ago.

* * *

The sun was higher in the sky, and the land had changed. What had been a sea of grass with a few patches of trees was now much greener. It might have been the season. Everything was greener, as if the rains had just ended, but there were also far more trees. The few small stands of trees of his own time were much more common here, larger and denser. John turned to Manny and asked him to tell the others that they would hunt elephants here.

He hoped there were elephants in this time. He wasn't sure he could explain a mammoth tusk. He was sure someone would notice a difference. They set up camp as the Maasai set out to scout the area. They had breakfast ready when he returned. Manny once again consulted with him and came to John with a very big smile on his face.

"He say there are many elephants here, Bwana. Many, many. He say there are bulls with big ivory. Very big, Bwana. He say there is good hunting here. He say there is water here. Many water holes." John thought about this. This must be a wetter time. The land seemed more fertile.

"This is good. We will hunt here." John made this pronouncement as if he had known this and that it had been his plan all along. Manny's smile was so broad that John thought the top of his head might fall off.

They set out after breakfast, Manny and John following the Maasai. It didn't take long. In a nearby stand of trees about a half mile away, a heard of elephant were feeding.

The men could hear them within the stand. They were feeding, which meant they were tearing the branches off the trees or simply pushing the entire trees over to get at the succulent leaves. The noise was tremendous. John tried to get Manny to ask the Maasai the number of elephants, but Manny simply answered, "Many."

John thought about what to do. He wasn't sure going into the stand with only one big gun and an unknown number of elephants was a good idea. Actually, he was pretty sure it was a bad idea. Maybe it would be better to try for them at or on their way to the watering hole. If they were feeding, they would need to drink soon, right?

He tried getting Manny to ask the tracker where the nearest watering hole was. He pointed to the grove. The Maasai could smell a water hole in the grove as the wind blew gently toward them. John couldn't smell a thing but took his word for it.

That complicated things. He had thought it was a rather good idea and was miffed that the world wasn't cooperating. He had a gun and pockets full of cartridges. If he was going to be a great white hunter, it was time for him to get on with it.

He took the big gun from Manny and handed him the Mauser, but it was hardly useful in this. He didn't think the elephant would even feel the smaller round.

He tried recalling what Blix had told him as they moved into the grove, but he had been very drunk. Blix had been adamant that John should not put too much faith in his 500. Even as one of the biggest guns in the world, it could not take down an elephant without proper shot placement. And most of the shots he described were small targets.

He had said that John should not try to take an elephant from the front with a head shot—even with the 500.

It was all bone. Ignore the old story about between the elephant's eyes. Try to spot the ear holes on the side and draw a line between them. If the head is angled at all to the side, you are almost certain to ruin the ivory on one side or the other. The tusk extended far up into the skull.

He warned John, "If you flub that shot, the elephant could literally walk away, ignoring the bullet in its head or charge forward and stomp you into paste." The only time Blix tried for a frontal was if it charged and then... "Well, you might as well try." His drunken shrug imparted no confidence.

It was much better to try taking the beast from the side. He said you could aim for the ear. He didn't favor brain shots at all. Blix preferred to shoot for the heart and lungs broadside. It would not drop it like a headshot, but it would die, and it was more forgiving of the angle.

By aiming behind the foreleg at the tip of the crease where it met the body, about a third of the way from the bottom, one was likely to get a good hit. In a last ditch, he talked about trying to hit its spine above the tail or the hip as it ran away. He also spoke of many an elephant's ass disappearing into the jungle never to be seen again.

As they moved into the grove, they found a trail probably leading to the water hole within. The Maasai went in front of them studying the tracks. He froze in place looking at one of them.

They came up beside him, and he pointed with the back end of his spear. One of the tracks was larger than the others. Manny pointed it out, the fine dust capturing the details of the deeper ridges of the large calluses worn down on the heel. "Bull, Bwana." The tracks were fresh in the soft powder. They had their quarry.

Moving in, they could hear the animals feeding, but it was hard to place their location. They heard one of them trumpet. Manny moved next to John and whispered in his ear, "Cow." The sight lines quickly became very short. They could not see more than fifteen yards, maybe twenty. The tracker froze. John followed his gaze to the left but saw nothing. They slowly moved up next to him. John wouldn't have seen it if it had not moved.

It was huge, but it blended into the background. All he could see was a patch of skin through the greenery. They moved to the right and got a better look. John had never seen anything like it. If he hadn't seen the dinosaurs, he would have been overwhelmed. But they were so close. He couldn't reach out and touch it, but he could see the pebbly surface of its skin.

Manny put his hand on John's shoulder, breaking the spell, and gently pulled him back. They retreated. "Cow, Bwana." The tracker led them deeper toward the pool at the heart of the grove.

As they got closer, the Maasai stopped and crouched. The rest of the group did the same. John listened harder than he ever had before. He heard the beating of his own heart, but then he heard *it*. He wasn't sure what it was at first. Then Manny raised his hand beside his ear and slowly made a strange waving gesture, rotating his hand back and forth. Then John realized what it was. They were hearing the sound of the elephants flapping their great ears back and forth to cool the blood running through them. The tracker knelt and pointed forward with his spear. It was time.

John crept forward as quietly as he could. Manny shadowed him. John did not know what he intended to do. The tracker came behind them. As they got closer, they stepped to the side so they would be in slightly heavier cover and peeked out of the brush into a small clearing containing a watering hole. It still had some water in it, but it was reduced in size, more than half dry. That left a muddy bank all around.

Two elephants stood by the water hole. The great bull was there, a true jumbo, and a smaller animal, one of the cows. His tusks were huge and curved. John had no idea of how to guess their weight. They were facing each other. The hunters had them broadside. The bull was at a slight angle toward them. He had not spotted them yet, but John realized they needed to act quickly before the bull smelled them.

John slowly raised the rifle, trying not to draw attention to himself. He thought about the ear shot but remembered what Blix had said. He aimed at the top of the crease behind the bull's left shoulder. He hesitated, but then the trigger broke and the gun roared, shoving him back. He tried bringing the barrels down again and getting back on the sights. The beast had not moved much, backing up but not really changing the shot.

He aimed a little farther forward for the shoulder. The big double roared again, and the bull bellowed as he fell on his side. The cow trumpeted wildly, and all of a sudden they heard echoing calls from what seemed all around them. There were a lot of elephants in this grove.

The cow was desperately trying to lift the bull back onto his feet with her tusk and trunk. The sight was piteous. John had never imagined animals could feel that way.

He heard crashing coming toward them and dropped flat in the bushes, hoping he would not be seen. It must not have been too bad an idea, as he saw his companions had done the same. It seemed as if the cows of the herd streamed into the clearing from all directions. Soon a dozen elephants surrounded the bull.

They managed to lift him onto his feet. He stood unsteadily, and surrounded by the cows of the herd, he began moving off at a limping gate, his staggering body being held up by his lovers on either side. They crashed away through the trees, flattening them in a wide trail.

John stayed there with his gun empty. He should have reloaded it when he had the chance. He got up and stared around. Opening the gun and ejecting the empty cases, he reloaded with two more solids.

He couldn't help but think about the expense and the rate at which he was going through them. The steel-jacketed lead bullets were so much more expensive than any ammunition he had ever bought at home. Nothing else could penetrate deeply enough, breaking through the heavy bones to strike home in the animals' vitals.

He thought about the beast he had seen in the deep past. He must find an even larger gun. Even the 500 felt paltry against the behemoth he had seen there.

John had shot an elephant but was not sure what to do now. He knew he hit it and probably in a good spot, but even after emptying his gun into the beast, it had walked away. The 500 did not seem so big anymore.

The tracker moved forward to where the bull had been. The rest came up behind to see what he was looking at. He pointed with his spear at a spray of blood on the foliage. Manny smiled broadly. "Sneeze, Bwana." If he was spewing blood out of his trunk when he breathed, then John had gotten him in a lung. They had the kill. All they had to do was be patient.

John took the canteen from the pocket on his belt. Without thinking, he offered it to Manny and the Maasai. They declined. He took a long swig from it and tried again. Now Manny accepted it and took a small swig from it very formally. Then the Maasai did the same, as if it had some greater meaning. As he was putting the canteen away John realized that this was the first time he had ever shared a drink with a Black man.

They moved away from the watering hole into a more anonymous part of the forest. They waited a good hour, surely more than long enough for the bull to expire. The tracker led the way. They moved slowly, not sure of what they would find.

The bull was lying on its side to the right of the trail they had broken through the forest. All the vegetation around it was flattened, as if the whole herd had milled around it, circling their bull. The odor of urine was strong. At first John thought the bull's bladder had let go. But no, the bull was covered in it. It looked as though every member of the herd had urinated on the big bull. He had not expected to see that.

The beast was very dead, surrounded by a pool of foamy blood that had been blown from his trunk. Still, it was impressive and majestic even in its death.

Butchering it was difficult. The tusk had to be carefully chopped from the animal's head. Manny did the work himself, not trusting the ivory to any of the men. The tusks extended almost two feet into the skull, and the bone had to be carefully chopped around it to free it. They were more than five feet long, even before they were cut from the skull, seven after they were freed. They were twenty inches in circumference at the widest point. They must have approached one hundred pounds a side of ivory.

They went back to their small camp. John worried about the man they had left behind in the future. He wanted to get this over with so they could return to him. They ate great steaks of elephant that night. They were slightly gamey and reminded him of venison.

Over the next week they hunted and bagged another bull elephant every day, which was almost unheard of. John never tried to split his shots to get a second, at least intentionally. He did not feel he could risk it with only a single gun. He did take one of them with a single shot from the side. It was standing still with a perfect shot at the ear. John decided to try for it, and it dropped flat as if a giant had poleaxed it.

That was good, because what came next gave him a real scare. John heard a crashing from their left and turned to see one of the cows charging them with her head down. He drew a bead on the center of its head, above the eyes, and fired.

He was rushed and hadn't prepared for the recoil. It put him on his ass, and he looked up in time to see the elephant's back end collapse under it. And then the front half of the animal came crashing down. John tried to reload the rifle, but his arm was numb and didn't seem to want to work. Fortunately, his shot had been true.

The only other time he tried for a headshot was out of necessity. They were trying to get a shot on a lone bull they had been tracking all day. He never seemed to stop moving and had led them on a merry chase. They finally found him but were having trouble getting a good shot. The men had gotten quite close during all of this, and the beast either caught wind of them or saw them.

Suddenly he was facing the hunters all flared up, his ears spread wide. They weren't twenty yards apart with the bull prancing sideways and shaking its head, trumpeting. John wasn't sure where to aim. Then the bull lowered his head, preparing to charge, and John fired.

The bull stepped back as if stunned but did not drop. He had missed. The beast turned, and as John brought the gun down again, he fired into the ear. The whole body jerked, and the elephant fell on his side as dead as a sack of potatoes. That was when John realized the value of a double. He could never have made that second shot if he had to work any type of action.

John had had enough for the moment. They had collected the ivory from eight elephants. None of the bulls were less than 80 pounds a side, and the largest must have been 140 pounds. The cow was smaller at sixty pounds a side but still respectable. They gathered everyone around in the center of their camp and triggered the device, returning them to their own time.

* * *

It was night, and on the open plain John could see the fire of their men less than half a mile distant. He had instructed them to keep it burning night and day. They left the ivory stacked in a pile and made their way to the light in the darkness.

John was glad they had returned. The injured man was not doing well. The jaws and claws of the dinosaur that attacked him had been dirty and carried some kind of sickness. The wounds were not closing, and the skin around them was red and raw. Infection had set in.

John thought back to all the men in the war who had died in the hospitals, consumed by sickness within their wounds. They had washed the injuries with gin and changed the bandages, but the sickness had already taken root.

Manny spoke to the tracker, and he turned, disappearing into the night. John did not know what to do for the injured man. They were stranded in the middle of the Maasai Mara, a week's travel on foot from the nearest hospital, and he was not sure when Blix would return to take them back to Nairobi. Perhaps if they could get the man back to a doctor they could cut away the sickened tissue to allow it to heal.

Sometime later the Maasai returned with a large pile of dung carried in his hands. Crouching by a lantern, he started pulling it apart, picking something out and putting it in his hand.

He returned to the man on the cot, and John saw that he held a bunch of maggots in his hand. Manny removed the bandages, and the Maasai began to put the maggots in the man's wounds. John wanted to object but had no idea of what to do. He had nothing else to offer. All they could do was wait, make sure he drank enough water, and try to get him to eat.

The next day they fetched the ivory back to the camp. All the men were pleased, but John's mind returned to the injured man. He had known these people for less than two weeks, but he already felt responsible for them. The man had almost died on John's trip into the past, and he might still pay the price for it.

Over the next few days they stayed in the camp. The man did not die but was still bedridden. They made sure he had water to drink, and he managed to take some stew. By the end of the week the wounds seemed to be improving. The Maasai added more maggots every day. They consumed the dying flesh and with it the infection.

At the end of the week they were able to pick the maggots out of the wounds and re-bandage. None of this seemed to have pained him, but John gathered that he could feel them squirming inside him. He was able to sit up now. John was beginning to hope he might live, but he would bear the scars for the rest of his life.

Manny brought John a necklace with one of the claws from the dinosaur that had attacked their camp. It was a big, hooked thing about four inches long. It hung from a leather cord. He very solemnly hung it around John's neck, and John tucked it into his shirt. Later he noticed that the man who had been attacked had one around his neck as well.

Some other odds and ends seemed to be popping up in the dress of the men. An odd bone here, a tooth there decorating anything from their clothing to their hair. Feathers seemed to be popular too. John wondered if that would become a problem, but they were all rather inconspicuous. They didn't really look that strange.

CHAPTER 31

Spear

Jenny Hamman, 31
Cretaceous

Her stomach rumbled. She had eaten the last half of her protein bar, which had not been enough. The night was still dark, but Jenny could sense the dawn lightening the sky even if she could not see it under the trees. She had cut ferns to make a bed and more to cover her last night, but she still felt cold and stiff.

She needed to find more food today, and she needed more of a weapon than the High Power. Her remaining ammunition would go fast if she ran into another predator, but the real problem was that it had no real stopping power. She could probably empty the gun into a predator in this time, and it would still charge in and kill her long before it died. She would never hunt a lion or even a leopard with a 9 millimeter. She needed something else.

As soon as it was light enough to see, she began looking around the woods for a young sapling. She needed something small enough that it wouldn't be too heavy. She didn't like a heavy spear.

Her leg hurt, and she took another of the antibiotics. She could see no sign of major infection, probably thanks to the modern medicines. Still, it slowed her down. It would take a while to heal, and she wouldn't be doing any running in the meantime.

Mid-morning she found something that might do. It was thin enough and straight enough that she wouldn't have to reshape it. It had enough length to give her a six-foot shaft. She knelt down and started chopping at the base with the large Bowie knife. It was slower going than if she had a proper hatchet. Once she felled the sapling, she measured it against her own height and cut it off.

While she was working she had been eyeing another tree. Would it be worth the effort? She was going to have to be a little sedentary for a while and could spare the time to work on it. The shape was actually pretty good. The tree was a conifer and too soft to do a truly proper job, but it would be better than nothing.

She began digging up the base of the tree and cut the roots. This took longer than Jenny had hoped, and she thought about giving up on the idea. She really wanted to find something to eat, and this wasn't getting her any closer. She decided to keep after it. Once the tree was down, she had to cut it off as well, more of a chore with this one, as it was thicker. She wished she had some type of saw.

The exercise had not been completely fruitless. As she moved around the forest, she noticed at least three different species of conifer. She had colleagues who would give their eye teeth for the chance to see these early trees themselves. The cones of many of the trees were starting to open. She picked large samples of all three species. It was getting awkward carrying everything.

Jenny found a spot away from any trail and started gathering wood for a small fire. The fire-starter made short work of the tinder she gathered, and soon she had a small fire. She set the pine cones around it and sat down with her back to a tree to begin working on her projects.

She stripped the bark from the shaft and started smoothing it. It didn't take much work to clean it up. She would be able to bind her grandfather's knife to it and have at least a functional spear. But before she did that, she needed it for her other project.

This took quite a bit more whittling. First she cleaned up the bottom, cutting away the roots and smoothing the round end. It was not a bad shape, about four inches around. The shaft was too thick. Holding the blade like a draw knife, she started shaving it down. It didn't take as long as she feared. Normally one would use a tree with a much harder wood. She left it a bit thicker than usual, as it was a softer wood and she did not trust it enough to make a thinner handle.

As she worked, she kept turning the pine cones next to the fire, trying to warm them evenly. She wished she had a better way to heat them. Eventually they opened up. Of the three species, two of them had nuts within the cone. It was the smallest cone that had the largest nuts. They were still smaller than the piñons from back home, at least on a good year. Perhaps it had been dry. She picked the nuts from them, keeping the two types separate.

She looked at them hesitantly. Not all species were edible. Still, it was worth a try. She took the larger nut and smelled it. She wasn't sure what she expected. She rubbed it on the tip of her tongue and then put it down. She waited but did not feel any numbness or other symptoms.

Finally, looking at it dubiously, she put it into her mouth and chewed. She held it in her mouth, moving it over her tongue, and then spit it out. Nothing frightening happened. It tasted like a nut. Fuck it. She peeled another and ate the thing. Waiting for some kind of pain, she went back to whittling. Her stomach hurt, but it was the same hunger she felt before.

The other nut did not seem to produce any harmful effects either. She gave up on caution and ate all of them. It took a lot of peeling, and it was not nearly enough to satisfy her hunger. Teasing her, it seemed to make her hunger worse.

Jenny got up and gathered more pine cones. She soon had a whole ring of cones around the small fire and continued whittling. When she was done, she got the idea to heat the ball end and the point over the fire to harden them. She was not sure how much it helped, but it was worth a try. It worked on spear points. Soon she had a functional knobkerrie. It was a good height to serve her as a walking stick, something she would not object to right now.

She turned the cones again and then set about binding her grandfather's knife to the shaft with para-cord. When she was done, she looked at her newest weapon. It was not a thing of beauty, but it did look dangerous. Afterward she turned to the water hole, wanting something more substantial in her stomach.

Jenny approached the shore not along one of the trails but through the brush. She was as quiet as she could manage, not wanting to scare anything away, but more importantly she was worried about hunters other than herself. She did not want to be the prey. It would be safer to hunt elsewhere, but she didn't have the time. It had been two days since her last real meal.

She could not spot anything else watching the water hole. It was still well before dark. It might be busier closer to sunset. She waited—and her waiting was rewarded.

They weren't too big. That was good. She wanted something small. She couldn't afford to carry meat with her, and she had no good way to preserve it. They were on the far side of the water hole.

She didn't really want to use her gun. She didn't have much ammo left, but she needed the meat. She would have to try making a better ranged weapon. She didn't see any practical way to build a bow. At least she hoped she would not be here long enough to have to do that.

Jenny slowly reached down and drew the pistol from the holster on her belt. Slowly bringing it up in front of her where she lay on her belly under a fern, she propped herself on both elbows as she sighted on the dinosaurs. She picked one and waited for it to be still. These animals were twitchy. They always seemed to be in motion.

The bark of the 9 millimeter was loud. She needed hearing protection. The rest of the herd moved so fast they seemed to vanish, leaving their companion behind. She worked her way around the water hole toward it. It was some type of ornithischian. She could not place the species. It was about the size of a dog.

She did a quick field dressing, leaving the offal well away from the waterhole to avoid contamination. Something would come along and clean up the pile of intestines for her.

Before she carried her prize away, she had an idea. She gathered a good bundle of long-stemmed ferns from around the water hole. With luck, they would be fibrous enough for her to weave them. Next, she picked up her kill and slung it across her shoulders. Holding one foreleg and the tail, she picked up her spear and made her way back to her little camp.

The fire had died in her absence, but the pine cones had opened. It was not hard to reignite the fire. She built it up larger, since she would need more coals. When the fire burned down, she laid the reptile wrapped in leaves in the ashes and covered it in more ash, then pushed more coals on top of it. Her hope was that the ash would insulate the bundle, and the coals would provide the heat to slow-cook the meat in its own skin.

It was a good idea in theory. She had mixed luck in the past with this technique. One advantage was that it would not give off much of an odor, other than that of the fire. In the meantime she looked at the ferns she gathered and started stripping them, splitting and pulling apart the long fibers. She might be able to work with this. As she worked, she munched on the pine nuts.

Jenny eventually had a workable sling. It was crude, and she wasn't sure how pliable it would stay as the fibers dried. It would probably not last long, but she could always make another. She kept the fire going and continued pushing new coals on top of her meal. It was starting to get dark by the time her dinner was ready to eat.

It was burnt, or part of it was, but it left more than enough to eat. She stuffed herself with as much as she could, then gathered up her new weapons and moved off into the night. She wanted to sleep somewhere else, away from the place she had cooked. She washed her hands in the dirt, trying to get rid of the smell of the greasy meat.

Thoughts kept coming about the theropods that had pursued her. She found a new place to curl up for the night, not wanting to sleep in the same location twice.

CHAPTER 32

Butcher

Jenny Hamman, 14
1984

The surprisingly heavy package was delivered by FedEx. Jenny's parents had to sign for it. They were getting used to this, which meant they made her open it in front of them so they could see what was sent this year. Inside was a heavy rolled bundle. Jenny stared at it, confused. Untying the strap around it, she unrolled the bundle on the dining room table to find something straight out of a serial killer's Christmas list.

It was every possible type of knife and edged weapon imaginable. There were *Psycho* knives, *Friday the 13th* knives, little knives, and even a cleaver out of *Texas Chainsaw Massacre*. All of them were made from gleaming stainless steel. Even the handles were steel. They were beautiful. This was going to be the best year ever.

Her mother stormed off. As she went, Jenny heard her say, "Enough is enough." While they were distracted, Jenny carried her newest toys out into the backyard.

If she was going to learn to be a ninja this year, she had better get started. She unrolled the holder on the ground, took out the coolest one she could find, and struck a ninja pose before throwing it at the largest tree. She missed. This was going to take some work. And where was the sword? She had all the knives she could ever want but no throwing stars or a proper sword. She wanted a pair of sickles or the sai the scary guy used in *The Octagon*. Chuck Norris was so cool. He could throw little daggers and take bad guys out just like that!

Jenny picked out another knife. This time it hit the tree handle-first and bounced back. She had to jump out of the way. Practice. She had to practice to be ready for this summer.

*   *   *

Jenny was waiting by the door, watching through the peep hole as Mr. Brown approached. She was dressed in her ninja uniform. Well, she was dressed in a black hoodie with the neck of her black turtleneck pulled up over her mouth and black sweats and shoes. She yanked the door open, taking Mr. Brown by surprise with her best ninja war cry as she struck her ninja stance.

His face was complete confusion as Jenny caught him completely off guard. She did the ninja quick draw, pulling the smallest knife from the sheath on her forearm that she had made out of duct tape and cardboard as she brandished it before him with another cry.

"Are you ready to go?" Mr. Brown asked as he looked down, baffled by what he was seeing.

"Yes! I am ready!" Jenny exclaimed as she came to the ninja stand-at-attention position.

"Good," he stated simply as he turned away and walked back to the car. Mr. Brown could ruin any mood. The weapon pack was already slung across Jenny's back, but as she exited, she reached behind the door and picked up the very non-ninja pink suitcase her mother had bought for her and trudged after him.

* * *

Once they arrived in Texas it was a long drive from the airport. They went straight to the house that Mr. Brown had rented them rooms in. The woman greeted them in a south Texas drawl. She called Jenny "precious." She even pinched her cheeks. Jenny didn't see any ninjas.

* * *

Jenny looked up at the sign that read, "Jo Bob's Wild Game Processing and BBQ." It could be a front for an underground ninja training camp, but she was losing hope.

A bell hanging above the door frame rang as they walked in. Along the wall were counters with cuts of meat under glass. In the middle of the room was a big display of breads and sausage. The walls all around were covered with trophy heads. Jenny had never seen so many different types of animals.

The man who came through the back door was not a ninja. He was fat. She had seen larger people on TV, on *That's Incredible*, but not in person. "So this is the little lady?" He came around the counter and bent over so they were face to face. "You are the one who wants to be a butcher?" Jenny turned and looked up at Mr. Brown. She felt betrayed. "Come on back here and I'll show you around."

* * *

Jo Bob looked at Jenny's knives one by one as he examined them, fingering the edges and looking at the point of the one that had a broken tip.

She felt the need to explain, "That one broke when it bounced off the tree and hit a rock." One of his eyebrows rose all the way to his hairline. Without saying a word, he went across the room and came back with a whetstone.

"You have a lot of work to do, little lady," Jo Bob announced as he motioned for her to sit on a stool in front of the whetstone.

* * *

The wild pig smelled. It hung by its rear legs from the hook on the ceiling. Jenny had washed it, so how could it smell so bad? She didn't think it could get worse until she opened the body cavity and the viscera spilled into the bin waiting underneath.

Oh, no—she couldn't help it. She vomited into the bin full of entrails.

"You need to hurry up with the evisceration's. We have twelve more to clean. Then we'll start on the primal cuts." Jo Bob laughed as Jenny dry heaved. *Asshole. New worst year ever.*

* * *

She was not allowed to come into the house after work each day. It had become a routine. She held her arms out straight as Mr. Brown sprayed her with the hose. The water ran red and a few other colors off her apron. He left Jenny alone with a stack of clean clothes on the porch to change into before she could come into the house for dinner. All her work clothes went into a bucket to be carried to the washing machine.

* * *

The exsanguinated carcass of the ibex hung head down over a tub full of blood. Jenny ran her hand over its long, curving horns. It was a beautiful specimen, a fully grown male with the largest horns she had ever seen. It was a shame the man had shot it broadside through the abdomen. The exit wound on the far side looked as if a bomb had blown out the side of the animal. What size gun had the man used? They would have to be careful stitching the skin back together to prepare it for mounting.

"They're assholes, but rich ones," Jo Bob laughed. "Can't stand them myself, but that's why I charge them twice what normal folks pay. They're all Yankees anyway. They got plenty of that East Coast money." He laughed again. "Do you know one of them wanted me to stuff his fancy deer and make it stand on its hind legs, growling like a bear?" More laughter. "I charged him triple. So you see here? We're going to cut from one leg all the way across to the other, like the inseam on your trousers... or your, err... women pants. Now watch here and we'll pull the skin off like a sock."

* * *

Robert Brown contemplated his fate and the events that had led him here. He had never seen so much grease in his life. He was still trying to find a menu item that they did not fry. The bread seemed to be the only thing in the restaurant they did not cook in bacon grease. He could feel his arteries clogging even as he sat at the table. A disturbing rumbling emanated from his stomach as it tried to digest what he had eaten.

"Can I get you anything else, sweetie?" The waitress looked down at him with a broad smile revealing only five teeth. It was disturbing. The amount of makeup she wore did not conceal her advancing age.

Frighteningly, she seemed to wear more makeup as his stay in this town progressed. He tried convincing himself that she was not flirting with him. That thought was too distressing. He went out of his way to be as polite and formal with her as possible, but she seemed to take this as some kind of courting. She spent far more time lavishing her attention on him than on any of the other customers. The glares from the others were getting uncomfortable.

As she smiled down on him, he was watching a 250-pound bearded man in overalls stare daggers at him. He did not fit in well here. He was very aware that he was the only person in the town who seemed to wear slacks and button-down dress shirts. He had removed his tie. Maybe he should get one of those baseball caps, maybe one with a tractor on it.

"No, I think I've had enough for now. Do you... is there... " She looked down at him with a sense of excitement. The mood from the rest of the room darkened even further. "Do you serve any food that you do not cook on your grill?"

She looked confused and had to stop and think for a bit. "I could bring you some grits! Would you like that, honey bun?"

He looked up at her in confusion. "What are grits?"

CHAPTER 33

Followed

Jenny Hamman, 31
Cretaceous

Jenny was lying on her back, her mind turning in circles. When she was busy, she could avoid thinking about where she was, the impossibility of it. But here in the night she had nothing to stop her mind from tying itself in knots. She was so lost in thought that she almost missed a faint sound.

It wasn't loud, as it was still a decent distance away. It was a bark. She knew that sound. She huddled there trying to think of what to do. Were they hunting in the area? Looking for animals bedded down for the night like her? Were they following her? Had they found her trail? What should she do?

Jenny slowly got up and retied her shoes. Staying here was not an option. If they picked up her trail, it would lead them right to her. She didn't have the firepower to fight. She couldn't shoot in the dark. Running was not an option. She gathered her things. She tried orienting herself. Which way had she come from?

Heading back down the trail from which she had come, she detoured by a tree with low limbs, then went back to intercept her old trail again. She then reversed course and went back to the tree.

Reaching up, she grabbed a branch and did a pullover, lifting herself up onto the branch. The hardest part was the spear. She could stick the knobkerrie through her belt, but the spear was almost impossible to climb with. She got as high as she could into the tree, trying to climb as quietly as possible, mostly by feel. If there had been fewer branches, it would have been impossible. She was as high as she could get in the dense upper part of the tree. She certainly could not see anything.

She found two branches that were on the same level and close enough together. She laid her spear across them and could sit with her back to the tree on the two branches with her legs on the spear. It wasn't overly uncomfortable, in a very relative sense. She might be here for a long time.

Jenny was not sure how long she waited. She never saw them. She heard them, a quiet coughing sound, then an answer. She thought they came down her trail, but it was hard to be sure. She heard a noise under her tree. They were here. At least one, maybe more, were right under her.

Would they fall for the idea that this was a loop where she had stopped by and continued on? Would they realize they had her trapped here in this tree? It seemed like an eternity, but she thought she heard them move off. She heard a bark in the direction of her little camp. They had found her sleeping place.

She was sure she had broken contact with them. Had they stumbled on her trail again? Perhaps at the water hole? Were they tracking her like any other animal? Had they smelled her cooking? Her fire? Had they heard the gunshot?

The last scenario was scary. Had they heard the shot and connected it to her and sought her out specifically? These things were assholes. Now her mind really was going wild. It was like the saying "You're not paranoid if they really *are* out to get you."

Jenny tied herself to a branch with the sling. It wasn't strong enough to support her full weight, but it might keep her from falling over sideways out of the tree.

She would be here for a while. How long though? They hunted at night, at least in the early part of it. Would they have to settle down once it got cold enough? Would they be forced to stop and settle down for the coldest hours before dawn? Or were they warm enough to hunt their prey all through the night?

How long would it take for them to get moving again in the morning? Should she make a break for it in the early dawn hours? Maybe retrace her steps to near the water hole where there were enough tracks to perhaps cover her while she took off in a different direction? Would they be lying in wait at the water hole? No matter what they were hunting, that was always a sound strategy.

Taking heart in the fact that everything they might want to hunt seemed to go into a torpor in the early predawn hours, they wouldn't expect her to be on the move then. She would wait and try to break contact in the early morning. With any luck, dawn would not reveal the entire pack camped at the bottom of her tree.

Jenny thought she got some sleep, dozing off a couple of times, only to start slipping sideways, waking up with a start. She was pretty-much exhausted by the time the sounds changed, signaling the approach of dawn.

She was very stiff, and her legs were asleep. It was challenging to climb down the tree. When she got down lower, she tried to scrutinize the ground beneath the tree. It was too dark to really see anything. Her real defense was the chill in the air. She stopped and waited, listening. No point in delaying.

When Jenny dropped onto the ground, she could barely see the shapes of the trees. The hunters could be anywhere. It was time to move.

She was as quiet as possible, but when you can't even see your own feet, stealth became more challenging. Slowly the sky lightened, but little of that made its way under the trees. Jenny headed east for no reason other than that was the way she needed to go. As she walked, the sun came up, and more light made its way down to her. She was able to pick up the pace.

Jenny walked with the knobkerrie in her hand like a cane and the spear in her other. As the morning warmed, her leg began loosening up. It still felt tight, but it didn't slow her down as much today. The wound was becoming more of a deep ache than a sharp pain.

She set a quick pace, valuing distance over stealth in these early-morning hours. This meant leaving her water hole behind. She had hoped to stay near it for a few more days until her leg got better, but it was too dangerous now. She had to move on.

Jenny walked for most of the day. In the late afternoon she slowed to gather pine cones once again. When she finally had to rest, she made a small fire to roast her armload of pine cones. She needed a better way to carry things.

She set to roasting the pine cones, and as they opened, she would shake the nuts out and begin roasting another set. Meanwhile she peeled and ate the nuts. It was not overly rewarding, but it did keep her busy and provided some sustenance. She didn't want to cook any meat today. Even the smell of the small fire caused her worry.

Jenny spent that night in a tree again. It was not a restful night. She wasn't sure she got any sleep, but she did not hear any sign of her pursuers. She was very tired when she climbed down from her perch early in the morning, tired enough to lie down on the cold ground and take a nap. She needed sleep.

CHAPTER 34

Return

John Hamman, 24
1919 Nairobi, British East Africa

The men kept up a small but smoky fire, feeding it with green brush every day so that Blix might find them in the vast plain. Nine days after their return to this time, they spotted his dust on the horizon as he slowly made his way toward them.

The men had a hearty meal of steaks and potatoes ready by the time Blix arrived. John had gone out and bagged some kind of large antelope the day before with the karabiner. It had large spiraling horns, and they saved the head. Blix admired it, saying that it was a very nice kudu.

He was much more admiring of the stack of ivory in the middle of the camp. They had tusks from eight elephants, none of them broken and all of them large. Even the ones that were obviously from a cow were sizable.

In his truck Blix had a larger number of tusks, but most of them were not as large. John thought by weight he had almost as much ivory as Blix, but John's tusks were larger, which made them much easier to work with and more valuable.

Blix eyed the group curiously, but Manny and the Maasai stood there proudly. He had left the men stranded in the middle of the Mara, a hundred miles from the nearest person, without a vehicle, and found them sitting on top of a pile of ivory.

In retrospect, maybe John had overdone it, taking only the largest bulls. Perhaps they should have taken some of the smaller animals. With all the hunting, the big jumbos were not as common in this time. John and his men had brought in a very impressive load, and on their first time out.

"Look, how in the hell did you find so many big bulls on foot?" Blix demanded.

John shrugged, trying to act natural. "The Maasai is a very good tracker, and Manny is a wonder. He is very good with the men." Blix continued to stare at him and John felt compelled to add, "We've had very good luck."

Blix ignored the steaks they cooked for him, went over and pulled out a bottle of the provisions he had left, and proceeded to get drunk. John wasn't sure if the man ever ate solid food.

John did not make any attempt to keep up with Blix that night. He watched Blix counting the number of men in the party, noting the one who was injured. The man was up now but still could not use his arm. It made John wonder if Blix had a bet with someone, even if it was only himself.

"I half expected to find your men standing guard over your dead body. Well, you're a goddamn white hunter now. What the hell are you going to do next?"

John was a little taken aback by the question. He really had not considered what his next move should be. "I suppose I need to sell all this ivory. Maybe buy another gun. It would have been nice to have another rifle. I suppose I'll have to find a place to live, and I'll need to get my own car."

Blix broke out laughing at the last statement so casually added. "There are plenty of lories around, but you won't find one for sale. You'll have to have one shipped in and that will take months." Blix continued chuckling at his naivety. "You might have to get by with a mule train. At least you don't have to buy petrol for them. Just don't let the lions eat them."

John thought Blix was finished talking as the man stared into the fire. "There are always guns around. Some fool will come out here thinking he can hunt elephants, and if the tusker doesn't stomp on the gun when it stomps on him, then voila—extra gun!"

Blix eyed John meaningfully when he said this and glanced at John's 500. John was beginning to question Blix's motivation for bringing him out here.

"No room at the club right now. Talk to Delamere. He can always find land for people. He'll try to make you a farmer. The trick is not to go broke and lose it." Blix stared into the fire as he ruminated. "A farm is too goddamn much work and will suck the life out of you. You'll have to find someone to run it for you." He drained another glass of gin and tonic water. "Good luck selling that load. Bunch of god damn thieving curry munchers. Those damn wogs are trying to tell everyone the price has collapsed. They're all in it together."

He took another long swallow of his gin and began telling John the story. The going rate for ivory was and always had been one pound sterling per pound of ivory, but a group of Indian merchants had been conspiring to set the price at one shilling and three pence. After that, Blix withdrew into a darker mood, staring into the fire and soon retiring into his tent.

The next day they packed up the camp and loaded into the truck, now even heavier with all the extra ivory. Soon they were lumbering along over the plains toward Nairobi. It was a slow trip, and they did not arrive until after dark. They dropped John off at the Norfolk, and he was very much looking forward to a real bath.

Soaking in a tub of hot soapy water and sipping from a glass of whiskey, John tried taking stock of recent events. It was hard to wrap his mind around the things he had seen. He almost fell asleep in the tub, but the thought of food roused him.

After changing into some clean clothes, John went downstairs to the dining room. It was not too late to get a meal and he had not eaten since breakfast. As he was finishing up, he felt a great slap on his back, and Blix sat down beside him. Blix was drinking whiskey this night. Did the man ever *eat*?

"You must come along to the club. They won't believe me if I tell them you're alive." Did he have a bet with someone there? After John finished his meal, they walked through Nairobi to the Muthaiga Club. There seemed to be a small party going on.

Lord Delamere approached John at the bar and congratulated him warmly on not having died. "I knew we'd see you again. I had a fine feeling about you." Had he won the bet? "And I hear you brought back a good load of ivory, some very big tusks. Good show."

Lord Delamere went on to explain that he had found a property for John. It had good farmland, and there was a village on the property. The previous owner had died in the war.

He was killed at the battle of Tanga early on. German General Paul von Lettow-Vorbek had given them a sound drubbing that day. He had then proceeded to lead them on a merry chase all over eastern Africa. They had never really been able to defeat his Schutztruppe until they surrendered in northern Rhodesia at the end of the war.

There were debts on the property, but it could be had for a fair price. And since John had not died, Lord Delamere wondered if he would be willing to take it on, as they needed a white man to take over the property.

It was located northwest of Nairobi, near the town of Nyeri at the base of the Aberdare Range and consisted of about 10,000 acres. It had water on it, but most of the water holes dried up seasonally, normal for the area.

A small population lived on the land in a village. The farm was farther from the town of Nyeri and consisted of a house and a few other structures. It was a bit more isolated than the other farms in the area. The property had debts but a good crop was growing. The title could be had cheaply, along with the debts, for anyone willing to accept them.

John had not been expecting this. He had never in his life heard of someone being offered 10,000 acres of land. Stories like that were old when his father was young. Back home, it seemed that every square foot was owned by someone. John didn't want to say no, but it seemed to be moving so fast. He told Lord Delamere that he would have to inspect the property. That seemed to please him, and he told John he could travel out that way with him when he returned to his own ranch.

John found Blix. "I'll see you tomorrow. I have to go back to the hotel to make some preparations."

"Nonsense. You must stay and have a drink with everyone." John's stomach turned over at the thought of another night of trying to keep up with the man.

John shook his head. "I have to go. I'll see you tomorrow when we sell the ivory."

"Yes, we must sell them together. We're the only two that brought in anything this month. We'll have those damn Indians by the short hairs!" He seemed very pleased at the thought. "When we are done here I'm going back to my farm. It's in the Ngong hills. It's not far from where Delamere is trying to settle you down. You must come and visit. You must meet my wife, Tanne." Blix slapped him heartily on the back as he left.

Escaping from the ongoing party at the club, John retired early, at least by his companions' standards, returning to his room at the Norfolk. It had been a long day, and he reflected on the recent events as he laid his head down on the pillow, but dreams soon claimed him, dreams of creatures grander than anything that had walked the earth for millions of years.

The next day John rose early and went to breakfast downstairs. The food was truly good here. He was told that the chef was French. The truck with Blix's ivory and his own was no longer out front. John asked the man at the desk and was told that Bwana Blixen had taken it to the market to be sold.

John was a little astonished as half of it was his. He gathered his things and quickly made his way toward the market. The lorry was easy to spot out in front of one of the larger shops. He went inside without any delay and was met with a tirade of what sounded like cursing in what he took to be Swedish. John could not speak a word of it, but the tone was unmistakable, and the tirade sounded rather inventive.

Blix had an Indian man in a turban pinned against the wall by the throat. As Blix was over six foot and as they were eye to eye, John looked down to see the man's feet dangling a good ten inches off the floor. In Blix's other hand was his revolver, the barrel of which was pressed down the man's throat. John turned back to look at the door, but this scene did not seem to have drawn any spectators as of yet.

"Blix, is everything okay?"

Nairobi may have been a frontier town, but John was sure the sound of a gunshot would draw at least some attention, if only out of curiosity.

"Good—you're here. This fine man was just telling me of the very fair price that he was going to pay for our ivory."

He cocked the hammer of his revolver. The man's eyes were as wide as saucers. He nodded vigorously until his turban fell down over his eyes. In the end, they were paid for their ivory. Blix had his men carry it in, and it was weighed and recorded.

John paid Blix his asking price for his help, which seemed rather high to John, but he did owe the man. Even then, a healthy sum remained, enough to equip himself and perhaps put a down payment on this farm he was being told of. Buying it seemed to be more about accepting the debts and obligations that came with it than about outright paying for it. This was a strange country.

Blix had his own negotiations to complete with the shopkeeper, which seemed to be about unpaid balances on his account versus what he called operating capital. But as he seemed to have gotten off on the right foot in their dealings, they quickly reached a settlement. Soon Blix was bidding John adieu and making him promise to come and visit. Blix said that he could not bear the boredom of the farm and that they would get in some hunting when John came to see them.

John watched Blix's lorry rumble down the street out of town and again thought about what a strange place this was.

Returning to the Norfolk, John was at last able to set about to his own plans. Sitting at the table in his room, he thought about what he needed to do. Idly, he played with the claw necklace as it sat on the table in front of him. He had taken it off the day before when he took his bath.

Maybe the farm was a good idea. He needed a place of his own, somewhere to hang his hat, as it were. More important were the two heads that they had saved, wrapped in tent canvas. He was going to need someplace private for his little treasures.

John was able to beg a pen and some stationery and sat down at the desk to compose his thoughts. He was going to need some things.

First he felt the need for more and bigger guns. The power of the 500 was amazing, but he wanted something with a little more reach. He didn't want to be so up close and personal.

The first letter he wrote was, once again, to Holland and Holland. He wanted something flat shooting in a magazine gun with enough power to do some damage. He wanted a telescopic sight mounted on the rifle. He was learning how little room he had for error in the shooting out here. The price would be painful. Weapons were something you should never compromise on. If you had need of a weapon, then you needed the best weapon you could have.

Next, he wanted something big. John couldn't lie— the encounter with Mokele-Mbembe had frightened him. He had no idea how to cope with something that big. He was thinking a cannon. He could not think of any way he could get hold of an artillery piece, but he might be able to get close. And so he composed a letter to an old friend from II Corps serving in the British Army of the Rhine. He was part of the occupying force in Germany and was slated to be transferred to the Inter-Allied Military Control Commission that would keep order in the country and enforce the terms of the Treaty of Versailles. If you couldn't turn to your old sergeant for help, then what was military service for?

Colour Sergeant Neils
Inter-Allied Military Control Commission
c/o Army Post Office, Cologne
Germany

Dear Colour Sergeant Neils,

How are you, Edward? I was pleased to hear of your acceptance into the IAMCC. It would seem the army still has a need for an old war horse like you when a task needs to get done. I won't beat around the bush, as I know you hate that.

I find myself in need of some help and as always turn to you to set me straight. I am involved in the hunting and control of the largest and most dangerous game in Africa. I find myself in need of a powerful rifle, something larger than anything available here.

As you are involved in supervising the disarmament, I wonder if you could find something and send it to me here in Africa. Do you recall the absolutely enormous rifle that we encountered at...

CHAPTER 35

CEO Hamman Corporation

1985 New York, NY

The CEO and president of the board of directors of the Hamman Corporation was on the phone. He heard a knock at his door. He hated being disturbed. He was the most powerful man in the building and should be obeyed. He had made it very clear that when he closed his door, he was not to be interrupted.

He ignored it but swore that he would terminate his secretary the moment he got off the phone. She would not be permitted to make this mistake again. The knock repeated. He couldn't believe it. No one would do this.

He had to excuse himself from the call and stormed to his office door. Whoever was on the other side would never work here or anywhere else again if he had his way. When he threw the door open, his secretary was standing on the other side wide-eyed. She was actually trembling. Her fear filled him with satisfaction.

"Sir... Mr. Cogburn is here."

"What? Today? Where is he? Call special security! Does he have an envelope with him? Call the board members! Get them here now! Close the building! Everyone out! I want the entire building emptied for the day. Send everyone home. Where is the envelope?"

Storming past the poor woman, he ran to the express elevator. He cursed its slowness all the way to the lobby. Hundreds of millions of dollars were at stake, and that was just for him. When the doors opened, he was already moving, yelling to the security desk, where a small, plain-looking man in a suit waited with an attaché case.

"Protocol one! Get him to the special conference room! Secure the package!" Guards scattered in all directions, moving to the doors and locking them. Two large men took the poor man by either arm and practically carried him into the depths of the building.

* * *

Five men stood around the table in a windowless room in the heart of the building. They were the only members of the board of directors onsite. The others who were unlucky enough to be out of the country would rue their misfortune. The room was soundproofed and electrically shielded. It was swept for bugs every day, and as the inner and outer doors were closed by the special security officers, they knew they were as alone and isolated as any person on the planet could be.

He turned to the man at his right and said, "Open the envelope."

All of them held their breaths as what was inside was read. Billions of dollars were on the line, not to mention their own personal fortunes.

No one understood how the envelopes could exist or hold the information that they did, but everything depended on them. At first they were incensed at the idea that instructions written by one man could overrule all of their authority, but as the envelopes were revealed one by one, no one could deny the information they held. Everyone in the room stood to make possibly hundreds of millions of dollars based on what was about to be read.

The questions that followed were predictable.

"What is a 'domain name'?"

"New Coke is a failure? What is 'New Coke'?" Could they short that?

"What the hell is 'Windows'?"

CHAPTER 36

Eggs

Jenny Hamman, 31
Cretaceous

Jenny couldn't hit anything. It was embarrassing. Finding good stones had proven harder than making the sling. This was a silty, dusty plain, notably short of large riverbeds full of nice, round stones. She finally found some jagged pieces and chipped at them until they were vaguely round. She was blaming the stones. They were not slipping smoothly from the pouch. It was throwing off her aim. That was her story and she was sticking to it.

Small game was abundant, this time boasting a great number of smaller dinosaur species. Some of them arguably had crossed the line into being birds. She could scare them up, but she could not seem to hit them on the run.

She had better luck searching for them in the early morning when there was enough light to see. She would find them curled up under patches of ferns. It was not a problem dispatching them in their sleep with her spear or with one good blow from her knobkerrie. She could roast them in their own skin, wrapped in leaves and buried in the ashes of her fire with coals on top to slow-cook them.

One thing lacking was any kind of seasoning. She dearly wished for some salt. Alternatively, if she placed a large rock in the middle of her fire and allowed it to heat, she could cook steaks on the hot stone, as if they were pan fried.

On the third day she found the eggs. It wasn't one nest. A dozen were scattered across the meadow. It was early in the morning. She found a fresh nest, recently constructed. The depression in the earth was still fresh. The walls of the nest were about a foot high, and the clutch was loosely covered by a mound of dirt in the middle.

Digging into the central mound, she found the eggs, which were about the size of ostrich eggs, around three pounds. She had no idea what species they were, some form of ornithischian, based on the tracks. She guessed they were of medium size. She took one of the eggs and covered the nest back up.

Making her way back into the trees, Jenny moved away from the hatching ground. Once she was a good distance away, she found a place where she could make a fire and sat down to cook her prize.

First she took her pocketknife, and holding the egg upright between her legs, she carefully made a small hole in the smaller end of it. She wished she had a pan to scramble it in. She preferred her eggs scrambled or cooked into an omelet.

A thought struck her as she looked down at the egg between her knees. Propping it so it would not spill, she went and found a reed. Cleaning it as well as she could, she slipped the end down through the hole in the top of the egg. She then put one hand on either side and began sliding them back and forth, making the reed spin. She stirred all through the egg with her magic wand.

Now to see if that had done anything. Once the fire was somewhat established, she set the egg upright next to it, with rocks behind it to reflect the heat. She turned the egg from time to time. With the size of the thing, cooking it might take a while.

Jenny's grandfather had taken her to a small family restaurant on several occasions that specialized in cooking breakfast. They made enormous omelets. Even sharing one, they had never been able to finish it. This would dwarf that meal. She wished he could be here with her right now to help her eat it. She wished she had some way to scramble it and cook it in a pan with cheese and a little ham. She kept turning it.

Somewhere out there was a man, but not the man she knew, not the kindly old man who had taken her to breakfast on a chilly Saturday morning—but a younger man. A man who had never met her. She wondered what he would be like. Would he be the same? When she met this man would she be able to see her grandfather in him?

When she thought it was getting close, she poked down into the center of the egg with her reed. No, it wasn't done yet. It took longer than she expected to cook all the way through. When it finally was done all the way through, she pulled it away from the fire. It was hot.

She propped it between her legs and tried to remove the shell. She had to use the pliers from her leather-man to break off pieces of the thick shell to expose—a nicely scrambled egg. She sliced into it, digging out a bite at a time. It needed salt. Other than its size, it was very much like a chicken egg.

When she was done, Jenny had eaten only about half of it. That left the bottom half of the eggshell with one more meal of saltless egg. There ought to be something she could do with the shell. Ostrich eggs had been used for all kinds of things back home. Could she cook in it? If she got another, maybe she could make a second canteen out of it. In Egypt they had been used as water carriers as far back as 4,000 BC. Well, she was in a time much earlier than that. Maybe she could steal a march on them and start a trend.

She was feeling very full and moved away from her cook site to find a nice place to relax in the morning sun. This would be the life if she didn't have a big wound in her leg and a deadly serious mission upon which the lives of many men, and her own, depended. Yeah, there *was* that little thing.

Her leg was getting better. It wasn't as sore now and was easier to put weight on. Soon she should start making her way to the river. It was out there somewhere. She would have to get another egg if only for the shell. It would be nice to be able to carry a bit more water. She guessed one of the same size would hold over a quart.

CHAPTER 37

Stowaways

John Hamman, 25
1920 Maasai Mara, British East Africa

Things had been going so well. It was just random luck they were nearby. Looking back, he should have suspected the monster was not alone, but as he was there huddled together in the night with his men, all he had been able to think about was getting them home and saving the life of the man who had been mauled.

A group of buff had been damaging the fields around one of the villages. The buffalo came in the night and would disappear back into the forest before dawn. The villagers were afraid to try pursuing them into the brush.

Most hunters did not like doing this kind of work. Most of their clients wanted trophy-size bulls with record sets of horns. Work like this was seen by them mainly as a chore. John had no such clients and found that it paid dividends to protect the locals and their crops. Even a small herd of buffalo or elephants could destroy a village's crops in a single night, leading to hunger for the entire village.

It had been a little sketchy, and there had been one charge at very close range when the body of the buffalo had knocked John tumbling across the ground before it fell dead from his shot. The big bull had snuck up the trail behind the hunters and only Manny's yell had alerted John as he turned to see the buff head down in full charge. He emptied both barrels into the bull, but even shot dead, its momentum had carried it into John, sending him flying.

He was ready to call it a day after that. Over the last week they had gotten four of the herd of buffalo. And John thought their job was about done.

The hunters had gotten back to the village, and John's ribs were feeling rather sore. He was ready for a drink and a good meal, but a man came running into the village. The villager was yelling and an intense back-and-forth ensued between him and Manny.

Manny turned to John and said, "Bwana, this man say his wife taken by Ghost Lion."

John grabbed his gun and reloaded the chambers. "Where?" It would seem their day was not over. They followed the man toward the river.

It had happened on the trail near the water. The man had heard his wife scream. When he ran up, all he could see was thrashing in the high grass off the trail, and then a crashing as she was dragged away through the brush. He tried following her screams, but they had ended, and all he found was a pile of viscera and a blood trail leading deeper into the woods.

It was a bit of a mystery. For some time, people had been finding strange kills. It was all different kinds of animals, all the way up to an elephant. That had surprised everyone. It was not normal for such a large cow still in its prime to be brought down.

The strangest part was the manner of the kills. They had been eviscerated and disemboweled. Then the lions, which was what everyone assumed them to be, had simply followed the animal until it died.

The odd thing was that lions were pretty well hunted out in the area. Some people thought it was a rhino because of the manner of the kills. Unfortunately, none of the kills found so far were fresh. All the animals had been heavily fed upon. By the time the different scavengers had gotten through with them, all tracks and other evidence of the original criminal were long gone.

They had the husband and the other men from the village wait where she had been taken from the trail. The hunters followed the drag marks through the grass and soon began picking up blood. The spot where she met her fate was marked by a scattered pile of her insides. They were partially chewed and then torn free. The body had been dragged farther into the trees.

The Maasai was hunkered down by the body. They didn't see any sign of the lion, and they turned to the Maasai. He was staring intently at the ground and pointed with the shaft of his spear. It was a three-toed footprint, like that of a bird but about ten inches long.

This was a problem. John thought back to that dark night, the attack, and what might have been lurking around them outside the fire light when they returned to this time.

They may have made a bit of a mess, and now this woman was dead because of their carelessness. The tracker and Manny walked carefully around the area.

When they returned, Manny announced, "Maybe five, Bwana. Maybe ten." So—they hunted as a pack. If they were pack hunters, he wasn't sure they could deal with this.

Suddenly John felt a lot less invincible holding his double. Manny had his karabiner. With some coaching, he had proven to be a decent shot. The Maasai stood there with his spear and shield, unfazed, but John's eyes went to the brush all around them.

Suddenly his hearing seemed to be very acute. Every sound seemed to bode danger, and this body felt more and more like a trap. That may have all been in his mind, but he got the feeling they were dealing with more than dumb brutes.

Saying nothing, John motioned for them to follow him back to the trail. He led, and the Maasai with his spear brought up the rear. John noticed the tracker's attention was directed to the rear as he waked backward while following the group.

They did not try to carry the body. That bothered John. It seemed wrong to leave her there to be devoured, but he was more worried about the living at that moment. It was anti-climactic, but John could not shake the feeling that they were being watched.

They gathered the other villagers, and Manny told them a pride of lions had killed the woman and that they must return to the village and stay within its walls until the rogue lions could be killed.

The day was growing late. The men made sure all of them were in their huts and would remain there with the doors blockaded throughout the night. John half expected some kind of attack, but the night passed quietly.

The next morning the Maasai could find no sign of the creatures. They cautioned the villagers to stay inside at night and not to leave the village unnecessarily. If they had to go for water, they needed to go as an armed group.

The hunting group left shortly after dawn, riding for Nairobi. John did not have a lorry yet. Quite a few cars were in the country, but none were for sale. He had been able to afford horses and a string of mules. Manny and John rode the horses, but the Maasai refused to even try. He stared disdainfully, so his mount became a pack animal.

It really didn't matter. It turned out that he could run at a faster pace than the horses could maintain throughout the day. In truth they tended to move at a walking pace with the porters leading the mules.

Today they were in a bit more of a hurry. Manny and John left the Maasai to look after the village. The porters and the mules remained behind as well. They rode two of the horses and brought a third along as a spare mount so John could change out midday. The horses were winded as they arrived in Nairobi near dark.

John went right to the store and caught the owner before he closed up shop for the night. He needed more firepower. The owner had recently gotten in a bunch of war surplus that arrived officially, or unofficially, from Europe.

It seemed that everyone from the man on the street to entire countries were broke and looking to sell anything they could. The table was covered with rifles. Mausers and all other forms of arms were stacked up like cordwood. They could be had for a pittance. Most of them were in quite a state. The war in the trenches had not been kind. If you wanted a seven-millimeter Mauser or an Enfield or any of a number of other more exotic arms, he had quite a hodgepodge to choose from.

Everyone had picked up something, but the taste here ran to bigger bores and more stopping power than the military rifles offered. John never thought he would find an 8 millimeter to be too small a gun.

He searched through the pile for anything he would trust his life to—for that matter, anything he could find ammo for. The pile—it was a pile—covered several large tables. If these were the better ones the store owner had on "display," John didn't want to think about what he might have stacked in the back.

He spotted something under one end of the pile on the last table. Its bore made it obvious as a shotgun. It was a pump. John had to get some help to unearth it from under the rest. He in fact found two. Looking through the rest of the pile from both sides, trying to spot the shorter weapons, John was able to dig up three more. He had five of the things.

As an American, he recognized them immediately as 1897 Winchester shotguns. The English had no interest in them at all, which showed that their taste was in fact not as well refined as they believed. Who could not appreciate the gifts given to the world by one of the greatest firearm designers of all time, John Moses Browning?

The problem was that the English idea of a shotgun was an elegant and very expensive double barrel with a good choke to shoot grouse in Scotland on a family estate. These were short riot guns with a cylinder bore.

The American forces under Pershing brought American shotguns with them. They even had a bayonet mount and a heat shield to allow you to grab the barrel when fighting with it. A lot of guards carried them and they had found their way into the line. It was strictly a short-range weapon, but once you actually got to the trenches it was fearsome.

The shop owner had cases of double ought buck for them in the new two-and-three-quarter-inch shells. That was nine round balls of pain with every pull of the trigger for his feathered friends. He was able to find enough ammunition to supply all five guns. It was getting quite late, and the shop owner was obviously losing patience with his customer.

Looking at the gun in his hands, John turned toward the pile of completely random war material. "Do you have any of the bayonets?" He had never seen a man's face turn so red.

He also purchased some cleaning supplies, oil, steel wool, and even sandpaper. He retired to a room at the hotel and spent most of the night stripping and cleaning the guns, trying to get them working. All of them were rusted. The war was not kind. None of them were pretty, but in the end John had all five working and feeding the shells smoothly. He wished he could have changed out a couple of the magazine springs, but they were as ready as he could make them.

John thought about trying to recruit other hunters to this little mission, but Blix was away, and frankly he didn't trust anyone else. He hadn't even told Blix about the device.

That was the way he wanted to keep it. John would have to clean up his own mess.

Dawn came early, and the hunters were already on their way back toward the village, loaded down with weapons and more shotgun shells then they had ever carried.

Looking through the piles of surplus, John had found a round leather case that opened to reveal a telescopic sight. It was a 3x Voightlander, made in Braunschweig.

He had never owned a rifle with a telescopic sight. It used a claw mount, hooking in the front and with a lever to lock it in at the rear. He had preceded to search through the entire stack of Mausers looking for one with sight bases that would fit it.

He found three fitted with bases. One was the wrong mount. Of the other two he picked the one with the better bore. The serial numbers did not match, of course, but at least it could be mounted, and it was cheap. John thought the shop owner might have given it to him just to get him out of the shop so he could go to bed.

It looked quite a sight, so worn and rusted that someone needed to put it out of its misery. He actually had to beat the bolt open to break it loose.

He wished he had gotten some sleep last night. It seemed that as soon as he got into bed, Manny was gently shaking him awake. He half-dozed in the saddle on the way back. It was almost dark when they arrived back at the village. John had improvised a sling with a piece of rope so he could carry one of the Winchesters across his lap as he rode. He was feeling rather jumpy. None of this sat well with him.

There had been trouble while they were gone. No one was hurt, but one of the outer corrals was attacked in the night, not long after sunset. The villagers heard quite a commotion. No one could see what happened, but something had gotten into the pen and the cattle had gone insane, breaking down the fence and running blindly out onto the plain.

That may have been what the predators wanted. Now they had an abundance of slow, stupid animals to hunt at their leisure. Maybe John was ascribing too much to them, but for some reason he feared these animals. Their tracks were everywhere in the corral. The hunters brushed the tracks out. They had to end this soon.

John picked the three men from the porters whom he judged most sound. He took them a little ways from the village to a clearing and began teaching them to shoot with the Winchesters.

He had varying degrees of success. It was not the custom to do this. John felt they all needed to be able to defend themselves and the camp—but mostly the training focused on not shooting John. They had to start somewhere.

While Manny continued with their training, John worked on the Gewehr 98. The action was still horribly pitted, and even cleaned and greased, it felt as though it had sand in it. He hoped it was safe to shoot.

He had to use up half the adjustment in the scope base, but he was able to center the scope with the rifle as he sighted down its bore. He took one of the empty cases from the twelve-gauge ammunition and set it up at 100 yards.

Setting the rifle across his pack, John settled in, and as carefully as he could, he sighted on the mark he had made in the middle of the crate. His eye was quite close to the scope, and when he fired the first shot it whacked him in the brow. Ow! Actually, he said a bit more than that. He would have to be more careful. He tried again, pulling the stock solidly into his shoulder, and managed not to whack himself in the face.

What was more interesting was that he found the second hole in the wood not an inch and a half from the first. Interesting. John fired three more times, and his group was only about two and a half inches. He looked at his new rifle with newfound respect.

This poor ugly thing had no right to shoot so well. He paced off the ranges to 400 yards. The range knob was... close. He would have to remember some small changes in hold. It actually shot a little high at the longer ranges. This had taken most of the day. They retired back to the village before it became dark.

The men took turns keeping watch by the window, mostly listening for sounds. The moon did not rise until late in the night. They accomplished nothing from this exercise except to reduce their sleep. No visitors came prowling in the night.

They were up early and started the search as soon as it was light. Problems quickly arose—too many tracks, too many trails disappeared into the brush. The cattle had run in to the night in all directions in a blind panic. The small group followed their tracker through the brush. It was a mess. They kept losing trails and having to double back.

By mid-morning they saw the birds. That was how they found the body of the cow. It had been disemboweled as with the other kills and was mostly devoured. The predators had come together to feed on it. From there the trails all moved off in one direction. They did not walk behind each other in one line leaving a single trail, but parallel, almost as if they were in a skirmish line. Did these things ever stop hunting? It also implied that they communicated with each other.

Midday arrived. John wasn't sure how far behind the hunters were. The dinosaurs had eaten. If they were like lions, they would look for water and then find a place to sleep off the meal.

The hunters followed one trail, keeping together, partly for safety, partly because John did not trust the men not to fire blindly through the brush in his direction. He wasn't sure he trusted them not to fire blindly toward him when he was in sight. The Maasai and Manny were the only ones he had any faith in.

The hunters were all armed with the shotguns, pockets full of shells. John thought he should get some kind of pouch or bag. He made damn sure all the safeties were on. He also had that old Mauser over his shoulder in case they got a longer shot. The Maasai carried his spear. John couldn't fault him for that. It seemed to serve him well.

Thinking on that, John drew the bayonet from the sheath hanging from the left side of his belt. He had to make new frogs to hang them from their belts. The originals were lost in the war, rotted away in the wet of the trenches.

John thought his little band looked like "right proper soldiers," all kitted out standing in line with their guns and bayonets hanging from their belts. They were very proud, trying their best to stand at proper attention. He should teach them some drills, just for fun of course.

John motioned with his bayonet, signaling for them to fix theirs as well. It added almost eighteen inches to what were short handy weapons. They were slightly more awkward but looked so much more fearsome.

The hunters understood spears. Even if they forgot to turn off their safeties, they would not be helpless. John really didn't want their first reaction to be wildly pulling the trigger and firing guns among the hunting team. He had more faith in them using it as a spear, and if they calmed down enough to find and disengage the safety, then they would hopefully be calm enough to shoot without hitting the rest of them—or more importantly, John himself.

The tracker moved in front, focused on the trail. John followed, focused much more on what was around them. Manny brought up the rear. It was in the middle of the afternoon when the trail approached a water hole. They were still a quarter of a mile out but were clearly making for it. John felt they were close.

He saw the Maasai in front drop to a knee, lowering his spear and shield as he dropped below the brush. He was not looking at the ground. His gaze was fixed to the right side at about a forty-five-degree angle. John knelt and motioned the others down. The Maasai was still focused in that one direction, almost like a pointing dog.

John motioned back to Manny to stay and pointed to the rear. Manny turned to guard their trail. Carefully John made his way up beside the tracker. His eyes were still set on a point through the bushes.

John could not see it. Slowly the tracker raised his head until he froze. In a moment he relaxed slightly, and

John did the same, slowly raising his head trying to make out the target.

Something was there. Then John saw it. Something popped up and moved in the wind. It turned to the right and then left. It was a feather. It lowered down again, about seventy-five yards away. Was that a sentry, guarding their trail?

What to do? John was sure they were near but did not think they could get closer with this one watching. Well, they could at least get this one.

John slowly set his shotgun down onto the ground and slipped the rifle off his shoulder. Pinching with his fingers to quiet it, he slowly flipped the flag safety to the fire position. It was already chambered. He moved the gun to low-ready and waited.

When John saw the Maasai relax, he lifted up to stand beside the tracker. John was a bit taller than where the Maasai was crouched. He stood straight, his sights locked on where the beast had risen before.

John peered through the scope. It was like looking through a straw, and he wished the field of view was a little wider. About four seconds later a head popped up, filling the image in the scope, and its eyes locked with John's. The trigger broke, and the head jerked and dropped back down. John heard squawks from the right and then the sound of animals crashing through the brush.

He slung the rifle back onto his shoulder and snatched up the shotgun. With his hand he made a chopping motion toward the right side of the trail. They must have at least gotten the idea, because the men began advancing into the brush on that side of the trail. John made for the spot he had fired at. He saw the Maasai disappear, flanking farther to the left.

The birdlike beast was down. The bullet had struck it in the muzzle on the left side and exploded out the back of its head. It was the same as the creature that had attacked their camp, sort of a cross between a crocodile and a stocky ostrich. One uninvited guest expelled from the party.

The group moved forward until they found a small clearing of beaten-down grass. Like a dog turned in circles to make itself a nest, it was flattened and looked as if they had all slept there together, huddled in a pile. All but the one on—watch? He had seen a prairie dog stand guard on its hind legs, looking for danger as the others foraged for food. If the predators were this smart, it could be a tricky problem.

They were not going to catch the others that day. The hunters backtracked the beast to where they had drunk at the water hole. They finally got good tracks. Manny announced confidently that there were six more.

The beasts had broken into a corral and had stampeded the cattle out of the corral and away from the village rather than killing one there. They hunted and killed one cow and then sought water. They returned along their own trail and made camp alongside it with one member watching the trail. If the hunting party had not seen the sentry, would it have woken the others and ambushed them?

They had been lucky to have spotted the guard and, in killing it, disrupted the beasts' plans. John did not like these animals.

CHAPTER 38

Dusty Saddle

Robert Brown, 49
1987 Broken Bow, OK

"Sell everything on August 17. Do not buy until October 26."

The room fell silent as this was read. The senior partners of the law firm looked nervously back and forth. What could this mean? Was there going to be some kind of correction? The market was stronger than anyone had ever seen. How could they justify such a major move? Was it worth it to risk missing out on two months of returns for some minor correction in the market?

As they debated this, Robert Brown was making notes, and thinking about where he could find a trauma surgeon who would be willing to teach private lessons.

This was insane. It seemed like every year it was something even more outrageous. Why would John Hamman want his granddaughter to have lessons from a surgeon or any of the other outlandish tasks he had been assigned? What kind of man left instructions in his will to buy hunting tags for his granddaughter? He had expected to be arranging for private schools, not hiring hunting guides in Wyoming. He didn't even hear the discussion of something called "Prozac."

* * *

The bar, The Dusty Saddle, was rustic. There was no wine. The beer came on tap and in only one selection. It was the only bar in the town.

Some of Robert's assignments had been harder than others. He was used to this part of the assignment, the initial surprise, the feeling that there was no way he could make this happen, followed by depression that he was going to lose his position, and always an epiphany that put him on the right track.

This one had been particularly difficult. He was at his wit's end after six weeks of searching for a suitable venue to meet the specifics of his task. He had been to more hospitals than he could remember and had met with dozens of retired trauma surgeons, who flatly turned him down. Apparently fears of the wrath of the AMA and malpractice lawyers ran deep. The futile search led him to be sitting in a low-rent redneck bar in Broken Bow, Oklahoma. He had been in the area to interview a man about a horse, as they say, and decided he wasn't who was needed for this job.

As Robert stared into his beer, he tried to imagine what he was doing here. What was all this for? When a client offered you, frankly, an extraordinary amount of money, you said, "Yes, sir!" Unless it was illegal... and even then, sometimes there were ways.

He could never make sense of it. Why him? Why was he shepherding a teenage girl around the country every summer? And why to these godforsaken places? John Hamman was well-known to be eccentric, but why should he insist that his granddaughter be dropped in the middle of the wilderness, learn how to shoot, or butcher exotic animals? None of it made any sense.

Robert took another long sip of the rather flat beer. He should refuse. He could quit. He could resign from the firm. Nothing was forcing him to go back. The pay was something obscene. The amount of money billed to the Hamman corporation was unheard of. It literally supported the entire firm, enough money to buy their silence.

And then there was the matter of the letters. They were not spoken of. That was the first and primary rule of the firm. No one spoke about them, where they came from, or how they could exist. He had tried to ask once, and it had almost resulted in his termination. Sometimes he wondered what he was involved in. Those were the questions that kept him awake in the night as he stared at the ceiling in a cold sweat.

Why him? He hated to admit it, but there nothing special about him. He couldn't fathom a single reason why he should have been specified to carry out these duties. He was clearly not the choice of the senior partners in the firm, but Hamman's will named him specifically. And now it appeared that he was going to be fired anyway.

As Robert sat at the bar and drowned his sorrows, one of the locals, a particularly worn-looking man, sat down next to him. Robert knew he was a local because the man knew everyone by name.

He turned to Robert and said, "Name's Cleveland. Don't know you." He held out his hand.

Robert shook it. "Robert."

"Talkative, aren't you?" asked Cleveland.

"Normally, yes, but right now I'm working my way through a problem I can't seem to solve. I'm contemplating returning to the home office tomorrow and admitting defeat to my very demanding, and less than patient, bosses."

"I've got some time, and I'm notoriously nosy. Why don't you lay it out for me and I'll see if I can help?"

Two hours later and after an unwise amount of alcohol, surprisingly Cleveland (or "Cleve," as his friends called him) actually had a lead. He made a call to a pal from the Veterans of Foreign Wars Post in town, who came down to the bar to meet with Robert on the promise of a free meal for a bit of conversation. Robert didn't hold out much hope, but he was stuck here for two days waiting on a flight.

Milton was a tall and rangy Hispanic or Native American. Robert couldn't tell which he was and didn't want to ask. He looked about as weathered as Cleveland but with a little more squint to his eye. He had that undefinable aura that made one think of Clint Eastwood in *High Plains Drifter*.

Cleveland told Robert he had been a truck driver in the army, but Milton obviously wasn't. Robert watched as he entered the bar and scanned the entire place. Every movement was planned before executed. Robert had heard you could pick out a predator when you saw one but had not believed it. He did now.

Milton ambled over and clapped Cleveland on the back.

"What's shakin', Cleve?"

"This here's the fella I was tellin' you about."

Robert held out his hand, and Milton took it and said, "I was given to understand that a free meal was included on this cruise."

Robert waved to the bartender and yelled, "Anything he wants, add it to my tab." He wasn't too worried about how large the bar tab got since he was on an expense account, and he had seen the checks the foundation regularly wrote for seemingly worthless things.

He took a leap of faith and explained the proposal to Milton, expecting to be laughed out of the bar. He wasn't too worried. This guy probably wouldn't be appropriate for the assignment anyway.

"I'm looking for someone to teach a seventeen-year-old girl an advanced trauma medicine course that includes minor surgical procedures, advanced first aid, and some trauma procedures. Does that sound like something you might be able to accomplish?"

Milton leaned back in his chair with a smile on his face and wryly commented that he would probably be able to put something together, depending on what Robert was talking about money-wise.

Robert smiled to himself. Of course, the only person who said yes was most likely not anywhere near qualified to fit the bill. "Milton, before we talk about money, tell me something about yourself. How are you qualified for this?"

Milton smiled. "Well, I was a Special Forces medic who did six tours in Vietnam and beaucoup other assignments to every shit hole this side of hell that you've never heard of. I've treated gunshots, stab wounds, burns, delivered babies, pulled teeth, performed appendectomies under a thatched roof, performed field amputations, and even saved a Montagnard Striker's life after he damn near got eaten by a tiger. For that matter, I killed the tiger as part of the deal." Milton pulled a gold chain from under his shirt that had one of the biggest tiger claws Robert had ever seen hanging from the end. "I've treated tropical parasites so nasty they'd turn your hair white, and not one in a hundred epidemiologists have ever heard of.

"As to the student, I've taught little brown people in third world shit holes who couldn't speak a word of English and generally thought electricity was some kind of magic. And I did it in a stinking swamp with other little brown people doing their damnedest to kill them and their patients. Think that about covers it?"

"If you're so skilled, what are you doing here? No offense, but I don't recall your name from when I researched the local hospital." Now Robert really was confused.

"When I got out, I thought I wanted to be a doctor. It wasn't the same. Medical school and the hospitals had too many rules. So I switched to veterinary medicine. It's interesting and nobody tells me what I am or am not qualified to do."

A smile started to form on Robert's face. "Milton, I think you might be my solution." Fifteen minutes later it was Milton who was smiling after Robert explained to him the monetary compensation.

CHAPTER 39

Teeth in the Night

Jenny Hamman, 31
Cretaceous

Jenny wasn't sure what woke her, some instinct that death was near. Perhaps it breathed on her. She opened her eyes but saw only darkness. The smell made her freeze. It was a fetid smell of rotten meat, the smell of a lion or hyena that fed on carrion.

She had covered herself with cut ferns, but she could turn her head slightly and look up where she saw patches of the stars through the trees on this moonless night. Then a shape moved above her and blotted out the stars. She heard a huffing sound, and that fetid breath blew down on her like a wind.

She drew her gun and fired up into the shadow looming above her. The flash from the muzzle of the High

Power lit up the inside of its mouth like a flashbulb, as she fired the gun down its throat. All she saw was teeth.

Jenny screamed, the sound lost as she pulled the trigger over and over, emptying the magazine of the gun as fast as she could. She pulled her arm back as the jaws snapped shut. In the flashes she saw a great head pull back. She kept firing, and then the slide locked back on the empty magazine.

She was engulfed in a darkness more complete than she had ever known, her night vision ruined. That void was filled with a roar. It was more than a sound. It surrounded her and shook her very core.

Blindly she grabbed for the spear that lay beside her as she slept, and crawled away through the ferns that covered the ground. Through the ringing in her ears she heard a crashing behind her as the great head smashed through the brush where she had been, its jaws closing on her resting place. Jenny made it to her feet and took off running.

She might have been safe if it hadn't been for the tree. She hit it straight on at full speed, and all she remembered was pain. Lying on her back, she had her spear and the empty gun was still in her hand. She felt it in the ground. It shook beneath her. The dinosaur was coming.

Jenny rolled over, trying to get to her feet and leaning on the spear. All she could see were blotches before her eyes from where the muzzle flash had blinded her.

She angled the spear blindly toward the monster—no time to do anything else. The spear's butt end braced into the ground as the dinosaur struck it like a semi-truck. She could not see what happened, but she felt the shaft bow as the spear buried itself deep somewhere in the beast's chest.

The spear did not stop it, but the tree above her did. A crash sounded above her, and broken limbs rained down. She heard the trunk crack as it repeated her misfortune.

Jenny clung blindly to her spear, and she was lifted into the air as the dinosaur reared back from the impact. She was thrown from side to side as it turned, trying to free itself from the tree and this thing clinging to its chest.

All she could do was hold on for dear life. Her only safety laid in staying out of the reach of its jaws. She felt its head come down on top of her, the scaly hide of its jowls crushing her against its own chest. It roared again in pain as the spear ground inside it. The beast swung around again, and there was nothing she could do.

Jenny was thrown, landing hard on the ground on her side. She saw a silhouette rise above her against the stars, and then it began falling. She dived blindly to the side as it threw itself to the ground, trying to crush whatever was hurting its chest.

The dinosaur rolled over like a horse, trying to crush its attacker with its own weight. She heard the spear snap and a roar of pain. Jenny pushed the button of the mag release with her thumb and got her last magazine into the gun.

She heard the animal roll to its feet and blindly pointed the gun toward it, not caring if she even hit anything. Turning her head away and burying her face in her arm, she pulled the trigger three times, lighting the scene with the flashes.

Jenny ran into the trees, barely able to see, and crashed through the underbrush. She hoped that her pursuer would be blinded by the muzzle flash as she fled deeper into the woods, where she hoped it could not follow.

CHAPTER 40

Site Y

Robert Oppenheimer, 39
August 1943 Los Alamos, NM

"Explain this!" Groves bellowed. The walls of the office seemed to vibrate like a great speaker amplifying his roar.

Robert wondered why he was always so studious about closing his doors in meetings for "security reasons," refusing to discuss anything until the door was closed, when he would then proceed to bellow and roar at the top of his lungs, as if no one in the building could hear him. All a spy would have to do was sit on a hill a mile away and he could have recorded half of the meetings.

Groves waved the papers back and forth as he towered over them, ignoring the fact that he had not shown them the contents. "What do you have to say for yourselves?"

Robert casually crossed his legs as he leaned back in his chair. He had become used to these types of encounters with the director of the project. Seth Neddermeyer was less composed. "What's wrong? What did we do?" Robert reached over and put his hand on Seth's arm before he could drop to his knees, begging for forgiveness.

"What I think my colleague is trying to say is that it would help us to answer you if you would clarify your question. What papers are you waving around there? Or are you trying to swat a fly?"

Groves's face turned as red as a tomato. At times like this his rather round torso seemed to swell like a balloon. Would his uniform one day split and start popping buttons like neutron from an atom? Without a word, Groves thrust the papers at them.

Taking them far too casually for Grove's liking, Robert began perusing through the several sheets. It was in a lovely flowing hand, undoubtedly that of a woman. It appeared to be a letter.

Turning back to the first sheet, he found it was addressed to himself, Neddermeyer, and several other members of the Los Alamos team. It named each of them, all department heads, and their group numbers. His brows furrowed, as that alone was a disturbing amount of information. Sometimes Leslie went off over completely trivial matters, but he might actually have cause this time. Flipping to the last page, it was signed "Jenny H."

"How did this arrive here?"

Groves picked up an envelope and threw it at him as if it were a weapon. Catching it, Robert looked at the address:

Site Y
Attn: Robert Oppenheimer

P. O. Box 1663

Santa Fe, New Mexico

The envelope had no return address. It had been mailed with a normal stamp from somewhere in New York City. This mystery went deeper and deeper. The term "Site Y" never appeared on external communications, and his name was not used openly. It was true that all mail and shipments went through the same post office box address, but the military designation for the site was never used.

"Read!" Groves was still looming over Robert, as he was wont to do. Leaning slightly to the side to escape the shadow, Robert proceeded to peruse the papers as his eyebrows steadily climbed higher on his forehead.

The letter was broken down into several sections, all dealing with problems they were struggling with. He turned back to the first one, titled "Implosion." It described something called "explosive lensing." As he read on, he began realizing that this could change everything. It addressed a number of completely original ideas, things that no one seemed to have considered. Could they compress a sub-critical solid spherical mass to a supercritical density with the shockwave of an explosion?

Robert had completely forgotten Groves until he once again moved to block the light. "Well?" Robert gathered that he had been asked this question several times as he was lost in thought. "Why are you receiving external letters about issues discussed in secret in half the divisions of the project? Can you explain yourself? Who is Jenny H?"

Robert Oppenheimer looked up stupidly at the director. He rarely felt stupid, even here, surrounded by some of the greatest minds in the world. "I don't know." It was perhaps the most inadequate answer he had ever given.

He looked again through the letter. A "P. S." at the end read, "Stop sharing with the British. England leaks like a sieve." Underneath that was added a "P. P. S." that read, "Be careful with the Demon Core!" Now what the hell was that supposed to mean?

He looked up, realizing that Groves was still yelling. By the color of his face, it was obvious that Groves was reaching criticality. Robert raised one finger, and Groves stopped mid-sentence. This only seemed to make things worse, like closing the pressure release valve on a boiler leading to a truly massive steam explosion.

"Leslie, shut up."

He turned back to the papers in his hands.

CHAPTER 41

Death in Tall Grass

John Hamman, 25
1920 Maasai Mara, British East Africa

It wasn't going well. Nothing seemed to be working. They tried all the usual ploys to hunt these things, but nothing seemed to work. John read about how people hunted lions, the different tricks they used. He heard even more stories from people here who had done it themselves. Nothing seemed to work with these beasts.

John and his men hunted the water holes. They staked out one of the creatures' kills, waiting for them to come back and feed. Nothing. They even tied a milking cow to a tree and waited all night long as it bayed for its calf. Nothing. They killed animals and poisoned their meat. Nothing. Actually that was not quite true. They had attracted hyenas, a pair of leopards, and even a whole pride of lions to the last trap. Half the pride was dead from the poison by the end of the day. But these damn dinosaurs did not seem to fall for any of the traps.

Since they ranged over vast distances, it seemed futile to try tracking the creatures. They did not seem to fall into any predictable habits. So far they had not killed any other villagers, although people were terrified to leave their villages and barricaded their doors at night.

The only good thing that the hunters had going for them was that everyone was still calling them the "ghost lions." No one had picked up on the fact that they were totally different beasts. Not yet.

The hunters worked hard to reinforce that. No one else needed to know about this little problem. So while everyone else went out hunting for trophy elephants, John and his crew stayed near these villages hunting the "ghost lions." Everyone thought they were crazy, and frankly money was getting tight with no ivory to show for day after day of hunting. John couldn't afford to keep this up forever. It was disheartening to see the despair in the eyes of the villagers when their entire herd of cattle disappeared in one night, only to be found one at a time torn apart as the dinosaurs fed on them.

The hunting party was tracking one of the missing cows. John had the idea that if the dinosaurs were hunting this scattered herd, sooner or later they would come for this cow. So they followed it day after day on foot, hoping they would get lucky. What they hadn't considered was that the dinosaurs might decide to hunt the men rather than the cow.

The cow was getting water. Tall grass surrounded the water hole on all sides. John and his hunters were well concealed watching the trail. It was a good place to hunt. It was a bad place to be hunted, but that thought had not crossed their minds. The men still thought they were the predators.

John did not hear it. It made no sound as it slipped through the grass, carefully placing one foot at a time. Its focus was on the game trail. The coloring on its feathers blended with the grass, but John picked up on a movement and was able to spot it in the grass on the other side of the trail. It had not yet seen the men and was intent on the trail the cow followed.

John had it. He slowly raised his shotgun and took aim down the barrel, placing the bead right on its head.

It paused in a gap in the grass, as if it were posing. John's finger tightened on the trigger. The bead on the end of his barrel was his whole world. Then the dinosaur turned and looked right at John. He froze, and the animal stood there, waiting.

A scream erupted from John's left as a second creature crashed into the Maasai, and John's head snapped around. The Maasai had his shield between himself and one of the dinosaurs. Its head whipped around the side, trying to bite at him. John watched as one of the hind legs came up and raked down along the shield, the large claw tearing a ragged gash.

John was trying to turn and fire on the brute when another one hit the Maasai from behind. All John caught was a blur of motion out of the corner of his eye before the impact. Its big claw landed in the middle of the Maasai's back, raking down as he screamed and collapsed under the weight of the monster pressing on his shield.

A shotgun went off behind them as Manny fired off to the right. John fired at the monster on top of the Maasai as its big hind leg came up past the shield and ripped him open the whole length of his stomach.

The Maasai thrust up into the beast's belly, and John's shot hit it high in the chest, knocking it off his tracker. The third beast fled back into the grass. John fired and thought he peppered it with buckshot. But it was too far away for a solid hit, and the dinosaur kept going.

John turned to his right as Manny fired another load into the creature on the right. It was down, dead on the ground. John turned back to the front, and the first one he saw was gone, as if it had never been there.

The Maasai sprawled in a pool of his own blood. He was still alive but refused to scream or cry out. It took all his strength to breathe, his eyes fixed on the sky. John pushed the intestines back into his stomach so they would at least be inside him, even though they were torn apart. They could all smell what was supposed to be inside them.

John and his men stood by helplessly. It took the Maasai a long time to die. Toward the end the pain seemed to ease. His breathing actually seemed to get easier. He started crooning something in his own language very softly as his eyes stared unseeing at the sky.

John looked to Manny. "He is singing, Bwana." They sat beside him until the song ended.

* * *

They were too far away. He had no hope of hitting them from here. John was on top of a plateau, looking down on the plain. Manny had been the one to spot them sneaking into position around a wildebeest herd. All they could do was watch as the dinosaurs circled their prey.

It was eerie to watch them ghost into position. All of it was planned as they surrounded the unsuspecting herd. The one in back moved in first, and then the flankers surrounded the herd on either side. The wildebeest didn't have a chance.

The dinosaur in front of the herd didn't show itself until the others were in position. As the wildebeest became agitated, they retreated away from the aggressor, placing themselves deeper in the trap. The attack came from the sides, as it did with John and his men. The panicked animals fled right into the fourth hunter waiting to their rear.

Two animals were down. A third was trying to run, but its intestines were dragging behind it and became caught in the brush. They could hear its bellows across the distance as the dinosaur stalked along behind it, trying to make it run onward. As John watched them play with the poor animal before killing it, he swore he would kill every one of these monsters.

This was how they hunted. This was how they had hunted John and his friends. This was how they had killed the Maasai. John had never learned to say the man's name.

How could he hunt them? How could he make *them* the prey?

* * *

The men borrowed half a dozen head of cattle. They herded them across the plain where the dinosaurs had been known to hunt and up a blind draw in the same escarpment they watched from.

They built a crude corral to contain the cattle. It dead-ended in a dry fall at the back of the small canyon and formed a twenty-five-foot sheer cliff over a small water hole. Everything was dry now, but in the rainy season water would run over the overhang and fall into the pool at the bottom, where it would run out the canyon. They already had a rope in the back leading down the cliff. John didn't want any trails leading back out of the entrance. Now they waited.

It was not a short time. The men were there for three days. John was ready to give up. He had decided the beasts had not found or were not interested in the trail they left.

By the second day the cattle were thirsty and mooing constantly to be let out. They had to go down and reinforce the fence to keep them from pushing it over. Much longer and they would have a canyon full of dead cattle. Then again, that might work too, but they had never seen the beasts feed on carrion. As far as John could tell, the dinosaurs made their own kills and had not returned to feed on any of them at a later time. They did not seem to be scavengers.

It was the third day. John was about ready to give up. It wasn't clear if they found the men's trail or if they heard or smelled the cattle. John was dozing with his hat pulled down over his eyes when the noise below picked up. His first thought was that they had attracted a lion, and he would have to shoot it and probably spoil the trap.

John grabbed the double and rolled over to peer over the edge. He froze. Something was peeking around the far bend in the grotto. He could glimpse its feathered head.

The cattle must smell it. They knew it was a predator, even if they had never seen its like. John sank lower until he could peek over the edge.

What were they going to do now? The canyon was narrow with a rocky bottom lacking any cover. They couldn't circle around or get on top of the plateau behind. They had seen corrals before but normally in a village. What would they make of this one here, unguarded? The beast's head did not move. John might have taken a shot at it, but it was a small target. He wanted all of them. He wanted to end this.

The head withdrew. John cursed silently. Were they leaving? He motioned all the others to the edge and made sure they had their heads down and out of view. They waited. John also was down and out of sight.

He listened to the cattle and waited, ready to sacrifice them all if he could kill all the dinosaurs. Would they send in one alone to spook the cattle and make them stampede? The men went out of their way to reinforce the fence. John didn't think the cattle could break through it.

Would the dinosaurs attempt to kill them in the corral and then feed on them there? That was John's hope. He needed them all in the canyon, with no cover and no way to get behind the hunting party.

The noise picked up below as the cattle sounded more frightened. The predators had come back. The cattle became more agitated. John could hear them pushing at the fence.

Then bedlam. It sounded like the cattle were going insane. One of the dinosaurs was right below in the corral with the cattle. John could hear the frightened prey ramming against the fence, throwing themselves against it. It might not matter if the dinosaur killed them—they might do the job themselves.

The dinosaur could not stand it any longer. The fear and panic of the cattle drove it into a frenzy. John listened to the cattle scream as the beast slaughtered all of them. It killed not just one but all the panic-stricken cattle trapped in the corral with it. Once it started, it could not stop killing until all beneath the men was silence.

John heard it feeding, ripping at the carcasses. Eventually he heard a barking sound from down the canyon and an answer from below. John waited as he heard more barks and snapping sounds from below.

He heard thumps as the dinosaur's companions jumped over the fence and landed amongst the bodies of the cattle. Listening carefully, John recalled hearing three of them jump and land inside the fence.

He heard more barking and snapping sounds from below as the beasts fought over the food. John wondered if they had a hierarchy in their pack, like that of wolves.

John looked over at his men and motioned for them to wait. He wanted the dinosaurs fat, bloated, and slow. They could eat all they wanted. He wanted their defenses down. The safer they felt, the bigger the surprise. If they wanted to gorge themselves and then go to sleep in the sun, that was fine with John. This was why he had brought so many cattle. The only thing better would be if the water hole was wet so that they could drink until they were bloated and fall into a deep sleep.

John waited, listening to them feed, the hate building in his heart. He thought about the woman from the village. He thought about her child. He thought about the Maasai, whose name he had never learned to say.

When the sounds slowed, he motioned to Manny and the other men. John did not want to risk them leaving to sleep elsewhere. He had the double. Manny had the karabiner that he had come to favor. The rest were armed with shotguns.

As one, they rose over the edge, looking down on what was below, like avenging angels passing judgment. All four were there. John fired both barrels at one and heard a whole volley of shots from either side of him.

The vengeful dinosaurs screamed up at them in defiance. One charged, already hit several times, and made a prodigious leap toward the cliff.

With a scream it hit below the ledge, its forelegs scrambling on the lip. John could hear the great claws on its hind legs scraping at the rock face below them. Its head snapped at John, trying to take his leg off.

John's gun was empty, but the man on his left fired a load of buckshot straight down the beast's throat. It slid over the edge, out of sight.

John walked to the edge and looked down at the carnal house of slaughter they had made.

It was done.

CHAPTER 42

Medic

Jenny Hamman, 17
1987 Broken Bow, OK

They had just gotten out of the back of the DHC-6 to the inevitable swirling dust that she was getting used to. "Why can't we ever go anywhere with a proper paved airport and gift shops?"

Robert pointed at a rangy old man with a battered pickup truck wearing an even more battered hat and a ponytail that made him look like some kind of cowboy hippie.

"That's you," Robert said with a smile on his face. He handed her a note with an address and phone number on it. "Here's my information. I'll be at the hotel in town. Let me know if you need anything that you don't have with you during your training. See you in three months."

Jenny looked up at Mr. Brown and then turned resignedly toward the pickup truck. The man said nothing to her as she approached so she just threw her bags into the bed of the truck. He pulled open the creaking door for her and she climbed into the cab. As he walked around to the driver's side, Jenny turned to look through the back window as she watched Mr. Brown get into a rather nice rental car and drive away. She was off for another summer, once again with no idea of what to expect.

* * *

The accommodations weren't the best, but they were a bit better than living under a survival shelter in the middle of a driving rainstorm. The training was initially a lot of books and diagrams and learning the names of parts of the body that she had never even contemplated before.

Milton explained the circulatory system and the pressure points to control bleeding. Most of the training consisted of, as Milton confidently explained, "Keeping the blood on the inside."

She enjoyed learning how to put in stitches. Milton shot a pig because it was mostly hairless and proceeded to make all manner of slices, jabs, and cuts all over the carcass, which Jenny then got to practice sewing back up. Milton even shot it with an arrow and made her remove it, along with the bullet.

At the end of the day Milton said, "Well, I reckon it's getting toward dinner time, so we'll start on the internal examination as we're going to process this big girl into dinner."

He handed her his belt knife and explained that he was going to walk her through gutting a pig and skinning it out.

"Can I use my knives?" Jenny asked.

Milton, with a quirky smile, said, "Sure—I don't see why not." Undoubtedly he thought she had a *My Little Pony* pocketknife or something along those lines. Jenny returned five minutes later, rolled out her knife roll with not a little bit of fanfare, and started expertly running a knife over a twelve-inch sharpening steel. Milton let out a low whistle as she got to work.

Jenny asked Milton to help her hang the carcass and get her a step stool. Thirty minutes later the pig had been proficiently and quickly separated into its component pieces.

She kept up a running commentary as she worked, identifying each organ by name and individually excising them.

"I guess we've learned that you aren't squeamish and know your way around the inside of a pig. Where'd you learn to do all that?"

"Jo Bob's Wild Game Processing and Barbecue in Texas. Spent three months working as an apprentice there last summer."

"Well, I'll be damned. I reckon we can speed up the training, as you already know more about a body than most second-year medical students."

* * *

The training did accelerate. Jenny almost tapped out when they started working on living animals. It wasn't the injuries or blood that bothered her. She was proud to help Milton save the horse that had gotten trapped in barbed wire.

But when they had no cases to treat, he saw no reason to delay her learning.

He brought in a goat and tied it to a stake. When he pulled out a sword, Jenny's eyes lit up. It wasn't exactly a proper ninja sword. Milton explained that it had come from a tribe called the Montagnard. He handed it to Jenny and told her to give the goat a good whack.

At last she had a sword! She leapt toward the goat, struck a dramatic ninja pose, and swung the sword, decapitating the animal in one smooth blow. She turned with a flourish and bowed to Milton in her best Japanese manner.

Milton stared at Jenny with his mouth open, undoubtedly at her incredible prowess.

"I don't think you quite grasp the nature of this exercise. That wasn't supposed to be dinner. And we can't sew that back on." He pointed to the decapitated head. "I think I have another one."

He once again went out back of the barn. This time he took the sword from Jenny and swung it himself, cutting deeply into the rear leg almost to the bone.

This was the first time Milton truly shocked Jenny. Slaughtering an animal for food was one thing, but cruelty was another. If she had been the one holding the sword right then, Milton might have been her target.

"You've got a bleeder! What do you do?" Milton yelled as the goat screamed and blood sprayed onto the floor of the barn.

Afterward, when they had finished sewing up the leg, which required both internal and external stitches, she was ready to make Milton her next patient. He had to explain that this was exactly how he was trained in the army. They learned to treat gunshot wounds by inflicting them on animals and trying to save their lives. Jenny didn't like it.

*　*　*

"You have to get the loop around the forelegs. Feel around for them." Jenny scowled at Milton. "You have to get deeper." Jenny was lying on her side with her arm deep up a cow's... lady parts... as it tried to give birth. Milton helpfully got behind her and pushed till she was shoulder-deep and her face was pressed against—best not to think about that, and best not to breathe. "Have you got it?"

Jenny scowled again. She knew he was laughing on the inside, taking far too much pleasure in this. *Asshole.*

*　*　*

Other exercises were not much better.

"It's time we started your training on different types of parasites."

Milton seemed far too pleased with this next phase of her education. Nothing that made him smile like that was ever good. He held out a glass filled with water. In it floated what looked like a flattened worm.

"Swallow it."

The evil bastard was grinning like a demon.

CHAPTER 43

Tracking

Jenny Hamman, 31
Cretaceous

Jenny sat with her back against the tree, shivering. Dawn slowly lightened the forest around her. She had not slept at all through the night. At first, as she ran she could hear the dinosaur's rampage behind her. As she got farther away the sound faded. It had not or could not pursue her. She found a place to hide mostly by feel and spent the night huddled in some bushes at the base of this tree.

She was cold and hungry and tired and pissed. She lost her weapons. All she had left was the High Power and a handful of rounds. Odd that she would value her spear more than a gun. The High Power had undoubtedly saved her life last night, but long term the spear held more promise of protection. And she had made it from her grandfather's knife. That loss hurt more than anything else.

It may not have been the wisest decision, but Jenny wasn't thinking overly rationally at the moment. She turned and started back along the way that she had come. It was slow going to back trail herself, but in the dark she had left more than a few signs of her passage. Eventually she did find her old camp. It hadn't been that far off. She had not run as far as she thought in the dark.

It was not yet midday when she found the site of the battle. She found her knobkerrie where she left it the previous night and felt better with it in her hand. It would be useless against what she had faced last night, but right now she needed to feel at least a little bit dangerous. The only cure for the feeling of helplessness was taking back some form of control over at least a part of her life.

Jenny searched the area, looking for any clue of what had happened in the dark. The broken shaft of her spear was on the ground where the animal had fallen upon it. She found no sign of the spear head, her grandfather's knife, or almost two feet of the shaft. On the ground was blood. The most interesting thing was a pool of foamy blood off to one side. It was not where the battle had taken place but a little bit away. Whatever it was, it had two feet of her spear in its lung.

She cut a circle around the camp and found where it had approached her in the night. It looked to be a chance encounter. She also found its trail where it had moved off. A good bit of blood spattered the ground, but they were small individual droplets.

Jenny had emptied more than a magazine of nine-millimeter into it. She had no hope of that affecting the dinosaur at all, but what was interesting was the amount of blood. It had bled more than she would have expected from all those wounds. Granted, it had a great deal of blood.

This would never weaken it. It was more a matter of her scientific curiosity. It spoke to the animal's blood pressure. There had been much speculation as to the heart size and blood pressure of some of the larger dinosaurs. Enough blood pressure was needed in the systaltic system to pump blood all the way up to the brain so that it would not pass out when it raised its head.

The numbers she had seen for the larger sauropods had been kind of crazy. But even the larger theropods had a greater difference in height between their hearts and heads than a giraffe, which would bleed profusely when shot. Assuming the heart was four-chambered, the blood pressure in the lungs could be lower, but Jenny wondered how much blood was pooling in its lungs right now.

She followed it for a good distance and had almost given up hope when she found a large spatter of foamy blood on a bush. She continued following its trail for the rest of the day. It was worse than tracking an elephant. The tracks were plain enough for a child to follow, but the beast could cover so much ground that it would just leave you behind in the dust.

She thought back to having followed a bull elephant in Tanzania for three weeks. It had led them on a merry chase for untold miles. They had followed its trail day after day and sometimes late into the night, following it even after dark by flashlight.

That was where she learned to fasten a light to the end of her walking stick so she could hold it along the ground at a low angle to cast the contour of the footprints into shadow, making them much more prominent. In some conditions it was actually easier to track like that in the dark.

She thought back to stories of the old white hunters who had followed trophy bulls for months at a time. There had been hunters who tried for years to get one specific elephant only to be outpaced whenever they got on its trail.

Jenny would have despaired if she had not found a pool of foamy blood from time to time. She followed it all day, stopping only when she lost the light and had to go off the trail to the side to find a place to sleep. She could not shake thoughts of the night before, but her body was so exhausted that she dropped off into a dreamless sleep the moment she settled down.

She found it the next day, lying where it had slept the night before. It had died in its sleep, its lungs finally filling with its own blood until it could no longer breathe.

It was big, a theropod of some type. She was reminded once again that the fossil records of Africa were not all that well documented. The head was large, and she couldn't help thinking of how she would have fit in the mouth in one bite. Looking at the teeth brought back nightmare images of that close encounter, her memories lit by the flashes from her gun.

The body had a long tail to counterbalance that head. The arms were larger than a T. rex, more fully developed. Thick downy feathers covered the body. It was thinner in the legs and faded out by the time it reached the knee. The lower leg was covered by a pebbly scale. A crest of longer dark, almost black, feathers ran down the length of its back. The lower body was a lighter gray, fading to black toward the tail. She climbed up on the neck to look closer at the large eye. It looked small in comparison to the head.

As she pulled the lid back, she realized how enormous it really was. The eyes didn't actually scale with the size of the animal. They were dictated by physics and the light they were meant to see in. This was a night hunter. Its great mass and the insolation of the feathers that covered it allowed it to hold heat deep into the night. It might even be warm-blooded. She wished she could saw a slice out of the leg bone. If only she had a microscope, she might be able to solve one of the great theories of her time.

Jenny set about cutting out her spear. The broken end protruded six inches from the dinosaur's chest. The spear would not move. She had to cut between the ribs for several feet in both directions before she could pry them apart enough to remove the spear head. It was good to hold her grandfather's knife once again. She had feared she had lost it, and with it her last connection to him.

She also cut out a large steak. She was hungry. She wished she could somehow take this thing with her, that the people back home could see this, study it. She wanted to spend weeks taking it apart. They could learn so much. But she had to move, as simply staying around here invited trouble.

Sooner or later something bigger would catch scent of this carcass. Part of her wanted to wait nearby and see what that might be. She looked again at the carcass wistfully, and her eyes fell on the teeth in its mouth...

She was a good two miles from the body before she stopped her march. Jenny was carrying the steak wrapped in the skin she had cut from the animal. It was heavy and awkward to carry. She might have overdone it, but damn it, she was hungry. She never thought well when she was hungry. She always overbought at the grocery store when she had not eaten.

Jenny built a fire and arranged a flat rock over it. As the rock heated, she went to cut some wood to make a tripod. Once her makeshift range was good and hot, she laid the large steak onto the rock and listened to it sizzle. Her mouth watered. She might have drooled a bit. The stone held plenty of heat.

Once the meat was nicely browned, she flipped it over. The sound of it cooking was gratifying, and the smell was divine. After it was nicely seared on all sides, she kicked the stones out of the way and spread out the coals a bit. She hung the steak above the coals from the tripod to cook slowly.

This was possibly the hardest part. She never had much patience. As she waited, she fingered the large tooth she had pried from its jaw. Turning it over and over in her hands, she reached up and placed her hand over her chest, feeling the tooth under the shirt hanging from the cord around her neck, the tooth she had carried most of her life. A cold realization dawned on her as she looked at the bloody tooth in her hand. This was hers. This was her. What she had done. What she was meant to do.

Jenny didn't know or understand what this meant. Maybe they should have sent her to school to study theoretical physics or some shit like that. Her hand clutched the tooth. This was real. Her other hand drifted down to the spear beside her. This was real. She was hungry. She focused on that as she stared into the fire.

When the meat was finally done, it was tender, like the finest roast beef, pink fading to red in the center and very juicy. It was a bit gamey and could use a little seasoning, but she didn't care. It was possibly the best meal she ever had. She had eaten only about a third of it before she sat back, feeling comfortably bloated.

CHAPTER 44

Fishing

John Hamman, 26
1921/Permian

The big rod was heavy. John swung the long pole above his head and whipped it forward, sending his hook far out into the darker water before the sand bar. He had a four-ounce lead weight and a bottom rig with a small fish that he had caught earlier as bait. He backed up, tightening his line as he set it in the pipe driven into the sand of the beach.

He looked to his left at his men spread out down the beach. All of them either had their lines in the water or were struggling with the rigging of their hooks. Manny was helping one man who did not seem to grasp the concept of how to attach the line.

John sat down in the deck chair under the shade of the big parasol, looking at his two rods. He hung his wide-brimmed straw hat on the back of the chair, careful to tie it to the frame. He had to move the big double rifle out of the way to open the picnic basket and retrieve a drink. Ice. All they were missing was ice. Unfortunately, that was in short supply, even in their own time.

Looking down the beach, one could see that none of the men were using the deck chairs. They brought enough for all of them, but the men preferred to squat on their haunches, staring intently at their poles, their eyes never leaving their rods.

John didn't think they grasped the idea that this was supposed to be relaxing. Damn it. They had gone to a lot of effort to steal those deck chairs and the parasols from that resort in the middle of the night. A chair wasn't that complex of a concept. He sighed. There really wasn't much to be done about it.

Manny returned and sat in the other chair. Maybe *sat* wasn't really the right word. He did put his bottom on it, but he lay back with his arms attached rigidly to his sides, his head locked forward, only his eyes moving. John didn't think he had ever seen someone more uncomfortable. At least he was trying, though.

John reached into the basket between them and handed Manny a bottle of beer. He stared at it with just his eyes, not knowing what to do. Finally he moved one arm to take the bottle then returned to his rigid sitting position.

John tried to toast him to get Manny to drink. Somehow he managed, holding the bottle in both hands, to take a small sip without moving his head from where it was frozen in his sitting posture. John would have laughed if it wasn't so frustrating.

The parasols, however, were a hit. Shade was an idea they understood, and the concept of a portable tree that they could move with them and sit in the shade of... John had really intended to return them, but at this point he might face a rebellion.

The strike was on John's first pole to the far right. The pole bent, and the reel spun, letting out line. He jumped out of the chair and ran over to the rig. He struggled to get the pole hooked to his belt. Then Manny's hands were there helping. Whatever was caught on the line fought hard. He couldn't feel much "head shake" in the line.

When John finally got it into the surf, close to the shore, where he could take a look, he was right. It was another lobster. At least that was what John called them. He preferred to think of them that way rather than as "sea scorpions," which they bore a greater resemblance to.

"Get the pole!" They had learned the creatures had spikes on the flat paddle-shaped tails that they would swat with. In the front they had large pincers on arms. They were almost as long as John was tall, and they roasted up nicely, like lobsters. The big arms and legs were larger and more succulent than any crab legs John had ever eaten.

Manny ran into the surf with a loop on a pole and secured the crustacean around its tail and began dragging it backward onto the beach. John ran up and brained it with a club.

Together they dragged it up the beach to the barbecue pit, where two of the men were grilling the catches. Manny and John exchanged a huge grin over the monstrosity. None of the tribe's men had ever heard of lobster before this trip, but it had quickly become a favorite, split open down the top and dipped in warm butter. John particularly liked the legs and claws.

It looked to be another good night. He picked up the butter crock and felt its weight. They would have to head back soon.

This had been a good idea. John struggled to get across the concept of a vacation. It was as alien to the men as the chairs. John wanted to get away from his modern Africa for a time.

The hunt for the "Ghost Lions" had been exhausting, and John could not get the tracker's death out of his mind. He had made a point of learning to say the names of all his remaining men. His tongue still tripped over some of them, and he provoked more than a bit of laughter at times when trying to use any of their names or words from their language. He was working on it. He couldn't have been too far off. They at least answered to their names.

John really should have been hunting ivory. The next payment on the land would be coming due soon, and all the time they spent cleaning up their little mess had not helped. The villagers were beyond grateful for the help, but that gratitude was not accepted as currency by the crown.

When they got back, John would start working on a big load of ivory. The hunting was good in the Stone Age, and he knew he could bring in more and bigger tusks than anyone else. Let them think he had been off hunting all this time, not lounging on the beach.

Coming up with a cover story for where they were hunting was sometimes more challenging than the elephants. Already, pointed questions were being asked. Maybe John should tell them he had been west over the border. Everyone would turn a blind eye to a little poaching now and then. After all, it wasn't British law being broken. It was as good a cover story as any, and no one really liked the Belgians.

Fishing here had been interesting. At first they lost a lot of lures. They needed a piano wire leader with a lot of these fish. One in particular had been a problem. John got to calling him "Bait Stealer," and from that point on, any time something large bit through their lines, they blamed Bait Stealer.

John thought they caught him on the fourth day. He had gotten fed up and made a leader from a short piece of chain and their largest hook. He baited it with a fish large enough that they could have eaten it themselves and used a bottle for a float. John tossed it out, and in less than half an hour the line started screaming out of the reel.

The struggle went on for several hours. John was almost dragged into the water three times. Manny and another man had to hold on to his belt to anchor him. Finally they landed it. He expected some kind of shark, but it was a giant fish, as heavy as two grown men.

Manny tried braining it to no avail. No matter what he did, all his blows bounced off the beast's armored head. Finally John yelled for him to shoot it. The big double rifle ended its struggles, and tying a rope around its tail, they hauled it onto the shore.

Now John knew what had bitten through all of their lines. The great parrot-like jaws acted like a pair of shears. The head was nothing but armored plates, and the body wasn't much better. It had been challenging to clean. That one fish was enough to feed them all for a day and a half. It had also convinced John against his plans to go swimming in the warm water. Oh, well—you couldn't have everything.

They sat around the fire that night, lazily staring into the flames and feeling pleasantly bloated. The whiskey burned John's throat but left a warm, contented feeling in his stomach as he thought about what a strange and wonderful life it was.

CHAPTER 45

Rebellion

Robert Brown, 50
1988 New York, NY

As the other partners discussed the future failure of the First Republic Bank of Texas and the completion of something called the TAT-8, Robert Brown stared down at the paper in his hands, almost forgotten by the others in the room. It must be some kind of mistake. They couldn't expect him to go there. It was too much.

"Separating ourselves from the Republic Bank is simple enough, but we have to think about the entire sector and the consequences for the region and the economy as a whole."

Years—it had been years. Every year he was expected to go off for months at a time, to ungodly remote locations. He had been loyal. He always did what he was told by the firm, and by these God damn letters. What were they? Where did they come from? How could Hamman have known all this? And why would he want his only grandchild to grow up this way at the far ends of the earth? And why did it always have to be *him*?

"The reach of this will be much greater than that. Look at real estate and all the sectors connected to it. The entire market value will collapse."

Was it even right, to do this to a child? There were ethical considerations. It wasn't all about him. There was safety. It wasn't safe to do these things to a child, to put her into these kinds of situations. What if something happened? There was liability. They could be sued.

"This is much bigger. Not only will our returns be astronomical, but think about its effects on international trade. It will tie the markets together like never before."

"I can't do this," he said softly. No one paid attention to him. Robert looked up at the animated conversation around him about AT&T and the coming Internet. More loudly he reiterated, "I can't do this!" This time a few heads turned to him, annoyed by the interruption of their discussion of hundreds of millions of dollars. "*I can't do this!*"

The room fell silent. All eyes turned toward him.

"Excuse me?" The president of the firm was glaring daggers at him. All the others in the room shriveled in their own chairs, despite not being the target themselves. No one could ever remember those words being uttered to the president of the firm before.

Robert stood up, his chair rolling back across the room. "I won't do this!" No one had ever said that in this room before. You could have heard a pin drop. He shook the papers at them. "You can't expect me to..."

"*Stop!*" The glare of the senior partner was focused on him like a laser beam. "You will *not* divulge any of your instructions. You will *not* place us in default of our contract. You *will* carry out your instructions to the letter and fulfill all of our obligations to this contractual agreement. "*Do you understand me, Mr. Brown?*" It was fairly certain that several hearts in the room actually stopped beating at this pronouncement.

"You can't make—" At this moment the president of the law firm stood up at the end of the table.

CHAPTER 46

River

Jenny Hamman, 31
Cretaceous

It was three days later when Jenny found the stream bed. It wasn't much to speak of, an erosion feature a couple of feet wide at first. It was dry, but it led her onward. Another half a mile on, it emptied into a proper stream bed with a rocky bottom. Still dry. She finally found rounded stones for her sling.

She followed the stream bed in hopes that it would lead her to the river. It was mostly dry, but from time to time there would be deeper pools that still maintained water. There were more animals here and of a greater variety.

The insect life also increased. Mosquitoes were becoming more of a problem. She had to camp well away from the sources of water, but they still seemed to find her in the night, buzzing around her.

She couldn't resist slapping at them in the dark, no matter how ineffectual it was. Rubin had always told her to let them land on her and start drinking before trying to kill them, but she couldn't stand them buzzing around her ears. Jenny wished she had a bottle of DEET. On the other hand, the strong smell might attract other problems.

She started seeing more ceratopsians steering clear of the larger varieties. They seemed very aggressive and moved in herds, but she also saw fighting between individuals. She wasn't sure if they were fighting for dominance, territory, or mating. Personality-wise, they seemed to be somewhere between cape buffalo and rhinos.

Some of the smaller varieties, on the other hand, were downright cute. As Jenny got closer to the river, she found that the land was crawling with Protoceratops. They seemed to be everywhere, foraging for food, digging burrows, mating, or just playing. They seemed to enjoy chasing each other apparently for the fun of it.

Slight differences in the shape of the head had been noted in the fossil record, and Jenny could now confirm they were based on the sexes. The Protoceratops were small, not much bigger than large dogs, and very cute, especially in the way they tended to wiggle and wag their tails.

On the second day of following the stream bed, Jenny found the river. She stood on a high bank, looking out over the river bottom. The river was low, with a ten-foot drop-off to a rocky bottom. The river was less than half its width with wide sandy shores on either side. It was still flowing, but with it being the dry season, it was far below its banks.

Jenny was feeling good about herself. She had made a new shaft for her spear and had also taken the time to weave a small basket on a shoulder strap to hold an egg. It made a nice canteen, with a small stopper in the top. It was good to carry a little extra water. She had also woven a satchel out of grasses to hang over her other shoulder.

She sat down on the edge of the bank with her back against a tree, her feet dangling over the edge. The sun was warm on her face. She took out half of a roasted Caudipteryx and tore off a leg. It was good but still needed lemon pepper.

She had made it. She was at the river. Now if she could only find that old man.

As she watched, a pair of pterosaurs came skimming down the river above the water. One dove down above the surface, dipping its head into the water and coming up with a fish. Flapping hard, it rejoined its companions.

Fish. Jenny liked a good steak, but it was getting old, particularly with the lack of even salt and pepper to add to the flavor. The water was low. The fish would be concentrated, but she would need to find a better place to fish from.

Following the river downstream, she found a bend where the river came all the way up to the bank on her side of the river. It was a good ten-foot drop to the water with good tree cover on top of the bank. It was as comfortable a fishing spot as she was likely to find, and it offered some protection from anything in the water. She had fishhooks and a couple of coils of line in her belt but nothing like a pole.

Jenny cut a young, green sapling to make herself a pole. It was not too bad, with a good bit of play at the end. She would use some of her grilled dinosaur as bait, but she wasn't sure about how to go about it. She would probably do better with a piece that was raw or rotting, depending on what she wanted to try catching. She assumed that strategies similar to what she would use at home would work here and hopefully lead to an equivalent result.

Jenny lowered her line into the water and let it drag through the current of the river. The water was muddy. Anything she caught would be based on smell. Would anything down there like roast chicken?

She sat back against a tree with the long pole between her legs and looked out over the river. It could almost be back home if it weren't for the pair of Triceratopses drinking on the other side. She wanted to take her boots off. This kind of fishing should be done barefoot with one's hat pulled down over your eyes while napping in the sun.

Somewhere out there was her grandfather, the same man who had taught her to fish with a homemade pole like this one. She had not caught anything that first day he taught her, but she loved being with him on the banks of the river in the warm sun as he told her stories of his time in Africa.

He at least caught a good-sized catfish. They grilled it over the fire that night. It had been so good, light and flaky, with lemon pepper. Jenny was seriously missing condiments. She mournfully thought back to the bag of spices in her pack that she had lost.

As she was lazily watching the river, Jenny heard a loud but low-pitched buzzing. At first she thought it was a hummingbird. Then it came into her line of sight, hovering above her. It was a dragonfly but larger than any she had ever seen. It must have been eight inches across.

The dragonfly hovered above her, as if studying her. Then it was joined by a second, and they began chasing each other. Young lovers? Who could say? She watched them chase each other over the water of the river until they disappeared out of sight.

Jenny had no idea what might be in the river. Visions of some of the strange, exotic fossils she had studied danced before her eyes as she watched the tip of her pole.

The outcome was far more mundane. Apparently she had traveled millions of years through time to catch a common gar. It looked exactly like something she would have pulled out of a river back home.

It was, in her time at least, an incredibly old form of fish, unchanged for many millions of years. And here she was holding one of its distant ancestors. It was a decently sized fish but no record. She had seen much larger ones pulled from the Red River back home. Wait—that wasn't accurate. This might be the first alligator gar ever caught. By definition, it was the current record.

It would make a tolerable meal if only Jenny could figure out how to make gar balls without oil to fry them in. In the end she gutted, deboned the fish, and cooked it spread out on top of its own skin. The tough skin and large scales made the perfect tray to roast and serve it on.

The dish needed creole seasoning, or at least a little butter. Eating it plain was a crime. It was bland and slightly oily. If she could soak it in milk overnight she could fix that. Still, it was filling and a welcome change from grilled dinosaur.

It was time to find her granddad. Jenny was close. She needed to find a big bend in the river. And she probably needed to get to the other side. That might be tricky unless she could find a place to cross. Without a doubt, far scarier things were lurking in the river than alligator gar. Even in her own day she would not care to swim across a river in Africa.

CHAPTER 47

Mokele-Mbembe

John Hamman, 30
1925/Cretaceous/Congo

The Congo was a very different landscape. It was a place of high plateaus and river basins. The game was plentiful and the ivory was good. Less of a problem for John, but it was becoming impossible to explain how he could take a quick jaunt from town and magically come back with a couple of tons of ivory in a land that everyone knew to be totally hunted out.

To be honest, he wanted to see more of this land, in this time and the past. Was it really poaching if he shot most of his ivory ten thousand years before a country like Belgium even existed, much less laid claim to this land?

Border patrols were less of a danger to him than others. As long as they spotted the patrols early enough, John's crew could duck back to an earlier time and travel for a few days to break their trail and lose their pursuers.

Sometimes he wondered what the patrol's trackers thought when they followed the trail of his group that had been spotted going into a grove of trees, only to have that trail dead end, leading nowhere.

The Belgians were not kind rulers. The native tribes of Kenya may not have been treated by the ideals of his homeland, of "all men created equal," but the abuse here was on a whole other level.

John and his men were often met with fear and mistrust until the local people learned they were from British East Africa. Being smugglers and wanted by the government created a bond with the local people, who feared the Belgians above all else.

Bringing trade goods and selling them fairly, or even giving them away, cemented the relationship. The local tribes helped John and his men to avoid the Belgian patrols. They would often hunt and kill rogue lions, buffalo, and elephants that were destroying crops and mauling or killing locals. A group of buff or elephants could destroy an entire crop in a single night and then disappear into the forest.

They had spent a week tracking a lion that killed more than a dozen people from this village. When they brought the pelt of the lion that had killed the chief's granddaughter, the chief cried and their friendship was sealed.

Drought consumed the land. For the second year it was dry, and the once-lush grasses were turning brown. The herds grew thin on what little grazing they could find. The milk did not come. The calves died. People were hungry.

John looked down at a child whose belly was swollen, not with food but with hunger. They had to do something to help these people. No amount of food they could share from their own supply would be enough.

The people of this land were the pygmies, the forest dwellers. They were indeed small of stature, living in scattered villages deep in the forest of the Congo River Basin. They normally avoided white intruders, preferring to slink away into the jungle.

This is what people thought of when they said, "deepest, darkest Africa." These people were barely beyond the Stone Age technology-wise. They had very few metal implements. A single metal pot might represent the fortune of a whole village. The trade goods from their supplies—pots, skillets, spoons, and knives—represented the majority of their contact with the outside world.

John could not stand to watch these simple people suffer. Seeing them abused was like seeing innocent children beaten. He had often thought that of all the places on earth, this most represented the Garden of Eden, free from the original sin carried by the men from the outside world.

He called to the chief, and they all sat down to speak of what must be done. With Manny translating, John explained that he would take them to a place where they could hunt game that would feed this and all the surrounding tribes. They must send for the best warriors and hunters from all the tribes and come together. John would take them all to a place with more game than they could imagine. In two days they would leave and come back with enough meat to feed all the villages. He hoped they could pull this off.

It was time. All the men who could be summoned stood in the clearing. They were armed with spears and bow and arrows, not one gun among them. The Belgians had never allowed firearms to escape their grasp. This was going to be interesting. John and his men would have to do most of the heavy lifting. He hoped that not too many people would get hurt.

John had the hunters all gather closely around his party. He set the device to take them into the past and pushed the button. A few seconds later a flash of light filled the clearing, and everything changed.

They were not in the same place, but it wasn't as different as one might think. The plants and trees were different, but the landscape was similar to where they had been. They were still in the middle of a dense forest.

He told the group that it was time to hunt. The trackers disappeared out into the forest seeking game. They would spread out and report back on anything nearby. John hoped they would not run into more than they could handle.

For the first three days they found mostly smaller game. They did kill one larger animal that weighed in at a bit more than a large elephant. They were pleased but needed more if they were to bring back enough for everyone in their own time.

On the fourth day one of the trackers came back telling of great beasts, "bigger than all the world." The man had found something. John hoped the group could handle whatever it was.

The other hunters remained behind in the camp as John, Manny, and the chief set out with the tracker to see these beasts. As John suspected, it was Mokele-Mbembe.

There were three of them, and they were enormous. Two were larger, and one was somewhat smaller, perhaps not fully grown. This was an embarrassment of riches. John had brought the hunters here, promising enough meat to feed all of their villages, and here it was.

But could they really kill something that large? John and his men had never attempted it before. It was like hunting a great whale. Men did it, but they used harpoon guns. John thought about trying to acquire one, but when he saw the weight, he could not find a way to do it. They were so large that they had to be mounted to turrets on a ship.

Now John wished he had something like that, maybe a small artillery piece or one of the smaller French models. He could not imagine how he would have explained that. If he went off to hunt towing a field piece, someone was bound to ask questions. They must make do with what they had or walk away and find smaller game.

John signaled them to move back. They had to pull the chief back into the woods, as he would not turn away from the sight of this beast "bigger than all the world." The chief stared at them wide-eyed as they talked it over. In the end, it was decided.

John turned to Manny. "Get the 'Big Gun.' Bring all the ammo." Manny was silent as he turned back toward the camp. John and the chief gathered all the warriors together as Manny returned with one porter carrying the 'Big Gun' and two more porters bearing two crates of ammunition for it.

Back in the old days there had been a white hunter who had a two-bore stopping rifle. This was in the age of black powder muzzle loaders. It fired a massive round ball of lead weighing half a pound. It was as close to a cannon as anyone had ever put a stock upon.

Being a muzzle loader, it had to be discharged from time to time if it had not been fired. One could not risk the black powder absorbing too much water from the air and becoming unreliable. If it had not been fired for a while, someone would have to discharge it so it could be cleaned and reloaded with fresh powder.

It became a test of their manhood for the black porters to fire the 'Big Gun'. One terrified man would hold it to his shoulder, and three more would stand behind him, trying to prop him up. When the gun fired, all four of them would go tumbling across the ground.

John had never seen the famous two-bore. He didn't think more than one such gun existed in the world. But the Big Gun, as they called it, might have given the two-bore a run for its money. It was not as large in the bore, but the power of the thing was enormous.

John had encountered them at the end of the war. The Germans built them to shoot at tanks. If they caught the tank at the right angle, at close enough range, they could actually penetrate the armor, sending their bullets rattling around the inside of the tank and bringing hell to the crews inside.

It was the only thing that could stop the behemoths short of an artillery piece and other than, of course, the regular failure of its engine, deep mud, a wide trench, tank traps, mines, or the death of its crew from the vapors of its own engine. But other than those things, the 'Big Gun' was the only infantry weapon that could stop one of the tanks. John was profoundly glad he had not been a tanker.

The Big Gun looked sort of like a Mauser, one that had grown four times its normal size. The thing weighed over forty pounds. It was over five and a half feet long and fired an enormous bullet. The cartridge was a 13.2x92mm. The Germans called it a "Tankgewehr." This was the true "Big Medicine." And John was not sure it would be enough. They had never tried to take one of the great beasts with it.

He was not sure of how to do this. This was their first try at one of these Mokele-Mbembe. He did not know how they would respond. Would they become aggressive and charge? Would they run away? If he didn't get a good shot, they might all turn and walk away faster than any of the hunters could run, and that would be the end of it.

John didn't even know if something so large could be killed at all. Was there a point where the size became so great that you simply could not do enough damage to it to bring it down? Could the bullets even penetrate through the bones?

John thought about the great spongy mass of bone in the top of an elephant's skull that could absorb rounds from his 500 Nitro Express, leaving the elephant completely unfazed. He had no faith in breaking any of the large bones or a shoulder. He wasn't even sure about the gun being able to make a spinal shot.

He would pump as many rounds as he could into where he thought the heart and lungs would be and hope he could shoot through the ribs of the great beast. With luck, some of his rounds would find their mark.

The rate of fire was not high. It was a single-shot rifle. John would have to load one round at a time. Honestly, he did not know how many times he could stand to fire the thing; its recoil was like nothing he had ever experienced.

Gathering the hunters, John announced they would hunt now. They would all attack one beast. John would shoot it, and if it tried to escape, they would attack it with their bows and spears. They must not let it trample them.

Manny translated all of this and tried to make it clear to the hunters. They would encircle it with the chief and attack when he did, not before. It wasn't much of a plan.

John didn't have any hope of their helping in any meaningful way, but they had to be a part of it. Manny would fire the 500 and John would fire the T-Gewehr. Those two would shoot as long as they could. If it charged, John would have to abandon the big rifle and they would run into the trees. Hopefully they would be able to trail the injured beast and find it dead, overcome by its wounds.

There was no point in waiting longer. They moved toward where they had last seen the giant dinosaurs in a long column of rather short warriors, led by John's men carrying the big guns and crates of ammunition, as they headed off for battle.

This would be very anticlimactic if the Mokele-Mbembe had decided to wander away as the hunters made their preparations. But no, they were still there in almost the same place the men had left them. They were still grazing, their long necks reaching into the tops of the trees or swinging back and forth along the ground grazing like some kind of great cows.

The hunters set up at the edge of the tree line, where they could retreat into the larger trees if needs arose. The chief took his men and spread them out. They would try for one of the larger beasts.

John and Manny would both shoot for the body. John was not happy with the angle, as it was facing more toward them. He wanted the shoulder out of the way. So they waited. The dinosaurs did not seem inclined to move. They did most of their reaching with their long necks.

Finally John sat down with his back against the tree, not making any effort to conceal himself, and watched the great beasts graze on trees as if they were bushes. He had never imagined such wonders. They should have brought cameras instead of guns.

Finally, as the dinosaurs seemed to exhaust the more tender parts of the plants within reach, they stepped back and turned to another area. This was the chance the men had been waiting for. The targets were now broadside, turned slightly away.

John got up and stepped behind the rifle. He laid down behind it and resigned himself to the pain that was to come. With the open box of ammunition beside him, he loaded one of the big rounds into the chamber and set three others beside it.

The tripod was tall enough to give John the elevation he needed. He looked up at Manny, who was standing erect with the double already loaded with two extra rounds between his fingers. John wished he didn't have to lie down behind this thing.

The two gun-bearing men exchanged uncertain looks and then turned back toward their target. John pretended it was an elephant and aimed his first shot behind its shoulder. He would spread out any following shots where he thought its lungs might be. If he got a chance, he would try a higher shot for the heart.

John pulled the gun back into his shoulder as hard as he could. It had a grip like a pistol. The stock was simply too big to grip in any normal way. He was stalling. He gritted his teeth and tried not to flinch.

Kaboom! John's ears rang even through the waxed cotton he had stuffed into them. That was not a fucking rifle. It should be on a carriage. John distantly heard Manny's second-round fire from the double.

John worked the bolt, ejecting the case, and reached for another, sliding it into the chamber and closing the bolt. He looked back, expecting to see the beast charging at him. He heard Manny's third shot, followed quickly by the fourth.

The unfazed dinosaur was standing there, chewing on a mouth full of ferns. It raised its head as if trying to understand the thunder. John fired again to the regret of his shoulder. He aimed farther back, trying for the lungs. When he looked back up again, the behemoth was still chewing, swinging its head from side to side as if looking for the source of the sound or perhaps the source of the slap of the bullet into its hide.

Red spots appeared on its side where they were hitting it. The patches were large and growing larger. Its heart was pumping great amounts of blood out of them.

John reloaded and fired again as he heard Manny fire twice with the big double. John got two more shots into it before the beast seemed to decide it had had enough of whatever was stinging it and started turning away.

This was when the chief commanded the warriors to attack, and a peppering of arrows and spears joined the wounds. John got off two more shots before the dinosaur started striding away, followed by the rest of its small herd.

They had taken their best shot, literally. John rolled over on his back and cradled his shoulder. He did not want to move his arm and was not certain he could. It was nice to look up at the sky. It became obscured by Manny's smiling face as he leaned over John. "Bwana?"

John motioned for Manny to sit down beside him, which he did, sitting cross-legged and cradling his own arm in his lap. John knew just how he felt. He had lost count of how many rounds Manny fired from the double. They would both be sore tonight.

The injured Mokele-Mbembe was not hard to track. Its tracks were deep, and nothing could hide them. John had never seen a blood trail like that. It seemed as if someone had poured buckets of blood along the trail. When the blood turned foamy, he knew they had it.

Soon they found a great pool of foamy blood where the beast had coughed it up, trying to clear its lungs, but the trail kept going. They followed it all day, but the blood trail never seemed to end. The hunters found several more spots where it had stopped and coughed up great foamy pools of blood. It began raining.

John wasn't sure their prey would succumb. It was like following a great bull elephant that could lead you on a merry chase for weeks across the plain. The party trudged onward in the steady rain.

Toward nightfall they finally found the beast lying on its side, dead, a huge pool of red foam under its head. Its lungs had finally filled with blood and ended it. They all stood around the beast, staring at this thing they had made. They had killed what was perhaps the greatest creature ever to have lived, at least on land. It was like having felled a mountain.

John sent back to have all their things packed and brought to this place. They had no way to move the beast. The men must come to it. Later, when their luggage had arrived, they bent the neck and tail around the body, making it as small as they could. It took all of the men to move the great neck and head. John had everyone climb on top of the beast. And they sat there, clinging to the spears in its side as John set the device. The light flashed—and everything changed.

* * *

Heat. They were sitting on top of soaking-wet dinosaur under the hot noonday sun. They were back, and they had enough meat to feed all the villagers if they could get it preserved before it all spoiled.

Not knowing exactly where they were, John sent the warriors out in all directions to spread the word to all of the villages to come and help with the butchering and smoking of the meat.

By the end of the day the entire corpse was swarming with pygmies crawling all over it, sawing through the hide and peeling it back to butcher the meat. The villagers built racks and smoky fires to dry the meat. By the next day, several villages' worth of people were camped there working around the clock preserving the meat. This went on for almost a week.

There had to be a better way. John had heard of whalers using great knives on long poles to dismember the whales they hunted. He read Moby Dick as a boy and had been fascinated by the stories of the whalers doing battle with the behemoths of the deep. Perhaps he could get some of the great flensing knives the book described.

They fed on great steaks. John hated to say it, but the meat was not very good. It was perhaps the toughest and most fibrous thing he had ever tasted. John taught the villagers to slow-cook it like a brisket back home, and that improved the taste immensely. All they were really missing was some sweet barbecue sauce.

John smiled as he considered that he could take credit for introducing Texas BBQ to the pygmy tribes of the Belgium Congo Basin.

CHAPTER 48

Lion

Robert Brown, 50
1988 Kenya

"Ahh!" He bolted upright. Something was in his ear! Robert almost knocked over the Coleman lantern burning on the small table as he fell out of his cot onto the hard ground. He was yelling and jumping up and down with his head to the side, trying to shake the bug loose before it ate his brain.

He could feel it crawling inside his head! With his pinky finger, he dug as deeply as he could in his ear. With a look of terror, Robert dug out a small beetle. He flung it far from himself as he screamed again. No one came this time. The other members of the safari had lost patience with him.

Robert sat on the edge of his cot, shaking and rocking back and forth. What was he doing here? He didn't belong here. There wasn't even a bathroom. He had to go to the bathroom. The packed clay of the ground was cold. He looked around for his slippers.

Working his feet in to the large fuzzy slippers arranged next to the cot, he gathered a roll of toilet paper, flashlight, and a small shovel.

When he had asked the professional hunter where he was going to set up the toilet, the man simply gestured to the broad plain that stretched as far as the eye could see. Smug South African bastard. He had probably supported apartheid. What was Robert doing here?

Juggling his collected items in his hands, he made his way out into the African night. At least no one would be watching him this time. They always sniggered and laughed. His paisley pajamas were not enough to keep him warm in the cold African night. How could it be so hot in the day and so cold at night?

Robert went behind some sort of tree. He was in a most awkward position, squatting over a small hole he had dug, with his pajamas and boxers down around his ankles—when he heard it.

It wasn't a growl as much as a low, slow rumble. Robert swung his light to the side to reveal a gigantic lion standing not twenty feet from him, its great golden eyes glowing in the pool of his light.

Robert screamed and tried to run, only to fall on his face with his pajamas around his ankles. This time it was a roar. He rolled over, pointing the light into the night to reveal the lion in midair sailing toward him, jaws wide.

The shot was deafening. A great weight landed on top of Robert. His ears rang. All he could hear was a high-pitched whining. He was pinned down under the monstrous lion and would surely be eaten at any second.

Robert squeezed his eyes tightly shut, waiting for the end. Nothing happened.

"You dead, lawyer man?"

Robert opened his eyes to see Jenny Hamman standing over him with the big rifle he had bought for her. The dead lion pinned him to the ground. All that could escape him was a whimper.

He realized he no longer needed to go to the bathroom.

CHAPTER 49

Ra III

Jenny Hamman, 31
Cretaceous

Jenny traveled south. It was as good a direction as any. It meant crossing smaller streams running into the river. Sometimes she would have to detour upstream to find a shallow, rocky place to cross. She didn't want to risk swimming across deeper water, especially near the larger river.

Jenny mostly kept her distance from the river, but she had to approach it several times a day to get water and check for a bend. She was also looking for a place to cross.

She hoped to catch sight of smoke or some other sign of her grandfather, but she might have to cross to the other side to locate him. Jenny would feel really foolish if she crossed and found that he was actually on this side all along.

How accurate was her information? Her landing had been west, not east, of the river, but she gathered that the device had a certain randomness, at least spatially. She sure hoped she was in the same time. Jenny didn't know what she would do if it was a year before her grandfather's arrival. For that matter, what if they were separated by a thousand years? She had to keep searching this section of the river. She traveled south and checked the river, looking for a bend, a place to cross, smoke.

Jenny really wasn't certain what would happen if she failed. As long as she was here, there technically wasn't a paradox. If she figured out how to use the device to return and went back to her own time, would she, on arrival, cease to exist? After all, her mother would have never been born, and therefore *she* would never have been born either. Or would she return to her own timeline when she had left off? Would it be a different world, one in which her grandfather had disappeared long ago? Would she be able to live out her life in that alternate timeline, a refuge from her own previous world?

Jenny had no way of knowing the answer to these questions, not without taking a gamble that she was not prepared to accept. No, Jenny had to find Granddad. And so she pressed on, traveling well back from the river. That was how she found the oxbow lake, or what was left of it.

It wasn't really a lake anymore. It had been filled in mostly with silt. There looked to be a small pond in the bend of it, or would be in wetter seasons. As it was, the dry lake bed formed a rich and fertile clearing, filled with sabal palms and ferns. The vegetation was dense and tall in places.

Smiling, Jenny made her way down into the green field in search of lunch. As she moved through the clearing, she looked for the young plants, less than a year old, whose growing cores would be tender and easy to harvest. She had to use her spear like an ax to harvest the plants.

It was a bit too long to be convenient for the task, awkward to swing. But the plants were young and soft and cut easily. Still, it was temping to dismount the blade from the shaft to be able once again to swing it like a machete. She had grown very attached to having a nice, long spear. But it didn't help her in this task.

The first warning she had was when she heard a chomping sound, followed by grinding and chewing noises as one of the palms ahead of her toppled. She had been in the process of stripping another section to its core to join the ones already filling her satchel. Jenny froze and slowly lifted her head above the ferns to find herself nose to nose with a Triceratops, or its close cousin.

Its beady eyes were fixed on her as it chewed its meal, the upper jaws spreading as the lower raised, grinding the fibrous core into meal. She flashed back to a similar moment when she had once been in the same position with a cape buffalo. For a moment they were both frozen like that—then she did what she had done the last time. She broke into a world-class sprint toward the tree line.

This had not been the best strategy with the buff, and it probably wasn't the best choice in this situation ether. Jenny heard a roar behind her, followed by crashing sounds as the ceratopsian charged after her.

She was smaller and could accelerate faster. She slipped through, between trunks of palms, and ducked around patches of heavier foliage. The trike sounded like a bulldozer as it smashed along, plowing through all these obstacles, its horn acting like a snowplow.

Reaching the edge of the vegetation, she struggled up the slope, ducking behind the first large tree as she continued running. A crash sounded right behind her as it impacted the trunk. At first she thought the conifer would be knocked over and fall on her. It did shudder all the way to the top and took on a decided lean, but it did not fall.

She hardly noticed as she continued on toward an even larger tree. Ducking behind that one, she finally turned to take stock of her pursuer.

She looked in time to jump behind the tree as the animal hit it in a full charge. The whole trunk, large enough that she could not reach halfway around it, shuddered but held against the full charge of the beast.

It backed up a bit, shaking its head, rotating back and forth on its short neck, slightly stunned. It glared at her from the other side of the tree. The head was so large she could almost see one eye on each side of the trunk. They were the mean, beady eyes of a rhino.

It started lunging to one side, and she moved around the other. At that moment it pulled back and lunged to her side. It turned into a chase. Jenny could corner and turn around the tree faster than the trike. If it tried building up any speed, she could dodge around to the other side, and it would overshoot the mark and have to turn around to face her again. It was a war of attrition; the loser would be the first to tire.

They were both panting, once again staring at each other from opposite sides of the tree. Jenny would give it this—it had more stubborn persistence than the buffalo. Maybe that was due to its smaller brain.

It pawed the ground in frustration and made a full charge straight into the tree. Pine needles and cones rained down from above as the whole tree shuck with the impact. That was the trike's parting shot as it backed up huffing and turned to tromp away with what remained of its dignity.

Jenny sat down with her back to the tree, panting, and took a long drink from her canteen. Gulping down the water left her feeling even more out of breath, and she had to lean her head back against the tree, closing her eyes to make the world stop spinning. *Cardio—never neglect your cardio.*

It took some time for Jenny to catch her breath. Eventually, using the tree and her spear, she levered herself up off the ground and onto her feet. She made her way on shaky legs away from the clearing. She was a little disturbed to find herself laughing. This was perhaps the only place in time where she could escape from a moment like that without it being captured on a cell phone.

It was on the second day heading south that she found the bend. Or just *a* bend? She could have easily missed it. From this side it was a sharp bend, and a quarter mile on, the river returned to its course. If she had traveled even another half a mile before detouring over to get water, she would have missed it completely.

This would be easier if she had been on the other side. It would have been a wall to run into rather than a gap to miss. She explored the bend enough to determine that it was a horseshoe, and a large one.

Was this it? It could be the wrong bend entirely. On the south side of it she tried climbing a tree, but the other side was a bluff. The bend was eating into a vertical wall, and the land was high enough that she could not see over it. She was hoping to see smoke, but if her grandfather was camped where he claimed in the note, it would be miles farther south. That was if this was even the right bend.

She had to get to the other side. Maybe she could wait by the river for someone on the other bank to come for water. It was a long river. She couldn't see that much of the opposite bank. They could easily miss each other. If they had a stream on their side, they might not even be coming to the river's edge for water. She wouldn't if she didn't have to.

She had seen a couple of herds of hadrosaurs. She had not seen any of the big predators, but she had seen their tracks. Jenny wondered if one day someone would dig up the prints of her boots in this mud. What would they make of them?

Great! Now she was stuck with the image of her Vibram sole preserved in the "Creation Science Museum." That's all she needed.

Jenny continued south along the river, looking for a place to cross. Two miles down, she climbed another tree. The land on the other side was higher and dominated by a volcanic bench. The river ran closer to it here, and the step on the other side looked drier and more open. But the land was higher, and she could not see very far.

Granddad was out there. She was close. She felt that she ought to be able to smell him from here. There was just that little thing of a river between them.

She thought about firing her pistol. It was far enough that she couldn't be sure he would hear her. The foliage would absorb the sound, and if she couldn't get at least above that bench on the far side, she didn't think the sound would carry.

Maybe she could try it at dawn when they might be gathering water. She only had a handful of rounds left. The nine-millimeter felt paltry, but it had already saved her life several times. Maybe she should start her own fire and try to draw their attention rather than to look for their camp.

That was a thought, but what could they do to help? He made no mention of their having boats. Bigger guns. They would have bigger guns, and that was never a bad thing. But it didn't address the bigger problem of crossing the river.

Beyond the bend the river was faster and became rockier. Some boulders protruded from the river, giving evidence of it shallowing. Probably basaltic blocks from where the river had undermined the other side. It wasn't quite a rapid, but it wasn't something she could wade across.

What she really wanted was a wide, shallow, rocky bed where it spread out enough that she could wade across and without any deep water for the larger monsters to hide in. But as Granddad always said, "If wishes were fishes..." He would generally insert some random comment about the relative rarity of steak or jelly jars of caviar. It had been funny at the time, when she was eight.

Back to the subject. She needed a boat. Could she build one? Could she build a boat big enough not to be eaten in one bite? Again, did she even know what was in the river?

Sadly, most of the aquatic fossils were from the sea, not rivers. She could categorically say there could be some big-ass shit living in that water. She had to get to the other side. There couldn't be that many big predators, right?

She did not want to swim. That was out. Could she build a boat? There were some rather impressive pine trees growing here. She could build a dugout canoe. Wait—could she? She would have to cut down a truly large tree. With no saw. With no ax. Maybe burn around the base? No way that could go wrong. Then she would have to dig it out. No adze. She had her grandfather's old knife. Great, but it wasn't any of the tools she needed.

She went and found herself a place to sulk, ahem, cook her lunch. She had a whole bag full of heart of palm. Great —the blandest food ever without a drop of tomato sauce for fifty million years. Why couldn't the damn things hurry up and evolve? She cut the palm into short sections and roasted them thoroughly until they were nicely brown. The browning at least gave them some flavor.

Could she build a raft? Now there was a thought. Her own *Kon-Tiki*. She loved that book. She liked the movie, but the book was better. Granddad had given her that book.

The protagonist had been one of her heroes, perhaps the first experimental anthropologist. It was a lot easier to cut down giant trees when they were balsa wood. She couldn't see herself doing that alone, and how would she propel it across the water? No, but it was a cool idea. She liked the thought of it.

That Norwegian had done a lot of cool things. Why couldn't the academic community see the value in demonstrating the possibility of contact being made between those cultures? He had done a lot of other things as well. He had tried proving that the Egyptians had crossed the Atlantic on a...

Wait a minute. *Ra II*, the first one, sank. Now that was a thought. Could she do that? It would help if she had a shit ton of rope, but then again if it weren't so large... canoe-sized. And it only had to hold together for a few hundred yards.

That horseshoe bend was a low lying, silty sandbar. The end of it was probably flooded and swampy at high water. Now it was dry, but it was covered with reeds drying yellow in the sun. She might not be able to cut down a giant tree, but Granddad's knife might make a dandy weed-whacker. She looked over at her spear and thought it would make a very serviceable scythe.

CHAPTER 50

Cryptozoologist

1956 Belgian Congo, Kenya

His parents did not approve of how he spent the money. He went to school, but rather than studying business or accounting, he insisted on studying zoology, taxonomy, paleontology, and folklore—nothing that would ever lead to a profession that would support him or a family.

The school didn't even have a degree plan for what he wanted to be. If he could find the evidence for his paper, they would be making him the head of his own department. His trust had matured, and it was time to finally make his mark.

The cryptozoologist arrived in Boma, at the mouth of the Congo River, as one of the few passengers aboard a freighter. It had once been the capital of the colony, founded as a port for the slave trade. It had not grown in charm.

Everyone he saw seemed to be sizing him up as to whether it would be worth the trouble of deboning him for the meat. He was able to find passage with a boat taking workers upriver to the rubber plantations.

As he watched them board the boat, he couldn't help but notice that the men were being guarded by white men with rifles. It would seem that the oppressive colonial regime had not yet given up its domestic slave trade. This was why the people must rise up together to stand against the corporations and capitalists who held them down in servitude.

The boats ran a regular route up the river, and he was able to stop along the way to speak with villagers along the river, catching the next boat a few days later. He was met with suspicion and more than a bit of fear.

He tried explaining to them that he was not one of their oppressors but one of the people, like them. He had received good marks in French but still struggled to make himself understood.

He showed them the pictures and drawing he prepared, and they seemed to cooperate, if only out of fear of offending him. At first he got nothing. They easily identified the normal animals found in the country today and showed no recognition of the special drawing that he had included.

It wasn't until he was far up the river that he began hearing stories of Mokele-Mbembe. People started identifying some of the special drawings, giving them African names. The sauropod drawing was recognized most often and identified as Mokele-Mbembe.

Sometimes they would have names for other prehistoric animals as well. They did not identify any of the fanciful drawings he also included. The people who responded to his drawings were always older and from farther upstream, deep in the basin. They told stories of dry years when all the people had come together to hunt great beasts as large as all the world.

Finally he found what he was looking for, a middle-aged woman who said she had eaten from a great beast. It was in her youth, before the rubber grower brought her here to work in the bar. She was from far upriver, beyond the falls. He had no way of telling what that meant.

The key thing was that, according to her stories, it was within her lifetime. Sauropods and other dinosaurs were alive in Africa within the last forty years! He had found it! If he could only get some kind of hard evidence that he could take back with him.

He journeyed more than a thousand miles up the Congo. It happened at Stanleyville, the last port below the cataracts that sealed the river from any travel beyond that point.

Stanley Falls and the town that grew up beneath them were named after Henry Morton Stanley, the first white man to explore the Congo River. They were a series of falls over more than sixty miles of the river, making it unnavigable. The falls barred any travel beyond them, requiring a long portage to bypass them. Beyond this was the darkest of Africa.

It was not until a narrow-gauge rail line was built around the rapids that any type of trade could be opened with the upper basin. Somewhere beyond, he would find Mokele-Mbembe.

As he got off the boat at the dock, he looked out at the falls. It was more a rapid than a single drop-off. He could see the local Wagenya natives fishing out in the water. They had built tripods out of logs in the middle of the rapids.

He was there trying to arrange travel on the rail line when he saw a man loading cargo from one of the rail cars onto a lorry. It was what was hanging around his neck that caught his attention: a claw. A big claw. Larger than anything he had ever seen or should ever be in this day and age. It was curved and over four inches long.

In his excitement he pulled the man aside and tried to question him. He was surprised to find that the man spoke passible English. The man was from Kenya and had terrible scars on his arm and chest. He said the claw was from the beast that had attacked him.

The cryptozoologist had seen claws like this before. He knew what it was, but that was impossible. He had seen those same claws in trays at the university. This was the claw of a dinosaur.

It was not a fossil. It had been cut from a living dinosaur. He had to have it. It was the proof that he needed, but the man would not part with it for blood or money. When he tried to take it, the man drew the machete from his belt.

He was able to take many pictures of it by having the man pose for the camera and then zooming in on the necklace.

He learned that the man was returning to Kenya by airplane that day. His village was west of Nairobi. After buying a good bit of the local beer, he was able to get the man to identify many of his pictures.

He had names for almost all of them. He identified Mokele-Mbembe, and he called the ceratopsian an "Emela-Ntouka," elephant-killer, but he said it had only one horn. That wasn't a problem. There were several known species with only one horn. He had just used a picture of the better-known Triceratops.

The man and his fellow villagers had hunted them, and the claw was from a creature that had attacked their camp. If he liked, he would take the cryptozoologist to his village.

Simi-Simi airport was about a half mile west of town. A DC-4 was loading for its return to Nairobi. The cryptozoologist was able to buy his way on board. It was mostly full of cargo, but he and the other men rode in the back in fold-down chairs along the cabin wall.

He did his best to question the man about the claw. The man told stories of hunting giant animals all over central Africa and described a number of species. Most of his descriptions matched, but there were anomalies.

He insisted that the animal that had attacked him was covered in feathers. That couldn't be right. Had dinosaurs somehow evolved into some kind of bird? Could it have been one of the giant flightless birds that were now extinct? But the bite was clearly from something with teeth, not any type of beak.

A lorry waited for the cargo, and they were soon on their way to the man's village. The cryptozoologist learned that they lived on a farm run by a great man, the Bwana.

It was in late afternoon when they arrived. It looked like any traditional village in Africa.

The cryptozoologist had his camera out. He wasn't sure what he was looking for until he saw a man with a necklace of teeth around his neck. No animal today had teeth that big. He got several pictures.

He saw two women pounding and grinding grain by hand. They were working on top of a bone. At first he thought that the anvil might be from an elephant's foot, but it was far too large. The villagers were shy, covering their faces, but the cryptozoologist's eyes were on the enormous foot bone.

Many of the villagers sported feathers he could not identify. He was speechless as he was led through the village.

An old man sat beneath an awning in a rocking chair. His guide led the cryptozoologist before him and explained that he was the chief. The guide would act as a translator, as the chief had no English.

"Why you here?" He was rather taken back by the abruptness of the question. He tried explaining that he was looking for the animal that the man's claw had come from. He started explaining who he was, but the old chief interrupted him.

"That beast dead long ago. Why you here?" Again, he tried explaining what he did and what he was trying to achieve but was interrupted again. "You no work for Bwana. Why you here?"

About then, another black man drove up in a jeep. He got out and hurried over. He was dressed in more modern clothing. He took one look at the stranger and spoke harshly to the man who had brought him there. A rapid exchange ensued between them.

The new arrival knelt by the old man and spoke to him. When he was done, the old chief spoke two words himself in English, "Go away."

"Now wait a minute. I'm from the University of California. You have—"

The new man stepped between him and the chief. "You leave now." A crowd was gathering around them.

They were looking more hostile. The smiles were gone from their faces.

"You can't just throw me out. I have questions. You have to—"

The chief stood leaning on a cane with a large round knob of wood at the top of it. "Go away."

Men seemed to close in on all sides. The cryptozoologist felt very vulnerable surrounded by hostile stares. He looked around in desperation, also looking up at the awning they stood under. It was skin, thin and semi-translucent. He realized that it was all one piece and was stretched over long bones, not poles. He was standing under a wing more than twenty feet wide.

He was grabbed by the arms as he was dragged away. He held the button down on his camera, capturing the great wing with the last of the roll of film, and was marched to the edge of the village and roughly pushed in the back. The man was holding a rifle now and cocked it meaningfully. "You leave now. You no come here again."

With no other choice, the cryptozoologist started walking down the dirt road away from the village. He was so close. He needed one of those bones, one of those teeth. At least he had the pictures. With them the bones could be identified. He could come back. He would get all the proof he needed. He was so close. He would prove it all.

* * *

The village was the enemy. They were aligned with the whites. Worse, the whites were kind and friendly toward them. Any village or group that was treated well was a target and had to be destroyed. The first step in driving out the English was to isolate them from all their supporters.

They had watched the lorry go by. They had not attacked—too many men in it. But this man was alone, a white man, one who visited the village of the hunter. This man must be in league with the hunter. It didn't matter. He was a white man. He was alone. So foolish. He didn't even have a gun.

They came out into the road in front of the lone white man in the fading light, machetes already out. He was afraid, turning to see the rest of the men behind him. He babbled nonsense about Marxism, about being one of them. He was not Mau Mau—he was white. They didn't care about anything else.

They would drive all the white men from this land. He tried to hold his fist up in some kind of gesture as he screamed that he was one of the people like them. The hand flew into the bushes with the first swing of the blade. He screamed. The screams went on for a long time.

They took everything that was on the body, including the camera.

CHAPTER 51

Last Trip

John Hamman, 43
1938 British East Africa

The large ranch-style house was looking good, with a great hall of a living room and a large fireplace—much more room than in the original building. They were starting on another structure out back. Eventually it would form an almost-enclosed courtyard behind the main house.

It had been a hot day. John went inside and poured water from the pitcher into a washing bowl and preceded to wipe away the sweat. The water felt good and cool on his skin. Enticing smells were drifting in from the cooking pit behind the house. Toweling himself off, John put his shirt back on and leaned out the door of the bathroom into the hallway, calling, "Manny!"

Manny's head popped sideways out of the kitchen doorway. "Bwana?"

"Dinner in one hour."

"Yes, Bwana." The head broke into a huge smile before disappearing back into the kitchen. John went down the hall and turned into the main room. He poured himself a not-too-small drink and sat back in one of the new chairs. When he sank into the big, soft overstuffed chair, it occurred to him that a man could get used to this. Taking a long sip of the whiskey, he leaned back, closing his eyes.

John was tired, but things were going well. The price of ivory continued going up. Everyone had to go farther afield now. New regulations almost shut down commercial ivory hunting in Kenya. Now it was all guided hunting trips. You had to go afield, often poaching in the Congo, to hunt unrestricted.

The herds were getting out of control again, at least by the standards of the farmers. John had seen how large the herds had once been before the white man decided to cull them to protect their crops. There was talk about opening up hunting in some of the districts.

The thing was—no large bulls were left. Only young animals remained. No more big ivory. John was having to go farther afield, or at least stay away longer to sell the idea of how he could come back with so many large tusks.

Let them think he was poaching in the Congo. He was sure they would charge him with illegal hunting if they could. It was hard to accuse him when he brought in tusks larger than anything seen in this country for over thirty years. Where else could he get them but by hunting over the border?

A strange defense: "My proof that I'm not breaking the law is that I'm breaking the law." In the meantime, the price of ivory continued to climb.

He was getting a lot of pressure from professional hunters to tell them where he was hunting. They wanted to take their clients there on safari.

There had been more than a few comments when the wealthy clients saw the tusks that John dropped off in the local shops, much larger than what had been found for them by their professional guides. The only reply was that John was hunting illegally over the border somewhere. Then what the hell were they doing going on safari here in this country? The whole thing was becoming a problem.

John took another long sip of his drink and ran the glass over his brow. Perhaps he should look for another line of work. At least the farm was starting to make a reliable profit.

They were digging up a lot of diamonds in South Africa. He heard once that you could find them on the beach back when the rush started. Maybe he could go on a little trip. They wouldn't miss a few, ten thousand years ago. But it was a long way to go, and they had just finished the house. He took another sip.

And it looked as if there was another war brewing. He could smell it. The Germans were going to start it again. Something in that bloodline had to march to the sound of a drum. Thank God he was about as far from it as a man could get. He was getting a bit old for it as well. They would have to play this next inning without him.

He needed a break. They had been working on the house for weeks. It was time for a vacation. "Hey, Manny!" He put some wind into it so that he could be heard in the kitchen.

He had started finishing off the drink when Manny called, "Bwana?" Jesus, did the man hover outside the door?

"Tell the men we go hunting. Have them pack food and equipment for a month. Pack all the guns. Don't forget the supplies. Tell them to be in the courtyard tomorrow, noontime."

"Ivory, Bwana?"

"No, vacation." Manny's face split into another wide grin, one that matched John's own as he sat back in the chair and finished his drink.

"Dinner soon, Bwana." John waved cheerfully as the liquor burned its way down his throat and made a warm, contented home in his belly.

CHAPTER 52

Last Letter

Robert Brown, 63
2001 New York, NY

All the people sitting at the table stared at the envelope, slightly yellowed at its edges. It was the last. They all knew it was the last one. There would be no more instructions.

After they carried out the contents of this letter, their contractual obligations would end. The fortunes of every person in the room had been founded on these mysterious envelopes and the secrets they contained. Now it was almost over.

The senior partner removed the papers from inside the envelope, and for the first time in several years there was an envelope within for Robert Brown.

The last few had been nothing more than instructions to encourage grants to fund his granddaughter's digs. Even that had not been necessary for some time. This envelope was quite a bit thicker. No one took notice as Robert went through the documents inside it.

It was a deed to a farm in Africa. There were also instructions on exactly when and how Jenny should take possession of the property. In other circumstances they would have raised eyebrows, but for the Hamman account it was surprisingly mundane. Robert made a few notes on his pad as he read, only half listening to the others in the background.

The senior partner was reading the instructions aloud. They concerned a merger of AOL and Time Warner, which would fail. A "dot com" crash. A scandal with Enron. There was also good news. Apple would release something called an "iPod." It would not be a failure. And Microsoft would build something called an "Xbox."

Everyone else in the room was totally focused on taking notes on these last and final instructions. By the end of the day, hundreds of millions of dollars would be in motion. Robert idly wondered if their own actions would bring about these collapses.

Sometimes he wondered how no one had ever questioned their financial dealings. Was it insider trading if they had knowledge before even the insiders were aware of it?

He was absorbed in his own study of the deed when the room grew silent. The senior partner was reading a prediction of a terrorist attack on America.

Robert felt as if someone were pouring ice water down the back of his spine. It included the exact date and time. It named the players who would conduct the attack and how it would be carried out. It spoke of the aftermath. The damage. How many people would die in the World Trade Center buildings that would be targeted. The shutting-down of all air travel. At that, people picked up pens that had been dropped to the table and began taking notes on the airlines. Robert had a feeling that a lot of shorts would be placed on those companies.

The discussion at the table turned to what this would mean for the economy and for different industries. Robert sat listening to his colleagues discussing leveraged negative indexes.

"We should tell them," Robert stated. The man sitting next to him glanced at Robert and then returned to the conversation. Robert stood up, drawing the attention of several of the partners. "We should tell them!" Now the conversations stopped, and all eyes turned to him. There was a long pregnant silence.

"Tell them what?" The stony gaze of the senior partner seemed to bore into Robert's soul.

"We have to warn them." Robert was beyond flinching under that gaze.

"How would you suggest we do that? Should we tell them we know the future? Should we explain to them we have magic envelopes written twenty years in the past that contain the exact dates and methods of this attack?"

No one had ever spoken of the envelopes, what they meant, or how they could be, not even among themselves. It was one subject that was strictly verboten, to even allow yourself to think about. No one wanted the answer.

"And how would you prove this? Would you tell them that every stock trade, every investment made by every person in this room was made with prior knowledge of the future, and therefore they should listen to us?"

People squirmed, uncomfortable in their chairs. "Would you show them the letters left to us by John Hamman? I assure you they are all not just shredded but burned, as this one will be before the end of the day." He turned back to the others at the table. Robert remained standing. The senior partner glanced up once more. "Sit down, Mr. Brown."

As the conversations resumed around him, Robert Brown turned and walked out of the conference room.

CHAPTER 53

Crossing

Jenny Hamman, 31
Cretaceous

Mowing took two days. At the end, Jenny cleared and gathered all the usable reeds on the bend in the river. This seemed like an almost sacrilegious act. Grasses were associated more with the Paleocene, but the order Poales actually extended back almost 115 million years. After the asteroid, they would be given to chance to spread across the entire earth.

Right now they were rare. It seemed wrong to strip the bank of this early example of Typhaceae reeds. It felt wrong to cut them all down, but she knew they would grow back from their roots with the coming of the next wet season.

She didn't feel too bad about camping there, as the entrance to this little island was rather narrow, and it at least felt less likely that wildlife would wander into the bend. Maybe that was wishful thinking. In truth, she was probably getting ahead of herself.

It turns out that a reed boat like this was not made out of reeds—it was made out of rope, or in this case twine. Lots and lots of it. It took two days to cut down all the reeds. Jenny spent a week making twine from anything she could find, mostly fibrous palm leaves. She had thought the blisters from swinging her spear like a scythe were bad. They were nothing in comparison to the blisters on her fingers from making twine.

After two days Jenny thought she had enough—wrong. When she started making the first bundle of reeds, she quickly learned how fast that twine went. Back at it, she spent another five days working on twine. One good thing—there were plenty of palm trees and other fibrous plants. The process was long and monotonous. She couldn't believe that the Cretaceous could be boring

Jenny wound up with five bundles, about six inches at their fattest, tapering to a point at each end. It took only a day to actually make the boat at that point. Both ends swept upward. It was about two and a half feet wide, somewhere between a canoe and a sit-on kayak.

She wanted it to be bigger, but there actually weren't that many reeds. She also made a paddle end for the butt of her spear. It didn't look very dignified. Jenny could feel the disproval radiating from it whenever she walked by and caught sight of it.

A total of twelve days to build a boat to cross something only slightly over one hundred yards wide. Jenny looked down at her blistered fingers and swollen knuckles. Maybe she should have swum.

During this time she mostly fished. More gar and several of something that looked kind of like a Hoplopteryx.

Jenny also took one quick foray inland to brain another chicken dinosaur in the early morning. And there were always sliced palm chips to munch on, devoid of salt or any kind of sauce.

During this time there was one incident when a herd of some type of hadrosaurs wandered down to the river to drink. It was interesting because they completely ignored her.

Jenny was able to walk among them, small enough that she didn't trigger their threat alarm. It might have helped that it was a mixed herd. She was able to count four different species. She guessed the survival advantages of a larger herd won out over their racial preadjust.

That gave credence to the idea that the wide variety of head shapes was evolved to identify other members of their own species for mating. It certainly made it easy for her to count and divide the herd. The only animals that were skittish around her were the young, and the adults would give her the side-eye anytime Jenny got to close to them.

It settled in her mind all the arguments about child rearing, but were these members of the herd, or had they attached themselves for protection? As far as she could tell, the gestation period inside the egg was very long, up to a year. That being the case, could a herd stay in proximity to a nest of eggs till hatching? The smart money was on these young simply attaching themselves to the nearest herd upon hatching.

They didn't seem to guard their nests, and the attrition rate of eggs was high. Jenny had seen and even been a part of that. So they laid and abandoned their eggs but protected the young that survived when they joined the nearest herd regardless of species. That explained the mixed nature of the herd.

They would probably favor reproducing with their own species, hence the dramatic differences in head shape. It was a mating signal resulting from the mixed nature of the herds. Jenny felt very proud of herself for clearing up this little debate that had raged in the academic community for... a paltry hundred years or so.

It was also interesting to watch the interactions with the smaller species of flying dinosaurs and even some land animals. The small birds—close enough to be called that anyway—traveled with the herd. They could be seen landing on the backs of larger animals, picking at ticks and other parasites.

Jenny made a note to do a tick check after this herd passed on and for several days after. The only real problem she had was shooing one cow away from her boat when she seemed intent on having a taste of it.

After half a day the herd moved on, but that led to the start of her troubles. Jenny had completed her little boat. She was very proud and lucky that this was the case.

She was pondering what to do next. A couple of issues stood out. Her grandfather's camp, if it was there at all, was several miles away. It would be best to attract his attention in some way before setting sail. And she had built her boat in the wrong place. Jenny would much rather cross the river somewhere much shallower, but the reeds were here. Also, there wasn't any place to land it on the other side.

She would have to go a good distance downstream to find where the river flowed away from the bluff on the opposite side, where there was a beach for her to land on.

Jenny had spotted a slope in the far bank that would offer access to the plain beyond, but that was maybe four miles downstream from where she was right now.

As she was pondering ways to contact her grandfather, some guests came to dinner. They were probably following the herd and must have thought they had them trapped here in this bend, but no, they had only her.

There were four of them, two young. Bigger theropods of some type. The arms were larger than the vestigial remains of the forelegs on the famous Tyrannosaurus rex. Their species really didn't matter, and Jenny didn't have time for any professional curiosity, as she was totally focused on pushing her little boat out into the current, right fucking now.

Climbing on top, she paddled for the far side of the stream. It wasn't really much of a race, not particularly dramatic, but the animals did wander down to the tip on the peninsula to stare at her as she floated against the far side of the river and was carried downstream out of sight. Jenny couldn't resist flicking them the bird as she rounded the corner, assholes. They glared back at her.

All that preparation and it was over just like that, or almost. Jenny had to find someplace she could put in on the far bank where she could reach that ramp leading to the plains on the far side.

Easy peasy. And her little boat did float well—it did not sink. Jenny wouldn't have wanted to cross the Atlantic Ocean in it, but it was good for the day. It was a little tipsier than she would have liked. Maybe she should have made it a bit wider. And paddling it was a bit of a pain with only one blade on her paddle. She had to keep switching sides, and the spear made a rather heavy paddle.

Jenny was inordinately proud of *Ra III*. She wished she could have made some kind of paint to put the name proudly on the side of her little craft.

Jenny paddled downstream, trying not to splash with the paddle. No need to draw attention to herself. Rounding the bend and a couple of miles more would bring her to the bank with the slope leading up to the gap in the rimrock. She could put in there before the rapids.

She mostly let the current carry her. She had not actually seen any massive animal life in the river, but she knew it was out there. Jenny had the image of the Lock Ness monster rising up in front of her.

She did see a splash as something bigger than anything she had caught on her line apparently found its dinner. There wasn't anything to see on the surface. It was a reminder that she wasn't alone in this river. If it weren't for the enormous terrifying monsters, it would be a perfect place for a kayaking trip.

Jenny started paddling slowly toward the side, trying to be careful sliding her paddle in smoothly and not pulling too hard.

Maybe it was the movement or the turning of her little boat. It might have been the shape. The water was muddy enough that she thought it keyed off the stokes of her paddle.

There was no warning. It must have been waiting on the bottom for something to pass by. All she knew was that the water exploded under her, lifting her little craft into the air as the jaws closed around it.

She yanked her legs back and rolled backward off her boat as the teeth closed around the center where she had sat. Jenny fell head-first into the water, still clutching her spear.

When her head emerged, coughing out river water, she saw the head of an enormous, absolutely huge crocodile. It had *Ra* in its mouth, holding it fully out of the water, thrashing it from side to side as the little boat was crushed in its jaws. Reeds flew everywhere.

All Jenny could do was float, trying to keep her head above water and cling to her spear. She didn't have a life vest or any type of flotation gear. Jenny made a few strokes toward the shore as she watched the beast fall back into the water, dragging her craft completely under. There was a thrashing in the water as it rolled over and over, trying to kill her poor boat.

Then the two halves of her little boat floated to the surface. It was a sad ending for the proud little ship that she had put so much work into.

The water was quiet. Jenny stopped moving. Where was it? It was terrifying to watch it destroy her little boat, but it was oh-so-much more frightening not to be able to see it.

She was still too far from shore. Could it see her? Could it hear her? Could it hear her heart beat through the water? It was certainly loud enough. Was it coming even now to swallow her whole from below? All Jenny could do was float there, trying to be quiet as she was carried into the rapids.

The rapids probably saved her from being killed right there. She tried swimming for the side. It wasn't a class-five rapids, but the current was strong. It was all she could do to make it in to the lee of a large bolder in the stream. Jenny clawed at the stone, trying to hang on to it until she got her foot onto a ledge and was able to drag herself like a half-drowned rat up onto the rock.

She still had her spear. Her satchel was gone. The boat was lost. And somewhere out there was one of the biggest river predators in this era. All she could do was cling to the sloping surface of this bolder and vomit river water.

Jenny looked out over the river. If she could swim to the shore, maybe the rapids would cover her splashing. It would be much harder for the animal to track her movements in this fast-moving water.

Jenny was about to try for the shore when she looked up river to see it staring at her. It was just the top of its head and eyes above the surface, but it was looking right at her and coming fast with the current.

Jenny struggled to her feet on the slippery rock. She had to prop herself up with the spear as she panted, still coughing. It went by her on the right side, still on the surface. Jenny could now see it all the way from its nose to the tip of its tail. The damn thing must have been forty feet long. Deinosuchus.

She reminded herself that it was actually an alligator, a direct ancestor to the ones in Florida, but really, really big. That was not a useful piece of information right now.

It turned and came back upstream in the lee of her rock. Not good. Not good. The Browning High Power was still in the holster on her leg by some miracle. Jenny drew the nine-millimeter without any real plan of what to do with it. She could see the beast's tail whipping back and forth from side to side. The current was no problem for it.

She needed a plan. They stared at each other. She had a little over half a magazine left in the Browning. It was right behind the stone. It wasn't a long shot to its head. Jenny didn't have any illusions about the nine-millimeter penetrating its skull, especially at this low angle. If she could hit it in its eye... well, that will make *anything* sit up and take notice.

Jenny took careful aim. If only she could stop shaking. She braced her dominant hand against her other arm, where she held the spear. *Crack!* It jumped. She hit its skull, and the bullet ricocheted off. She tried again, missing the eye. On the third shot its head dipped underwater for a second. She thought she had actually done it, but then it reemerged, that glaring eye unhurt.

It dropped back slightly. Jenny could see the serpentine movement of its tail broaden. It was coming. It would whip that tail and send itself lunging forward onto her rock. Jenny had one more shot.

Kaboom! She fell backward on her ass, almost falling off the rock. That was not her pop gun. The concussion almost knocked her over. Jenny looked up to see the croc roll on its side, thrashing in the water. Its tail whipped as it completed the roll, spasming in agony.

She looked to her right up on the bluff and saw— people. There was a flash from someone lying on the rim, and another concussion hit her like a wall. *Kaboom!* Looking toward it was worse. Her ears rang as they took the full force of the report of the... rifle? What the fuck were they firing? It sounded louder than a 50 BMG.

The croc was thrashing in the water drifting downstream in its death throes as the river turned red around it. She looked up again and covered her ears as the rifle—really a cannon—fired again. *Fuck*.

Jenny got to her feet and looked up at her saviors. There were several standing there on the rim waving. The man behind the cannon rose up on his knees and waved her toward them.

What the hell—what else was she going to do? Jenny re-holstered the Browning, making sure it clicked into place securely. She took a deep breath and jumped into the water, holding her spear as she paddled for shore.

Jenny drifted a good way before reaching the shore, dragging herself onto the bank, feeling like a drowned rat and probably looking worse. Her clothes were in tatters, shredded on the rocks, and she was covered in mud from the bank of the river.

By the time she trudged back upstream toward the slope leading down to the river bank, she was exhausted. She was met at the riverside by five Black men. It was hard to tell, but she thought they looked Kikuyu.

"We were very happy that the crocodile did not eat you, Memsahib."

"Alligator," she said, and he stared at her blankly. "It's actually an alligator." They didn't have that word. She sighed. They were apparently more amazed at her survival than at the fact she was there at all.

That was one of the very refreshing things about the tribes she really missed from her trips here in her youth. They lived in the now. Of course, she was here. She was standing in front of them. What more explanation did they need than that? But the crocodile—that was something they would tell stories of around the fire, for they had seen it with their own eyes.

"Bwana waits for you, Memsahib." As he pointed up to the ridge. The other men went about filling their containers with water. Of course, he was. He couldn't possibly have roused himself to walk down and say hello. *Asshole*.

Jenny looked up at the man standing on the top of the escarpment next to his... cannon. The climb up to the escarpment seemed impossible long. Jenny had to stop to catch her breath before she reached the top.

He was about fifty yards off to one side standing next to the biggest rifle she had ever seen. It was resting on its bipod and looked to be almost as long as he was tall.

He could have walked over and given her a hug, but he simply stood there. Jenny walked over to him until they were a few feet apart. *To hell with it*. She reached out and snatched him in to a big hug. It had been so long. She had never had the chance to say goodbye.

He was clearly startled by this woman who had appeared out of nowhere and now had her face buried in his chest as she clung to him. She might have been crying—she wasn't sure. He still smelled the same as she remembered. Once she had herself a little more under control, Jenny leaned back and wiped her eyes.

The man, her grandfather, looked down at her more confused than ever. She just had to do it.

"Doctor Livingston, I presume."

He stared at her open-mouthed. *Oh, come on. She'd been sitting on that one for a month.*

He was confused, "Who are you? And what are you doing here?"

Be patient. Do not kill him. You've come all the way to save him and yourself. Don't kill him now. Remember—he has no idea what is happening. It was "old him" who planned all this.

Long sigh. "I'm your granddaughter. I'm here to rescue you."

"I don't have a granddaughter." A pause. "At least I don't think I do." Of course, he focused on that. Try again.

"You don't have a granddaughter—yet. That's why I'm here, to make sure you make it back to fix that. I'm here to rescue you." She didn't remember him being this slow.

"Young lady, we just saved you. Pardon me, but you don't appear to be in any condition to rescue anyone." He looked her up and down again and his eyes fixed on her spear. She turned it so he could see it better. "Is that my knife?" He pointed at the blade lashed to the shaft.

"No, it's *my* knife now. You left it to me. No take-backs." Could the man not focus? He reached behind him and drew his own knife, turning it over in his hands to examine it. She helpfully lowered hers down beside it so he could see. They were the same, right down to the nick in the brass spine where "Red" Hamman had deflected another blade in a knife fight in Abilene.

"Exactly what kind of rescue is this supposed to be?"

Jenny rolled her eyes. *Don't kill him. You really shouldn't kill him. If he dies, you might cease to exist. Hold on to that thought. He doesn't know anything.* She reached into the pouch on the left side of her belt and pulled out a shrink-wrapped package with the two batteries and a cable. She held them proudly before her.

He looked down at them for a long moment and then back up at her confused. "They're your batteries," she explained. "I brought them here for you!"

"They're small."

Jenny managed not to shoot him. *Look at my self-control.*

"They're NiCad. Batteries have gotten smaller over the years. Trust me... trust you. You sent them, whatever. Just take them," Jenny said as she planted them in his hand and then stood back with a supremely satisfied smile on her face. She had done it!

"How did you get here?"

"You sent me. Or you arranged for it. You were dead by then." That raised his eyebrows. Served him right. "It was a long time from now. Millions and millions of years and another sixty or so to boot." Let him chew on that and swallow it. Right about then the porters reached the top of the escarpment.

"Camp now, Bwana?" They had wide-smiling faces. Jenny couldn't help smiling back.

"Yes, camp now. You'd best come along with us. I guess we'll sort this all out there."

CHAPTER 54

SEC

Richard M. Helms
1970 Langley, VA

"I'll see what I can do. Take care. I was so sorry to hear about your wife.... I'm sure she's at peace now. I'll speak to you soon." The director of the Central Intelligence Agency hung up the phone and stared at it.

That old man was still kicking. Still running his empire, which was all to the good. How much money had been funneled through it over the years? Hell, sometimes you didn't even have to provide the funding for projects. There were times that old man paid for operations on his own. He couldn't think of anyone else who had ever done that. Maybe Hughes, but even he didn't have as much money as Hamman.

The most interesting thing was that, unlike Hughes, the old man was never in the spotlight. No one knew about his money. That could be very useful. *Let's see what we can do about keeping it that way.* He began making notes.

Pushing the button on the intercom, he said, "Martha, could you bring me the register on the SEC and a list of any files we might have on their staff? You might also check discretely and see what the FBI has." He intentionally did not use the word *ask*. That would have instructed her to make a formal inquiry, which was a common enough practice, but when he asked her to "see what they had," it was an instruction to use a more indirect source to access the files.

"Right away, Mr. Helms. Would you like me to bring in some coffee?"

"Yes, please, Martha." She was even older then him and very formal. He had inherited her from his predecessor, Marshall Carter. No one really knew how long she had been with the agency. There was a theory that Congress had commissioned her construction in World War II for the OSS (Office of Strategic Services), like one of the great battleships. He had never been able to find the paperwork on it, but the documents were probably sitting alongside the Manhattan Project. He chuckled to himself, but it got him thinking. Where did the old man get his stock tips from?

About that time a small thin woman, who might have once been five foot, came into his office carrying a tray with a tea set. She filled his mug for him, adding a pinch of salt. "So the SEC thinks they can look into John? Would you like me to leave the pot, Mr. Helms?"

She was the only person he had ever heard refer to John Hamman by his christened name. "Yes, that might be best, and the word is they are opening an investigation. Martha, where does Old Man Hamman get his information?"

She froze for a moment. "I'm sure I don't know, Mr. Helms, but I've never known him to be wrong. And I've never known anyone who ignored him to be right." She finished picking up the tray. "Will there be anything else, Mr. Helms?"

"No, please bring in the files when they arrive." She turned and left him even more curious. He had inherited the old man as he had inherited Martha. Artifacts from an earlier time, their stories lost in myth and legend. That would have sounded way too dramatic if it hadn't been true.

Hamman had been around since before World War II. He had been a running partner of William "Wild Bill" Donovan. The story went that they had met when they were both smuggling Jews out of Europe before the war had really gotten rolling. Donovan had helped him find a law firm to handle their visas and travel documents.

Somehow Hamman had known about the importance of uranium and had worked with Bill to secure the ore in the Congo. It had been key to the Manhattan Project. Without it, the US would never have been able to finish the bomb in time for it to be used in the war. He had spent the entire war working with the OSS, mostly in Africa.

After the war, the old boys' club of the OSS had fallen out of favor. Truman did not want them. Donovan had written to FDR of the importance of continuing an intelligence program, but by then his wife was running the presidency. Truman didn't want an American gestapo, or if there was going to be one, he wanted it to be one he controlled. It went through a number of iterations, but ultimately Allen Dulles was chosen to head the new agency.

Dulles had worked under Donovan in the war. And the story went that Hamman had continued feeding information to Donovan, who had the ear of Dulles. There was a story that he was behind preventing the Soviet takeover of Iran and had helped fund the coup that had installed the Shaw.

When Donovan became ill and eventually died, Hamman had tried to convince Dulles that the US should not place missiles in Italy and Turkey, claiming it would force the Soviets to place missiles in Cuba. This had caused a bit of an uproar, as the plans for those deployments had not been well known. Eisenhower had dismissed these warnings.

Hamman had been a supporter of Eisenhower's and Dulles's plans to invade Cuba at the Bay of Pigs, believing that it was critical to avoid greater problems in the future. Kennedy and his new administration were not enthusiastic. After Kennedy lost his nerve, Hamman tried to warn them again that the Soviets would be emboldened to place missiles in Cuba. But now Kennedy had replaced Dulles with McCone. He was eventually able to get him to sortie a U2 over Cuba, but by then the first set of missiles was already in place, and all the world knew what followed.

Those were only the highlights. The partnership had continued all these years through several projects in South

America. Recently he had been warning of the potential rise in the drug trade. He seemed to believe it could become a national security concern. The damnedest thing was that he always seemed to turn out to be right in the end. He had predicted the missile crisis three years before Castro had met with the Russians to sign the agreement.

There was a brief knock on the door, and Martha brought in the first set of files. *Now let's see what we have here on this gentleman from the SEC.* He sat back, opening the first of the folders.

CHAPTER 55

Fort

John, 43, and Jenny Hamman, 31
Cretaceous

The camp was more of a fort than anything else. They had clearly been busy. It was set up back from the river on clear land. There were a number of mud brick huts around a central cooking and work area. There was a... wall. No, it was really a screen made from woven branches between poles. Jenny couldn't imagine it stopping anything sizable. It was about eight feet tall and hid most of the camp. Getting closer, she could see firing slots in it. There were two small guard towers with lookouts at opposite corners.

The whole camp was surrounded by a sea of stakes of different sizes and hedgehogs of sharpened spikes like tank traps. It was odd to see a military camp built to protect against animals rather than rifle fire.

As they got closer, John started pointing out pit traps in the ground surrounding the fort. They were surprisingly small and didn't make a lot of sense to her until he explained it.

One couldn't really dig a pit trap big enough for the larger dinosaurs, but it was possible to dig a prairie dog hole. They were only about four feet deep with spikes in the side walls angled downward.

He wasn't even sure those were necessary. Covered with branches and camouflaged, it was big enough only for a foot, the idea being that when one of the big theropods stepped into it, it would lose its balance and fall over, breaking its leg. At that point the animal would be helpless and basically dead.

John led her around to one side of the fort, where a group of men were working to dismember the corpse of a dinosaur that had fallen prey to one of his prairie dog holes.

He had gotten the idea early on when one had approached the camp and circled it, trying to decide what it was. He had set his men to digging the traps around the walls at about the distance that it had circled.

Men waved to them as they entered through a gate that again was made of woven branches sliding to the side behind the wall. None of this made any sense to Jenny until she saw what was on the inside.

They had to step around and through another area of sharpened stakes on the inside of the fence. Now she understood its purpose. It really was just a screen to hide the second set of stakes. It was an invitation to the smaller animals to jump over the top of it only to find a nasty surprise waiting on the other side.

They passed a group of men digging a well. By the looks of it, they had not hit a water table yet, hence the reason they were still making regular trips to the river. Lucky. If she had arrived a week later, they might not have found her at the river.

John led her to one of the open-sided sheds beside one of the central huts. People were sitting in the shade working on different projects. He planted himself down in a camp chair, and someone brought Jenny a folding stool. She heard him ask one of the men in Kikuyu to bring them some provisions. After that, they sat there staring at each other.

Jenny didn't think either of them knew where to begin. She was staring at a younger version of her grandfather, whom she had known as an old man. Now he sat in front of her at perhaps forty, strong and virile, at the height of his adventures.

About then, his man returned with two tumblers filled with something delightfully brown. The smell alone hit her like a hammer. The first sip burned going down. She gave a little gasp as the world got just a little bit better, the aches and pains a little less.

Jenny wanted to kill him. She had been struggling her way across this landscape to save his life, only to find him set up like a little king, comfortably sipping whiskey in the shade. She really did want to kill him. She wanted to sit in his lap and have him hold her in his arms and tell her that everything would be okay.

Jenny then looked up at a tall Black man who walked up and took station behind her grandfather on his right. He looked strangely familiar. She dismissed it. There was no way she could have ever met him. Looking up at the man, her grandfather addressed him: "Manny, meet my granddaughter. She has come to save us."

The man's face split into a huge smile. "That is good, Bwana."

"So a dead me sent you here to save me—after I was already dead?" It was infuriating, but Jenny had to admit she was actually enjoying his confusion.

"That's right. It was all your idea. To be clear, you died when I was a child. Here—I can prove it." She reached into one of her few remaining pockets and pulled out her phone. This would *really* blow his mind. It was a brand-new Nokia. A 9210, almost a small computer. Jenny was inordinately proud of it. She opened it to reveal a small color screen and a QWERTY keyboard. "Check this out." She turned it on and waited. Nothing happened.

"It's very nice... . What is it?" She didn't hit him.

Shit, it was wet. She opened it and pulled out the battery. "It got wet in the river. I need to dry it out and maybe recharge it... . Look—it's really cool. You'll see. It does everything. It's a computer."

He looked up at her skeptically. "A computer— someone who does calculations? Like an accountant?"

Jenny did not break the irreplaceable device from the far future over his head. "More like an entire building full of them. I've got a lot of stuff stored on here." He still looked skeptical.

Changing subjects, he looked at the vacuum-wrapped package she had brought him with two battery packs of NiCad batteries and a pair of small metal cans with screw-on lids. He seemed to be more impressed with the plastic than with anything else.

Losing patience with him, she reached forward and took it from his hands. Her pocket knife made short work of the seal as she cut off the end. This elicited a squawk of protest from him as she destroyed what was a wonder in his eyes. The contents spilled out into his lap.

He reached down and picked up one of the cans that had fallen into the dirt. With a sense of excitement, he unscrewed the end, and a spool of... film slid out. Unrolling the first few inches, he peered at it as he held it up to the sky. A smile spread across his face. Quickly he rewound it, sliding it back into the canister. Jenny was losing patience again. "What is it?" she asked.

"I don't know. But it's from the future! I'll have to get one of the machines to read it." She looked at him, confused. "It's the new microfilm they are publishing newspapers on. I need a projector machine. Where can I get a projector machine?" Standing up, he said, "I have to go back!" Only then did he glance down at her. "What will *you* do? Are you going home to your own time? We've only just met. I have so many questions to ask you."

Everything was happening too fast. Jenny realized she was about to lose him. Again. She hadn't exactly been nice to him and couldn't help poking at him, but she didn't want to let him go. She had missed him so much over the years, even if he wasn't the kindly old man she knew as a child.

Jenny was exhausted. All she wanted to do was take off what was left of her boots and prop her feet up. "For god's sake, sit down. We literally have all the time in the world. Stop being an asshole! Sit down and be a gentleman. Take off my boots and rub my feet like you did when I was a kid."

"You know, you're not exactly dressed," he said. For the first time he realized that she was wearing pants, and if that weren't scandalous enough, they weren't in the best of shape. They were torn till they were little more than shorts. The rocks in the river had not been kind. She let out a huff of irritation and propped her feet up on a convenient crate. It probably served as a table for his meals.

"Rub!" she said. With a look of annoyance, he pulled his chair up across from her and began unlacing her boots. "You know, there's about to be another war when you get back."

He grimaced. "I've been in wars before. I was in the Great War. I think I'm going to sit this one out right where I am. I'm getting a little too old for those games."

"You may not have a choice. This one is going to make the First World War look like a prelude. It was a skirmish in comparison to what's coming." That soured his face. "And besides, I haven't seen you in twenty years. Tell me how you've been doing."

He looked confused again. "Well, we finished building the house."

"Seen it. It's nice."

He seemed startled by that but composed himself to continue. "The ivory is going well, but I'm thinking about trying to hunt for diamonds."

"Kimberlite pipes."

He stopped rubbing again. The man could not focus and looked even more confused now. "Excuse me?"

"It's where they come from—old volcanoes." She took another sip of her drink, and the Manny fellow stepped forward to refill her glass. Jenny couldn't help but smile up at him.

"I thought they found them on the beach in the sand."

She rolled her eyes. "At first, but those have washed down from higher up. It's not like they grow there. They come from many miles under the ground."

The conversation went on like that for some time until he said, "I really would like to get to know you better, but I have to get my men back home. One of them is sick. He broke his leg. I thought he was going to be all right, but infection has set in. If we get him back to the town, the doctor might be able to save his life if he can survive the amputation."

"The what? Let me see him." That was right—he had said something about an injured man in the letter. Jenny started pulling her boots back on with a groan. The man was under another of the awnings, resting on a cot. When they pulled the blankets back, she could see the puss seeping through the bandages.

Amputation, my ass. We'll see what modern antibiotics could do. He was only semiconscious, but they were able to get him to drink some water and swallow the pills. Jenny started explaining the regimen of drugs he would have to take. Hopefully her supply would be enough to kill the infection. "Do not let some butcher at him unless the infection returns after you run out of drugs."

The men had been gathering in the center of the compound with all their supplies and trophies. Jenny couldn't believe that all of this was about to come to an end. Looking at him, "If you will be kind enough to set the device to return me to my time, I guess I'll be off." She reached down for the time travel device where it had been in the front cargo pocket of her right pants leg.

It wasn't there. All that remained was torn fabric. She had been carrying that thing for weeks, and now it was gone. Jenny stared down at the torn fabric. Her mind went numb. Distantly she could hear her grandfather asking her what was wrong, but it was drowned out by the buzzing in her head. Now she was trapped.

"It's gone." That was all she could get out as she pointed to the torn fabric of her pants. Eventually he came to understand her meaning and became very quiet. "Can you send me back with *your* device?"

"No, it doesn't work that way," he replied. "You don't set your return. You simply activate it. It's like a rubber band stretched backward through time. When it's released, it snaps back to where it came from, taking everything around it with it." He was very somber as this sank in.

Jenny's heart was racing. She felt out of breath, as if she were hyperventilating. What was she going to do? She couldn't stay here.

"There is no way back to your time, but the device I have can take us all back to mine," John said. Jenny might have been in a bit of shock. There was no way home. She couldn't get back to her world, to her life.

To be trapped in the 1930s? Was that any better than staying here with the dinosaurs? It was practically the Dark Ages.

"It's going to be all right. We'll look after you." He led her to the center of the compound with the other men. He put his arm around her, and she leaned her head on his chest, the way she used to as a child, as tears rolled down her cheeks.

Jenny felt a comforting hand on her back as Manny said, "Do not worry, Bibi. All is as God wishes it." There was a beep, and everything changed.

CHAPTER 56

Investments

Thomas Sowell, 80
Hoover Institution, Stanford University
2010

An older distinguished Black man sat wrapped in a sweater at his desk in a small office. The hour was late. He was perhaps the only one remaining in the building.

Yes, here was another one. They had sold at exactly the peak of the market. He added the name to the list. While he sat at his desk, the lamp's green shade shielded his eyes as he looked down at the pool of light and the list.

Corporations, dates, and trades, some of the largest and most profitable investments ever made. All the investments had been named in the paper he had written... nine years ago. It had been nine years ago in this very room. It had been a warm spring day, the window was cracked open, and one could hear students down on the quad. Now the room seemed cold as he sat at his desk late into the night. Shivers ran up and down his spine as he looked down at the list in front of him. What had he stepped into that day?

The man had made an appointment by phone. He had been some kind of lawyer and had wanted to commission a study. It was rather pointless, but the check that he brought with him had an impressive number of zeros in it, even for an economist. It really wasn't more than a thought exercise.

Make believe you could go back in time with all the knowledge you have today of economic history. How much money could you make if you knew exactly what to buy, what to sell, and exactly when to do it?—which was a completely meaningless question. The answer was, of course, as much as you wanted.

If you were God with omnipotent knowledge of the future, you could place thousands of trades a day on every peak and dip, so the whole question becomes pointless. But that wasn't what he wanted. The man wanted to commission a list of the greatest peaks and dips of the most important stocks with the potential for the highest gains broken down year by year. He wanted the top five trades that could be made every year.

He had asked the man if he had invented a time machine. He had meant it as a joke, but it had not elicited any laughter. The man had stared at him blankly and then changed the subject to compensation. The numbers the lawyer had proposed had more than distracted him.

So—he had done it. He did the research and wrote the white paper as requested. The greatest investment opportunities from 1938 to that day, in 2001. Considering how he had been paid, he included yearly analysis of the growth and the percentages by which you could outperform the S+P 500 and all other indexes.

The results were as ridiculous as you would expect. In fact, the numbers were even higher than he might have guessed. What anyone could do with such a study—he could not imagine. It was an interesting thought experiment.

When he deposited the check, he thought back to when he was a child growing up in Harlem and how he had to drop out of high school for lack of money. If he had only a fraction of that check back then...

Now he was doing a study of different funds and corporations and their performance relative to the indexes. For fun, he was going to include the percentage below the optimum that they could have made in that calendar year. He had thought to use the results from that paper as a theoretical benchmark. That mutual fund X had performed 7 percent better than the index but still returned less than 48 percent of what could have been achieved if they had followed this optimized strategy.

On examining different companies, he came across one that had hit the nail on the head. They had bought and sold at exactly the moments he had selected in his paper. All he could think was *Wow—someone had really called it right that day*! Then he found another. It was a different corporation, but it had also nailed another investment at exactly the point he had himself selected.

There were, of course, thousands of investment firms with very fine minds working in them. So it became a game, going back through that old newspaper and seeing if anyone had made the same call he had.

That was when he started becoming frightened. In every case a corporation had traded large blocks of stock on exactly the points he had specified. When the names had started repeating, he spilled his coffee.

It had taken several days to track down who owned all these corporations. It was like peeling an onion or taking apart one of those nested Russian dolls. There always seemed to be another shell corporation—until finally they all seemed to converge. The Hamman Corporation.

Someone from all the way back in the thirties had followed his investment plan to the letter. "Ha ha! My goodness—you haven't invented a time machine, have you?" The man had just given him a blank stare.

He went to a shelf and started sifting through an old stack of appointment books. Finding the one from 2001, he sat back at the desk, his knees creaking almost as much as the chair. It was in the springtime in the afternoon. Yes, here it was, 3:30 on May 7. Robert Brown of... He could see the man in his mind's eye, brown hair, not large, a simple suit. You wouldn't have been able to pick him out of a lineup with countless others like him. He could almost see the moment he had risen from behind his desk as the man had extended his hand to him. "I'm Robert Brown. I represent the Hamman corporation. We would like to commission a... "

As the memory faded, he looked down at the entry in his day planner. He leaned back in his chair, taking off his glasses, slowly methodically cleaning them as he thought.

Placing them back on his nose, he slowly and deliberately tore the page from his planner and added it to the stack of papers on his desk. It was the first one to be fed into the shredder as one by one he cleared all his notes off the desk.

Turning his chair, he looked out his window at the university below, quiet and peaceful late in the night, and tried to pretend that the world was the same as it had been the day before.

CHAPTER 57

FBI

Robert Brown, 63
October 2001 Washington, DC
J. Edgar Hoover Building

Robert brown sat in the chair. It wasn't made of metal. It wasn't bolted to the floor. There was no ring in the table. And there were no handcuffs run through it restraining him. There might as well have been. It was a very nice, if plain room, but the door did not open without a pass key. The card hanging around his neck from a lanyard said "Visitor." That was a courtesy.

He thought about asking if he were free to leave. He would advise clients to do so, but that would put an end to the polite fiction that they were all indulging in. He knew the answer to the question, and that was enough.

He mused that he was probably listed as a person of interest. The truth was that he was a prime suspect in connection to the attack. He had made himself so.

They were being very careful with him. That was not a courtesy. They knew he was a lawyer. They knew that he had worked his whole life at one of the top law firms in the nation if not the world. A very private law firm. One he was no longer employed at.

Robert smiled, wondering what they were making of that. The partners had done the work for him of separating themselves. He didn't think the FBI had any grounds for a warrant for the firm. As tempting as it was, he was being very careful not to give them any excuses.

Many of the question were about the firm. They seemed to hope that he would be eager to sell them out. He was sure that they were making things very interesting for the senior partners right now. Hopefully no one there would do anything silly. They were all very good lawyers.

There were layers of separation, protection. Client confidentiality. Every company, every shell was its own client. They were all handled by different lawyers from different groups. It would be hard to penetrate, and even if they did, it would be hard to make sense of it. He could hardly make sense of what they had done over the years. At most they could be accused of making obscene amounts of money.

Robert just had to wait. They didn't have anything actionable on him or he would not be in this room. He was an upstanding citizen who had made a report. See something, say something. The problem was that his report had been vague but accurate. And he could offer no explanation for his knowledge, so he didn't even try.

The men who met with him in August had been polite. They had smiled. They dutifully took down all of the information he had given them. They had tried to question him, but he offered no further information and made no further statement.

The men who had come to see him in September had not been smiling. Robert had been waiting for them dressed in his best suit with his briefcase ready to go. He did not think they were expecting that when they arrived at five o'clock in the morning, but that had set the stage for the rest of the interaction.

Everything since then had been dreadfully boring. All of their interviews had been very polite and very formal. Robert had lost count. Was this the fifth or the sixth time that they had "invited" him to come in to help them "answer some questions"?

He really wasn't sure what they made of all this. He wasn't sure he cared. He had clearly come into some kind of information. He had dutifully reported it. They wanted that connection. but he didn't have anything to tell them.

By now he was sure that they knew everything there was to know about him. He was a very boring lawyer. They had no right to any information about the firm or its clients.

He was sure they were trying to piece together his work. Best of luck with that. He had never paid for anything in his own name—all transactions related to his work had been through the firm. Robert wondered what they would make of that. There were blank holes in his life without even a charge for takeout.

Robert supposed that it could look suspicious if one were inclined to think the worst of someone. It didn't matter. They had nothing on him, and as long as he gave them nothing, they could be as suspicious as they wanted. He had time.

His mind wandered to the young woman around whom all of this revolved. He had carried out his final instructions before he left the firm. He had prepared all the papers for the transfer of the property in Africa. He had made sure that all her travel plans were prepared for her take possession of the property in February.

Robert had shaken her hand, and she had hugged him instead as they said goodbye. When she walked out the door he wondered if he would ever see her again. By the end of the day there would be no connection between them. It would be as if they had never met.

He was brought back to the present as the door opened and a man walked in carrying a stack of folders. Robert sighed.

CHAPTER 58

Answers

Robert Brown, 64
October 2002 Kenya Africa
Northwest of Nairobi

It had taken a year before they would let him leave the country. He had been a "person of interest." No one could understand how he had predicted the attack on the airlines. He could give no explanation.

For the last year he had been under a microscope. The FBI had found nothing. There was nothing of any kind linking him in any way to the attack. As vague as he had been about the exact details, he had given them more than enough information for them to have stopped it if they had listened to him. For all of their efforts to tie him in some way to the attack, he was exactly what he seemed to be—a very boring lawyer.

Robert had not been able to watch as Jenny Hamman had left in February to take possession of the property. He did not want to risk any connection being made to her. As far as they knew, she was merely another client of the firm.

He could not say why, but he had a strange feeling that everything depended on this. He knew she had flown into Nairobi and then... nothing. Jenny Hamman had been missing for almost a year. She had never returned to the United States. As far as he could discreetly determine, she had not been seen anywhere. It was as if she had dropped off the face of the earth.

The firm he had worked at his entire career had fired him. They had directly forbidden him from contacting the FBI, but they couldn't say that. They had to make up other reasons for removing him as a partner. They had done everything in their power to distance themselves from him. They couldn't tell the FBI why, but they implied that he was behaving in a less than stable manner.

In one interrogation after another, they didn't use that term. He just repeated himself over and over again, or if the questioning became too aggressive, he just sat mutely. He was a very good lawyer and knew what to say and, more importantly, when not to speak. In the end they could do nothing. He didn't know how they wrote it up, but by then they had much bigger fish to chase down.

So here he was in a rented car with a map on his lap. Northwest of Nairobi. That was... to the left and up? This had to be the road. There weren't that many. Maybe a little farther.

It was late in the day when he pulled up in front of the hunting lodge that was the last place Jenny Hamman had been seen. He sat there in the car, staring at the wooden gate in the mud-brick wall around the large house. He didn't know what if anything he would find here.

He got out of the car, and as he approached the gate, he heard sort of a barking or coughing sound and a scratching from the other side. "Hello? Is anyone home?" He could see the shadow of a... dog? It was scratching at the corner of the gate where the wood had clearly been repaired.

There were sounds of someone approaching. He heard a voice speaking something he did not understand and making shooing sounds from the other side of the gate. The scratching noise stopped, and the heavy gate swung open enough to reveal the face of a young Black man. A huge grin split his face, revealing broad white teeth.

"Mr. Brown, we did not know when you would come." Looking down to the side, he said to the dog, "Shoo! Go, go! Mr. Brown must come in. You cannot go out." Looking back up to Robert, he added, "Come, come. Do not let her out." He motioned Robert in through a crack in the gate.

He squeezed through as the man closed it behind him, sliding a bolt home. Robert looked down to see—a dinosaur. He stared at it. His mind seemed to be stuck. There was a dinosaur. Of course, there was a dinosaur. Why shouldn't there be? With everything else over the years, what else would you expect?

It was a bit larger than a dog. It had a bony shield on its head but no rhino horns, and a beak like a parrot. Didn't this kind have rhino horns? Maybe three of them? It stood there looking up at him expectantly, like a dog. Its short, thick tail wagged back and forth, causing the whole body to wiggle. It was a dinosaur, and it was cute.

"Never mind her. She is hungry. Here—give her this." He handed Robert a fruit from a large pocket on his vest. He took it, looking at the dinosaur dubiously. "Do not hand it to her. Toss it to her. Her beak is sharp." The wiggling was almost uncontrollable now that the dinosaur could see the fruit. He dropped it toward the dinosaur, holding his hand well out of reach. It gave a little hop with its forelegs, tilted its head back, and caught the fruit midair. The dinosaur immediately began chewing on it enthusiastically. The young man took the chance to usher him away, leading Robert to the house.

"My grandfather has been waiting for you. She said you would come."

"Jenny Hamman? She's here?" A wave of relief flowed over him.

"No, Bibi. Bibi from before. She knew you would come." With that, he led Robert up onto the porch to where a very old African man sat in a chair made from woven rattan. "He has come, Grandfather. Mr. Brown has come."

The old man looked up at Robert with eyes that seemed to bore into him. His voice was still strong, if a little rough. "You are her friend. Bibi say you will come. Bibi did not say when. Only after she had gone."

The young man motioned for Robert to sit in the other chair. He went to stand behind his grandfather, who looked up and spoke softly in his own language to his grandson, who went quickly inside the house.

As they sat on the porch, there was a loud squawk and a... chicken? It jumped up onto the railing of the porch. A chicken with teeth and a tail? It squawked or barked again, and the old man threw something to it from the folds of his robe. Its head snapped out on its long neck, plucking the treat out of the air.

"Hi-hi." He shooed it away with his cane.

It turned and jumped down off the railing. His grandson returned with a wooden box and placed it in his lap. "Bibi, tell Bwana you are a good man. Bwana say this is for you." There was a thick envelope in the box with Robert's name written on the front of it in a hand he knew. He looked down at the envelope in his hands, as so many others. Opening it, he found a letter and a number of documents. Included were the deed to this farm and the stock certificates to the Hamman corporation.

Dear Mr. Brown,

Thank you for caring for my granddaughter. She has told me what a help you were to her. Please accept these as a token of my appreciation. Inside you will find the deed to this farm. We were very happy here. I hope you will look after it and her pets. And her garden. She was very proud of it and all the special things in it. There is nothing like it in the world today.

I ask you to look after and protect the village and the people who live upon this land. It was theirs long before we came. They have watched over it from time immemorial. Please watch over and protect them, as they have been loyal friends and supporters from the beginning

There are also all one hundred shares of stock of the Hamman Corporation. You are now the sole owner. It has served its purpose. I cannot leave you any more secrets from the times to come. Our insight ended when the woman you knew as my granddaughter left and came to me in the hour of my need.

She was very happy to have had the chance to see you one last time before she passed on. And even though she could not tell you how much you had meant to her, please know you were very special to her, and she valued your friendship greatly. And she never really meant it when she kicked you in your leg.

John Hamman

The house was large and spacious and filled with wonderful things, souvenirs from across time. Things that had disappeared from this world long before the first man was born. But what most struck him were the little things that made it a home.

There were pictures of them posing with hunting trophies, fantastic animals no modern man had ever seen. But the ones that most affected him were the ones of Jenny and her grandfather. They were both young and strong, as he remembered her, and as he had never known the man. In those photos on the walls and mantels, he could see her with her daughter. Watch them grow. See her grow old.

On the mantel was one last picture of them together as the old couple he had met so long ago. He was holding her, looking down toward her, and her head was leaned against his shoulder, a contented smile on her face.

In the center of the mantel over the great fireplace, in a place of prominence, was a shadow box holding a large knife, its blade old and darkened but well cared for. Its handle was made from some kind of horn, and there was a strip of brass now shading to green along the back of the blade. The knife rested in the box on two pins, and there was an empty space below it with two more matching pins as if there was once a pair.

"I wonder where that's from." As he looked at it, he felt something bump and rub against his leg. Looking down, he saw it was the little rhino-like dinosaur. He absently reached down and scratched her neck behind the bony shield on her head.

She let out a deep purr of ecstasy while he scratched her itch as she rubbed her head against his leg.

Epilogue

The Time Machine

Roger Hoffman, 66
2025

The drink burned going down his throat. For a moment he thought his stomach was going to rebel. Wasn't it supposed to get easier? He looked at the glasses lined up in front of him on the bar. The world felt unsteady around him as he swayed slightly.

They had laughed at him. Members of the audience had stood up and said that his graphs and data were impossible and that he had forged the results of the test. It had been a blind test sent to three different laboratories. None of them knew what they were testing or why.

The isotope ratios proved beyond any doubt the age, over eighty-five million years. And the post-atomic nucleolar contamination proved beyond any doubt that the metal had been smelted after the Hiroshima and Nagasaki bombs.

It was totally contradictory. That was true. He admitted that. But it made all their explanations impossible as well. No one could have fired a gun into the ground, lodging the bullet there. The lead was provable more than eighty million years old. The rock around it was undisturbed. The vertebra was broken before fossilization. The metals were contaminated by fallout from early nuclear bombs. That was also proven without a doubt from not one but two separate laboratories also working blind with no idea of the purpose of the test. In fact, the date of the smelting was unequivocally in 1948.

These were facts. A bullet was manufactured in 1948. Somehow that bullet was transported 85 million years into the past to the mid-Cretaceous. There, that bullet was used to kill a dinosaur. That dinosaur was buried by sediment on a mud flat and fossilized over millions of years. The bullet had remained embedded in the skeleton, undisturbed, when his team excavated it.

It didn't help that his whole team had disavowed themselves from any involvement in his theories. None of them had made any statement contradicting him, but no one was willing to give up their career to support him.

He had the proof, but they refused to acknowledge it. He thought that if he came here and presented all his evidence, they would have to see.

He reached for the rest of his drink, but his hand was stopped by another. "Perhaps that would not be a good idea, Professor Hoffman. My employer would very much like to have a meeting with you." He was a tall man, not in any way memorable, wearing a well-tailored but plain suit.

"Who?" The world swayed slightly as he turned to look at the man. He had to grasp the edge of the bar to help steady himself.

"Please come with me, Professor." He took him by the arm and helped him down off the stool. "Please do not forget your briefcase." Hoffman dutifully picked it up, holding it to his chest as if protecting it, as the man led him outside.

A large limousine pulled up silently before them. It was one of those new electric models from Tesla. He had never seen a Tesla limo before. The man opened the door and helped him inside.

He had to close his eyes for a moment when he sat down to stop the spinning. When his stomach settled, he slowly opened them again and found that he was looking at one of the most recognizable faces on the planet. Elon Musk was sitting across from him.

"Professor, I was at your presentation this morning. I found your data to be very interesting. You've peaked my interest. I'm sorry my men lost track of you. You left the auditorium rather abruptly." He leaned forward with the boyish eagerness that he was famous for. "Could I see the bullet?" Hoffman just stared at him. "The bullet—I believe you have it in your briefcase." He looked pointedly at the case that the professor was still hugging to his chest.

Roger Hoffman blinked again, trying to catch up with the conversation. He looked down at the case he was holding and set it in his lap, almost fumbling the briefcase while trying to open it. Musk reached out and stopped it from falling to the floor of the car.

Looking inside, Hoffman picked up the sealed glass case containing the thing that had both made his career and destroyed it simultaneously. Musk reached forward and took it from his hand. Hoffman let out a squeak of protest. Musk held up a hand, quieting him as he turned the sealed case over and over in his hands. "May I have this?"

"What? But I need that. It's my proof. I... " Hoffman stammered till he was cut off.

"Don't worry about any of that. I'm sure we can privately fund all of your research far better than that institution. In fact, I would very much like for you to expand your excavations. I would like for you to excavate the whole area where this was found. I'm sure we can provide you with everything you need. I already have a team searching for... other anomalies. I find this all very interesting. It opens up whole new possibilities that I had never considered before."

Hoffman stared at him. "Why? What do you care about archaeology? I thought you wanted to build rockets so you could go to Mars." He couldn't keep the scorn out of his voice.

"Professor, you misunderstand me. My interest is not in the past. I'm interested in shaping the future. And a little head start might be very helpful in the present." Musk stared intently into the case he held in his hands, lost in his own thought and plans.

As Roger Hoffman watched the man across from him, he didn't know what this would mean, but deep down he had a feeling this would have a profound effect on much more than his own career.

__Afterword__

I have been getting some questions from my readers about the knife. Many of the questions center around if there should be one knife or two at the end of the story. Let's begin with the history of the knife.

It was forged by James Black, a blacksmith in Arkansas. James Black claimed to have forged the knife for Jim Bowie. There are many stories about this man. It's said that he was very secretive about his heat-treatment methods. IIe would hang up curtains when he quenched and tempered his knives. It is said that they never broke.

There are also serious questions about all of this. All of his claims may be false. There is no proof that he ever met Jim Bowie. I chose to believe the legend. At least it makes for a good story.

The knife was sold to her grandfather's grandfather; I guess her great-great-grandfather, as he passed through Arkansas on his way to Texas. He became a Texas Ranger and carried it in the Texas Revolutionary War. He carried it throughout his life, and a knife fight in Abilene is mentioned.

It passed down through the family to her grandfather, John Hamman, who carried it through two World Wars. Her grandfather carried it when Jenny knew him as a child, and he taught her to skin her first game with it.

The knife was taken from its resting place on the mantel and placed in Jenny's pack before she went back in time. And yet it is still sitting on the mantel when Robert Brown comes to the lodge at the end of the story. And there is only one knife on the mantel at that time. However, there is space for two.

Let me spell it out for you, as this is an ongoing argument between me and one of my friends. There is only one knife. Because of the oddities of time travel, its history overlaps with itself. So, there is a time when two knives are present. They are the same knife at two different periods in its history.

Let's, for the sake of the conversation, call them by different names: John's knife and Jenny's knife. John's knife is carried by John Hamman in WWI and on many adventures back and forth through time.

In 1938, he went back in time and, through misfortune, was trapped there. He is rescued by Jenny, and he returns with Jenny and his knife to 1938. He carried his knife throughout World War Two and the Cold War years until his death as Jenny's elderly grandfather.

The knife remains on the mantle till an elderly Manny removes it and places it in Jenny's pack. At this point, it becomes "Jenny's knife."

Jenny is sent back through time by elderly Manny. She has the knife, now her knife, and carries it on her search for her grandfather. When they meet, she is carrying an older version of "his knife." She has lost the time machine, which is where its story ends, but her grandfather still has the earlier version of the machine, and they are able to return together to 1938.

At this point, John has "his knife," and she has an older version of the same knife. So, the history of the knife overlaps with itself from 1938 to 2002. There are two different versions of the same knife together at the same time, one older than the other. But there is only ONE knife.

After the deaths of Jenny and John Hamman, the two knives, versions of the same knife, wait on the mantel. The knife Manny takes from the mantle is John's knife as it begins its journey back in time with Jenny.

The knife that remains and is found by Robert Brown is "Jenny's knife." It has lived through this long journey through time and remains the sole remaining knife on the mantelpiece. It is the knife, the sole knife, the one and only knife. There was only ever one knife, and once the journey was over, there was once again the one and only knife.

This explanation seems exhaustive. It is. This has been an ongoing argument between myself and my friend, Tom. He believes, erroneously, that there should be two knives at the end of the story. And he feels other readers will share in his mistaken understanding of the timeline. I hope this settles it and proves once and for all that my math is better than his.

On another note, in case it was unclear, there is only one time machine. It follows a similar journey, but it is lost in the river. That is where its journey ends.

One of the interesting things about time travel is that cause does not have to precede effect. The creation of the time machine, presumably by a fictional character that might possibly resemble Elon Musk—please don't sue me—is inspired by a piece of evidence made possible by its own existence. The discovery of this 65,000,000-year-old bullet inspired the research that led to the creation of the time machine by a company, Time X.

A time traveler goes back to film WWI, and despite wearing modern ballistic plates and a helmet, he has the bad luck to catch an eight-millimeter machine-gun bullet to the face.

The time machine he used was found by John Hamman and is used throughout all of his adventures, including the little issue he had in 1938, all the way through 2002. At that point, Manny uses it to send Jenny back to save him from his mishap. She loses it in the river and returns with him to 1938. Again, there is only one time machine.

They meet in the distant past and are thrown together in 1938 on the brink of World War Two. Together, they do all they can for their country and the world, and their actions form the timeline we know today. They are part of history. Their lives intertwine from there, resulting in the birth of her own mother. Jenny dies before she is ever born. But before her death, she was able to secure the appointment of a young Robert Brown, her childhood friend, to the law firm that they employed, ensuring his future.

With her knowledge of what she went through and what her younger self will one day face, they were able to leave instructions to prepare her younger self for the challenges ahead. After her death, an elderly John Hamman does his best to care for and guide his granddaughter, but he knows he will die long before she grows into the woman he came to love. He knows all the perils before her. He does all that he can to provide for her and prepare her for what awaits in her future.

I am following the idea that there is only one timeline. That, what is done in the past is part of the past. I do not admit the idea of multiple timelines or multiple universes spawned from every decision in every moment.

This raises the question of paradox. What would have happened if Jenny had failed? You could as well ask, what if Jenny had given in to her impulses and shot her grandfather? I think the answer is simply that she didn't.

If she had failed, the story might simply be that John Hamman disappeared on safari in 1938 with all his men. Not an unheard-of story. No daughter. No Jenny. No larger story. History would have turned out however it turned out. If the Tyrannosaurus rex had not been shot, then the time machine might never have existed.

All of these raise the question of free will. Was Jenny free to shoot her grandfather, or to fail for that matter? I think yes. Free will existed at the time. The choices that were made, the events that happened, were no less real, and no more certain, in that moment than the choices we make today. Looking back through the lens of history, we see the past as a fait accompli. Whereas at the time it was a desperate struggle with an uncertain outcome.

There are other ways I could have gone in this book. Perhaps one day I will write a multiverse time travel book with a thousand versions of one character, but for now this one was hard enough to keep straight through the course of history.

Weaving the story into existing history was by far the most interesting part of the book. I went to some pains to find details of the people, places, and times that they went through. I invite you to look up any or all of the historic characters mentioned. John, Jenny, Robert, and Manny are all fictional characters, but you will find all the historical figures they interacted with in their own place and time, and the lives they lived are as fascinating as any story I could ever tell.

I tried my best to find key moments where they might have influenced the course of events, and moments where things might have gone wrong.

I became fascinated with the idea of moments when people they brushed up against might have discovered their secret, and how they might have reacted. This led to what I think are some of the funniest parts of the book, interludes where we get brief glimpses of their history and the people who encountered them. What would you do if you met a time traveler and discovered their secret? Maybe that will be the next book.

Regarding dinosaurs, I am not a paleontologist. Reaching out to people in this field, I sent them whole list of questions, and I got back...crickets. I can't really blame them. They probably get letters like this all the time. I imagine they have their own dumpster dedicated to letters like mine. They probably have a filter built specially into their email to filter out people like me. I wound up leaning heavily on three books, a handful of papers I found online, and an awful lot of Googling. Wikipedia was my best friend.

I quickly ran into a few problems. There is a distinct lack of paleontology being done in Africa. If you want to know something about North America, the answers are right there. First, there is a much longer tradition of study in America. We have been digging up dinosaur bones here for over one hundred and fifty years.

Africa is more of a mystery. There has been as little work done there. There isn't funding, and frankly, you might get your head cut off in a civil war. This is a shame because there are surely fascinating things to be found there. The bottom line is that I took a lot of liberties with the species of dinosaurs.

My reasoning ran something like this. We don't know what was there, but we know what was everywhere else, so it might not be exactly the same species, but something might have evolved into the same niche.

So, I basically stole real dinosaurs from all over the world, but left her a little unsure about the exact species. One question that intrigued me was, would even a trained paleontologist be able to identify the exact species of dinosaur if she saw it in real life? Would we even have an example of that exact species? What about the real animal would surprise them? I thought these questions were fascinating.

If you find yourself being chased by a pack of overgrown Utah raptors in the middle of the African plain... I advise you to just roll with it and ask questions later. If you wake up in the middle of the night to something like an allosaurus leaning down over you, I advise you to run, not argue with it over the fossil record. And triceratops were everywhere, so why not there?

I look forward to the book being picked apart by experts and even enthusiastic amateurs. I would love to hear from you, but if you wanted the book to be more accurate, you should have answered my letter.

If you would like to help a struggling author out, leave a review wherever you found this book. It really helps with the algorithm.

Also, if you have liked this book, you might enjoy listening to it as an audiobook. And lets be honest, its safer to listen to an audiobook when you are driving then to read a physical novel. So buy the audiobook and save a life. The life you save might even be your own. So far, the audio version is available on Spotify and on Kobo. I hope to have a version on Audible soon. Look for it there.

www.ingramcontent.com/pod-product-compliance
Lightning Source LLC
Chambersburg PA
CBHW031132260626
47153CB00021B/26